# DON'T LET ME GO

DON'T LE

T ME GO

KEVIN CHRISTOPHER SNIPES

HARPER
An Imprint of HarperCollins*Publishers*

ALSO BY KEVIN CHRISTOPHER SNIPES
Milo and Marcos at the End of the World

Don't Let Me Go
Copyright © 2025 by Kevin Christopher Snipes. All rights reserved. Manufactured in Harrisonburg, VA, United States of America.
No part of this book may be used or reproduced in any manner whatsoever without written permission except in the case of brief quotations embodied in critical articles and reviews. For information, address HarperCollins Publishers, 195 Broadway, New York, NY 10007.
www.epicreads.com

Library of Congress Cataloging-in-Publication Data
Names: Snipes, Kevin Christopher, author.
Title: Don't let me go / Kevin Christopher Snipes.
Other titles: Do not let me go
Description: First edition. | New York : Harper, 2025. | Audience term: Teenagers | Audience: Ages 13 up. | Audience: Grades 10–12. | Summary: "Two star-crossed boys are trapped in a millennium-spanning cycle of reincarnation that always ends in their untimely tragic deaths and the only solution may be to never see each other again"— Provided by publisher.
Identifiers: LCCN 2024034916 | ISBN 9780063062610 (hardcover)
Subjects: CYAC: Gay people—Fiction. | Reincarnation—Fiction. | Science fiction. | Romance stories. | LCGFT: Gay fiction. | Science fiction. | Romance fiction. | Novels.
Classification: LCC PZ7.1.S65738 Do 2025 | DDC [Fic]—dc23
LC record available at https://lccn.loc.gov/2024034916

Typography by Julia Feingold
25 26 27 28 29 LBC 5 4 3 2 1

First Edition

"It isn't possible to love and to part. You will wish that it was. You can transmute love, ignore it, muddle it, but you can never pull it out of you. I know by experience that the poets are right: love is eternal."

—E. M. FORSTER, *A Room with a View*

DON'T LET ME GO

POMPEII, ITALY

(AD 79)

CHAPTER 1

LUCIUS

If there was ever a time when I didn't love Marcus, I don't remember. From the moment I could speak, I saved all my words for him. From the moment I could walk, my legs carried me in his direction. Even now, after all these years, when I'm in a crowded temple or the busy streets of the Forum, his face is the first thing my eyes seek out, just as his voice is the only music that delights my ears. He is so much a part of me that I scarcely know how to exist without him.

"Stop it," Marcus grumbles. His sleep-heavy eyes flutter open as his lips curl into a mischievous smile. There's more light in that smile than in all the morning sun streaming through the tiny window of the squalid room we've rented over Faustus's tavern.

"Stop what?" I ask, stroking a strand of his fine tawny hair away from his brow.

"You're doing it again."

"Doing what?"

Marcus slides his strong hand up my back, sending an exquisite shiver down my spine, before arriving at my head and clasping a tight fistful of my black curls in his grip. I gasp, breathing pleasure into the air, as he pulls me onto my back. Then the sturdy weight of his body is pressing down on me as his mouth closes on mine, still tasting of honey and wine.

"I've told you to stop watching me sleep," he whispers, his lips so close, it's impossible to know if his words on my mouth count as speech or a new form of kissing.

"You tell me a lot of things," I answer, biting his lower lip when I can no longer bear its absence.

"And you should listen to all of it."

"If I did that," I counter, wrapping my legs around his waist, "we wouldn't be here now, would we?"

He has no answer for that. At least, not an answer of words. He shuts my mouth with a kiss, and I surrender to him. Just as I've always surrendered.

The first time we made love was supposed to be the last.

That was two years ago. Pompeii was sweltering under the oppression of a searingly hot July, and the city reeked of piss even more than usual. Marcus and I were sixteen and bored, so we escaped our tutors, as we were wont to do when the midday heat made them drowsy with lethargy, slipped outside the city walls, and spent the day swimming in the bay.

Later, behind the privacy of the rocks, we dried ourselves in the sun. It was there I tried and failed not to stare at his sun-kissed form, more perfect than any statue of Apollo. It was there we first gave in to each other. Without words. Without shame. Just his strong arm around my waist and my body welcoming his as the shore welcomes the sea.

In the blushing aftermath, Marcus became adamant that what we'd shared was nothing of significance—a moment of trivial pleasure, a thing to pass the time, or, if we wanted to cast a more noble light on our assignation, a testament to our unique closeness and to the friendship that had kept us by each other's sides for sixteen years.

But, he said, it would never happen again.

That was his resolution, and it lasted until the following day, when he sought me out in the public baths, where we once again found each other in the damp heat of an empty steam room. The next day it was in a secluded street behind the Temple of Venus. The day after that it was among the grape arbors of his father's vineyard.

So it was that in the months that followed, we became thieves of time, stealing an hour here, an hour there, sometimes an entire night when we were feeling bold, despite the mounting suspicions of our families. It was also in those months that we stopped pretending that we were merely passing the time, that Marcus didn't own my soul as surely as I owned his. Instead, we began pretending something else, something far more impossible: that what we had could last forever.

"I have to go," Marcus sighs, slowly pulling his mouth away from mine, as if it required all his strength to forsake my lips. Spent but still wanting more, neither of us has the will to move, let alone part. Instead, Marcus's body sinks into mine, his head resting over my heart.

We've stayed out later than we should, considering the scoldings we're bound to receive when we return to our homes. But it's an indulgence we've allowed ourselves because it's my birthday and because of the other thing. The thing neither of us wishes to speak of but that we both know we won't be able to avoid much longer.

"We have the room until noon," I remind him, running my fingers through his hair, which always smells faintly of sweat, muskroot, and myrrh.

"My father wants me to go with him to inspect Gaius Lucretius's vineyard this afternoon."

"You mean your father wants you to go with him to inspect Gaius Lucretius's daughter."

Marcus frowns. This isn't a conversation that either of us wants to have. Not on my birthday. Not any day. Not when there are so many sweeter things we could be whispering to each other. Like how his hair in this moment looks like burnished bronze gleaming in firelight. Or how his eyes are bluer than the Bay of Naples. Or how his heart is half my own.

But we've put off this talk for too long already.

"They say Lucretia is very beautiful," Marcus answers simply.

"Lucretia could have the face of a horse and the brain of a mackerel, and your father would still expect you to marry her."

Marcus's shoulders tense. He knows I'm right. Gaius Lucretius owns one of the largest vineyards in Pompeii, second only to that of Marcus's father, and he has no heirs except his daughter. A marriage between their two families, therefore, would be not only convenient but highly lucrative.

"We must all marry sometime or other," Marcus sighs. Then, extracting himself from my embrace, he rises from the bed to dress. Without the furnace of his body to warm me, I feel the chill of the early autumn air. It's subtle but pervading. Not unlike loneliness.

We must all marry sometime or other.

It's a statement not worth refuting.

The stories of Jupiter and Ganymede, of Hercules and Hylas, may be known to every man in this city. Such loves may be celebrated as the true and rightful passions of the gods and their favorites, but nonetheless they are passions that most Pompeiians prefer to witness in their poetry, not their neighbors.

Hypocrites.

There's hardly a youth who hasn't played Patroclus to another boy's Achilles in some fevered moment of desire, and yet there isn't a single elder in the entire city who wouldn't condemn a man as unfit for public office if he dared to play the wife instead of taking one.

But that's the way of the world, isn't it? What is pure and noble between a god and his cupbearer on the heights of Olympus is sullied and unspeakable when it occurs between two merchants' sons.

There's no surprise in this, and so there's nothing to say as I watch Marcus sit on our bed and don his sandals in the late-morning light. From the first time that our hearts marked each other as our own, we've known there is only one way for our story to end.

"I'll see you later tonight if I can," he whispers, leaning across the bed to kiss me.

Our lips touch, and it occurs to me that the next time I see him, the next time that he is in my arms, he may very well be betrothed to another. How long until he is wed? Until I am wed? Until wives and children and obligations fill up our lives so that there is no longer room for each other? Until this kiss and all our kisses are nothing but distant memories of some other life we once led?

Pushing those thoughts away, I clasp his cheeks between my palms and hold his face against mine. If this is the last time that I will call him my own, truly my own and no one else's, then I want to hold on to this moment. I want it carved in marble. Or written in song. A kiss between two boys captured in time forever.

Marcus gently pries my fingers from his cheeks. He kisses my left hand, then my right, then folds them both against my chest directly over my heart. My heart that will never be anything but his.

Then, without a word, he's gone.

The noonday sun is warm on my face as I wander through the busy stalls and shops of the market district. There's nothing I want to buy, but when your soul is heavy, it's better sometimes to be adrift in a crowd than to be a prisoner of your own solitude.

I should head home, make an appearance before my family starts to worry, but I'm not in the mood for Mother's prying eyes or pointed questions. Father, thankfully, is in Naples today, hiring more fishing boats to add to his fleet, or else I'd have to endure his scrutiny too.

I wonder if he'll be home in time for my birthday feast tonight. I shouldn't count on it. Not content to be the most successful garum merchant in Pompeii, my father recently declared it his intention to become the largest distributor of fermented fish sauce in all of Rome's wide empire. He's even started marketing a special garum made without shellfish to sell to the Jews so that no household on the peninsula will be without Titus Flavius Maximus's special sauce.

Father is a mediocre man of great ambitions. And whether I like it or not, those ambitions extend to me. Someday I shall inherit his "empire." That is the life that he has decreed for me. A life of commerce and condiments.

Crossing the square, I pass a wine vendor, whose shelves of amphorae bring to mind an afternoon of bliss I once spent with Marcus in his father's storeroom, our ruby-red lips stained with wine and kisses.

I wonder if Marcus has left for the Lucretian vineyard yet. If so, is he thinking of me? Or is he even now steeling himself against the future by erasing all traces of me from his heart?

The thought of someday being nothing more to Marcus than a youthful indiscretion—a half-forgotten memory—is enough to bring tears to my eyes.

Why didn't I try to stop this marriage when I had the chance?

For months, the threat of Lucretia has loomed in the distance, casting a shadow over our happiness, but I held my tongue. I stayed quiet even though all I wanted was to beg Marcus to refuse the match. To refuse every match his father might make on his behalf.

Even now, the blood pounding in my ears is telling me to run. To find him. To stop him before it's too late.

But I don't. Not because I fear his father's wrath or even the wrath of my own father. No, what I fear is far worse and at the same time far simpler. I fear the truth.

If I asked Marcus to choose me above everything else—above family, duty, reputation—what would he say?

For my part, I know that if he asked me to, I would turn my back on the world and forsake everything for him. But would he do the same? Would he risk the ridicule and the censure of his friends and family for me? For us?

I'm afraid to ask for fear of what his answer might be, so I delude myself that we have no option but to submit to the careful lives that our parents have planned for us. The lie that we have no choice hurts less than the truth that we do and that Marcus won't choose me.

Pushing aside this thought, I turn onto the main thoroughfare and head north toward the Forum. As I do, my feet stumble, and I'm forced to steady myself against the nearest storefront to keep from tripping. When I resume my walk, I stumble a second time, at which point I realize that it's not my distracted thoughts or tired feet that are at fault but the ground itself that has started to shake.

A clay amphora topples from a merchant's passing cart and shatters on the street. A whimpering dog scurries inside its master's shop and hides under a table. All around me, the early-afternoon shoppers steady themselves against the sides of buildings or cast nervous glances at their companions as they cling to one another in surprise.

I force myself to stay calm. Earthquakes are as common as thunderstorms in Pompeii. I've grown so accustomed to them over the years, they've become easier to ignore than the persistent stench of anchovies that pervades my father's clothes.

There's nothing to do but wait. If this earthquake is like the others, it will soon spend its anger, and the city will be no worse for wear save for a few cracked plates and broken vases.

But as the minutes pass, the shaking increases, and a terrible doubt takes root in the back of my mind.

Something is wrong.

There's a strange fury to this earthquake, a violence I have never known before. As if the earth itself is in a rage against its own existence.

I close my eyes and offer a quick prayer to the gods.

To my great surprise, the world around me grows still. I'm hardly presumptuous enough to think my prayers alone have placated the great divinities, but I'm relieved nonetheless to open my eyes and find the world as it was: silent and unmoving.

Then I hear it. A sound unlike anything my ears have heard before. Like the heavens are being torn asunder.

A woman in the street collapses to her knees and points toward the northern horizon, her face twisted and white with terror. I follow her gaze, and there in the distance, rising far beyond the walls of our city, I see a thing that I have no name for but that every instinct in my body knows is death.

Vesuvius, the mountain that has watched over our city since the time of the Oscans, is exploding. Like some ungodly furnace, it vomits a burning column of smoke and fire into the air.

My mind struggles to understand what I'm seeing, but understanding is gone. All I can do is stare in horror as the mountain belches its foul contents up into a dark cloud that consumes the sky, blanketing the horizon and blacking out the sun. A false night falls over the city, but instead of stars, the sky is filled with ash and smoke.

When the stones begin to rain from the sky, I run.

ORLANDO, FLORIDA

(THE PRESENT)

CHAPTER 2

RILEY

I'm trying to run, but my entire body is paralyzed. Why can't I move? I have to get out of here. I have to find Marcus. He's in danger. We're all in terrible—

"Riley?"

I open my eyes. Someone's leaning over me. A girl. Her curly mane of auburn hair falls around a freckled face that's twisted in worry. She looks familiar, but it's difficult to focus. My head feels like it's filled with fog.

"Riley, can you hear me?"

Riley? Is she talking to me? Is that my name? It sounds familiar but also wrong.

I stare into her anxious eyes—eyes I know I should trust—and force myself to concentrate.

"Riley, it's me. Audrey."

Something clicks in my brain. *Audrey.* Of course! She's Audrey O'Shea. And I'm Riley. Riley . . . uh . . . Anderson? No. Evanston? Iverson! My name is Riley Iverson!

How the hell did I forget *that*?

"Hey . . ." I say, my voice coming out weak and strained as if I've just learned to talk.

"Oh, thank God," Audrey sighs in relief. "Are you okay?"

I'm not quite sure how to answer that. The last thing I remember is running frantically through the streets. Now I appear to be lying on my back in a patch of dead grass, feeling like someone's just sucker punched the back of my skull.

When I don't respond to Audrey's question, two more people lean over me. Their concerned expressions suggest they also know me, but I'm having trouble placing them. The girl is petite with clear olive skin and wide blue-green eyes, and her hair is covered by a lavender headscarf. The boy is also on the smaller side. He's Asian and wearing makeup, and his fine black hair is styled into a majestic swoop that would make the members of any boy band jealous.

Except . . . hold on . . . that's *wrong*. "He" is wrong. Their pronouns are they/them. Because that's Duy. Duy Nguyen. And the girl is Tala . . . Youssef.

Duy, Tala, and Audrey—my friends.

"What happened?" I ask as I stare up at their faces in confusion. If I'm having trouble remembering the three most important people in my life, something must be seriously wrong with me.

"You fainted," Tala answers, squeezing my hand.

"I what?"

"You fainted," Duy repeats, picking a stray leaf out of my hair. "You just, like, passed out."

Huh. Okay. Interesting.

Fainting would definitely explain the whole waking-up-on-the-ground thing. Except I've never fainted in my life. Did I forget to eat lunch this afternoon? Or did I lose my balance and bang my head when that earthquake hit?

Wait. What am I saying? What earthquake?

This is Florida. We don't get earthquakes.

At least I *think* this is Florida.

That's not something that would normally be up for debate, as I've never left the state. But I'm having a hard time shaking off the impression that a minute ago, I was somewhere else. Italy, I think? Yeah, I was in Italy and—

"Whoa! What do you think you're doing?" Audrey asks, placing a restraining hand on my shoulder when I try to sit up.

I'm looking for the volcano. I know that's insane. But a part of me is certain that if I turn my head to the horizon, I'll see it looming in the distance, spewing stones and smoke into the sky.

On instinct I sniff the air. But instead of the suffocating smell of sulfur, it's the buttery aroma of freshly popped popcorn that hits my nostrils. Then I hear the incessant chipper polka of a merry-go-round mingling with the excited shouts from the Tilt-A-Whirl.

"The summer carnival!" I exclaim, letting out a sigh of relief as the world around me finally starts to make sense. "I'm at the summer carnival."

"Umm . . . *yeah*," Audrey replies, as if that should be obvious.

Whew. That's a load off my mind. For a second, I thought . . .

Actually, I don't know *what* I thought.

I must have had a nightmare. An insanely vivid, detailed, and *terrifying* nightmare. But at least I know where I am now. I'd recognize these garishly striped booths and blinking arcade lights anywhere. My friends and I have been coming here at the start of every summer for years. It's more out of habit than for actual amusement, though Tala's love of funnel cakes is as genuine as it is ferocious.

"Are you okay?" Audrey asks, still studying me. Lowering her voice, she adds, "You've been eating, right?"

My cheeks burn. "Yes, I've been eating."

Jesus Christ, you go through one tiny anorexia phase, and for the rest of your life everyone's the Food Police.

"Is that the truth?" Audrey demands, giving me a suspicious once-over.

It is. But before I can say so, a raucous and all-too-familiar shriek of laughter erupts nearby, causing the hairs on the back of my neck to stand on end. I peer over Audrey's shoulder and spot a group of teenage boys clustered around the shooting gallery. They're aiming air rifles at spinning targets while they thump each other on the back, hooting and hollering like wild apes.

I recognize them instantly. With their matching buzz cuts, blue varsity jackets, and gleeful howling, the Olympus High Thunderbolts (as our school's football team is unoriginally named) are as impossible to miss as they are to avoid. And after some of my run-ins with those testosterone-fueled assholes, I try pretty hard to avoid them.

Thankfully, none of them seem to have noticed me.

Though I suppose it's possible that they saw me faint and simply don't care. That's honestly the more likely scenario, given that most of the entitled jerks who go to my school wouldn't bother to pour water on me if I was on fire. Unless, that is, they thought it would make for a good Instagram story. In which case they *might* pour water on me but only after setting me on fire in the first place.

Such are the joys of being gay in the Central Florida public school system.

"Maybe you shouldn't get up just yet?" Tala suggests as I force myself to stand. But if the Thunderbolts haven't noticed me, I want to make a discreet retreat before they do.

"It's okay," I assure her, wiping the grass stains off my jeans. "I'm fine."

At least, I *think* I'm fine. I don't feel sick or unsteady. Whatever made me faint seems to have passed. Of course, if I'd lost a leg or was bleeding out of both eyes, I'd still insist I was fine if there was the slightest chance that any of my classmates might be watching. That's

High School Survival 101. Never show weakness and never give your enemies any ammunition they can use against you.

I learned that lesson the hard way. Freshman year, I made the mistake of dying my hair pink for Halloween, then spent the next six months dodging various nicknames like Barbie Boy, Bubblelicious, and Gem and the Homo-Grams.

"Do you want us to call your dad?" Audrey asks, looking very much unconvinced by my supposed recovery.

"Or 911?" Duy suggests.

"How many fingers am I holding up?" Tala demands, shoving her hand in my face. "What's the date?"

"Guys, I'm fine!" I insist, casting a nervous glance at the shooting gallery, where my Cro-Magnon classmates are, thankfully, too occupied shooting metal ducks to notice the commotion my friends are making. "Seriously, I'm sorry if I freaked you out, but I'm good! There's nothing wrong with me. See?"

I spin in place while waving my arms over my head to demonstrate that I have both balance *and* full control over my motor functions. Almost immediately, though, I regret that decision, as it's apparent from my friends' horrified expressions that I must look like a malfunctioning robot attempting to fight off a swarm of invisible bees.

"Is this what a stroke looks like?" Duy asks.

"I'm googling stroke symptoms," Tala says, already typing on her phone.

"*Guys*," I groan in exasperation. "I'm *fine!*"

Behind me I hear an awkward chuckle, and for a second, I'm afraid the Thunderbolts have spotted me. Bracing myself, I turn around for a fight. But instead of a rowdy football team, I find myself face-to-face with—

"Marcus?"

I don't believe it. It's him. The boy from my dream. He's wearing cargo shorts and a turquoise polo instead of a tunic and sandals, but I'd recognize him anywhere. The same athletic build. The same dark blond hair. The same piercing blue eyes. I *know* those eyes. I know *him*.

At least... I think I do.

The boy, though, just blinks in confusion.

"Uh... no," he replies. "I'm Jackson."

For a good ten seconds, his words are meaningless. Then, in a flash, it hits me.

Jackson is Jackson Haines. Duy's new neighbor.

Duy's been obsessed with him ever since he moved here from Tallahassee at the end of the school year. For the past week, Duy's been blowing up our group text with updates about their every fleeting interaction with their "hot new neighbor," who apparently likes to jog every morning with his shirt off.

Duy's last update had been that they'd invited Jackson to join us at the carnival this afternoon. A decision I wasn't too thrilled about. I don't like strangers infiltrating our friend group before I've had the chance to vet them. Especially not strangers who are clearly overconfident jocks with an exhibitionist streak.

In fact, I distinctly remember standing in line for funnel cakes with Audrey and Tala and complaining about Duy's tendency to gravitate toward such problematic sports bros just as they arrived at the carnival with Jackson in tow.

After that, though, things get a bit... hazy. Not to mention X-rated. That dream I had was *intense* in more ways than one.

Oh crap. What if I was talking in my sleep while I was passed out? My friends might have heard everything. Worse, Jackson might have. No wonder he looks nervous. He probably thinks I'm some deranged sex freak.

"Oh. Um. Nice to meet you," I mumble, trying to keep my cheeks from flushing in embarrassment.

Again, Jackson blinks uncertainly. "Um . . . we've already met."

Out of the corner of my eye, I catch Duy, Tala, and Audrey exchange anxious glances.

"We have?" I ask.

"Yeah. About five minutes ago. Right before you fainted."

"Oh."

I'm starting to think Tala might be right. Maybe I am having a stroke.

"I remember," I lie, not wanting my friends to worry about me any more than they already are. "I just got a little confused from the fainting."

Jackson nods. "No worries, dude. I'm just glad I was able to catch you."

"Catch me?"

"You kind of swooned," Duy interjects. "Like, right into his arms."

"I swooned?"

"Actually, first you said, 'Oh, wow,' and *then* you swooned," Tala clarifies, rather unhelpfully.

I'm mortified. Fainting is bad enough. But swooning? Over a boy I've just met? That is fucking embarrassing. Jackson's not even my type! I mean, sure, he might be a 10 on the conventional beauty scale, but these entitled Abercrombie and Fitch clones are nothing but trouble. Trust me, I know their type. They call each other "dude" and "bro," and they think the whole universe revolves around them because everyone treats them like fucking gods. They also make up 90 percent of the jerks at our school who seem to take endless pleasure in calling Audrey a dyke, or asking Tala offensive questions about her hijab, or mocking Duy's pronouns.

These people are the enemy. And the best thing you can do when you encounter one of these walking Ken Dolls in the wild is keep your distance. Because as cute and clueless as they might seem, they will eventually turn on you. It's only a matter of time.

"You okay, dude?" Jackson asks when I continue to stare at him, now with thinly veiled hostility. "I brought you some water if you need it. Figured you might be dehydrated."

"Thanks, *dude*, but I'm fine," I retort, ignoring the bottle in his outstretched hand. Despite my fainting and my dreams, I refuse to appear thirsty. For water or for him. "Should we go on some rides?"

My friends look dubious. Before they can protest, though, I start off in the direction of the Ferris wheel. I realize I'm being a bit of a jerk, but I'm humiliated.

I can't believe I *swooned* over a boy. Is there anything more cringe than losing your mind—not to mention total consciousness—over some guy you've just met?

At least, I *think* we've just met.

Maybe I'm still disoriented from fainting, but I can't shake the feeling that there's something familiar about Jackson. When I first turned around and saw him standing there, when I saw those insanely blue eyes of his, I had the strangest feeling of déjà vu. Like I knew him. And not just from my dream.

But that's impossible. Jackson and I are total strangers. We've never met before.

Have we?

CHAPTER 3

JACKSON

Not gonna lie, I'm not loving this day. Then again, this entire year has been one giant clusterfuck. Why should today be any different?

I told Aunt Rachel I wasn't in the mood to go to a carnival. But Duy has been so persistent about hanging out, and my aunt was clearly tired of seeing me mope around the house, so here I am, sitting in awkward silence on a graffitied picnic table at a third-rate funfair while this Riley guy gives me the cold shoulder.

The curvy redheaded girl (Audra or Audrey?) said she was worried about his blood sugar, so she asked me to look after him while she and the others went to get snacks, even though Riley insisted he was fine about a thousand times.

Maybe that's why he's sulking. I don't like people making a fuss over me either. Then again, given the side-eye he's been shooting me ever since we sat down, I'm starting to think maybe something else is going on. He seems kind of on edge around me.

Shit. I wonder if he knows who I am. He doesn't look like he follows football, but maybe he heard about what happened in Tallahassee?

"Everything okay?" I ask when I catch him scrutinizing me out of the corner of his eye for the third time in under a minute.

"What?" he asks, looking startled. The sun has begun to set, but I can still see him blush under the glare of the Ferris wheel's neon lights. "Oh. Yeah. Everything's fine."

He nervously pushes a curl of jet-black hair out of his face, then scans the carnival for his friends. With his distressed gray jeans, black T-shirt, and beaded bracelets, he looks like he'd be more comfortable at some underground indie concert than an amusement park. I wonder if he's also been dragged here against his will.

"Have you ever been to Orlando before?" he asks, turning back and narrowing his gaze at me as if I'm a puzzle he's trying to solve. His eyes are green and sharp—like glass. They have an almost spooky way of demanding your attention.

"Orlando?" I repeat. "Yeah. I've been here a couple of times."

"You have?" He sits up straighter.

"Uh . . . yeah. My parents took me to Disney and Universal when I was a kid."

"Oh," Riley sighs, and turns away in disappointment.

Guess that was the wrong answer? I'm not sure what the right answer would've been. All I know is I feel like I'm failing a test that I didn't even know I was supposed to take.

Then again, failing is something I'm good at. I've failed my parents as a son. I've failed Micaela as a boyfriend. I failed my coach and my team and my school. Hell, I bet most people back in Tally would say I failed the whole damn city.

"Have you ever been to Italy?"

Riley's question catches me off guard. "Italy? Uh. No."

"Oh."

Once again, my answer disappoints him. I don't like losing whatever game we're playing, so I add, "I've always wanted to go, though."

Riley nods and chews his lower lip as he mulls over my response. I'm not sure where these questions are coming from or where they're going, but to avoid another awkward exchange that leaves me feeling like I've flunked my midterm, I change the subject.

"Thanks again for letting me join you and your friends tonight. I haven't gone out much since I moved here, so I appreciate the invite."

Riley shrugs. "It was all Duy."

"Yeah, he seems like a cool dude."

Riley's green-glass eyes turn back to me with a cutting glare. "*They*."

"What?"

"Duy is nonbinary."

Shit. Right. I knew that. Aunt Rachel told me Duy wasn't a boy when he—fuck—when *they* dropped off that welcome-to-the-neighborhood cake.

"Sorry," I say. "I'm still getting used to the whole pronoun thing. We didn't have any trans students at my school in Tallahassee."

Riley shakes his head and snorts. "Okay, first off, Duy is nonbinary, not trans. Some nonbinary people identify as trans, but some do not. Duy does not. Second, I can one hundred percent guarantee that you had trans students at your school. If you didn't know about them, it's because they didn't feel safe telling you."

Fuck. This guy's not giving me an inch. I should probably stop talking. But I don't want him thinking I'm some ignorant redneck. Before I can say anything, though, Duy and the two girls return, their arms overflowing with junk food.

"Okay," the redhead announces, "we got you hot dogs for protein, French fries for starch, Diet Coke for caffeine, funnel cakes in case your blood sugar is low, popcorn and pretzels 'cause why not, and, last but not least, a giant fried pickle because that's the closest thing we could find to a vegetable."

Riley stares at the mountain of food that's just been dumped in front of him and shakes his head.

"Seriously, Audrey? You expect me to eat all this?"

"I told you it was too much," the other girl, the one with the cute button nose, says to her friend. (Tara? Tala? I've got to get better with names.)

"We're covering all the bases," Audrey answers as she plucks a French fry from its basket. With her bell-bottom jeans, beaded necklace, and white flowy blouse, she's rocking a sixties flower-power look pretty hard tonight. But it suits her. As does Tara's/Tala's mixed-and-matched ensemble of lavender jeans, blue blouse, and maroon leather jacket, which I could see Micaela wanting to borrow.

"Please tell me you're going to help me eat all this?" Riley pleads, pushing the pile of food toward his friends, who have seated themselves at the table.

"Well, if you don't want the funnel cake . . ." Tara/Tala says, reaching for the fried dough.

Audrey raises an eyebrow. "Really, T.?"

"It's only my third."

"Yeah, your third in ten minutes. You still have powder on your nose from the last one."

Audrey leans forward and kisses the sugar off her nose. And before I can stop myself, I blurt out, "Oh! You two are a couple?"

Audrey narrows her hazel eyes at me. "Yeah. *And?*"

"No. Nothing," I cover, trying to downplay my surprise. "I just didn't, um, know. Duy didn't tell me."

Audrey nods, her face and body relaxing as Tara/Tala takes her hand. "Audrey and I have been together for two years."

"Two and a half," Audrey corrects her.

"You can't count those first six months."

"Oh my gosh, Tala, how many times do we have to have this conversation?" Audrey groans melodramatically. "They count. They absolutely count. We went on *multiple* dates."

"Yes, but I didn't *know* they were dates. I just thought you really liked hanging out with me and holding hands."

"You're *such* a little liar!" Audrey laughs, pulling her girlfriend into a hug.

I turn from the cuddling girls to Duy, who casually plucks a speck of lint off Riley's shoulder in the same way that Micaela used to pick grass off my football jersey.

"So, are all four of you . . . um . . ." I realize too late that I have no idea how to finish this question.

"Yes," Riley growls. "We're all 'um.' Very, *very* 'um.'"

Shit. I genuinely didn't mean to offend anyone. I just wasn't expecting everyone I met tonight to be gay.

"Cool," I say, trying to shrug off my awkwardness. "That's—cool."

"Glad we have your approval," Riley shoots back.

Tala shoots him a scolding look. "Be nice, Ri."

"What? He started it."

"I'm sorry," I say, wishing I would just stop talking. "I didn't mean anything by it."

"It's okay," Duy assures me, flashing me an amused smile as they adjust the red silk scarf around their neck, the only pop of color in their otherwise all-black ensemble of crop top and short shorts. "We totally acknowledge that your sporty football life back in the conservative wasteland that is Tallahassee might have shielded you from close contact with amazingly fabulous people like us. So, just for today, you get a pass. But for the record, Riley and Audrey identify as gay, Tala is bi, and I'm queer/nonbinary with a preference for guys who look like Henry Golding or Regé-Jean Page. Got all that?"

"Got it." With everyone sharing their sexuality, it strikes me that I should do the same, so I add, "I'm straight."

The group stares at me, and once again I find myself wishing I'd kept my mouth shut.

"That was probably obvious," I say.

Fixing me with his green eyes, Riley grabs one of the hot dogs and pointedly tears the end off with his teeth. "There were clues."

CHAPTER 4

RILEY

After being force-fed my weight in carnival food over the past half an hour, I can safely say that I never want to see another funnel cake or fried pickle for as long as I live. I know my friends are just looking out for me, but honestly, I feel worse now than I did after I fainted. My insides are practically on the verge of exploding.

"Okay, now that we've refueled Riley," Audrey says as she hops up from the picnic bench, "who's ready for the Death Drop?"

My stomach makes an inhuman-sounding groan, and I stare at her with unrestrained incredulity. "Are you joking?"

The Death Drop is a so-called ride where people are slowly raised three hundred feet into the air and then sadistically and violently dropped to the earth at fifty miles per hour. It's never been my favorite attraction, and given my current condition, I would be out of my mind to think that I could ride it and not end up covered in my own vomit.

Not that Audrey seems to register that fact.

"What's the matter?" she asks, looking genuinely perplexed.

I indicate the enormous swath of grease-stained wrappers strewn across the table in front of me.

"*Oh,*" she says as the light of realization dawns in her eyes. "Right."

She bites her lower lip in disappointment, and I watch the same disappointment spread to Duy's and Tala's faces. My friends have always been amateur adrenaline junkies, and the Death Drop is one of their all-time-favorite fixes.

"You guys should go on it without me," I suggest, not wanting to deprive them of one of the few genuine pleasures that this carnival has to offer. I've already spoiled enough of the fun with my fainting.

"Don't be silly," Tala protests. "We're not going to leave you."

"For the one-millionth time, *I'm fine*."

"But what if you faint again?" Duy asks.

I roll my eyes. But before I can respond, Jackson jumps in.

"I can watch him," he announces, much to my surprise. "If the three of you want to ride this death thing, I'm happy to stay here and keep an eye on Riley."

I'm not quite sure how to respond to this. On the one hand, I don't love the infantilizing implication that I'm some child who needs a babysitter. On the other, it is unexpectedly thoughtful of Jackson to stay with me so my friends can get in their extreme thrills. It's not the kind of behavior that I expect from these walking Ken Dolls. And Jackson certainly doesn't have any reason to be nice to me, especially not after the way I've been sniping at him.

Of course, he could just be trying to redeem himself after all his problematic comments; it's hard to say. I'm usually better at reading people and figuring out what their deal is, but Jackson is proving more difficult than I expected.

"Are you sure you're okay staying with Riley?" Audrey asks, though I can tell from the gleam of excitement in her eyes that she's already mentally accepted Jackson's offer.

"Yeah. It's all good," he assures her. "You guys go have fun."

My friends don't need any further convincing. After quickly deciding that we'll meet back up in front of the Ferris wheel in half an hour, they link arms and practically skip off into the night. Though not before Duy shouts parting instructions at Jackson to toss me into the dunking booth if I get too moody.

Jackson chuckles and turns his attention back to me. "Your friends seem really great."

"They're certainly something," I answer, avoiding his gaze. While I'm grateful that my friends' evening hasn't been ruined, I'm not exactly over the moon to spend the next thirty minutes alone with a dude-bro like Jackson. What are we supposed to talk about? His workout routine? Protein shakes? How hot Sydney Sweeney is?

Ugh. I'd rather go back to being unconscious.

"I need to walk off some of this junk food," I announce, rising from the picnic table and half hoping he'll take the hint and not follow. "I'm about to go into a sugar coma."

"Good idea," he says, hopping up like a faithful golden retriever and falling into step beside me as I walk away. I should've known I wouldn't escape so easily.

Stuck with my "sitter," I wander aimlessly down the carnival's main thoroughfare, passing various tents and booths that offer cotton candy, Skee-Ball, fresh lemonade, and face painting. I'm praying there are enough loud noises and twinkling lights to keep Jackson distracted, but it's not long before he's back to attempting another round of awkward small talk.

"So, uh, how did you and your friends meet?" he asks as he chews on the straw of his fountain drink.

"At school," I answer. "Tala, Audrey, and I met when we were freshmen. The year after that, Duy came along, and we sort of took them under our wing. We figured if the four of us wanted to survive high school, it would be in our best interest to stick together."

"Stick together against what?"

"People like you."

Jackson stops in his tracks and tilts his head in confusion. "What do you mean?"

"I mean at my school, people like you seem to take a lot of pleasure in making life really uncomfortable for people like me and my friends.

And because this is Florida and the state is run by Republicans whose mission in life is to make the world unbearable for queer teens, people like you get away with it pretty much all the time. Which means that in addition to stressing about finals and the SAT, my friends and I have the added pressure of walking around with targets on our backs, wondering when the next asshole is going to say or do something to ruin our day. And we get to do this every day of every week of every year until we're old enough to graduate and get the fuck out of Florida."

Jackson opens his mouth to say something, and I prepare myself for the usual stream of protests that I get from defensive straight people: that they personally have never bullied anyone, that not all straight people are the enemy, et cetera, et cetera. I've heard it all before, and I'm ready for whatever Jackson says next.

To my surprise, though, Jackson just shakes his head and says, "Fuck, dude, that sucks. I'm sorry you have to deal with that."

Unprepared for the earnestness of his apology and the total lack of defensiveness in his response, I feel all my scathing rejoinders die on my tongue.

"Thanks," I hear myself say.

Jackson nods, and we continue our stroll. We're both silent, and it occurs to me in that silence that I was (perhaps) intentionally trying to goad Jackson with my comments. What can I say? I wanted to piss him off so he'd reveal his true colors. And I suppose, in a way, he did. It just wasn't a color I was expecting.

Not that I'm ready to make peace with him yet. I still don't trust him. Mainly because I can't shake the feeling that my dream was some kind of warning. Like my subconscious was telling me, *Yes, he's hot, but be careful. There's danger around the corner.*

Except Jackson doesn't seem dangerous. Oddly familiar, yes. But dangerous? The more time I spend with him, the harder it gets to justify my initial impression that he's just another sports-bro who's hell-bent on ruining my life. If I'm honest, I don't know *what* he is, aside from Duy's new neighbor.

I guess what I'm saying is the jury's still out on Jackson Haines.

"So, are you and Duy, like, a couple?" he asks.

"Duy?" I laugh, surprised by his question. "No, not at all. They're like my sibling. Also, I'm pretty sure I'm not their type. Duy's only into guys with six-packs and pecs. You know, guys who could be Greek gods or underwear models. Guys like you."

Guys like you? Did I hit my fucking head when I fainted? Why would I say that out loud?

Jackson lets out a snort of laughter, and I feel my entire face burn.

"A Greek god or an underwear model, huh?"

"I didn't mean you *specifically*," I backtrack. "I meant someone *like* you."

"Like me?"

"Sporty. Athletic. You know what I mean. Don't act like this is the first time someone has pointed out that you're—"

"That I'm what?"

"Annoying, Jackson. You're very, *very* annoying."

Jackson laughs, and his laughter is so open and good-natured, it makes me feel warm all over. Then, just as suddenly, Jackson stops and stares down guiltily at his Nikes, as if he isn't sure if he's allowed to laugh.

Odd. He did the same thing earlier when he mentioned that he used to play football at his old school, and Duy joked that the only sports they like to watch is the volleyball sequence in *Top Gun*. Jackson laughed, then immediately stopped himself.

Now he's done it again. He keeps walking back his happiness. Like he doesn't trust it. Or like he doesn't think he deserves it.

"So... Duy said you live with your aunt?" I ask, hoping to ease his awkwardness with a change of topic.

Jackson nods. "Yeah. I moved in with my aunt about a week ago."

"But your parents are still in Tallahassee?"

"Yep."

"How come they didn't move to Orlando with you? Or are they planning to move down later this summer?"

Jackson shrugs nonchalantly, but avoids my eyes. "It's kind of up in the air at the moment."

"What does that mean?"

"My dad's a doctor. Physical medicine and rehab. He works a lot with Florida State, so it's not exactly convenient for him to pack up and move his practice. Besides, I'll only be here for a year before I head off to college, so it doesn't really make sense for him and my mom to move just for my sake, you know?"

"Sure," I concede. "But then why did *you* move here?"

Another shrug. "Better schools."

"Better schools?" I scoff. "Here?"

"Yeah."

"Do you mean, like, better for football?"

Jackson doesn't answer. He finishes off his soda and effortlessly tosses the cup into a nearby trash can. I'm not sure if I should repeat my question or let the subject drop. But before I can decide, the matter becomes moot. A raucous cackling splits the air, and when I turn to look, I see the Olympus football team bounding down the thoroughfare like a pack of overcaffeinated hyenas.

"Crap," I growl under my breath. If the Thunderbolts spot me, they're going to say something. Because they *always* say something. And I'm really not in the mood for some classic schoolyard bullying on my first week of summer break.

Without thinking, I grab Jackson's hand and pull him into the nearest tent. I close the flap behind us, shutting out the light and noise of the outside world and shrouding us in darkness. Jackson starts to protest, but I shush him and press my ear to the tent flap to listen for the Thunderbolts. It's not long before I hear their laughter. It's wild and rowdy and hungry for attention—the exact opposite of Jackson's.

The whooping grows louder until the voices sound like they're right in front of us. Holding my breath, I silently pray to the universe that none of the boys saw me sneak inside this tent. It seems to work. The howling moves on, gradually fading into the din of the carnival.

"Okay," I say, letting out a sigh of relief as I peek out from behind the flap. "We're good."

Jackson doesn't say anything. He just stares at me for a confused second, then looks down at his hand—which I'm holding.

My cheeks burn as the memory of my dream washes over me. Jackson and I in bed. His weight on top of me. His lips stealing kisses. His hands caressing me *everywhere*.

"Sorry!" I blurt out, dropping his hand like it's on fire.

"Uh, no problem," he mumbles, shooting me a forced smile that barely masks his own discomfort.

I don't know what possessed me to grab his hand like that or pull him into the tent with me. It's not like the Thunderbolts would've messed with someone like Jackson. If anything, they would've taken one look at his biceps and crowned him their new bro-king.

"I take it those guys go to your school?" he asks, still not speaking above a whisper.

"Yeah." I nod.

"They're the ones you were talking about earlier, the ones who mess with you and your friends?"

"Only when they have nothing better to do," I joke in an attempt to brush off his concern. The last thing I need is a straight boy's pity. But, like most oblivious straight boys, Jackson doesn't take the hint.

"Are you okay?" he presses.

"Me? Yeah. I'm fine. Really. It's not a big deal."

"Are you sure? You seem kind of—"

"I'm *fine*," I snap.

Jackson opens his mouth to say something, then thinks better of it. He nods unconvincingly and kicks at the grass.

Crap. I think I hurt his feelings.

"Sorry," I whisper. "I know you're trying to be nice."

"It's fine. My father always says I never know when to keep my mouth shut."

"I really am okay," I tell him. "I don't know why I made us hide. Those guys probably wouldn't have done anything. I just didn't want to deal with the hassle if they did. Not that I can't take of myself. But somedays it's just easier to avoid certain situations and save yourself a lot of bullshit, you know?"

Jackson nods. "Yeah, I do." And something about the way the light goes out in his eyes makes me think he means it.

"Anyway, we should probably head back to the Ferris wheel..."

I reach for the tent flap, but as I do, a voice suddenly calls out from the darkness. "Who seeks to know the future from the great Madame Carlotta?"

Jackson and I nearly jump out of our skins. We spin around and see a woman seated at a small table in the very back of the tent. A large crystal ball gleams in front of her, illuminated by thick red candles that she's slowly lighting one by one.

"Holy crap," I gasp as I attempt to catch my breath. Has she been here the entire time?

"Do not be afraid, my children!" the woman exclaims dramatically, beckoning us closer with a gesture that causes the many bangles on her wrist to jangle together. She appears to be in her late forties with sunburned cheeks and a mane of long black hair. Despite the early June heat, she's wearing about ten shawls, each one embroidered with moons and stars. "Madame Carlotta knows all. Madame Carlotta sees all. Madame Carlotta reveals all!"

"Madame Carlotta" has an accent that sounds like a mishmash of Greek, Indian, and Arabic. Which is to say, totally fake. In fact, I'm pretty sure she's the actress who played Cleopatra last year in the Orlando Shakespeare Company's production of *Antony and Cleopatra*.

"Thanks," I say, giving her an apologetic smile as I start to back toward the exit, "but we just came in here by accident. We're good."

"Ah, but are you? Is your future as secure as you think? Or does calamity await upon the horizon? Only the cards know for sure." With a flourish, Madame Carlotta spreads a tarot deck on her table. "Plus, for one night only, I'm offering a two-for-one special. Just for couples."

Couples?

I shoot a quick glance at Jackson, fully expecting him to contradict her with a vigorous defense of his heterosexuality. It's how every macho guy at my school would respond to even the slightest implication that he might be queer. Jackson, though, just stares at the ground and awkwardly clears his throat. I guess the fact that he's not tripping over himself to assert his straightness is another indication that he's not as awful as I first thought. Although part of me wishes he didn't look quite so mortified at the suggestion that he might be my boyfriend.

"I think your crystal ball's a bit dusty," I shoot back at our hostess before pushing my way out of the musty tent and into the open air.

I don't wait to see if Jackson follows. Between my swooning, the hand-holding, and him being mistaken for my boyfriend, he's had a lot of queer shit thrown at him. I honestly wouldn't blame him if he needed some space. Hell, I wouldn't blame him if he disappeared for the rest of the summer and then showed up on the first day of school acting like we'd never met.

Actually, that's not true. I would 100 percent blame him if he pulled that shit because no one's masculinity should be that fragile. But a very small part of me would also understand.

"That was weird," Jackson says as he hurries after me and once again falls into step beside me.

"Yeah. Weird," I repeat, relieved to see he's not as fragile as I feared.

"Fortune tellers always give me the creeps," he adds, folding his arms across his chest as if fighting off a shiver.

"Really?" I ask. "Why?"

"I don't know." He shrugs. "They've always freaked me out. All that talk about peering into the future and seeing doom on the horizon."

"You know she's not *actually* a fortune teller," I remind him. "I mean, if she could really predict the future, I'm pretty sure she'd be a millionaire lounging in her mansion in Hawaii instead of working in a tent that smells like patchouli and piss."

Jackson chuckles. "Yeah, I know. It's more the *idea* of fortune tellers that makes me uncomfortable. I don't like thinking there could be someone out there who knows my future."

"Why not?"

Jackson considers. "I guess because if someone knows the future, then that means nothing we do matters. Because our future's already written. Which means we're all just trapped in these lives that we don't really have any control over because they're not even our own. They're something that already exists. And we've just been slotted into them without any say in the matter. In which case, life is kind of pointless."

I think it's safe to say that when I woke up this morning, the last thing I expected to hear today was a rumination on free will versus predestination courtesy of a walking Ken Doll. Even more surprising, I think I actually agree with Jackson.

"That makes a lot of sense," I tell him.

"Right?"

"Although, for the record," I clarify, "if I was about to walk into some epic *Titanic*-level disaster, I wouldn't mind a little heads-up from a psychic."

"Even if you couldn't change anything?" Jackson asks.

"Yeah, even if I couldn't change anything."

"How come?"

"Honestly, Jackson? I just really hate surprises."

CHAPTER 5

JACKSON

Aunt Rachel is sitting in the garage that doubles as her studio enjoying a glass of wine and the cool night breeze when I pull into the driveway a little before ten.

I'm not used to being home so early. Especially on a Saturday. Back in Tally, games and after-parties usually kept me out well past midnight. But those days are over. Now I'm a guy who goes to second-rate carnivals and chauffeurs his neighbor home in time for curfew.

"Thanks for the ride," Duy chirps as they hop out of my Jeep.

"No problem. Thanks again for inviting me out tonight."

"Of course! Also, if you're not doing anything tomorrow, we're all going to Rink-O-Rama around noon."

"Rink-O-*what?*" I ask.

"Rink-O-Rama. It's a skating rink. And on Sundays they do a whole *Xanadu* tribute and play Olivia Newton-John nonstop. It's *amazing*. You have to join us."

"Oh," I say, not expecting to field another offer to hang quite so soon.

Tonight was fun. Mostly. But I'm not sure it's something I want to repeat. My plan for getting through my senior year without any more drama is to keep my head down and fly under the radar as much as possible until graduation. Somehow, I think that might prove difficult if I keep spending time with Duy and their crew.

Besides, I'm not really in the market for new friends.

"Let me check with my aunt," I hedge. "I think we have plans tomorrow."

"Oh, really?" Duy pouts in disappointment. "Well, if anything changes, you know where to find me. Also, you have my number."

I do. I actually have everyone's number from tonight. Duy insisted on adding me to their group text before we left the carnival.

"Night, Miss Haines!" Duy calls to my aunt, giving her an enthusiastic wave as they stroll across the lawn to their own house.

"Night, Duy," Aunt Rachel calls back. "Thanks again for the bánh xoai."

"My pleasure!"

There's a second lawn chair set up next to my aunt's in the garage, so after grabbing a Coke out of the minifridge, I plop down beside her.

"You have a good time tonight, kiddo?" she asks, setting aside the magazine she was skimming. She's wearing her navy-blue coveralls, and her brown hair is pulled up into a red bandanna, giving her a real Rosie the Riveter vibe. She must have been sculpting earlier.

"Yeah. Carnival was fun."

"See?" she crows, breaking into a wide grin. "I told you the world wouldn't end if you left your room for *one* night."

I can't help smiling. Despite her tendency to exaggerate about anything and everything, Rachel has always been my favorite aunt.

She's almost ten years younger than my father, and because of that they've never been especially close. Even so, from the moment I was born, Rachel and I just clicked. I think it's because, in a family of overachievers and perfectionists, my aunt is the one person I'm related to who thinks that you should be allowed to enjoy life and not spend every waking second trying to conquer it.

That's what my father does. Conquer.

When he was growing up, his one goal in life was to play for the NFL. He ate, slept, and breathed football. By all accounts, he was damn good at it too. Everyone was convinced he'd go pro. That is until a knee injury in college sidelined his dreams of glory.

Even then, he didn't lose his drive. He just switched his focus, channeling all his energy into sports medicine and building up the state's most successful physical therapy and rehab center. Now when the Seminoles' quarterback tears his ACL or the Dolphins' wide receiver dislocates his shoulder, they come to my father, and he gets them back on the gridiron. Because Dr. Wyatt Haines is a man who gets results.

My mother isn't much different, at least when it comes to ambition. She spent her teens and twenties dominating the pageant circuit in the hopes of becoming Miss Florida and, ultimately, Miss America. She never managed to take home the big crown, but she did eventually take home my dad, becoming Mrs. Holly Haines in the process. Now she runs a successful real estate agency catering to footballers and other newly rich sports professionals looking to buy retirement homes for their parents in the Florida panhandle.

Then there's Aunt Rachel.

My father always says Aunt Rachel could've been a really successful artist if she'd had a bit more ambition and approached her sculpting the way that he approached medicine. But world domination has never been Rachel's thing. Sure, she might be only an adjunct art professor at a community college who spends her weekends sculpting in her garage. But unlike my parents, Aunt Rachel seems genuinely happy with the life she's built for herself. She doesn't need a trophy or an empire to prove her worth to the world. Or to herself.

Is it any wonder I wanted to live with her after everything that went down in December?

"Did I hear Duy invite you to go skating tomorrow?" my aunt asks, finishing off the last of her wine.

"Yeah. He did—*they* did."

"That was nice of them."

"Mm-hmm."

"Did I also hear you say that you wouldn't be able to go because you and I have some vague mystery plans that I am unaware of?"

Shit. I was hoping Aunt Rachel didn't hear that part. "Yeah, sorry. I shouldn't have lied."

"No, please, don't apologize. I just wanted to make sure I hadn't scheduled important bonding time with my nephew and then forgotten. You know I'm a senile old crone who can barely remember what day it is."

I roll my eyes. "You're thirty-eight."

"I'm thirty-*four*!" she barks, swatting my shoulder with her magazine.

"Ow! Okay! Sorry!"

"Thirty-*eight*." She snorts. "You're lucky you're so good-looking, kiddo, because your manners are crap."

For a second, I think I'm off the hook. Then Aunt Rachel fixes me with one of her sideways glances. "So what's going on? Why don't you want to hang out with Duy? Did you not have a good time tonight?"

"It's not that," I say.

Despite my initial hesitation about going out, I am glad I went. After Riley and I met back up with his friends, we spent the rest of the night hopping from ride to ride and playing games. Duy lost half an hour (and a ridiculous amount of money) to a ring toss trying to win a giant purple octopus; Audrey managed to get banned from the bumper cars for "reckless driving"; and Tala ate four funnel cakes, after which she complained of a stomachache that she insisted was completely unrelated.

It was a bizarre and ridiculous evening. But despite my current "situation," I think I actually enjoyed myself. And that's the problem.

"Did you not get along with Duy?" my aunt presses when I continue to stare down at the bottle of Coke in my lap. "I know they're a bit different from the kids you're used to."

"No, I like Duy and their friends. They were weird but interesting. Especially this one guy, Riley. He made me laugh. They all did."

"Okay . . . so you hung out with funny, interesting people and had a good time. I totally understand why you wouldn't want to do *that* again."

"Come on, Aunt Rach. I'm only gonna be here in Orlando for, what, a year? There's no point in making friends."

"A year's a long time to go it alone, kiddo."

"I'll survive."

Aunt Rachel's mouth twists into a frown. "So that's the plan? You're going to spend your senior year alone with no one for company other than your insanely cool, vibrantly young, breathtakingly glamorous aunt?"

"I thought you were a senile crone?"

Aunt Rachel swats me with the magazine again.

"Ow!"

"Jackson, you can't spend the rest of your life hiding in your room," she says, her tone once more tinged with concern.

"That's not what I'm doing," I protest. Even though, yeah, that's exactly what I'm doing.

My aunt shakes her head, then takes my chin in her hand and forces me to meet her dark brown eyes. "Look, kiddo, I know you've had a rough couple of months, and I fully support your decision to move in with me and make a fresh start. But for the past week, all I've seen you do is play video games and eat microwaved Hot Pockets. You can't keep hiding from the world."

"I'm not," I insist. "I'm just . . . taking a pause."

Aunt Rachel lets go of my face and sighs. "Sometimes, Jackson, we stumble in life. And you can let that stumble define who you are and sabotage any chance of future happiness, or you can try to move past it and build a new life for yourself in a new city with new friends who are funny and smart and just the right amount of weird. I personally think the latter is the better option, but I will support you no matter what you do because you are my nephew and I love you and I just want to see you happy. You know you're allowed to be happy, right?"

I'm not sure that's true, but I appreciate her saying it.

"I know," I tell her. "I'll try."

Aunt Rachel nods and smiles. "That's all any of us can do."

CHAPTER 6

RILEY

When I get home from the carnival, Dad is waiting for me in the living room practically vibrating with excitement, like a kid on Christmas morning.

"What do you think?" he asks, his eyes twinkling behind his thick glasses as he thrusts a cobalt-blue suit in my face. I'm starting my internship at the ACLU in a week, and this suit is obviously intended as a bribe to get me amped about a long summer of paralegal work.

"Um. Wow. Thanks," I say, doing my best to muster the appropriate level of enthusiasm. With its slim lapels and subtle pinstripe, the suit is admittedly quite stylish. It's also, however, an unfortunate reminder of just how much a person's taste can change.

Case in point: When I was ten, Dad asked me what I wanted to be when I grew up, and because he was my hero, I told him that I wanted to be just like him—I wanted to be a lawyer.

To clarify, Dad isn't the gross kind of lawyer who spends his days helping corporations avoid paying taxes. He's a civil rights attorney. And for the past twelve years he's worked for the ACLU, fighting for criminal justice reform, free speech, immigrants' rights, voting rights, and (of course) LGBTQ+ rights.

I still remember as a kid eagerly listening to him talk about all the cases he was working on and all the people he was trying to help. He was so passionate about his work and even more passionate about instilling that passion in me, his one and only child. And for a while, I shared his passion.

To my ten-year-old brain, my dad was Superman. Only instead of tearing his suit off before heading out to fight injustice, my dad put one on. Even after all these years, Dad's enthusiasm for his work is still infectious. And as cheesy as it sounds, he's still my hero. The only trouble is, now that it's my turn to don a suit and help save the world from injustice, I'm having second thoughts. More than second thoughts.

I *know* I don't want to be a lawyer. I've actually known this for quite some time. I just haven't found the right opportunity to tell my dad and break his heart.

"Do you like the color?" he asks, noticing my hesitation. "I know you're more into blacks and grays, but I thought something with a little color could be fun."

"The color's great," I say as a fresh wave of guilt washes over me. "You *really* didn't need to do this."

"Of course I did! It's not every day that my son comes to work with me."

I force myself to smile, and Dad laughs one of his good-natured laughs.

"Don't worry, I'll try not to embarrass you too much at the office," he jokes, slapping me on the back. Though, to be honest, I'm far more concerned about embarrassing him.

I've inherited a lot of things from my dad (his curly black hair, his aversion to tomatoes, his love of classic *Doctor Who*), but an unwavering optimism about the world isn't one of them. But that's Greg Iverson. He goes to work every day believing that he can make a difference.

Me? I'm not so sure.

Given everything that's happened over the past few years, it seems to me that America is one giant dumpster fire, and things are only getting worse. Especially for people like me and my friends. And while I know it's important not to lose hope and to keep fighting prejudice and inequality, most days it feels like my time would be equally well spent banging my head against a large rock. Because for every Greg Iverson fighting for queer rights, there are a hundred lawyers and politicians on the other side of the aisle trying to take them away.

It's exhausting. We might be on the right side of history, but most of the time it feels like we're also on the losing side. And honestly? I'm not sure we'll ever win.

But how do I tell my dad that? How do I say, *Hey, you know everything you've spent your entire life fighting for? Well, I think it's all been a waste of time, and this country and humanity are doomed. But thanks for the snazzy suit!*

"Why don't you head upstairs and try it on?" Dad suggests, still grinning with pride. "Make sure it fits."

"I'm actually kind of tired," I lie. "I think I'm just going to go to bed."

"Oh," he says, unable to hide his disappointment.

I don't want to hurt his feelings, so I shoot him a conciliatory smile and add, "I'm also kind of sweaty and gross from the carnival. I don't want to stink up the suit. But I'll try it on first thing tomorrow. After I've showered."

Dad nods, accepting the compromise. Then, feigning a few expertly crafted yawns, I carry the suit upstairs to my room and promptly shove it into the back of my closet.

Almost immediately, though, my guilt overtakes me. Even if the suit is a reminder of the potentially exhausting future that Dad has laid out for me, it's still a thoughtful gift. A thoughtful gift from a kind and compassionate father to his thankless child who's a terrible son and an even worse homosexual.

Seriously, how many queer teenagers would kill to have a parent who's this excited for their child to follow in their footsteps and work alongside them to fight for queer rights? I hate that I'm so ungrateful.

But sometimes I feel like I answered a question when I was ten, and that answer determined the entire rest of my life.

It's like what Jackson said at the carnival tonight. If the story of your life has already been written, can you even call it your life?

With that depressing thought, I decide not to wait until morning to wash up and head to the bathroom. A hot shower is one of the few things that can lift my spirits when I start to sink into one of my existential black holes. And a few minutes later, with the warm water washing the sweat and stress of the day down the drain, I do feel a little less fatalistic about my future.

I also find myself thinking about Jackson.

I still can't figure him out. On the one hand, he was exactly what I expected from a walking Ken Doll: clueless, privileged, awkward around queer people. But on the other hand, he was thoughtful and compassionate and ready to own his mistakes. He also laughed at my jokes, which indicates a higher-than-average intelligence.

That being said, he looked really uncomfortable when Duy insisted that he save all our numbers in his phone. He clearly wasn't ready for that level of commitment.

I bet he's already deleted us from his contacts. In fact, I bet none of us sees or hears from Jackson Haines for the rest of the summer.

Not that I care.

Sure, overall, he seemed like a not-terrible guy. I didn't mind hanging out with him. If I'm honest, I also didn't mind his piercing blue eyes. Or his ridiculously toned biceps. Or his strong but surprisingly soft hands. Or . . .

Crap.

I don't need to look between my legs to know what the situation is down there. I can feel all the blood in my body rushing to a certain extremity.

What is wrong with me? There's literally nothing more mortifying or clichéd than crushing on a straight boy. And yet my stupid body has decided to betray me all because Jackson has a cute smile and a tight ass.

"Traitor!" I hiss at my erection.

There's no way I'm going to indulge my body's problematic taste in boys. Instead, I turn the water temperature down as low as it will go. Sure enough, it takes only about ten seconds of waterboarding my groin with ice-cold water to get my libido under control.

With my hormones in check, I step out of the shower and dry myself off, thankful for the warmth of my towel. Then I head back to my room, where I slip on a clean pair of boxers and consider trying on the new suit so I can show Dad that I'm not the world's shittiest son. Before I can make it to my closet, though, my phone buzzes. Much to my surprise, I see the group text has a message from its newest member.

JACKSON: Had fun tonight. Looking forward to skating tomorrow if the offer still stands.

Huh. Okay. Interesting.

Duy must have invited Jackson to Rink-O-Rama. I should've expected that.

What I wouldn't have expected was for Jackson to accept.

Or that I would be so excited that he did. I can feel my heart racing in my chest. Which is ridiculous, because I so don't care one way or the other if I ever see Jackson again.

Which isn't to say that if *he* wanted to hang out, I'd be against the idea. I could see a future where we might be friends. Maybe. We do sort of seem to have a connection, at least when it comes to hating psychics and predestination.

Is that why I can't shake the feeling that we've met before? Because he's some sort of kindred spirit?

Oh my God, what the hell am I saying? Kindred spirit? That's ridiculous. I literally just met the guy. I barely know him!

But if that's true, why did I have that very inappropriate dream where I was going on and on about how he was the other half of my soul?

Somehow chalking it up to physical attraction doesn't seem like a good enough explanation. Not for such a vivid and elaborate dream. There must be a practical reason why Jackson seems so familiar.

I know this mystery is going to keep me up all night unless I get to the bottom of it, so I grab my laptop off my desk and flop down onto my bed, hoping that a quick search of his socials might provide me with a clue as to where I've seen him before.

There are three people named Jackson Haines on X but none of them are high-school students. Next I try Instagram, but he doesn't seem to have a profile there either. Same for TikTok and Snapchat. In fact, as far as I can tell, Jackson Haines has no social media presence whatsoever.

Which is odd*. Even serial killers have fan accounts.*

I decide to try an old-fashioned Google search, but it turns out Jackson Haines is an annoyingly common name (as well as a nineteenth-century figure skater). I narrow the search parameters to Jackson Haines *and* Tallahassee *and* football *(which are the only things I know about him), and the first result that comes up is a link to a news story from December with the headline "Friday Night Lights (Out)." Next to it is a thumbnail of Jackson in a football uniform with the rest of his team, the Tallahassee Wolverines.*

I click the link, and it takes me to the website of a Tallahassee newspaper. I start to skim the article, but I don't need to read more than the first few paragraphs to realize two very important things.

One, I definitely know who Jackson Haines is.

And two, I was right not to trust him.

CHAPTER 7

JACKSON

When I get back to Aunt Rachel's after my morning run, it's almost ten. Which is late for me. Normally, I'm up and out of the house at the crack of dawn. It's part of the daily regimen that my father devised for me after I made running back freshman year, and I've maintained it ever since, even over these past few months. My days playing for the Wolverines might be ancient history, but with all the changes in my life, it's been comforting to have a routine to fall back on.

Today is the first day I've broken that routine. My internal alarm clock, which is always so adamant about waking me up with the sun, must have decided to let me sleep in. Not that I'm complaining. Maybe it was my talk with Aunt Rachel or maybe it was hanging out with Duy and Riley and the others, but I slept better last night than I have in months.

"What time are you heading out to meet your friends?" my aunt asks, nibbling a piece of buttered toast as she finishes a late breakfast in the kitchen.

"I'm supposed to go over and collect Duy in an hour," I answer as I pour myself a large glass of orange juice, which I immediately polish off in one long satisfying gulp.

"Roller-skating and Olivia Newton-John." Aunt Rachel chuckles. "Everything old is new again."

"Or maybe everything old is still old, and Duy and their friends have really bad taste."

"Duy? Bad taste?" My aunt shakes her head. "Have you seen the outfits that kid makes? They're going to be the next Oscar de la Renta."

"I have no idea who that is."

"Oh, go shower. Your teenage funk is stinking up my kitchen."

Laughing, I lean over my aunt's chair and wrap her in a sweaty bear hug. "Love you."

"Gross! You're getting boy smell on my favorite robe. Go away!"

I grab a piece of toast and head off to my room, which technically is Aunt Rachel's guest room. With the exception of my Xbox and some clothes, I haven't unpacked any of the boxes that I brought with me from Tallahassee, and when I see them stacked haphazardly against the wall, it occurs to me that I should get around to that. After all, I am gonna be here for a while.

I peel off my sweat-stained tank top and toss it into my hamper along with my shorts and underwear. I'm smelling pretty ripe after my run, but before heading to the shower, I check my phone to see if I have any new messages. When I texted the group chat last night to say I was down to hang today, Tala wrote back, *Great!* Audrey sent a thumbs-up. And Duy replied with *Yay* spelled with about twenty-five *y*'s and a string of emojis that meant they were either really excited or having a stroke.

The only person who didn't text back was Riley.

That surprised me. I felt like the two of us had a connection. Not at first, obviously. But by the end of the night, it felt like we were vibing. Like we got each other. It's odd he hasn't responded.

Then again, maybe he doesn't want me to come? I did say a lot of asinine things last night. It might've pissed him off more than I realized. Maybe I should text him. Just to make sure we're good.

Wait. Hold up. *What am I doing?*

Why am I acting like some girl who got stood up by her prom date?

Riley doesn't owe me a response. It was Duy who invited me. For all I know, Riley isn't even coming. I need to *chill*.

I toss my phone onto my unmade bed and head down the hall to the guest bathroom where I take a quick shower. Once I finish drying off, I wrap a towel around my waist and return to my room just in time to hear my phone buzz with an incoming text. Despite my previous instructions to myself to chill, I can't help checking to see if it's Riley.

It's not. But I don't have time to be disappointed, because after four long weeks of silence, Micaela has finally sent me a message.

MICAELA: Hey.

It's just that one word. With a period. But given how I treated her, it's more than I deserve.

She was the one person who stood by me despite everything that happened in December. And how did I repay her? By ignoring her calls and shutting her out of my life. Even then it took her months to dump my ass. And that was only after I told her I was moving to Orlando.

Hey, I write back.

I'm not sure what else to say. What can you say to someone whose heart you broke?

I don't think I was ever in love with Micaela, but we were good together. At least in the beginning. We'd been friends for years before we'd started dating, so in a way, it almost seemed inevitable that we'd end up together. She was a cheerleader; I was a running back. We were at all the same games and all the same parties. We were both on strict diets but couldn't resist Taco Bell on our cheat days. It just made sense to be together.

Everything with Micaela was easy. Effortless. Until it wasn't.

How's Orlando? she texts back.

JACKSON: Okay. Different.

MICAELA: Good different or bad different?

JACKSON: Just different-different.

Micaela sends me the confused-face emoji, and I chuckle because I know in real life, she makes that exact same scrunched-up expression.

How are you? I text back without thinking, then instantly regret it. What can she possibly say to that? *Great! My boyfriend ghosted me for an entire semester, then moved to a different city. #Blessed. #BestLife.*

After a longer pause than usual, she responds. Heading off to cheer camp this afternoon.

Aren't you a bit old for camp? I joke, hoping to keep things light.

Ha-ha, she types instead of using the laughing emoji, which is how I know she's being sarcastic. I'm one of the instructors.

JACKSON: Ah. So you'll be molding the next generation of cheerleaders?

MICAELA: I like to think of them as cheer warriors.

JACKSON: Sounds intense.

MICAELA: Just doing God's work.

Like I said, easy. Even after our awkward breakup and a month of not talking, we're able to fall into our old routine like no time's passed.

MICAELA: Do you think you'll come back to Tally for a visit this summer?

Her question catches me off guard. I'm not sure how to respond. Is she asking because she wants to see me? Because she's hoping we might get back together? I don't want to lead her on or make her think that's a possibility, but I also don't want to hurt her any more than I already have.

I don't know, I type back noncommittally. Right now, vagueness seems like the best course of action. Or inaction.

MICAELA: What about your birthday?

JACKSON: I'll probably spend it here with Aunt Rachel.

MICAELA: That's so sad.

She's not wrong. I always figured that when I turned eighteen, I'd throw a huge house party, invite all the guys from the team, maybe hire a DJ. Micaela would be there, of course, along with the rest of the cheer squad. There'd be too much smoking and drinking, and the neighbors would complain about the noise. My parents, though, would conveniently be out of town because despite their insistence on excellence, they also understand that every once in a while, champions need to celebrate.

But I'm not a champion. Not anymore. And I never will be again.

How the mighty have fallen, I text.

I mean it as a joke. But as soon as I hit send, the truth of that statement hits me with the force of a linebacker. I suspect it's hitting Micaela the same way. She doesn't text back for what feels like an eternity, and when she does, all she says is Sorry. Mom's nagging me to finish packing. Got to go.

There's so much more I want to say to her, so much I want to apologize for. But I don't know where to begin. Thanks for checking up on me, I type.

She doesn't respond.

Maybe it's for the best. Even if I have no desire to get back together with her, a part of me wishes we could still be friends. But I don't think that would be good for either of us. I moved to Orlando so we could have a clean break. It's what I need and what I'm sure Micaela needs. There's no point in clinging to the past.

An abrupt and angry banging on my bedroom door jolts me out of my self-pitying spiral, and without thinking, I call out, "Come in."

The door swings open and Riley enters, his face screwed into a scowl and his shoulders tensed. He looks like someone ready for a fight.

"We need to talk," he barks—then stops in his tracks.

I'm not sure why he's staring at me like a deer in headlights until I realize that the only thing I'm wearing is a damp bath towel. Three years in a locker room have pretty much made me numb to nudity (especially my own). Riley, though, is clearly uncomfortable.

"My bad," I apologize. "Just got out of the shower."

I grab a pair of underwear out of my dresser and slide them on under the towel while Riley stares at the floor. It's kind of funny how freaked out he is.

"All clear," I assure him after pulling on some chinos and a pink polo.

Riley cautiously glances up from the carpet to confirm I'm no longer naked. Satisfied, he shakes off his awkwardness and grumbles, "Sorry," though he sounds more annoyed than contrite. "Your aunt let me in."

"That's okay. What's up? What did you want to talk to me about?"

Riley fixes me with his sharp green eyes. "Devon Sanderson."

I can feel the color drain from my face. "What?"

"Devon Sanderson," he repeats. "You know, the kid that you and your friends put in the hospital."

CHAPTER 8

RILEY

"Well?" I ask when Jackson continues to stare at me in silence.

After reading about Jackson in the Tallahassee newspaper last night, I found five more articles about him and his football team, including one in the *Orlando Sentinel*. That's where I must have seen his picture and why he seemed so familiar.

I considered forwarding the article to my friends—they should definitely know what kind of guy Jackson is. But I decided to hold off until I confronted him. I want to hear with my own ears what he has to say for himself.

Jackson, though, doesn't look like he's in the mood to talk. He doesn't look like he's in the mood for anything. As he sits on the edge of his bed, his whole body deflates in shame.

"You heard?" he finally manages to ask.

"Yeah. I heard."

"Do the others know?"

"Uh . . . no," I say, slightly taken aback that *that's* his first concern. Jackson looks up at me, his eyes hopeful. Until I add, "Not *yet*."

Nodding, he hangs his head in defeat. He looks so crushed—so miserable—that a part of me wants to rush to his side and give him a hug. Then I remember the photo of Devon Sanderson in his hospital bed, and I remind myself that Jackson isn't the victim here.

"I'm really sorry about what happened to Devon," he says, his voice almost a whisper.

"So why did you do it?" I snap.

Jackson shakes his head. "Does it matter?"

"It does to me."

Jackson looks up in surprise. I'm surprised too. I don't know where this burning need to hear his side of the story is coming from. If Duy or Tala or Audrey had hurt someone, I'd give them every opportunity to explain themselves. But I've known Jackson for less than twenty-four hours. I shouldn't care why he did what he did or what excuses he might have. And yet I can't help myself—I need him to explain.

"Did you ever feel like you were living the wrong life?" Jackson asks. His question catches me off guard, and when I don't answer, he continues. "I've been playing football ever since I learned to walk. I don't even remember deciding it was something I wanted to do. My father played when he was in college. So did my grandfather. There was never any question that I'd play too. Football was . . . in my blood."

He says that last part like he's discussing a congenital disorder instead of a family pastime. "You didn't enjoy playing?" I ask, wondering where this is leading.

Jackson shrugs. "I liked making my father proud. And I wasn't particularly good at anything else, so it didn't really matter if I enjoyed playing or not. It's what I did. I never really felt like I had a choice."

I nod. Only last night, I was lamenting the fact that my life didn't feel like my own and wondering if it ever would. I guess I'm not the only one struggling under the weight of other people's expectations.

Be that as it may, I'm still not any closer to understanding what happened to Devon.

"What does all this have to do with . . ."

"Right, sorry," Jackson apologizes. "I'm getting to that. It's just kind of hard to talk about."

"Take your time," I tell him, my voice coming out far kinder than I intend.

Jackson shoots me a grateful look. "Devon was a freshman. He joined the team in the fall and wasn't the best player. That's not an excuse for what happened. But it—it made him a target."

I nod, intimately aware of how bullying starts. And how it can end.

"You see, we were on a pretty hot winning streak last year," Jackson continues. "We had a real chance of making it all the way to the state final and taking home the trophy for the first time in something like twenty-five years. It was all anyone at school talked about. Hell, it was all anyone in Tallahassee talked about. Even Devon."

Jackson pauses and lets out a defeated sigh. "But Devon . . . he kept messing up. Little mistakes. Nothing major. But the guys on the team began to get afraid that one of Devon's 'little mistakes' was gonna cost us the championship. They started hazing him, usually at parties after our games. I think some of the guys legitimately thought they were toughening him up, you know? That they were helping him. Or teaching him a lesson. But the other half? The other half just wanted to punish him."

"What did they do?" I ask. The articles online had mentioned the hazing, but they hadn't gone into specifics.

"They'd make him down a six-pack and then do push-ups until he puked. Or they'd get him so drunk that he passed out and then they'd drive him out of town and dump him in some random farmer's field in just his underwear. Devon never said anything. He never complained. He was so desperate for the guys to like him that he went along with whatever they told him to do. He wanted to prove he was one of us. He didn't want to let down the team."

The word *team* seems to stick in Jackson's throat. He shakes his head in disgust.

"I should've stopped it," he confesses, staring down at his hands as if he'd like to wring his own neck. "Whenever the guys started in on Devon, I'd always make some excuse and leave the room. I never participated. I *swear*."

Much to my own surprise, I hear myself say, "I believe you."

Jackson looks relieved. But his relief doesn't last long. He turns inward again, his face clouding over in self-recrimination.

"I still knew it was happening. I knew it was wrong. Devon was getting hurt, and I didn't say a thing. I did nothing."

"And then Devon ended up in the hospital," I finish for him.

Jackson nods and shuts his eyes like he's shutting out the world.

"Yeah. One night in December, right after we'd made the finals, the team was celebrating at Kris Kaplan's house. His parents were out of town, so we had the place to ourselves. I was upstairs in one of the bedrooms with my girlfriend, Micaela. We were just hanging out when we heard all this shouting coming from downstairs. We went to the living room to see what was happening, and when we got there, there was a crowd of people standing around Devon. He was on the floor. Not breathing.

"People were freaking out. No one knew what to do, so I called 911. An ambulance came, and the paramedics got Devon breathing again and then took him to the hospital. We found out later that he had alcohol poisoning. Apparently, the guys on the team had made him drink so much, it almost shut down his heart."

I didn't know Jackson had been the one to call 911. None of the articles had mentioned that. Just like none of them had mentioned that Jackson was the one person on the team who hadn't bullied Devon. They'd said the whole team had been involved.

"Is that why you moved to Orlando?" I ask. "Because of what happened to Devon?"

To my surprise, Jackson shakes his head no.

"After Devon was hospitalized, there was a police investigation. The guys on the team wanted to cover their asses, so they told the police that Devon had a drinking problem, that he had a history of getting wasted. They claimed no one else at the party had been drinking. That Devon had shown up drunk and no one had given him any alcohol."

I stare at Jackson incredulously. "And the police believed them?"

Jackson shrugs. "Nobody wanted to see the team that was one game away from bringing home the championship trophy get disqualified. The police accepted the story. So did our coach. And the school. No one at the party got in any trouble. Except Devon. He got kicked off the team and suspended from school for the rest of the semester."

"Jesus Christ," I growl.

"I know."

"That is seriously fucked up." Then I recall what I read last night and realize something in Jackson's story doesn't add up. "Wait a second. The *Orlando Sentinel* said that your entire team got suspended for hazing Devon."

Jackson nods. "We did."

"But if your team lied about what happened, and the police believed them, how did the school find out the truth?"

"Because I went to the principal and told him."

I stare at Jackson in surprise. That piece of information was *definitely* not in any of the articles.

"I had to," he continues. "I couldn't let Devon take the blame. Not after everything we did to him. I mean, we almost *killed* him, and *he* was the one being punished? It was bullshit. So a few days before we were supposed to play in the final, I told Coach Barnes and Principal DeSoto what happened. They had no choice but to suspend everyone. Which meant we had to forfeit the championship."

Jackson lets out a bitter scoff. "The guys were furious when they found out. They thought I was a traitor, and they weren't the only ones. Everyone—students, teachers, hell, even the lunch lady—they all looked at me like I'd betrayed my team. And my school. And the whole fucking city. Micaela was the only one who stood by me. But everyone else?"

Jackson's face burns with anger.

"Even my parents acted like I'd betrayed them. My father was furious. He said I should've kept my mouth shut, played ball, and protected my team. He told me I had deliberately sabotaged any chance of a career in the NFL. That I'd flushed my entire future down the toilet over nothing. That's what a kid in the hospital was to him. Nothing."

Jackson releases an exhausted sigh that seems to come straight from his soul. "*That's* when I decided to move to Orlando."

I hardly know what to say. It's inconceivable to me that anyone—let alone Jackson's parents—could hear everything that had happened and still decide that Jackson was the villain of the story. And all because he was brave enough to tell the truth.

"I'm sorry you went through that," I tell him, hoping he knows how sincerely I mean it. "I can't imagine what it must have been like to have to change schools and move across the state all because you did the right thing and everyone hated you for it."

Jackson waves away my apology. "I *didn't* do the right thing. I let the guys torture Devon for months. I let them put him in the hospital. As far as I'm concerned, whatever shit comes my way, I deserve it. I had so many chances to stick up for Devon and stop the bullying, and I didn't. Because it was easier to look in the other direction. Because I was a coward."

I can't believe how much I misjudged Jackson. I thought he was just another entitled jock, someone who smashed up people's lives and didn't care about the consequences. But seeing the regret on his face and hearing the ache in his voice, I know I was wrong.

"That's not true," I say, crossing to his bed and sitting down beside him. "You're not a coward."

"A kid almost died because of me."

"But he didn't. Because *you* called 911."

"And if I'd stopped the bullying when it started, I wouldn't have had to call 911 in the first place."

I can't disagree with that. Just like I can't absolve Jackson of the guilt he feels. He's going to have to live with that for a long time. Even so, I can still be here for him.

"Do you know why I came over here this morning?" I ask. "I wanted to confront you. I wanted to learn every awful thing about you so I could tell my friends exactly who you are and what you're capable of. And do you know who you are?"

Jackson tenses. His entire body is on edge in preparation of the blow it's anticipating.

"You're a boy who made a mistake," I tell him. "A mistake you'll probably regret for the rest of your life. But also a mistake you tried to make right when no one else would. Even though it cost you your friends and your family and your future in football. *That's* who Jackson Haines is. *That's* what you're capable of."

I put my hand on his shoulder and give it a squeeze.

Jackson looks startled. For a second, I'm worried that he thinks I might be hitting on him. (Why are straight boys so fragile?) Then the hard, exhausted lines of his face soften into gratitude, and he pulls me into a hug.

CHAPTER 9

JACKSON

The rule for eating food that's fallen on the floor is the same as the rule for hugging another dude: Anything under five seconds is okay. Anything more and you shouldn't be surprised if you get funny looks.

I've been hugging Riley for a full minute now, and honestly, I couldn't care less about rules. It feels good to be held. It's been so long since I've been close to anyone. Since I've let anyone get this close. I'd almost forgotten what it's like to be touched. I don't care if it's by a guy—even a gay guy. Riley is comforting. For the first time in a long time, I feel like I can *relax*. Like the world isn't crashing down on me.

I know that doesn't make any sense. I only met him yesterday. And ten minutes ago, he was ready to tear me a new asshole.

But he didn't. He stood there and listened to me tell him about the worst thing I've ever done. And when I finished, he didn't look at me like I was a monster or tell me to stay the hell away from him. He offered to be my friend.

Is it any wonder I can't stop hugging him?

"Thank you," I say, giving him one final squeeze before pulling away. As much as I'm enjoying this moment, I don't want to make him uncomfortable. Or give him the wrong idea.

"No problem," he replies, blushing slightly and avoiding my eyes. "We should probably grab Duy and head over to Rink-O-Rama. Audrey and Tala will be there soon, and Audrey does *not* like to be kept waiting."

Riley slides off my bed, but I don't follow. Instead, I feel a sinking feeling in the pit of my stomach.

"Are you coming?" Riley asks.

I open my mouth but can't form the words to answer. Riley must notice my apprehension because without missing a beat he says, "Don't worry. I won't tell anyone about what happened in Tallahassee."

That's exactly my worry. But Riley's willingness to keep my secret somehow makes me feel worse than the thought of it getting out.

"I don't want to put you in that position," I protest. "I don't want you to lie to your friends."

"I'm not going to lie. I'm just not going to volunteer certain information. If my friends want to know about you, they can do their own stalking. They have Google."

He's right. It's only a matter of time before someone looks me up on the internet. I should probably be up front and tell the others about Devon before they hear it from someone else. But I'm not sure I have it in me right now. I'm pretty drained from telling Riley.

"You sure you don't mind?" I ask.

"I don't mind," he says, flashing me a smile. "You deserve your chance at a fresh start."

Whether or not I deserve a fresh start remains to be seen, but an hour later, I'm at Rink-O-Rama. In terms of venues where I might relaunch my life, it seems as good a spot as any.

The old Jackson wouldn't be caught dead in a place like this. He wasn't a fan of skating rinks, especially not ones that seem way too excited to bring back the eighties.

The walls are covered in oversize murals featuring painted caricatures of Molly Ringwald, Winona Ryder, and a bunch of other old actors I don't recognize. Hot-pink and turquoise-blue LEDs line the ceiling and provide the only lighting—except for the giant mirror ball hanging over the center of the rink. As for the music? So far, the only songs I've heard have been by some band called ELO, which Duy told me stands for Electric Light Orchestra.

Despite all this, New Jackson is trying to keep an open mind. Old Jackson might have been too cool for a retro roller rink, but Old Jackson also made really shitty life choices and wound up miserable, so I should probably stop listening to him.

"Come on, pretty boy, hurry up," Audrey barks, skating around the bench where I'm seated. I'm struggling to lace up my skates for the second time after missing an eyelet on the first attempt.

"Almost done."

"Take your time," Tala advises, sipping the root beer she purchased at the concession stand. "Safety first."

She and Audrey must really be into skating. Or maybe they're just into old eighties movies, because they've both dressed up for the occasion. Audrey is wearing a collarless white shirt, tan vest, and blue jeans. She's also parted her hair down the middle in order to look more like Michael Beck, who's apparently one of the stars of *Xanadu*. Meanwhile Tala is wearing a calf-length pink dress and knee-high white roller skates, which I'm told is what Olivia Newton-John wore in the movie. She's even got on a golden hijab that she says matches the exact shade of Olivia's hair.

Of course, the prize for Most Unique Costume would have to go to Duy. They're wearing a woman's World War II uniform that they've sewn from scratch. Supposedly, it's an exact replica of what Olivia Newton-John wore in the movie's flashback/dream sequence. I don't really know. Duy tried to explain the plot of *Xanadu* to me, but I'm pretty certain they were messing with me. The story sounds too bonkers to be a real movie.

"All set," I announce, finally finishing with my laces. I push myself off the bench—and my feet immediately slip out from under me.

"Whoa there!" Audrey exclaims, catching me before I fall on my ass.

"I'm okay," I assure her, though I'm finding it harder than I expected to stay upright. Both of my feet seem determined to escape in opposite directions.

"Have you ever skated before?" Tala asks, popping up beside me to steady me.

"Uh . . . yeah. Of course. It's been a while, though."

"How long?" Audrey demands.

"Um, maybe ten years, give or take?"

Audrey shakes her head. "Oh, boy."

"You might want to take it slow," Tala suggests, adopting the sort of tone that's usually reserved for addressing small children. "Maybe stick to the side of the rink? That way if you start to fall, you'll be able to catch yourself."

Wow. Okay. Not gonna lie, New Jackson is not loving this part of his fresh start. Finding out that I'm somehow the least athletically coordinated member of the group isn't a great boost to my ego.

"Is everything okay?" Riley asks, returning from the restrooms with Duy.

Audrey sighs in exasperation. "Jackson doesn't know how to skate."

"I can skate," I insist with a confidence that turns out to be sorely unearned because a second later my legs buckle. Both Riley and Duy have to grab hold of me to keep me from face-planting onto the carpet.

Luckily, no one can see how embarrassed I am because, without warning, the lights in the rink suddenly dim, leaving us in almost total darkness. At first, I assume it's a power outage. Then I notice two things: The mirror ball is still sparkling, and a wave of applause is erupting around me.

"It's starting!" Tala squeals.

The applause morphs from a general cheering into a deliberate, almost synchronized clapping. It reminds me of one of Micaela's cheer routines. Everyone in the rink is doing it. Staff, customers, *everyone*.

"What's going on?" I shout over the noise.

"They're about to play 'Xanadu'!" Riley shouts back.

"The movie?"

"No." He laughs. "The song."

I stare at him in incomprehension. "All this is for a song?"

"It's not just any song," Duy informs me. "It's literally one of *the* greatest pop songs in movie history *ever*."

The crowd seems to agree. As soon as Olivia Newton-John's voice sings out over the sound system, skaters flock to the rink like their lives depend on it.

"Come on!" Audrey shouts, grabbing Tala's hand and pulling her to the rink, where the LED lights are now pulsing in flashes of neon pink and blue.

I can tell Riley and Duy want to be on the floor with their friends, but they're stuck propping me up.

"It's okay," I shout. "I'll sit this one out."

"What? Don't be silly!" Duy shouts back. "This song is the whole reason we came. They only play it once an hour."

"I think Tala's right. I need to take it slow. You two go without me."

"No," Duy snaps, grabbing my left hand. "Just hold on to Riley and me. You'll be fine."

"Yeah," Riley says, taking my other hand and shooting me a grin. "We've got you."

Before I can protest, Riley and Duy steer me onto the rink. We merge with the throng of skaters who seem to have been training their whole lives for this moment. Everyone is executing spins and leaps like they're goddamn Olympic pros. Meanwhile, I'm concentrating so hard on *not* falling down that I don't even care what people think about the fact that I'm holding hands with two boys. I mean, one boy and one Duy.

"You're doing great!" Riley yells over the music.

Great is an overstatement, but I appreciate the encouragement. We circle the rink a couple of times, and after a few near stumbles, I start to feel more confident. Though not as confident as Tala and Audrey, who are holding hands and weaving gracefully in and out of the crowd. They're really fast, or maybe I'm just embarrassingly slow, because they manage to lap us twice. On their third approach, they slow down and separate. Tala skates over to Duy and links her arm around their free arm while Audrey rolls alongside Riley and does the same with him.

"We thought we'd give you a hand!" Tala shouts.

"Literally!" Audrey adds.

From opposite ends of our human chain, Tala and Audrey begin to pull us all forward. Since we got onto the rink, Duy and Riley have been so focused on keeping me upright that we haven't had the chance to gain much momentum. With Tala and Audrey acting like a pair of engines, though, we finally start to pick up speed. It's both exhilarating and terrifying.

"You okay?" Riley asks, clocking my expression.

"Yeah. I'm okay."

"You want to try skating on your own?" he asks, offering me an encouraging smile.

I'm a long way from becoming a skating prodigy, but I no longer feel like a complete idiot on wheels. And with Olivia Newton-John belting what I can only assume is the climax of the song, the driving beat has me feeling oddly confident. Maybe Duy's right about its pop-musical greatness. It certainly makes me feel like I could fly—or at least not fall.

Or maybe that's just Riley and his friends.

"Okay, on the count of three," Riley instructs the group. "One. Two. *Three*."

Duy and Riley release my hands. The others fall back, and I push myself forward, uncertain and unsteady, but on my own two feet.

CHAPTER 10

RILEY

"Thanks for today," Jackson says, taking a hearty bite of his bacon double cheeseburger. "After these past couple months, I needed it."

"Thank Duy. They invited you," I remind him, sipping my Diet Coke.

After several hours of skating (and only a few near collisions), Jackson and I are resting our weary and blistered feet in the Rink-O-Rama café while we wait for Duy, Tala, and Audrey to finish competing in the limbo tournament.

"I will thank them," Jackson replies. "Though right now, Duy looks a little busy."

I follow Jackson's gaze over to the rink where a recently disqualified Duy stands on the sidelines chatting with a striking Black boy who's rocking a platinum-blond Afro and a zebra-print muscle tee that does indeed show off his muscles. I can't hear what they're saying over the wail of Olivia Newton-John's "Magic," but from their body language, I can tell there is definitely some hard-core flirting going on.

"Looks like someone made a friend," Jackson says with a grin.

"Duy's *always* making friends," I grumble. "They collect people like strays."

"People like me?"

"*Exactly* like you."

Jackson laughs, and I can't help cracking a smile myself. There's something infectious about Jackson's happiness when he chooses to show it—something he's been a lot more comfortable doing ever since our rather intense conversation this morning.

"I'm actually a little jealous at how easily Duy makes friends," I confess, poking at my fried chicken sandwich. "I don't know if you've noticed, but I don't exactly have, like, the best people skills."

Jackson raises an eyebrow. "You don't say."

"Screw you," I retort as I toss a fry at his head.

Jackson dodges it and laughs. And once again, I find myself basking in his joy.

"So, what about you?" Jackson asks, taking another bite of his burger.

"What about me what?"

"What kind of guys are you into?"

His question catches me off guard, and I choke on my soda.

"What?" I sputter after finally managing to swallow.

"You told me yesterday that Duy was into Greek gods and underwear models. What about you? What's your type?" he asks, casually dipping a French fry into a tiny container of aioli, then tossing it into his mouth. "Maybe we can find someone here for you to practice your 'people skills' on."

"I don't have a type," I retort, eager to shut down this line of conversation.

"Okay, but what kind of guys do you generally go for?"

"I don't go for anyone. I don't date."

Jackson pulls a face like he's just caught a whiff of rotting fish. "What do you mean, you don't date? Everyone dates."

"Not *everyone*. And not me."

"Why? What have you got against dating?"

"It's a waste of time," I sigh. "Even if I manage to find someone at school that I'm actually into—and, let's be honest, the odds of that happening at Olympus are about a trillion to one—I'll just have to break up with him when I go off to college, so what's the point of dating?"

"Um . . . it's *fun*?"

I bite a fry in two and scoff. "Maybe for you. You're straight and hot. You've got options."

"You're not exactly ugly."

"That's not the point," I reply, though the compliment doesn't go unnoticed. "The point is, as one of the few out guys at my school, I'm already a target. Walking around with a boyfriend would be like painting a permanent bull's-eye on my back."

"Don't Tala and Audrey go to your school?"

"Yeah, and when they're there, they keep the PDAs to a minimum."

Jackson takes another bite of his burger and mulls over my words. "Okay, I get that dating is tricky for you. But if you don't date, how are you gonna meet someone and fall in love?"

"I don't believe in love."

Jackson pauses mid-bite and stares at me like I have two heads. Which is pretty much the reaction I get whenever I make this particular confession. It's also why I didn't want to have this conversation in the first place.

"How can you not believe in love?"

Where to begin?

I could tell him the story of how my mom left my dad and me when I was six because, and I quote, she "never wanted to settle down," then moved to Boston, promptly got remarried, and gave birth to my two half sisters, Addison and Arianna, neither of whom I've ever met.

Or I could tell him the story of Alex fucking Vargas and how freshman year he obliterated my heart and put me into the hospital. Either story on its own would absolutely justify my complete and utter distrust in love. But I'm not going to trauma-dump all my problems on Jackson.

"I just don't believe in love," I insist with a shrug.

"But people fall in love all the time."

"People are *horny* all the time. There's a difference."

Jackson looks unconvinced. "So you have zero interest in a boyfriend? Like, at all?"

I roll my eyes and take a sip of my Diet Coke. "I have about as much interest in having a boyfriend as most guys have in being my boyfriend."

Jackson laughs. "Well, just so you know, if I were gay—"

"Don't," I cut him off.

"Don't what?"

"Don't say if you were gay, you'd date me. I *hate* when straight guys say crap like that. It's *so* condescending."

Jackson blinks in confusion. "That's not what I was gonna say."

I feel my cheeks burn. "You weren't?"

"Uh. No. I was gonna say that if I were gay, I'd probably hold off on dating too. At least until I'd gone off to college or moved somewhere like New York. That's a pretty gay city, right? So you might feel safer. And you'd have more options."

Well, this is fucking mortifying. Not only would Jackson *not* want to date me if he were gay, but apparently he doesn't think *anyone* in Florida would want to date me and I need to move to *another state* to get a man.

"Gay people are perfectly capable of existing outside of New York," I huff.

"Oh, I know—"

"Also, queer people shouldn't have to move to a big city to feel safe," I add even more adamantly, trying to put *him* on the defensive before he notices I've turned even pinker than his aioli. "We should be able to date wherever we want and not worry about being harassed."

"Yeah. No. Of course, I only meant—"

"In fact, maybe if more queer people didn't have to flee to big cities because their hometowns were so unwelcoming, we could start to build up queer communities where they're needed and could do some good. Then we might finally have a chance of transforming America from the homophobic wasteland that it is into a progressive, twenty-first-century country where everyone is safe to love who they want no matter where they live. And maybe our straight allies could start stepping up to make that happen instead of telling us to move to New York."

I aim that last comment directly at Jackson, who looks appropriately tongue-tied. I know I'm deliberately twisting his words because I'm embarrassed that he rejected me (even if it was only hypothetically), but I'd rather be prickly than pathetic. Also, as we've established, I don't have great people skills.

"Wow," Jackson says, before shaking his head and letting out one of his warm, full-bodied laughs. "Have you ever thought of becoming a lawyer? Because you *really* like to argue."

In the presence of his bighearted smile, I find it impossible to hold on to my manufactured indignation. It evaporates in an instant, leaving me humbled and not a little embarrassed by my outburst.

"Sorry about that," I mumble.

"No, dude, don't apologize. You went from passionately defending your right *not* to date to passionately defending your right *to* date in sixty seconds flat. I'm seriously impressed."

Now it's my turn to laugh. "Yeah. Well, I think it takes more to be a lawyer than having ragingly strong opinions and loving the sound of your own voice."

Jackson grins and pops his last fry into his mouth. "I don't know. I'd be scared to face off against you in court."

For some reason, this strikes me as one of the nicest things anyone has ever said to me.

"I'm actually starting an internship with the ACLU in a week. My dad set it up for me. He's a lawyer there, and he *really* wants me to follow in his footsteps."

"That's great," Jackson exclaims. The face I make must indicate that I think otherwise, because almost immediately he adds, "Isn't it?"

"You'd think, but . . ."

"But what?"

I shrug. "Do you remember earlier this morning when you asked if I ever felt like I was living the wrong life?" I don't need to say anything more. Jackson nods.

"Ah. Gotcha."

"Yeah."

"Okay, so we've established that you don't want to be a lawyer, *and* you don't want a boyfriend or love, *and* you don't want to move to New York," Jackson says as he enumerates these items on his fingers before flashing me a mischievous smile. "What *do* you want?"

I shake my head and let out a long sigh. "Great fucking question."

This isn't the first time someone has pointed out that when it comes to what I *don't* want, I have the unrelenting certainty of a boomer, but when it comes to what I do want out of life, I'm about as clueless as a newborn babe.

It doesn't help that all my friends seem to have come out of the womb knowing exactly who they are and what they want to do with their lives. Audrey is going to be a singer like her dad. Duy wants to work in fashion. Tala has her heart set on becoming a therapist.

But me? You'd think by this point in my life I'd have found something that I'm passionate about. Some vocation or calling or even a hobby that I could obsess over and build my personality and/or future around. But I haven't.

"There's got to be something you want," Jackson presses.

I shake my head. "You sound like Tala. She told me she read this article online that said in order to be a healthy, happy, functional human being, you can't know only what you don't want out of life. You also have to know what you do want. The way Tala explained it, you can't go through life just saying no to everything—'No, I don't want this.' 'No, I don't like that.' For every no, there has to be an accompanying yes. 'No, I don't want this, but *yes*, I do want that.' Otherwise you reject everything life has to offer, and you end up sad, miserable, and alone."

Jackson nods. "Sounds like good advice."

"Yeah, it is. Only . . ."

"Only what?"

"I've never been able to find anything to say yes to."

Jackson scrutinizes me with his deep blue eyes. *Eyes bluer than the Bay of Naples*, I can't help thinking.

"That's okay," he finally says, shooting me an encouraging smile. "You're in high school. You've got time."

"Yeah," I agree. Though after almost eighteen years, I can't help worrying that time is exactly what I'm running out of. I can feel my life turning into one giant *no*, and I'm nervous that I'll never find anything that makes me say *yes*.

"Of course, if you want my advice," Jackson continues, stealing some fries off my plate now that his are all gone, "I think you should reconsider the whole anti-love thing."

"Oh, really?" I ask, raising an eyebrow. "And why's that?"

Jackson shrugs. "I think you'd make a really good boyfriend."

I feel the heat rise in my cheeks. And when I open my mouth, my throat is so dry, I need to take a sip of my Diet Coke before I can speak.

"Why do you think *that*?" I eventually manage to ask.

"Well, from what I've seen, you're really protective of the people you care about. And you don't take shit from anyone. I feel like if some asshole tried to mess with anyone you were dating, you'd lay them out in ten seconds flat. Or you'd tell them off so badly they'd never show their face in public again."

"You're telling me I'd make a good boyfriend because I'm scary?"

"Um, *yeah*. Have you met you? You're terrifying." Jackson laughs. "But you're also a good person. This morning when I told you about what happened in Tallahassee, you were really there for me. In fact, you're the first person that I've met in a long time who's made me feel like—I don't know—like my life isn't a total disaster. Like there's a chance everything might turn out okay."

"Oh," I say, staring down at my chicken sandwich. It's becoming increasingly difficult to look at Jackson.

"I mean it," he insists. "You're a special guy, Riley. You're smart and you're funny. And despite the fact that I'm kind of terrified of you, I know you've got a big heart. I think any guy would be lucky to be your boyfriend."

My cheeks are burning so hard, I don't know what to say.

It's not like this is the first time I've ever received a compliment. My friends and my dad have made similar attempts to bolster my self-esteem over the years, but then they're legally obligated to tell me what a catch I am.

Jackson, though, isn't a friend or a parent. Jackson is Jackson. I've known him for less than twenty-four hours. His opinion should mean nothing to me. Yet for some reason, his words leave me speechless.

Maybe that's because they make me believe things about myself that I stopped believing a long time ago.

"Sorry," Jackson says, noticing my silence. "I didn't mean to embarrass you."

"It's okay," I answer once I remember how my mouth works. "And thanks."

"No problem." Jackson nods. Then, grinning cockily, he reaches across the table and grabs another handful of fries off my plate. "I was just buttering you up so you'd let me steal your fries."

"All yours." I laugh, pushing my plate to him.

"Sweet!"

Jackson beams in excitement, and I can't help smiling back. I don't know if he's right about not giving up on love or about me making a good boyfriend. In fact, I'm pretty sure he's wrong on both counts. But that doesn't matter. Right now, I'm okay with settling for being a good friend. Because after a lifetime of saying no, friendship with Jackson is definitely something I can say yes to.

I'm still thinking about Jackson's words as I crawl into bed later that night. I can't believe how much I misjudged him. Only yesterday, I was convinced he was trouble, someone to be avoided at all costs. Now I find myself wondering when I'll get to see him again.

Unfortunately, that won't be for a while. Tomorrow, Dad begins the one (and only) week of summer vacation he allows himself. We'll be going to St. Augustine to stay with my grandparents, who have a condo on the beach. It's a trip I normally look forward to, though right now, I can't help thinking that the timing kind of sucks.

I wonder if Dad would let me stay here in Orlando without him . . .

Wait. What am I saying? That's *ridiculous*.

I can't bail on our summer vacation because I want to hang out with a guy I just met. Is my self-esteem really so low that I'd abandon my family just to spend a few more days with a boy who gave me a couple of compliments?

Granted, they were pretty great compliments. And if you think about it, is it really that crazy to want to spend time with someone who seems determined to see only the best in you?

Who knows? Maybe if I keep hanging out with Jackson, I might actually start to see myself the way he sees me. Because that Riley—the Riley he seems to think I am—sounds like a pretty great guy. I have no clue if he's real, but maybe with Jackson's help, he could be.

Could that be why I've felt such an intense connection with him since the carnival? Because, for whatever reason, he's able to see me more clearly than I can see myself? Just like I'm able to see the real him?

Lying in the dark of my bedroom, I smile at that thought and listen to the thunderclouds growling outside. A summer storm is moving in, sending raindrops the size of golf balls splattering against my window. Normally I'd find the noise distracting and wouldn't be able to sleep, but I must have worn myself out at the rink today because I'm suddenly aware of how exhausted I am.

With a yawn, I close my eyes and listen to the *plonk, plonk, plonk* of the rain. A heaviness steals across my body, and I feel myself being pulled down into sleep.

I think of Jackson. I hear the storm. And the screams begin.

POMPEII, ITALY

(AD 79)

CHAPTER 11

LUCIUS

I run.

I run faster than I've ever run before as a storm of rocks falls upon the city. Horses shriek, overturning their carts in the streets, and terrified children huddle in doorways screaming for their parents. A voice shouts for everyone to take cover while another orders everyone to abandon the city.

Everything is pandemonium.

Racing like a hunted animal, I turn down my street, fighting against a frightened crowd who are fleeing in the opposite direction. Some of the people are clutching hastily packed bags, no doubt filled with whatever gold or valuables they managed to grab before forsaking their homes. It occurs to me that my family might already have done the same, that I'm wasting precious time running to an empty house when I should be making my way out of the city, but I need to make certain.

My brother, Quintus, is only six, and my sister, Flavia, is not yet two. If Mother is out shopping or visiting neighbors, then my siblings will have no one to carry them to safety except their nurse. And purchased loyalty can go only so far in times of catastrophe.

I push forward against the clamoring tide of bodies, and after what feels like hours, I reach my house. My mother, thank the gods, is outside, shouting instructions at the servants to calm our horses and load our cart with provisions.

My tutor Philodorus carries Quintus, who wails into his shoulder, while the wet nurse rocks Flavia in her arms. My relief at seeing my family is as overwhelming as it is fleeting. None of us will truly be safe until we are out of the city and as far away as possible from the mountain of death.

"Lucius!" Mother shouts, catching sight of me. Her fine golden hair, always so impeccably coiffed, is wild in the wind as she rushes across the street to me. It reminds me of fire dancing on a breeze. She pulls me into an embrace, and the sheer force of her love is almost unbearable. I feel as though I'm a child of four, and all I want is to hide in her arms as I did when thunderstorms used to chase me from my bed.

But there's no time for fear or comfort. There's no time for anything. Except, perhaps, the most important things.

"Thank the gods you're here!" She weeps as the sky falls around us. The air is thick with a cloying, noxious smell that burns my eyes and lungs. Meanwhile, the streets are filling up with rocks that continue to batter our heads like burning hail.

"Is everyone all right?" I ask.

"We're fine. But we need to get out of the city. I'm just taking a few—"

Mother turns to Leonidas, who has served our family for years, and he answers her unspoken question with a nod. "The cart is ready, Lady Julia."

"Then let's make haste!"

Mother turns to go and attempts to pull me after her, but my feet refuse to follow. I have a different journey to take, one I've postponed only so I could be sure of my family's safety.

"Come on, Lucius, don't dawdle!"

"Go without me," I say, my voice surprisingly calm despite the surrounding storm.

"What?" she gasps, her eyes wild with panic.

"Go without me," I repeat, this time with urgency. "I'll meet you at our villa in Sorrento, but there's something I have to do."

Mother's hand flashes out, quick as a talon, and clasps my wrist in a crushing grip. "Are you mad? We have to go *now*, Lucius! The world is ending!"

She's right. Nonetheless, I know what I must do.

"You have Leonidas and Philodorus. They'll make sure you get out of the city. Just head toward the South Gate and keep to the wider streets."

"I'm not leaving without you!"

I pull myself free from her iron grip and back away.

"I'm sorry," I say, my voice starting to tremble. Her face etched with terror is so pitiful that if I stay a moment longer, I know I'll lose my resolve. I cast a quick glance at my brother and sister, both of whom are too petrified to even notice me, and hope against hope that this won't be the last time we're all together.

Then I turn from my mother's pleading eyes and run into the darkness of the dying city in search of Marcus.

The streets are cluttered with rocks as I make my way toward his family's villa. With every step, my feet sink deeper into the rubble, and still more stones continue to fall from the sky, piling higher and higher, burying everything.

The air grows thick with ash. It's like breathing sand, and it coats my body in a heavy gray soot. At least there are no longer any crowds to fight against. The streets are deserted—everyone has either taken refuge in their homes or fled.

It occurs to me that Marcus might be among those who have fled. But I can't leave Pompeii until I'm certain he's not at his villa.

Another great tremor shakes the earth, and I stumble as I turn down the narrow alley that I've used so often when sneaking off to be with Marcus. It's cramped and dark but the high walls on both sides provide a temporary shelter from the sky's relentless barrage of rocks. Pausing to catch my breath, I wipe the ash from my burning eyes, and, to my surprise, I see a light up ahead—a torch moving through the darkness. Its weak flame struggles against the storm but it's bright enough that I can make out that familiar head of golden-bronze hair.

"Marcus!" I shout, rushing toward him.

He looks like a ghost. There's scarcely an inch of his body not stained with ash. Even so, I throw my arms around him and clutch him to me, scarcely daring to believe my eyes or my good fortune.

"What are you doing out here? Why aren't you with your family?" he shouts over the roaring winds, staring into my eyes as if to assure himself that I'm not some fevered illusion.

"I was coming to find you!" I answer. "Why aren't you with *your* family?"

"Because I was coming to find *you*!"

Despite the panic in my bones and the devastation whirling around us, I find myself weeping with joy as he once again pulls me into his arms.

In a city of chaos, with death raining from the sky, Marcus came for me.

At the end of the world, he chose me.

"We have to get out of the city!" he hollers, breaking our embrace. "Everyone is evacuating!"

He takes my hand. Then together we leave the narrow alley and clamber onto the wide avenue that cuts through the eastern half of the city. Much to our dismay, we find it almost completely buried in debris. Rocks are raining down even faster than before, as if Vesuvius won't be content until it's vomited every stone out of the belly of the earth and smothered every inch of our city. We try wading our way through the sea of stones, but it's up to our shins. If the rocks were heavier, we could walk on top of them, but with every step, we sink into their crippling embrace.

Running is no longer possible. We are half blind from the ash and tripping over our own bruised feet. I try not to panic, but a voice in the back of my head is growing louder with every faltering footstep.

We're running out of time.

"I need to rest," Marcus says through choking coughs as he steadies himself against the wall of a house. "I have to catch my breath."

I would give him the air from my lungs if I could, but at this moment I can barely breathe myself. With every greedy gasp for air I take, my throat burns with pain.

We're running out of time.

We need to find shelter. The city's battered buildings might be a death trap, but out here, exposed to the elements, we won't survive much longer.

I cast a hopeful glance up the street and catch sight of the Temple of the Sibylline Oracle. It's one of the few great sacrileges for a man to enter the inner sanctum uninvited. And the high priestess is a woman as feared as she is respected. But I have greater fears at this moment, and the temple door is open.

"Come on!" I shout as I put my arm around Marcus's waist, then pull him upright.

Wading through the rubble and fighting against the wind, we force our tired feet onward until we're climbing the temple steps and pushing ourselves inside. Then, with the last of our strength, we shut the heavy wooden door against the warring elements and collapse onto the cold marble floor.

The temple is still and quiet. And the air is cleaner. But even in this sacred place, the falling stones are forcing their terrible pollution through cracks in the ceiling.

"We shouldn't have stopped," Marcus laments. In the darkness, with only a torch to light his ash-stained face, he looks like some ancient terror spawned from a nightmare. "We need to keep going."

"We wouldn't have made it another ten steps," I say, gasping to catch my breath. "Besides, we don't know if we'd be any safer outside the city."

"We'd be farther away from the mountain."

"There are other mountains. Maybe they're all exploding. Maybe this is the end."

Marcus is silent. He turns his face from me, but when next he speaks, I can hear the panic in his voice.

"Is this the end?"

I have no answer. It seems impossible, and yet if the gods wanted to bring an end to the age of man, the horrors I've seen today would be more than sufficient.

We're running out of time.

"What was that?" Marcus asks, jolting up straight as his eyes dart toward the entryway that leads off into the temple's inner sanctum. "Did you hear that?"

Lost in thought, I hadn't heard a thing, but I cock my head and listen. Aside from the storm outside, I hear nothing. I'm about to tell Marcus this when a faint groaning from deep within the temple echoes throughout the darkness.

"Do you think someone else is here?" Marcus asks.

Having found the temple's outer door open and all its lamps overturned or extinguished, I'd assumed the place was abandoned. But perhaps others have sought refuge here. Others who might be able to help us or whom we might be able to help.

Rising to our feet, we take each other's hands and carefully step forward into the inner sanctum. Our dying torch struggles to light our way, and once or twice our feet stumble on the uneven floor that has been unleveled by the earthquakes. Slowly, though, our eyes begin to adjust to the shadowy blackness. I spy cracks splintering like spiderwebs across not only the temple walls but the central columns as well. One has already collapsed. Like a giant oak tree of stone, it lies uprooted on the floor, shattered to pieces.

And under one of those pieces lies a body.

A woman's body. A wild mane of bloodred hair obscures her face, but the purple tunic bedecked with a large golden brooch in the shape of a wolf's head is familiar enough. I have often seen the wearer of these things at a distance, passing solemnly through the streets of Pompeii with her handmaidens.

"It's the high priestess," Marcus exclaims, darting to her side. "We have to help her."

I don't move. Because I can see what he does not or will not. The priestess is dead. The great life that once flowed through her veins is now spilling out in thick pools of crimson blood under her twisted, broken body.

But Marcus is undaunted. He sets down the torch and tries to lift the heavy slab of column. When those exertions fail, he attempts to pull the priestess's body out from under the crushing weight.

"Marcus, she's gone," I whisper. "There's nothing we can do. She's already—"

"*You . . .*" a voice whispers in the darkness.

I stare at the high priestess, my eyes wide in amazement. That a body so broken and drained of blood should still contain life seems an impossibility. How great must her will to live be that even in this state, she is able to hold off death?

"Save your strength," Marcus bids her, leaning in close to wipe her wild, bloody hair from her face. "We'll help you."

"*I knew . . . you two . . . would come,*" the dying woman answers in a halting, desperate whisper.

Marcus looks at me in surprise, and the priestess's strange pronouncement leaves me equally confused. She can't have expected us.

Marcus and I would never have set foot in this temple if necessity had not driven us here.

Perhaps she's rambling. Or mad. In either case, she's probably too far gone to know what she says. Already she's sunk back into a silence and stillness that have all the signs of death.

"Priestess?" Marcus whispers, placing a cautious hand on her shoulder in an attempt to rouse her. "Priestess, can you—"

The priestess's hand shoots out like a snake darting to strike at a startled hare and closes on Marcus's wrist. At the same time, one black eye in her bloodstained face opens and fixes him with its ferocious gaze.

"*Die!*" the priestess commands, spitting the word with rage. "*You ... must ... die!*"

White with terror, Marcus pries his wrist free and scrambles backward on his haunches, cutting a frenzied wake through the pool of blood. I rush to his side and wrap my arms around his trembling body as we both stare at the convulsing priestess. Her twisting form writhes in the throes of death, yet her piercing black eye never leaves us.

Even when she at last goes stiff and the unmistakable death rattle breaks from her lips to announce her passing, her unseeing, unforgiving eye remains fixed on Marcus and me. Judging us. Accusing us. Condemning us.

"I don't want to die," Marcus whispers, his voice small but full of fear.

In the presence of death and with the high priestess's words ringing in his ears as surely as her blood lingers on his hands, Marcus is falling to pieces. Whatever strength he possessed has fled his body. I can feel him quaking in my arms as if his own soul longs to escape its mortal prison. "I don't want to die ..."

"We won't," I assure him, though I scarcely believe my own words. I have no idea what Marcus or I could have done to offend the priestess to such a degree that she would use her final words to demand our deaths, but her vehemence leaves no mistake that she meant every word.

"We won't die," I repeat, taking his trembling hands in mine and kissing them in the hopes that the touch of my lips might impart some sliver of courage to him even as my own is fading.

As if in defiance of my words, a violent tremor grips the temple. It shakes the building to its foundation, sending stonework crashing to the floor and reminding us—as if we needed reminding—of the endless devastation awaiting us outside.

Marcus releases a sob and pulls me to him, crushing me in a desperate embrace. His chest heaves against mine as warm tears run down his cheeks, staining both our faces.

"I don't want to die," he repeats even more frantically. "And I don't want to marry Lucretia. I want to be with you. *Just you.*"

"I want to be with you too." I gasp, choking back my own tears. "Just you. Forever."

Another tremor shakes the temple, and another column cracks. It splits in half as it collapses, taking with it a chunk of the roof, which crashes in front of us, scattering masonry across the floor and extinguishing our torch. Whatever protection we had from the elements is gone. Rock and ash spill through the wound in the ceiling, poisoning the air around us and turning our sanctuary into a trap.

A sharp animal instinct urges me to flee, but Marcus clutches me to him even tighter.

"Don't let me go," he begs, holding on to me as if his life depends on it.

He's always been larger and stronger than me, his body a shelter against the world that I've sought comfort in so many times that it almost feels like home. Even so, I wrap myself around him, as if my thin frame might somehow protect him from the wrath of the gods.

"I won't let you go," I promise. "Do you hear me? You are my blood and my heart and my soul. If I had a thousand lives, I would spend them all with you. Because you *are* my life. And neither the gods nor death will *ever* tear us apart. I swear it. Our hearts are bound—forever."

"Forever," Marcus repeats, pressing his forehead to mine. Our lips find each other in the darkness. He tastes of ash and tears, but I don't care. Whatever comes next, at least we are together. And in this terrible, terrifying moment, that feels like victory.

Then more of the ceiling collapses.

Marcus and I huddle closer, each of us attempting to shield the other from the onslaught of stone and violence. It's getting harder to breathe. The air is pungent. It burns my eyes and stings my lungs. I bury my face against Marcus as he buries himself against me. I can feel our bodies growing numb with fear and exhaustion. We're both straining to breathe, struggling to stay conscious. But it's a losing battle.

We've run out of time.

Beaten and battered by the storm, I no longer have the strength to open my eyes. My limbs grow heavy with soot and fatigue, so much so that I can barely feel Marcus in my arms. One by one, my senses abandon me until only my ears are left to tie me to this life.

I hear the mountain rage in the distance. I hear the sky fall. I hear the city dying. And through it all, like the clearest bell, I hear Marcus, his voice repeating the same desperate refrain over and over and over again.

Don't let me go . . .
Don't let me go . . .
Don't let me go . . .

ORLANDO, FLORIDA

(THE PRESENT)

CHAPTER 12

JACKSON

I'm drenched in sweat when I return from my morning run. It's barely nine but last night's storm has left the air so hot and thick, it's like moving through soup. It's not the kind of day you'd want to be outside if you can avoid it. Which is why I'm surprised to see Riley in my driveway. He's pacing nervously next to his Prius, his face twisted with worry. But when he sees me, his entire expression melts into palpable relief.

"Hey, what's up?" I ask as I make my way over to him. I wish I were wearing a shirt to wipe some of the sweat off my face, but I settle for the back of my hand. "Did I forget we had plans?"

Riley looks down at his scuffed-up Chucks like he's suddenly too shy to meet my eyes. "No. Sorry. I didn't mean to ambush you. I tried calling but . . ."

"Oh. Yeah. I don't bring my phone when I run."

"Right. Of course. Makes sense."

He's still not looking at me, and the tension radiating out of him is starting to make me tense. "Is everything okay?"

"Yeah." He nods unconvincingly. "Yeah. I—sorry—I don't know why I'm here. I mean, I know *why* I'm here. But now I feel *really* stupid."

"What's going on?"

Riley shakes his head and lets out a sardonic snort, like even he can't believe what he's about to say. "I sort of—I sort of had a nightmare. Last night. A really *intense* nightmare. About us. Or people who looked like us. I mean, it *was* us, but it also wasn't. You know what I mean?"

"Not really..."

Riley sighs. "It doesn't matter. The point is, we were in Italy in my dream. But we were in ancient Roman times. And there was this huge volcano that erupted. And you and I..."

"You and I what?"

"We *died*."

"Oh." That's definitely a weird thing for someone to dream about. But I still don't see why he's so upset.

"I know. I *know*," he says, shaking his head again. "It's ridiculous. I don't even know why I'm telling you except... except it felt so real, Jackson. I felt us *dying*." Despite the hot-soup air, Riley shivers. "And then, when I woke up—I don't know. I knew it was a dream, but part of me still felt like I was in danger. And that *you* were in danger. And I—" He finally forces himself to look at me, and his green eyes are full of concern. "I just wanted to make sure you were okay."

I'm not quite sure what to say.

Part of me wants to laugh. No one's ever rushed over to my house to check if I've died overnight in a volcano eruption before. But the other part of me is oddly flattered. It's touching how worked up Riley is. I can tell he's worried about me. And despite knowing how bonkers he would sound, he still came over and risked making a fool of himself to see if I was okay.

If that's not a good friend, I don't know what is.

Riley, though, must mistake my silence for annoyance. He flushes, and his cheeks burn so pink, they're almost crimson.

"I shouldn't have come," he mumbles. "This is so fucking stupid. Forget I said anything."

He turns to get into his car, but he's so rattled, he drops his keys.

"Dude, where are you going?" I ask, forcing a laugh and putting a hopefully not too whiffy arm around his shoulder. "Come on inside. We'll have some breakfast."

"No, I need to get home."

"You don't need to go anywhere," I insist. I don't want him driving when he's this upset. Especially when the reason he's so upset is because he was worried about me. "My aunt started teaching summer classes at her community college today, so no one's here, and I've got nothing to do. Let's hang out. You came all this way to save me from a volcano, right? Well, now you can save me from a boring Monday."

Before he can protest, I steer Riley inside and lead him to the kitchen, savoring the refreshing chill of the AC along the way. At the sink, I fill up two glasses of water and hand one to Riley, who still looks skittish. Like any second he might dash out of the house.

"So," I begin after a satisfying gulp that empties half my glass, "tell me more about this dream."

I want to be supportive and show him that I'm taking his feelings seriously. If his nightmare upset him, we should talk about it. But Riley gives me a dismissive shrug. "There's really nothing more to tell," he says before sipping at his glass.

"Sure there is. Give me some context. What were we doing in the dream before we died?"

Riley chokes on his water, and a second later, he's fighting off a full-on coughing fit.

"Are you okay?" I ask.

"Yeah. Water just went down the wrong pipe," he wheezes, still trying to catch his breath. "I'm fine."

He doesn't look fine. He looks like he wants to run and hide or be anywhere other than here with me. I'm guessing he's embarrassed about almost being killed by a glass of water, so I try to take his mind off it by asking him again about his dream. For some reason, though, my question seems to make him even more uncomfortable.

"We were just friends," he mumbles. "In the dream. We were just . . . hanging out."

"Just hanging out? In ancient Rome?"

"Pompeii, actually. It's a coastal city on the Bay of Naples that got wiped off the map when Mount Vesuvius erupted in 79."

"Okay, Google."

Riley blushes. "I did a paper on it for my world history class last year."

"Okay, well, *that* explains why you dreamed about Italy."

"Yeah, maybe," Riley agrees, though the skepticism in his voice doesn't match his words.

"So what were you and I doing in Pompeii? You know, *before* the volcano erupted?"

Riley hesitates and again I'd swear his cheeks color. "You were . . . getting ready to meet your fiancée."

"My fiancée? Nice. Was she hot?"

Riley scowls. "Does it matter?"

"Hey," I say, unable to keep from laughing. "I'm just curious what kind of love life you've concocted for Dream Jackson."

"Dream Jackson's love life is *fine*. Trust me. He has no complaints about—"

Riley stops himself and stares at the floor. Nervously, he grabs his glass and drains what's left of his water. I'm afraid he might choke again. But when he sets down the empty glass, he seems to have pulled himself together.

"It was just a dream. It doesn't mean anything."

"No, of course," I agree. "I'm just trying to understand what happened. Get all the details."

"I don't remember much more," Riley sighs. "Seriously, the whole thing is so hazy now. I can't really tell you anything."

I nod, though I'm not sure I believe him. "Okay. Well, if you ever do remember more or you want to talk about it . . ."

"It's fine. *I'm* fine. It's probably just stress. I'm starting that internship in a week, so my brain is just freaking out and being a drama queen about it."

"Yeah. Could be," I concede, remembering some of my own sleepless nights from these past few months. "When I was going through all that stuff with Devon, I had nightmares all the time."

"You did?"

"Yeah. I mean, I didn't dream about volcanoes or time traveling. It was the usual anxiety dreams, you know? People yelling at me. Feeling trapped. It was more stressful than scary. But it wasn't fun."

My words seem to have a reassuring effect on Riley. "When did the nightmares stop?" he asks.

"When I moved in with Aunt Rachel."

Although that's not exactly true. My first week in Orlando, I still had plenty of restless evenings. I don't think I truly had my first solid night of sleep until after I went to the carnival. After I met Riley.

Maybe it's the breeze of the AC on my damp back or maybe it's the unpleasant memory of those sleepless nights back in Tallahassee, but a shiver creeps across my skin. For some reason, I suddenly feel . . . *exposed*.

Though that's probably because I'm standing around in nothing but my running shorts, smelling like a dirty locker room.

"Anyway, um, I'm gonna grab a quick shower," I announce, edging toward the hall. "Make yourself at home. When I get back, I'll make us some breakfast."

Riley arches an eyebrow and smirks. "You cook?"

"I can pour two bowls of cereal like a pro."

Riley laughs. "Go shower. I'll cook breakfast."

"What? No. You don't have to do that."

"Please. I'm the one who came over uninvited and made you listen to my ludicrous dream. It's the least I can do."

CHAPTER 13

RILEY

If there's an upside to having a mom who abandoned you and a dad who works sixty-plus-hour weeks, it's that you learn to cook for yourself at a very young age. My culinary repertoire isn't expansive or impressive, but when push comes to shove, I can make some damn tasty cinnamon banana pancakes. And after the morning I've had, it's honestly a relief to be doing something so mundane.

I'm still a little freaked out by my dream. Correction—my *second* dream. But maybe it's like I told Jackson. Maybe my brain is stressing about my internship, so it's creating nightmares out of a bunch of random facts I learned for my history paper. That seems logical. Mostly.

Though I'd feel a lot better if I could forget the burning hatred in that crazy priestess's eye. Or the screams of all those frightened people. Or the sickening stench of sulfur.

"Wow, those pancakes smell *amazing*," Jackson gushes as he returns to the kitchen. Fresh out of the shower, he doesn't smell so bad himself: a mixture of soap and citrus. He's wearing a pair of tan cargo shorts and a black tank top that still manages to show off all his muscles. But at least his current outfit is less revealing and distracting than those ridiculously tiny running shorts.

Not that I noticed.

"Breakfast is served," I announce with a flourish, setting the platter of pancakes onto the kitchen table.

When we're both seated, I scoop two pancakes onto each of our plates. Jackson sniffs at his breakfast like an excited puppy and picks up his fork. Then, remembering something, he hops out of his chair and rushes to the fridge.

"There's already butter and syrup here on the table," I tell him.

"I know. But you forgot the most important ingredient."

Jackson rummages through the shelves, releases a cry of victory, and returns to the table with a canister of Reddi-Wip.

"Seriously?" I say, not bothering to hide my disdain.

"What?" Jackson asks.

"We're having breakfast. Not dessert."

"Dude, pancakes are the dessert of breakfast."

Shaking my head, I watch in horror as Jackson smothers his pancakes in enough butter and syrup to send a diabetic into hyperglycemic shock, before capping the whole thing off with a heaping mountain of whipped cream.

"You are *such* a boy," I scoff, rolling my eyes.

"A growing boy," he counters, shoving half a pancake into his mouth. Almost immediately, his eyes go wide, and he releases a moan of approval that's so intense, I can only describe it as pornographic. "Fuck, dude, this is *incredible*."

My cheeks flush with pride. Seeing Jackson enjoying himself so completely, I can't help catching some of his happiness.

"Glad you approve," I say, taking a small bite of my own pancake. (No butter, no syrup, and definitely no whipped cream, thank you very much. My work stands on its own.)

Jackson swallows another mouthful and unleashes another orgasmic moan. This time I can't stop myself from laughing. "Do you need to be alone with your pancakes?" I ask.

"What? I'm enjoying my breakfast."

"Your enjoyment is *obscene*."

Jackson gasps in faux indignation. "Are you slut-shaming me?"

"Yeah. I am. And I'm not afraid to say it. You're a pancake slut."

"That's *Mr.* Pancake Slut, and don't you forget it."

As if to prove his point, Jackson crams an entire pancake in his mouth. We both burst out laughing, and I feel the last of my anxiety leave my body. In fact, I feel so good right now, it seems almost inconceivable that I let myself get so bent out of shape over something as ridiculous as a couple of silly dreams.

Seriously, who drives all the way over to someone's house (after leaving them a stalkerish number of voicemails) all because of a nightmare? I must have been out of my mind.

I *was* out of my mind. At least, that's how I felt when I woke up this morning. Like something terrible had happened. Or was about to happen. And the only thing that I could think to do—the only thing that I thought would make things better—was find Jackson.

Oddly enough, now that I'm here with him, everything *is* better. In less than an hour, I've gone from traumatized to tranquil to tickled. And Jackson did that.

Maybe *that's* why I keep dreaming about him in these weird disaster scenarios. Because on some level, my subconscious knows that he's the person you want by your side in a crisis. Because Jackson has the rare ability to make everything better. Or at any rate, to make *me* better.

"By the way, I've been thinking about the situation with your dad," he announces, wiping his mouth with a napkin and pushing aside the plate he's licked clean.

"What situation?" I ask, thrown by his non sequitur.

"The work situation. You said you thought your nightmare might be stress related? Because you're starting that internship?"

"Oh. Yeah. Right," I agree, though I'm not sure where he's going with this.

"And the reason this internship is freaking you out is that you don't want to be a lawyer, right?"

"Right. Well, not anymore."

"Not anymore?"

"When I was a kid, I thought being a lawyer was the most important thing a person could be. But as I got older, I started realizing how many problems there are in the world. And the idea of having to fight all those battles for the rest of my life . . . it just feels *exhausting*."

Jackson nods. "Sure. I get that."

"It's not that I don't want to do good or help people," I explain. "I'm just not sure that being a lawyer is the best way for me to do that. But I also don't want to disappoint my dad. He's really excited for me to start working with him. And, as we've already established, I have literally no idea what else I want to do with my life."

"You could make pancakes for a living," Jackson jokes. "I'd buy them."

He flashes me a smile, but I can't quite smile back. It's hard to joke about the future when yours isn't looking so bright.

"Okay, so, here's how I see it," Jackson says, dropping the humor and getting down to business. "You're pretty sure you don't want to be a lawyer, but maybe not a hundred percent sure. So I'm thinking, maybe you try this internship for the summer and see how it goes. Who knows? Maybe you'll be surprised. Maybe you'll discover you actually like practicing law. In which case, an internship at the ACLU will look totally badass on your résumé when you have to apply to colleges in the fall."

"And if I hate it?" I ask, which seems the more likely scenario.

"Then you go to your father and say, 'Hey, I gave this internship my best shot, but I don't think being a lawyer is for me.'"

"Just like that?"

"Why not? Is your father a reasonable man?"

"Yeah," I concede. "He is."

"Okay, so, if after a summer of putting in the work, you tell him that lawyering isn't for you, he'll know you're speaking from experience, and he'll understand. Then you'll have your entire senior year to figure out what it is that you really want to do with your life."

The simplicity of Jackson's solution is as surprising as it is sound. I'm honestly embarrassed that I didn't think of it myself.

"That's really good advice," I tell him.

"Try not to sound so surprised," he chides. "Mr. Pancake Slut is more than just a pretty face, you know."

Evidently feeling quite pleased with himself, Jackson begins loading a second helping of pancakes onto his plate.

"And, hey, if you do decide that law isn't for you but you're still nervous about telling your father, I can help you through it. I know from experience what it's like to have to disappoint a parent, so if you want me there for moral support or in case things go sideways, just say the word, and I'm there."

The generosity of his offer surprises me. Although it shouldn't. Jackson has spent the past two days proving what a good person he is. And what a good friend he can be. Still, I'm touched by his kindness. "You'd do that?"

"Of course. If you think it'll help," he says after swallowing another whipped-cream-smothered bite. Then he pauses and shoots me a crafty look. "But I do have one condition."

"What's that?" I ask, already suspicious.

Jackson picks up the Reddi-Wip and holds the can over my barely touched pancakes.

"Absolutely not," I say, pulling my plate away.

Jackson's jaw drops. "Wow. *Really?*"

Given that yesterday I barged into his house to accuse him of being a terrible person and today I showed up to tell him I dreamed about his death, I decide that a small concession might be in order.

"Okay, but just a little," I relent as I slide my plate back toward him.

"Totally," he agrees before *burying* my pancakes under an avalanche of whipped cream.

I grab at the canister to try to salvage what's left of my breakfast, but Jackson refuses to let go. We struggle over the Reddi-Wip, Jackson laughing, me cursing. I can't pry the can out of his grip, but I am able to turn it around and aim the nozzle in a new direction—Jackson's face.

"Oh. My. God," he sputters, letting go of the can to wipe the thick ribbons of cream from his eyes, nose, and mouth.

Now it's my turn to burst out laughing. Jackson is definitely going to need a second shower this morning. And even though it's technically his own fault for desecrating the sanctity of my breakfast, I decide to be magnanimous in victory. I set the Reddi-Wip down on the table to fetch him some napkins—at which point I realize I've made a huge tactical mistake. Before I can correct it, Jackson scoops up the canister with a devilish grin.

"*Don't* think about it," I warn him.

Jackson nods innocently. But I can see the wheels turning in his head.

A second before he lunges at me, I bolt to the other side of the kitchen where I grab a batter-stained spatula out of the sink and brandish it like a sword.

"Jackson, *stop*," I order.

He laughs and tosses the Reddi-Wip between his hands. "Sorry, dude. I'm gonna have to cream you."

"You're being a child."

"Definitely."

Jackson rushes me, but I'm too quick. I slip out of the kitchen, race down the hallway, and sprint out the front door. My plan is to lock myself in my car until Jackson tires of this game. Unfortunately, I'm only halfway across the yard when I remember that Jackson plays football. Or rather, I remember this when he tackles me from behind and slams me to the ground.

Cackling like a wild man, Jackson crawls on top of me, straddles my waist, and pins me down. He then holds the Reddi-Wip directly over my head as I beg for mercy through gasps of laughter.

"Jackson, get off, I'm serious!!" I chortle.

"Say *ah*," he instructs, lowering the can to my face.

I close my eyes, preparing to get blasted with sticky sweetness. But before Jackson can let me have it, I hear a voice pointedly clear its throat.

Risking a peek, I look across the expanse of Jackson's yard to see Duy standing in their driveway. They're holding an overflowing blue recycle bin and staring at Jackson and me with one eyebrow arched in curiosity.

"Hey, Duy," I say, giving him a feeble wave of embarrassment.

"Hey, Riley. Hey, Jackson. What's going on over there?"

Looking like a naughty child who's been caught with his hand in the cookie jar, Jackson blushes awkwardly and climbs off me. "Just having a good old-fashioned food fight."

"Uh-huh." There's a long, oddly protracted silence. Then Duy shrugs, sets the recycle bin on the curb, and heads back toward their garage.

"See you tonight!" Jackson calls as Duy disappears inside.

"What's tonight?" I ask, lying back on the grass, still attempting to catch my breath.

"Duy and I are gonna watch *Xanadu*."

"You are?"

Jackson shrugs. "Yeah. I figured I should check it out. You know, since you and your friends are *obsessed* with it. You should join us."

I'm flattered by the invitation, but my excitement is short-lived.

"I wish I could, but I'm heading out of town this afternoon. My dad and I are driving up to St. Augustine for the week to visit my grandparents."

"Oh. Really? That's too bad." To my surprise, Jackson looks as disappointed as I feel.

"Yeah. In fact, I should probably get back to my house and pack. My dad's got to be wondering where I am."

"Right. Sure," Jackson says as he offers me his hand and helps me off the ground. "Well, thanks for breakfast. I hope you and your dad have a great vacation."

"Thanks," I answer, brushing the grass off my jeans. "Enjoy your movie night with Duy. Although I should warn you, the music and the idea of *Xanadu* are a lot better than the actual movie. You might want to lower your expectations. Like, *really* lower them."

Jackson chuckles. "Thanks for the warning."

"No problem."

Even though our conversation is clearly over, neither of us moves to leave. Maybe it's because we both know that when we do, it'll be at least a week before we see each other again. Whatever the reason, there's only so long we can stand here in silence before it starts to feel weird, so reluctantly I say goodbye and head for my Prius. Not that I get very far. I've only taken two steps when Jackson calls my name.

Thinking I forgot something, I turn back—only to receive a face full of Reddi-Wip.

"Gotcha."

Unable to suppress a smile, I wipe the cream from my eyes and see Jackson beaming proudly.

"Are we good now?" I ask.

Jackson considers. Then, with a grin, he runs a finger across my cheek, scoops up a dab of whipped cream, and pops it into his mouth.

"We're good."

CHAPTER 14

JACKSON

Riley was right. *Xanadu* is kind of unwatchable. Even Duy, who was the one who suggested I come over and watch the movie, checks out halfway through the film and spends the next forty-five minutes texting on their phone. Not that I blame them.

"Well," I yawn when the credits roll after what feels like a short eternity. "That is one movie I will *never* forget."

"I know, right? What a mess!" Duy laughs, finally putting their phone down on the glass coffee table. "But kind of a brilliant mess. Like, how many drugs must the people who made this film have been on? I'm guessing *all* the drugs."

"For sure." I chuckle. Despite the epic badness of the movie, I had a good time tonight. Duy might not have said a lot, but what they did say was always entertaining.

"Anyway, thanks for coming over for movie night. Sorry I was so distracted."

"No worries," I assure them. "Looked like you and someone were having an important conversation."

"That remains to be seen," Duy replies with a cryptic smile.

Before I can ask what they mean, Ms. Nguyen pokes her head into the living room to remind Duy that it's almost ten. Duy rolls their eyes at the mention of their curfew, but I take the hint not to overstay my welcome. I thank Ms. Nguyen for her hospitality, hop off the sofa, and make my way to the door.

The night air is muggy when I step outside. But Duy lingers in the doorway, letting a cool breeze of AC escape into the soupy Florida evening.

"I'm glad you and Riley are becoming friends," they announce just as I'm about to stroll away.

The comment comes out of the blue, and for some reason, it stops me in my tracks. Duy's tone and smile seem genuine. But the words feel pointed as they hang in the air between us. Almost like a challenge. Or a test.

"Uh . . . yeah. Me too."

"Riley doesn't have many. Friends, that is," Duy explains. "He's kind of got major trust issues on account of some drama that went down his first year at Olympus. I don't know all the details. I wasn't there. But suffice it to say, Riley has a hard time trusting people. Especially boys. That's one of the reasons I'm always trying to introduce him to new people and expand our friend group. I know he thinks it's because I'm boy crazy, and, whatever, maybe sometimes I am, but nine times out of ten, the boys I bring around are for him. Because I'm worried about him and about how closed off he's getting."

"Oh," I say, unsure how else I'm supposed to respond.

"Don't get me wrong," Duy continues. "Audrey, Tala, and I love him. But we can't be his whole life. He needs to start opening up and stop pushing away anyone who tries to get close. Because as much as Riley likes to play the cynical loner who looks down on humanity, he needs people. He needs friends. He needs—" Duy stops and studies me carefully. "*Good* friends. Riley needs *good* friends."

I'm not exactly sure what Duy means by *good friends*. But I've seen firsthand everything they're describing. Riley is definitely someone with a lot of walls, and if I can help break some of them down, I'm more than happy to do it.

"Of course," I agree. "Riley's a great guy. I'd like to be his friend."

Duy continues to study me, their dark eyes scrutinizing my face like they're trying to peer inside my brain. "Good," they conclude. "Glad we're on the same page. Because if you hurt him, I swear to Diane von Furstenberg, I will *end* you."

"Wh-what?" I stammer, caught off guard by Duy's abrupt threat. But Duy just smiles.

"Anyway, thanks for coming over! Tonight was so much fun! Byeeeeeee!"

With an effusive wave, Duy shuts the door in my face.

For a solid ten seconds I'm too surprised to move. Mainly because I have no idea what just happened.

I get people wanting to look out for their friends. And wanting to protect them. But that conversation was just *weird*. I mean, Duy's acting like Mr. Adams did the first time I came over to pick up Micaela for a date. Except, oddly, I'm way more scared of Duy than I ever was of Mr. Adams.

I wonder if Duy found out about Devon. That would explain their sudden need to lay down the law. Or maybe they got worried when they saw me roughhousing with Riley this morning. Do they think I was picking on him? Or bullying him?

Oh, crap. Does *Riley* think I was bullying him?

I was only horsing around. But maybe I took things too far? I did knock the wind out of him with that tackle. And I haven't heard from him all day.

Shit, do I need to apologize? If not for the tackle, then for something else I did?

By the time I get back to Aunt Rachel's house and shut my bedroom door, I'm questioning every interaction that I've had with Riley over the past three days. Aside from a few stupid remarks that I made when we first met, I don't think I've done anything wrong. But if Duy's concerned about my behavior, maybe there's something I'm not seeing?

With a sigh, I flop down onto my bed and stare at the ceiling. There's no way I'm gonna be able to sleep while I'm worried I've done something to hurt Riley. So even though it's after ten, I shoot him a quick text. Nothing dramatic, just How's St. Augustine?, to see how he responds.

Almost immediately, my phone buzzes with his reply.

RILEY: I'm already sunburned and at dinner my grandfather asked me to explain what a throuple is. Other than that, I'm good.

My body relaxes. If there's one thing I learned from dating Micaela, it's that people who are mad at you don't text back. And they certainly don't text back with jokes. That means whatever prompted Duy's warning, it's not something I've done to Riley. It's something they're afraid I'll do in the future. Like stop being Riley's friend.

But since I have zero plans to do that, there's no problem. Everything's okay.

JACKSON: What are you up to now?

RILEY: Not much. Dad and grandparents are asleep. I'm sitting out on the balcony looking at the ocean and listening to music.

JACKSON: Sounds nice. Send me a pic.

RILEY: Of me?

JACKSON: No, dude, the ocean. I know what you look like.

Riley sends me the middle-finger emoji. Then a few seconds later, a photo comes through. At least, I think it's a photo. It looks more like a completely black square.

JACKSON: What's that?

RILEY: The ocean. At night. What'd you think it'd look like?

Ha-ha, I type. Though I can't help smiling. Since breaking up with Micaela, I've missed having someone to text with before bed. It makes a nice change from staring at the ceiling while my brain plays a highlight reel of all my greatest mistakes. Even so, I should probably say good night. I don't want to bother Riley on his vacation. The guy's gotta have better things to do with his time than entertain me. But before I can tell him that I'll talk to him later, a new text pops up asking what I thought of *Xanadu*, and my decision to wrap things up goes straight out the window.

Oh, man, I think that movie BROKE my brain! I reply, feeling oddly excited at the prospect of keeping our conversation going.

JACKSON: Seriously. How did it get made? It's SO bad.

RILEY: Some might say it's so bad, it's good.

JACKSON: That's not a thing, dude.

RILEY: Actually, dude, that's the definition of camp.

I have no idea what this means.

JACKSON: What do you mean camp? Like summer camp?

RILEY: What? No. CAMP.

Like the queer art form.

JACKSON: Like cheerleading camp?

RILEY: Seriously???

I'm so lost, but I'm also shaking so hard with laughter that I'm afraid I'm gonna wake Aunt Rachel.

For the next ten minutes, Riley attempts to explain what he calls "the concept of queer aesthetics" before giving up and letting me change the topic to something that doesn't hurt my head—movies. I try to convince him that Zack Snyder's director's cut of *Justice League* is a modern-day masterpiece. He then spends the next half hour explaining why I'm wrong.

Have you even seen it? I ask when he's done typing out his exclamation-point-heavy tirade.

RILEY: I don't need to see it to know it's garbage!

JACKSON: You can't have an opinion about something you haven't seen.

RILEY: I'm gay. I have an opinion about EVERYTHING.

Again, I can't help laughing. Riley's intensity would be terrifying if it weren't hilarious. It reminds me of a video that I saw a couple of days ago on TikTok where a large golden retriever is being terrorized by a tiny, adorable hedgehog. I find the video and send it to Riley.

RILEY: Is this supposed to be us?

JACKSON: Maybe . . .

RILEY: Let me guess. You're the big hapless dog and I'm the spiky little monster?

JACKSON: Your words, dude. Not mine.

RILEY: Have you seen the video of the baby pig who gets adopted by a bunch of wild turkeys and then grows up thinking he's a turkey?

JACKSON: No, but that sounds amazing. Send it now.

He does, and for the next few hours, Riley and I swap our favorite videos back and forth.

He sends me a video about a color-blind kid whose parents surprise him with a special pair of glasses that allow him to see color for the first time; I send him a video about a German shepherd losing its ever-loving mind after being reunited with a soldier who'd been deployed to Afghanistan for a year.

He sends me a video about a flock of ravens that visit a depressed woman's backyard every day and help her get through the pandemic. I send him a video of a little girl opening a birthday card and learning that the foster family she'd been living with wants to adopt her.

Half the videos have me cracking up with laughter, and the other half have me tearing up with emotion. Which is odd. I'm not a crier. If fact, I spent the past few months deliberately making myself as numb as possible just so I could get through the day.

Then again, maybe that's why everything is coming out now. Not that I mind. It's oddly freeing to let myself feel again. And to share those feelings with Riley.

Damn, we're sappy, I text, wiping a tear from my eye after a particularly moving video about a lion that's reunited with the zookeeper who rescued it as a cub.

The sappiest, Riley replies. **And the sleepiest.**

I can't disagree. Curled up in bed, in the cozy dark of my room, I'm finding it harder and harder to keep my eyes open. Stifling a yawn, I check the clock on my phone and immediately bolt up from my pillow.

Holy crap, I text. **Just saw the time. Is it really that late?**

Riley's response is to send me a photo. It's the ocean again, only instead of a black square like before, the picture shows a sliver of bright orange sun rising over the blue water into a hazy pink sky.

I can't believe it's dawn.

JACKSON: Wow. I didn't mean to keep you up all night.

RILEY: No worries. But I think that video I wanted to send you about the sassy sea lions will have to wait. I should probably get some sleep.

JACKSON: Yeah. Me too.

RILEY: Text you later?

JACKSON: For sure, dude. Get some rest.

RILEY: Will do, bro.

Chuckling to myself, I set my phone down on the nightstand. I can't believe how late it is. Or, I guess, how early? I don't even remember the last time I stayed up all night talking to someone. This might be the first.

I lie down and pull the sheet up around my chest. I'm on the verge of drifting off when I hear my phone buzz. I take a look and smile.

RILEY: Okay, ONE more video . . .

CHAPTER 15

RILEY

I'm not a lawyer, but I'm pretty sure it is criminally unprofessional to be this tired. Especially as it's only my first day on the job here at the ACLU. I've already downed three cups of coffee but, despite this, it's taking all my strength not to lay my head on my laptop and conk out.

Thankfully, my duties so far have consisted almost entirely of filing and photocopying, and not (for example) arguing a case in front of the Supreme Court that could determine the future of civil liberties. Still, I feel incredibly guilty. I might not want to devote the rest of my life to the law, but, per Jackson's plan, I do want to give this internship a fair chance.

Unfortunately, it seems that I also want to stay up until three every night texting with Jackson. That's how I spent my entire week of vacation in St. Augustine—chatting with Jackson all night, then drowsing by the condo pool all day.

I should've forced myself to go to bed early when I got back to Orlando yesterday, but once again, I couldn't stop myself from texting until dawn. Which is why I'm currently yawning so hard that I almost unhook my jaw.

"Someone needs some coffee," Dad observes dryly as he looks up from his desk on the other side of the office. "Why don't you grab a cup from the break room and stretch your legs? I think Charmaine brought doughnuts if you need some sugar."

I have no idea who Charmaine is. I'm sure I met her during my tour of the office this morning, but right now, I'm way too tired to put a face with a name. I also doubt a fourth cup of coffee will help if the already dangerous levels of caffeine coursing through my veins aren't doing the job, but I've got to try something.

"Good idea," I say, setting aside my laptop and rising from the (far too comfortable) sofa that I've been working from. "You want me to grab you anything?"

"Maybe a jelly if there are any left?"

I stop in the doorway and stare at him in incomprehension. "You want a jelly coffee?"

Dad blinks in confusion. "No, Riley. A doughnut. I want a jelly doughnut."

Yikes. I must be more exhausted than I thought. There is no way my brain is this dumb.

"I know," I say, covering with a forced laugh. "I was joking." Then I hurry out of the office before Dad can call bullshit on such an obvious lie.

I can't keep up these all-night texting sessions with Jackson. I've *got* to start going to bed at a reasonable hour. Though if the last week is any indication of my self-control, that'll be easier said than done.

Over the past few days, Jackson and I have progressed from swapping memes and TikToks to swapping stories about our lives, which is proving just as—if not more—entertaining. Not to mention informative. Seriously, I now know so much about Jackson Haines, I could write his biography.

I know that when he was six, he was terrified of the Tooth Fairy and slept with a baseball bat under his bed to defend his teeth.

I know that when he was ten, he discovered that girls really wanted to kiss him, so at recess he started charging them a dollar per smooch.

I know that freshman year, he won first prize at his school's Halloween carnival by dressing up in his mom's old pageant gown and tiara.

Every story that he tells me makes me want to learn more about him. And the more he opens up about his life, the more I want to open up about mine.

Already I've told him about my mom leaving when I was six, about the half sisters I've never met, about coming out to my dad at twelve and the mortifying STI lecture he gave me with *visual aids*.

I'm honestly shocked at how much I've told him. I've never really been one to talk about myself. My life has always struck me as too messy or sad or boring to share with anyone. But with Jackson, I don't feel that way. He doesn't make my life or me feel small or pointless. Just the opposite, in fact. He makes me feel interesting and important. It's actually quite intoxicating. I haven't had someone show this much interest in me since I dated Alex Vargas.

Not that you could call what Alex and I did *dating*. Alex certainly didn't.

He was a junior when I was a freshman. He was tall, brooding, and (more important) *deeply* in the closet. During the day, he kept his distance from me at school. He never wanted to hang out in public or be seen in the same room with me.

At night, though, it was a different story.

At night, Alex could be sweet and flirty, especially over the phone. We would text until dawn, and for a while our mutual obsession with each other seemed almost magical. I even managed to convince myself that we were in a sexy *Romeo and Juliet*–style situation where no one could be allowed to discover our "forbidden love." It made all the sneaking around seem exciting and fun instead of what it actually was: pathetic.

We might have gone on like that all year, with Alex ignoring me by day and hooking up with me by night. But one day, in the parking lot after school, some of the guys from the Thunderbolts started harassing me about my hair, which I'd dyed pink for Halloween.

Alex came out of the building and saw what was happening. But instead of coming to my defense or trying to extricate me from the situation, he kept on walking. Just got in his car and left me to fend for myself against six guys who were twice my size.

Thankfully, Audrey came to my rescue. She scared off the Thunderbolts with some devastating put-downs, and we've been best friends ever since.

Alex, meanwhile, dumped me.

According to the text he sent me later that night, I wasn't "discreet" enough. Apparently, me almost getting my ass kicked by half the school's homophobic football team was my own fault. I was "asking for it." And since I clearly didn't care how my actions affected *him*, Alex decided it was best that we no longer had anything to do with each other.

In hindsight, I know that getting dumped was a blessing in disguise. A guy who cared so little about me that he'd leave me in a potentially dangerous situation without a backward glance is definitely *not* boyfriend material.

At the time, though, getting dumped like that really fucking hurt. Alex was my first (almost) boyfriend. And those nights we spent texting each other until the sun came up had been some of the happiest weeks of my life.

I'd almost forgotten how happy it made me to share my life with someone until Jackson came along.

Not that the situation with Jackson is *anything* like the situation with Alex.

Jackson's not my secret boyfriend. *Obviously.* He's not texting me for hours every night because he's got a crush on me and hopes to get in my pants.

And I don't want to get in his! Because I don't crush on straight boys. And Jackson is straight.

Straight and bored.

Straight and bored and lonely.

Seriously, as amazing as getting to know Jackson has been, I'm not fooling myself that our time together is anything other than a summer friendship of convenience. Once school starts in the fall and he makes a bunch of new friends in the popular crowd, I'm sure he'll find someone else to share his favorite cat videos with.

Probably some annoyingly pretty cheerleader who's just like his ex-girlfriend.

Which is fine! Obviously. He's allowed to have a girlfriend.

Like I said, Jackson's not Alex. Jackson and I are not a couple. We're just friends.

I mean, do we have amazing chemistry and a surprisingly strong connection? Sure.

Do I find myself occasionally thinking about him and replaying the R-rated parts of that incredibly steamy dream where we pledged our undying devotion to each other? Guilty.

Has this past week been one of the best weeks of my life in a long, *long* time, and does the thought of having more weeks with someone as funny and thoughtful and handsome as Jackson make the world seem like an infinitely less shitty place to live in? Absolutely.

But all that just means . . .

It means . . .

Oh, fuck.

I have a crush on Jackson.

CHAPTER 16

JACKSON

"Are you even watching this movie?" my aunt asks with an exasperated huff.

I look up from my phone and see her staring at me from the other end of the couch, her arms folded across her chest and an amused smirk on her face. When we were cleaning up after dinner, she asked if I wanted to watch a movie since it was Friday night and neither of us had any plans. I suggested the latest Zack Snyder zombie thriller, and Aunt Rachel agreed to give it a try, even though she's not a fan of horror or gore.

"I'm watching," I tell her, somewhat confused by her question and tone.

Aunt Rachel's left eyebrow arches so high, she looks like the suspicion emoji. "Really?"

"Yes."

"Then what's the last thing that happened?"

I turn to the TV to refresh my memory, but Aunt Rachel has paused the film at a point where the entire screen is black. I try to remember what was going on with the zombies, but that proves more difficult than it should. I really *was* paying attention. At least, at first. But a couple of minutes into the movie, Riley texted me, and I suppose I got distracted.

But that's only because Riley's been acting so weird lately.

Ever since he got back from St. Augustine, he's been insanely slow to respond to my texts. Like molasses in winter slow. And when he does respond, his answers are always short and blunt. Without any warning, we went from texting nonstop every night to texting only a handful of times during the day. I was starting to get nervous again that I'd said or done something to offend him, but earlier tonight, a few minutes into the movie, he texted me to say that he and his friends have plans to go somewhere "really cool" tomorrow and asked if I wanted to tag along.

I've been pumping him for details, more to make sure he's not mad at me than because of any real curiosity, but he's being surprisingly cagey. He keeps insisting that if he tells me, I won't come, and I keep telling him that I'm so bored, I'm down for anything. Even so, he won't give me a hint, so I've been trying to bribe/cajole/weasel some clues out of him. Which is why I haven't necessarily been giving this zombie flick my undivided attention.

"Well?" Aunt Rachel asks, still waiting for my answer.

"The last thing that happened was the zombie attack on the Empire State Building," I tell her. I know that was early in the film, but I don't think anything important has happened since then.

"The attack on the Empire State Building?" she repeats, her poker face giving nothing away. "Interesting. Is that your final answer?"

"Yep. Final answer."

Aunt Rachel reaches for the remote and hits play. There's a swell of orchestral music, and the movie's end credits roll.

Holy crap. I missed the entire movie.

I turn back to my aunt, expecting her to look annoyed that I made her sit through a two-and-a-half-hour gorefest when she'd wanted to watch the new *Pride and Prejudice* remake. But she just grins a smug little grin.

"*So . . .*" she coos. "Who's the girl?"

My cheeks flush with heat. "What?"

"Jackson, you've been texting nonstop for *two* hours, and you haven't stopped smiling *once*."

"I'm texting a friend," I protest.

"Ooh, a *friend*."

"A *boy* friend," I clarify, then immediately realize what I said. "Not a *boyfriend*. A boy *friend*. Fuck. A friend who's a boy. Riley. One of the guys I went with to the carnival and Rink-O-Rama. You know, Duy's friend."

Aunt Rachel looks momentarily thrown. "Oh. Huh. Okay."

"He's been going through some personal stuff, trying to figure out what he wants to do with his life," I hear myself explain in a voice that's oddly defensive. "I've been helping him out."

I'm not sure why I feel the need to volunteer that information or justify my friendship with Riley. It's not like we're doing anything wrong. Aunt Rachel's the one who misread the situation and made it weird.

"Riley, huh? Well, that's great, kiddo!" Her face breaks into a delighted smile. "You've made a friend. I'm proud of you."

Aunt Rachel squeezes my knee, and the heat of my cheeks burns twice as hard. Eight-year-olds get complimented on their ability to make friends. I'm almost eighteen. Is the bar really so low for me that my family is now proud when I display basic social skills?

"Okay, you're being weird," I say just as my phone buzzes with an incoming text. "I'm gonna need you to stop."

"I'm not being weird. I'm excited. You very wisely took my advice about making friends, and it's clearly improved your life."

My phone buzzes again, and Aunt Rachel's smile grows ever smugger.

I roll my eyes and hop off the sofa. "I'm going to bed. I'll see you in the morning."

"Okay, kiddo. Have a good night," she trills in a singsong tone as my phone buzzes for a third time. "Tell Riley good night for me!"

I don't bother to dignify the remark with a response. Instead, I head to my room, shut the door, and flop down onto my bed, where I see that my last three messages aren't, in fact, from Riley. They're from Micaela.

MICAELA: Crushed the first week of cheer camp.

MICAELA: Pretty sure I've been elected their new queen.

The third text is a photo of a football field covered in a sea of mostly preteen girls and pom-poms. At the very center is Micaela. She's flashing that thousand-megawatt smile that makes her stand out in any crowd.

I can't help smiling back at her photo. And her texts. Despite the awkwardness of our last exchange (not to mention the awkwardness of the past six months), Micaela seems determined to be a part of my life. That means a lot.

Congratulations, Your Majesty, I text, trying to keep things breezy so I don't screw up and hurt her feelings like I did last time. Will you be using your new powers for good or for evil?

MICAELA: For good, of course. The Kingdom of Cheer is a joyous and beneficent place.

JACKSON: As long as you always get your way?

MICAELA: Let's just say it will behoove my people to keep their queen happy.

JACKSON: Good to know.

MICAELA: So how are you? Do anything exciting this week?

JACKSON: Not really. Watched movies with Aunt Rachel. Looked for a job.
Went roller-skating.

MICAELA: Skating? Like, around your neighborhood?

JACKSON: No. At this place called Rink-O-Rama. They had an eighties night. It was a whole thing.

MICAELA: You are literally blowing my mind right now.

JACKSON: I think there's an emoji for that.

MICAELA: For real? Skating?
In public? Who are you?

JACKSON: I'm going with Jackson 2.0.

MICAELA: Ha! Does Jackson 2.0 have any pics?

I actually have an amazing photo of Riley and me at the rink. We're standing between some blue fluorescent bulbs, so the lighting is dramatic but also flattering. We look like we're members of a boy band posing for our album cover. If I hadn't deleted all my social media, I'd definitely make it my profile pic.

Sending now, I text Micaela.

I start to attach the photo, but before I hit send, something stops me.

It's my smile. Looking at the photo, I can sort of see what my aunt meant earlier. For the first time in a long time, I look happy. Really, *really* happy.

Maybe too happy?

It's possible I'm overthinking things, but if Micaela had moved halfway across the state because she needed "space" and "a new start," I'm not sure I'd want to see a photo of her looking ridiculously happy with another guy.

Not that this photo of Riley and me is anything like that. He's a friend.

All the same, I don't want Micaela to think I replaced her overnight with a new set of friends or that I'm rubbing my newfound happiness in her face. Especially since I'm the reason she was unhappy for so long.

I'm waiting, she texts.

I can't risk hurting Micaela's feelings again. Not when things finally seem to be getting back to normal between us. Which means there's only one thing to do. Using the photo editor on my phone, I crop Riley out of the picture and send her the shot of just me.

She writes back immediately.

MICAELA: Wow, looks like Jackson 2.0 is having a lot of fun.

JACKSON: He is. Though Jackson 2.0 is not a good skater.

MICAELA: Aww. Don't worry. The next time I'm in Orlando, I'll give you some lessons.

JACKSON: You're on.

Based on Micaela's reaction, it's safe to say that cutting Riley out of the picture was definitely the smart thing to do, and I'm momentarily flooded with relief. But as I stare at the cropped image on my phone, I can't help feeling something else. Something that feels a lot like guilt.

Which is weird. Because I did the right thing, didn't I? I protected Micaela from getting hurt.

So why do I feel like shit?

CHAPTER 17

RILEY

Jackson looks like a deer in headlights. Then again, I'm pretty sure I looked the same way the first time I stepped foot in a gay bar. I probably should've given him a heads-up that we were coming to Heartbeats. But truthfully, I wanted to see his honest reaction.

Ever since my realization that my crush on Jackson has morphed from the superficially physical to the full-on emotional, I've been trying to think of a way to cure myself of the attraction. I've kept our texting to a minimum and refused to think about the steamier and more romantic moments from my two dreams, but it hasn't been enough. So when Audrey suggested an afternoon of drag-queen karaoke, it occurred to me that this could prove the perfect opportunity to get over my feelings for Jackson.

I figured if we took him to Heartbeats without any advance warning, then his inner dude-bro might emerge, and he might freak out and refuse to go inside, which would be super-shitty and cause me to lose all respect for him, but it would provide me with the much-needed reminder that Jackson isn't queer.

"Are you sure I'm allowed to be here?" he asks, gaping nervously at the brightly clad, big-bewigged drag queens like they're creatures from another planet, as we wind our way through the Saturday-brunch crowd.

"Why wouldn't you be allowed here?" I ask.

"I don't know. 'Cause I'm straight?"

"Straight people are allowed in gay bars," Audrey explains with a groan as we slide into a U-shaped booth near the stage. She's been warming up to Jackson ever since Rink-O-Rama, but her patience for hetero-nonsense goes only so far. "It's straight people who like to exclude queer people from things—like bathrooms and civil rights—not the other way around."

"Right. Yeah. Sorry," Jackson says, looking suitably chastised.

"For the record, I wanted to tell you where we were going," Tala confides, shooting him a sympathetic smile. "I was outvoted."

"I thought the surprise would be fun," I lie.

"No, it's cool," Jackson says, casting another nervous glance around the room. "First time for everything, right?"

Despite my hope that the bar would freak him out and make him unworthy of my crush, I can't help being relieved to see Jackson so open to the experience. Then again, I should've known he would be. He's been nothing but totally accepting of my friends and me since the day we met. And Heartbeats isn't exactly Sodom and Gomorrah.

At night, the club models itself after a romantic speakeasy. They keep the lighting low, and patrons have to be over twenty-one to get in. During the day, though, anyone is welcome, and the place takes on a more casual diner vibe. In fact, on a morning like today, there's actually very little to alert a random passerby that this is a queer establishment. Except, of course, for all the drag queens.

"So . . . we're here to watch drag queens sing karaoke?" Jackson asks after our bouffant-coiffed server takes our food order.

"No, the drag queens work the bar and host the show," I clarify. "Sometimes one of them will do a number. But for the most part, they're here to encourage other people to get up and sing."

"Or *discourage* people if they don't happen to approve of your song choice or if you're a *little* off-key," Duy grumbles, no doubt recalling the time they made the mistake of attempting to perform opera. "There are some *very* judgy queens in this room."

"The roasting is all in good fun," I assure Jackson. "Mostly. Except when it's devastating."

"I'm gonna sign up for a slot," Audrey announces, scooting out of the booth. "Riley, I'll put you down to go after me? Your usual?"

"Sounds good."

"Jackson?"

Jackson's eyes go wide with panic. "Me?"

"Yeah," Audrey says. "Do you want to sing something?"

"No. God—*no.*"

His horror is so palpable, it makes the entire table laugh.

"It's all right," Tala assures him. "You don't have to. Duy and I never sing."

"Not anymore," Duy mumbles.

Jackson exhales in relief, looking like a man who was just pardoned from death row.

"I take it you're not a fan of karaoke?" I ask as Audrey heads off to add our names to the sign-up sheet.

"Not really. I went once with Micaela for her birthday. Did not go well."

"Ooh, tell us everything," Duy demands, leaning forward in excitement.

Jackson lets out an embarrassed laugh. "So, have you guys ever seen one of those cheesy rom-coms where someone goes to a karaoke bar and at first they're really stiff and awkward but then magically, after thirty seconds, they somehow get confident, and by the end of the song, the whole room is cheering for them and singing along?"

We collectively nod.

"Right, so picture that. Except in my case, I started off bad and then somehow managed to get worse until some guy who worked at the bar came up onto the stage and took my mic away."

Tala's jaw drops. "They can do that?"

"Apparently, if you're bad enough, yeah."

"No way," I say, trying to stifle my laughter. "You're making that up."

Jackson shrugs, which makes me laugh even harder. If my plan was to convince myself to like him *less*, it's so far a total failure.

"I'm glad my pain and humiliation is so amusing," Jackson teases, playfully ramming his shoulder into mine. "I take it you're some sort of musical prodigy?"

"Me? No," I protest. "I like singing, but Audrey's the one with the voice. We all tell her she's going to be famous someday."

"Yes, my girlfriend is *incredibly* talented," Tala boasts. "But Riley here is *also* talented, whether he chooses to believe it or not."

"I'm fine," I say. "I can carry a tune."

"Come on," Tala insists, "you're literally the only person Audrey has ever deigned to duet with. And she doesn't like to share the stage with anyone."

"Audrey likes singing with me because she knows I won't question her artistic choices or steal the spotlight."

"Oh my God, your low self-esteem is so *boring*." Duy groans. "Can we please talk about something more interesting?"

"Sure." I laugh, relieved to have the focus diverted from me and my supposed singing talents. As much as I appreciate Tala's words of encouragement, praise makes me uncomfortable. I'd almost rather be insulted so I can get offended and tell someone off than receive a compliment that I don't think I'll be able to live up to.

"Okay, so, very important question," Duy announces, looking across the booth at Jackson and me. "Do either of you have any plans tomorrow?"

Jackson and I shake our heads.

"Awesome. I need you both to come over and model for my portfolio."

Jackson furrows his brow in confusion.

"Don't worry," Duy insists. "It'll be super-fun."

I roll my eyes at this whopper of a falsehood. "Allow me to translate what Duy means by 'fun,'" I say. "They want us to come over and stand in the hot sun for six hours wearing whatever elaborate outfits they've concocted while they sit in the shade with an ice-cold pitcher of boba taking seven *thousand* photos and yelling at us to, 'Look better!'"

Jackson chuckles as if he thinks I'm exaggerating, but I know whereof I speak. One of the few perks of being as thin as I am is that most clothes look good on me, so over the years I've helped Duy build up their fashion portfolio for colleges by modeling some of the outfits they've designed.

The last time I volunteered, though, I almost got heatstroke, and I vowed never to do it again. Duy's one of my best friends and one of the most talented people I know, but when it comes to their clothes and getting the exact right shot, they can be an infuriating perfectionist.

"Ha! Riley's such a *kidder!*" Duy laughs in an attempt to brush aside my all-too-accurate criticism. "It's actually *a lot* of fun. And the pitcher of boba is for everyone. You just can't have any while you're wearing the clothes."

"So you just need me to model some clothes while you take my picture?" Jackson asks.

"Exactly."

"I don't have to get naked or anything, do I?"

At the thought of Jackson in nothing but his birthday suit, I feel my face flush. I immediately try to block out the image. Though if my dreams are accurate, I've already seen *plenty*.

"Oh my gosh, of course not!" Duy laughs. "This shoot is about how good people look *in* my clothes. Not how good you'd look without any."

Now it's Jackson's turn to blush. "Just checking," he mumbles. "I guess I'm in if Riley's in."

Duy turns and flashes me a wide but pointed smile that makes it clear that I better not screw this up for them. Models like Jackson don't come along every day.

"Sure," I sigh. "I'm in."

"Yay!" Duy squeals. "This is going to be so much fun! You're going to *love* the outfits. Just don't eat anything for the next twenty-four hours. The camera adds ten pounds."

"Duy!" Tala whispers, shooting them a warning look that I can only assume means *Maybe don't tell your friend who once had an eating disorder not to eat.*

"Kidding!" Duy exclaims, turning slightly pink. "Everyone looks great. No one needs to worry about their figure. All bodies are beautiful!"

I shake my head and let out an annoyed snort, which I instantly regret when Jackson clocks it.

"Am I missing something?" he asks.

Of all the things we've discussed during our late-night texting sessions, my (very) brief flirtation with anorexia is not one of them, and I plan to keep it that way. I already have my dad and my friends playing Food Police; I don't need Jackson worrying about my weight or giving me concerned looks anytime I happen to skip a meal.

Thankfully, Tala notices my discomfort and deftly changes the subject. "Speaking of beautiful bodies, isn't that the boy from Rink-O-Rama that you were flirting with?"

Duy sits up ramrod-straight and instinctively smooths down their hair. "Where?"

"Over by the bar."

Duy covertly looks over their shoulder and gasps. "Oh my God, it's Caleb!"

"Who's Caleb?" Jackson asks.

Duy leans over the table and whispers conspiratorially, "Caleb Holzinger. The boy I've been texting for *two weeks*. He goes to a fancy private school in Winter Park but he's super-down-to-earth. I want to suck off his face and live in his biceps."

Jackson and I steal a quick glance at Caleb, whose brooding eyes, strong jaw, and languorous posture remind me of a figure in a Pre-Raphaelite painting. If guys in Pre-Raphaelite paintings wore crop tops and camo pants.

"He's cute," Jackson observes with a nod of approval.

The comment surprises me. I didn't think straight boys noticed how other guys looked. Or if they did, I didn't think their bro-code permitted them to admit it in public.

More to the point, I can't help wondering who else Jackson might think is cute.

"Yes, Caleb *is* cute," Tala agrees. "And based on some light Instagram stalking that Duy and I have been doing, we know that Caleb is also witty, smart, socially conscious, and the first ever trans president of his school's GSA. But for some reason Duy's not interested in asking him out."

"I never said I wasn't *interested*," Duy huffs. "I just said I was keeping my options open. You know, in case I meet Michael B. Jordan or Manny Jacinto."

Tala gives Duy a pitying look and gently squeezes their hand. "You know that's literally never going to happen?"

"Why don't you go say hello?" Jackson suggests. "I mean, if you've been texting, why not?"

Duy shrugs with feigned indifference, but I can tell it's just a cover for their nerves. The more Duy likes a boy, the more self-conscious they get. And given the sudden dip in Duy's otherwise insanely high levels of confidence, they must be into Caleb a lot.

"You all need to stop being so thirsty," Duy retorts. "Just because Caleb and I have been texting every day doesn't mean he *likes me* likes me."

These words hit a little too close to home, and I can feel my cheeks burn. It takes all my strength not to look at Jackson.

"Oh my gosh, are you serious?" Tala exclaims. "Until you made me read your entire text history with Caleb, I never knew the eggplant emoji could be used like that. Trust me, he *likes* you."

"But what if I ask him out and he says no?" Duy groans. "Or what if he says yes, and it ends up being a total disaster, and I die of mortification after being rejected by literally the hottest boy on the whole entire planet? No offense, Jackson."

"All great points," Tala concedes. "I'm going to counter with what if Caleb says yes and you have a great time and you get to make out with that sexy face for the rest of the year?"

Duy glances over at Caleb, whose face in the bar's soft lighting does look particularly kissable.

"Ugh, *fine*," Duy relents. "I'll talk to him. But you're coming with me."

"Me? Why?" Tala asks.

"Because I need to make it look like we're going to the ladies' room to fix our makeup and I just happened to run into him."

"Or you could just walk up to him and say hello."

"Oh my God, T., you are so naive," Duy scoffs. "No wonder you didn't notice you were dating Audrey for six months."

Before Tala can protest, Duy grabs her by the arm and pulls her up from the booth.

"Wow," Jackson exclaims as he watches the two of them disappear into the crowd. "Duy does not take no for an answer, do they?"

"Not really." I'm still feeling a little awkward after Duy's reminder that texting does not necessarily equal romance, but I'm trying not to show it. "It's kind of the best thing about them. Also maybe the worst."

"Tomorrow should be fun, then."

"Oh, you have no idea what you're in for."

Jackson grins and begins counting off on his fingers. "Carnivals, roller discos, drag-queen karaoke, modeling—do you and your friends ever do anything, I don't know, normal?"

"Normal?"

"Yeah. Do you ever just chill at home and watch a game?"

"Oh, I see the confusion. I think the word you're looking for is *boring*."

Jackson laughs one of his big, full-body laughs. And despite my confusion about my ever-increasing attraction to him, I can't help laughing back.

"Well, bless my soul," a drag queen drawls in a thick Southern accent as she sashays past our table patting her enormous red beehive wig. "Aren't you two the cutest little couple I ever did see."

My shoulders stiffen. If there's one thing guaranteed to make a straight boy freak out in a gay bar, it's having his sexuality questioned. And even though that was absolutely my original intention in bringing Jackson here, I don't think I could bear to see that happen now. In fact, I'm almost certain it would break my heart.

Jackson, though, only laughs. "Why do people keep thinking we're a couple?"

"I have no idea!" I force myself to laugh back.

"For real, that's the third time someone has thought we were dating."

"It is?" I remember the fortune teller at the carnival but—

"My aunt said the same thing last night," Jackson clarifies.

Oh. Huh. That's...interesting. "Why did your aunt think we were dating?" I ask, trying not to sound like swarms of butterflies are flapping inside my chest.

"Because I was texting you so much. She thought you were a girl."

"Oh."

"It's crazy this keeps happening, right?"

"Yeah," I say, turning away so he can't see my face. "Crazy."

CHAPTER 18

JACKSON

Riley wasn't kidding about Audrey—the girl's got some serious pipes. She's only halfway through her rendition of "To Love Somebody," strutting across the stage in her black faux-leather jacket and high-heeled boots, and already all the people in the bar are on their feet cheering her on like she's a legit rock star.

"*In my pain, I see your face again, it's burning in my mind,*" she wails into the microphone, her voice tinged with a raspy growl that earns her another burst of applause.

"Dude, she's so good!" I shout to Riley over the music.

"I know!"

"How long has she been singing?"

"All her life! Her dad's a singer—mostly local gigs—so she grew up performing with him. It's in her blood!"

That's for sure. I don't think I've ever seen anyone own a stage the way Audrey's dominating hers right now. When she gets to the chorus, the entire room joins in. Even the very judgy drag queens, who up until now have been unimpressed with the caliber of performers, are waving their wigs in the air.

In fact, the only person not singing is Tala. She's too in awe of Audrey's talent to do anything more than stare at the stage, a huge, lovestruck grin spread across her face. It reminds me of the way Micaela used to look at me during my games.

"*The wa-a-a-a-a-a-a-ay I love you!*"

Audrey finishes with a vocal flourish that would put Kelly Clarkson to shame, and the whole bar loses its mind. It's like being at the Super Bowl and watching your team come from behind to win the game with a last-second touchdown. People are legitimately losing their shit.

"Why did I agree to go on *after* her?" Riley groans beside me as he watches Audrey soak up the almost-deafening applause.

"Don't worry," I assure him. "You're gonna be great."

"No, what I'm going to do is hide in the bathroom until they skip me."

"Whoa, whoa, whoa, not so fast" I say, grabbing his arm as he tries to slip away into the crowd. "You don't get to trick me into coming to a gay bar because you want to sing karaoke and then *not* sing karaoke. You owe me a show."

"Rain check."

"Nope. Sorry, dude. You're getting up there."

Miss Understood, the drag queen who thought Riley and I were a couple, takes to the stage and resumes her emcee duties, demanding another round of applause for the vocal pyrotechnics of Audrey O'Shea.

"I can't follow *that*," Riley pleads, looking like he might actually be sick. "I'll get crucified. You saw how the drag queens made that twink cry when he messed up the lyrics to 'Jolene.'"

I laugh and drape my arm around his shoulder to keep him from running off. "I'll make you a deal. You go up and sing, and no matter what happens, I promise I will cheer for you like you're Harry Styles and I'm your biggest fan."

Riley tilts his head and looks at me with surprised eyes. "You will?"

"Absolutely."

Onstage, Miss Understood announces it's time for the next singer. She looks at the sign-up sheet and calls Riley's name.

"You've got this," I tell him, giving his shoulder a squeeze when I feel him tense.

"You better clap your ass off," he grumbles.

I give him an encouraging push toward the stage as Audrey returns to our booth. She joins Duy, Tala, and me in cheering Riley on, but I can tell his confidence is still shaken. As he takes his place behind the mic stand, he keeps his eyes down and his shoulders hunched. He's shrinking into himself.

"Go, Riley!" I shout.

The opening chords of Queen's "Who Wants to Live Forever" begin to play, and Riley takes a deep breath.

"There's no time for us, there's no place for us," he begins, his voice coming out thin and hesitant. I'm hoping he'll loosen up or at least sing loud enough for the mic to pick up his voice. But even if he doesn't, I'll keep my word. I'm gonna cheer for him like I'm his number one fan.

Because I am.

Riley's been an incredible friend since I moved to Orlando. I keep having to remind myself that I met him only two weeks ago because I feel so comfortable around him. Like I've known him my whole life.

For some reason, the dude just gets me. And I get him. We click.

It's actually a little disturbing how much we click. During our late-night texting sessions, I've told him things that I've never told anyone. I don't mean deep dark secrets. He already knows my secrets. I mean silly, stupid stuff. It's like all my life I've been storing up these stories about myself and now I finally have someone to share them with. Someone I *want* to share them with. And he wants to hear them. Just like I want to learn everything about him . . .

"Who wants to live forever? Who wants to live forever?" Riley sings, his voice growing in confidence as he reaches the second chorus. He doesn't have Audrey's swagger or showmanship, but there's something

compelling about his performance. He closes his eyes the way some singers do when they're really feeling the music, and his entire body seems to relax and expand like the song is filling him up—likes he's becoming one with the music.

Lost in his performance, Riley is more self-assured, more alive, more *himself*. It's like getting a glimpse into his soul. A soul that is strong and beautiful and *familiar* ...

Something stirs in the back of my mind. A buried memory pushes itself to the surface. Images of people and places I only half recognize flicker in front of my eyes like a flip book with the pages out of order.

It makes my head spin.

I try to steady myself against the table, to focus on Riley until the dizziness passes, but I can't seem to concentrate. The world is going sideways.

"Jackson?"

My legs give out under me. I collapse to the floor, the weight of my own body pulling me down as the world goes dark.

Somehow, though, I can still see Riley, his face leaning over me, his clear green eyes staring into mine.

Those eyes ...

"Jackson?"

I've seen those eyes before.

"Are you all right?"

I've met Riley before.

"Can you hear me?"

I know him.

LONDON, ENGLAND

(MAY 10, 1941)

CHAPTER 19

JACK HARTNELL

Truth is, people can get used to anything. Look at Myrtle. Nine months ago, every time the Germans dropped their bombs, she would scream her head off and scramble for the nearest shelter faster than you could say "God save the King." Tonight, she just lights up a smoke, not even bothering to look up at the planes buzzing overhead.

Why should she? The Germans never bother with Piccadilly. All the girls who work the streets 'round here know that. Even the sounds of the bombs dropping on the other side of the river hardly warrant their consideration.

It's all a bit old hat now, innit? I mean, every other night, the same routine: The sun goes down, the air-raid sirens go off, a dozen planes courtesy of Herr Hitler fly up the Thames and blow up a few buildings. Then they pop back across the Channel, and we all get on with our lives. Start to finish, the whole thing only lasts an hour. I suppose that's what they mean on the radio about "German efficiency."

"All right there, Myrtle?" I shout over the din, tipping my cap to her as Charlie and I make our way past the fountain with the flying baby on top. Myrtle told me once it's not actually a flying baby. It's some Greek lad named Eros who's the god of love or something. That's why all the tarts hang around it.

"Slow night." Myrtle yawns and flicks a bit of ash off the sleeve of her coat as another loud boom echoes in the distance. Only ten minutes ago, Charlie and me saw the Germans hit Tower Bridge on our way across the river. Watched the Constable Tower go up in flames and everything. That last explosion sounded closer, though. Maybe London Bridge? Or Southwark?

The Germans always go for bridges.

"Why don't you go inside, have a warm-up?" I ask as a gust of wind causes Myrtle to shiver. It's a bit nippy for May, and the streets were emptier than usual even before the air-raid sirens sent everyone ducking for cover.

"Nah," Myrtle says with a shrug. "Business'll pick up once the all-clear sounds. Don't want to miss my Prince Charming now, do I?"

"You're a credit to your profession."

"I do what I can."

Myrtle takes another drag and casts a glance over at the eastern sky, where ribbons of smoke curl up into the air like fat snakes from the flames below. Poor bastards. Hope whoever's getting it tonight are keeping their heads down.

Charlie pulls on my sleeve, impatient for us to be on our way. He still gets nervous on nights like this, and I can see his green eyes grow wider every time another bomb shakes the air.

"Ready to shove off?" I ask, shooting him a smile as I put my arm 'round his shoulder. He likes when I do that. And I don't mind it so much myself.

Charlie nods, and we wave farewell to Myrtle as I lead us north onto Regent Street.

"You got your sack?" I ask. Though I ain't really asking. I watched him tuck it under his coat before we left our digs. But I try to keep Charlie's mind occupied whenever we're about to do a job. Otherwise, his nerves get the better of him and he's a bit useless.

"I've got it," he says.

"Good lad. I think we're in for quite a haul tonight."

"Where are we going?"

"Someplace special."

"Can't you tell?"

"It's a surprise," I tease him. "For your birthday."

Charlie's eyes narrow like a cat's. When you grow up on the streets, surprises are rarely a good thing.

"Don't make that face. When have I ever steered us wrong?" I ask.

Charlie considers, then flashes me that shy little smile of his. "All right, Jack."

I suppose you could say, like the bombs, that smile's something else I've gotten used to. Lord knows, when Charlie first came along, I wasn't looking for no "partner in crime" (as Myrtle calls him). In fact, I'd been doing all right on my own if I do say so myself. But that's the thing about Charlie, innit? He's got a way of growing on you.

We were twelve when we met. I'd been on the streets 'bout two years then, scrounging for food and nicking things by day; dossing where I could at night. I don't mind admitting those were some dodgy days. Even so, the streets weren't half as rough as home.

My old man was a boxer. Used to fight at Vauxhall under the name Bruisin' Bill. Made a decent bit of money at it too, I'm told. Only trouble was, he liked to practice his punches on my mum and me. Mum didn't seem to mind taking it. Like I said, people can get used to anything. But it struck me at the time that a black eye and a broken arm weren't things a body should get used too.

So I left.

For a while I ran around with some of the neighborhood gangs in Bermondsey. The boys were older, sixteen, seventeen, but they didn't mind having me around. Thanks to my dad, I knew how to throw (and take) a punch. Plus, I was useful.

My special skill was squeezing myself through tight spaces (iron gates, open windows, et cetera), then unlatching the door so the other boys could turn a place over. I also made a pretty good lookout. With my blue eyes and my curly bronze hair that turned kind of golden-like in the summer, people said I looked like a right little cherub. Coppers would pass me on the street and not give me a second glance.

The other boys weren't so lucky, though. Most of them got pinched and went off to the workhouses. But by then, I could look after myself.

To be honest, I preferred being on my own. Other people had their uses, but in the end, you couldn't count on anyone but yourself. Best not to get attached, I said.

But one day in the early fall, I was nicking apples from the Borough Market when I got this funny-like sensation on the back of my neck. Like I was being watched. I thought it might be a cop, but when I turned around, all I saw was this skinny dark-haired boy staring at me from across the stalls. He was about my age, with big green eyes that had this way of burrowing into you. Like they could see into your soul.

If his clothes had been shabbier, I'd have taken him for another street kid. But he had on a proper cap and jacket, and his shoes didn't have no holes that I could see, so I reckoned he must be the son of the grocer and was about ten seconds from screaming his head off.

But he didn't say a word.

He just stared at me. Like he was waiting to see what I'd do next.

If I'm honest, it spooked me. I shoved a few more apples in my pockets, then did a runner before he could give me away.

It was a warm September day, and as I didn't have nothing better to do, I went down to the river to watch the boats. I used to reckon that when I got older, I'd get me a job on one of those boats. You know, spend my days cruising up and down the Thames, delivering cargo. I've always liked the water even though I've never learned to swim proper.

I was thinking I might head over to the Surrey docks to see if there was any work going when I felt that funny sensation on the back of my neck again. Sure enough, when I turned around, there was the boy. Standing under a tree not twenty feet away, watching me.

I thought about giving him a good ticking-off, but there were people about, and I didn't want to risk making a scene. So I satisfied myself by giving him a dirty look complete with the appropriate hand gestures and decided to shove off.

I kept myself pretty busy for the next few hours. Then, when the sun started going down, I made my way back over to Bermondsey. The railway arch by the Peek Freans factory was (and still is, I reckon) a good place to set up camp for the night, provided you got there early and claimed your spot. Nobody bothered you under the arch, and in bad weather, you had a bit of shelter over your head. Also, a few weeks earlier, someone had dumped a bunch of empty orange crates there that were about the size of mattresses and not half bad for sleeping in.

I'd just claimed one of these prize crates—by which I mean one that *didn't* reek of piss—and was about to tuck into the eel pie I'd pinched when I noticed the boy was back. I don't know how he'd managed to follow me. I hadn't seen him since the Thames. But there he was, standing under a streetlamp, still staring at me with his big green eyes.

I ain't proud of what I did next, but I'd had enough of the me-and-my-shadow routine, so I picked up a rock and chucked it at him. It hit his foot, and he jumped back like a startled dog. I threw another, hoping to send him packing, and this one hit him square in the shoulder. But instead of crying out or running for cover, he just stood there, not taking his eyes off me.

At that point, I said, *Right, enough's enough.* I hopped out of my crate and marched myself over to him.

"*Oi!*" I shouted, trying to look nothing like a cherub. "What sort of game are you playing at?"

The boy flinched. He opened his mouth to say something but must've changed his mind because all he did was hang his head like a dog what knows he's in for a beating.

"Well?" I barked. "What're you following me for?"

The boy shrugged and kept staring at his shoes.

"Why've you been tailing me all day?"

Another shrug.

"Ain't you got a home to go to?"

The boy shook his head.

"What about parents?"

Another shake.

"You all alone, then?"

The boy nodded.

"Well, what you want me to do about it?" I snapped in exasperation. "I ain't the bloody Salvation Army."

The boy didn't answer. He just stared at the cobblestones.

Up close I could see that his clothes had once been pretty nice, but now the sleeves and collar were edged with dirt, and his wool jacket was stained. His face was dirty, and while I reckoned he'd always been a bit on the scrawny side, something about the way his clothes hung off his body made me suspect it'd been a while since he'd had a proper meal.

I didn't like the thought of that.

Maybe it was the way he sniffled and buried his hands in his pockets to keep them warm. Maybe it was the way he reminded me of myself back when I was first starting out. Maybe I just have a thing for strays. Whatever the reason, I couldn't help feeling right sorry for the lad.

Except... no, that wasn't it. It wasn't that I felt sorry for him. I felt *responsible*.

Hang me if I could tell you why. It didn't make no bloody sense. I mean, who was he to me? Just another urchin on the street. London's full of them. It weren't any skin off my nose if he went hungry. It's a cruel world. And the sooner he got used to that fact, the better off he'd be.

Even so, I found myself saying, "All right, one night. You can doss with me under the arch for *one* night. After that, you're on your own. Got it?"

To this day I ain't forgotten the look on his face. His eyes lit up like it was Christmas and he was Tiny Tim. And his smile did this funny thing to my heart because a second later I was also smiling. Damned if I could tell you why. All I knew was that, in that moment, his happiness made me happy.

"Right, follow me," I told him, heading back under the arch.

It'd be a bit cramped with two of us in my crate, but I told myself I could make do. After all, it was only for one night.

As we were settling in, I remembered the eel pie I had in my pocket and I asked the boy if he was hungry. The boy nodded, so I broke the pie in two and gave him half. He devoured it in one bite, and once again I found I couldn't stop myself from smiling.

I know I said you can't depend on other people. And I stand by that. Even so, it occurred to me under the arch that there might be worse things in this world than having someone depend on you.

"You got a name?" I asked as the first stars started to appear in the night sky.

Wiping the crumbs off his mouth, he answered, "Charlie."

That was six years ago, and Charlie and me have been together ever since. He still follows me wherever I go. Still refuses to sleep unless he's by my side. Still looks at me like he'd be lost without me.

And I suppose, if I'm honest, I'd be lost without him.

I asked him once, not too long ago, why he'd been so keen to follow me home that day he spotted me at the market. He said he didn't know. Just that he'd had "a feeling."

I asked him what kind of feeling, and he said, "Like we belong together."

ORLANDO, FLORIDA

(THE PRESENT)

CHAPTER 20

JACKSON

"He's awake!"

I can hear the relief in Charlie's voice, but I'm not sure who he's talking to. My head feels like it's full of wet cement. It's a struggle to even open my eyes. And when I do, the world is upside down.

"Jackson, are you all right?"

Jackson? Why's he calling me Jackson? And why am I on the floor?

I don't recognize this room. Are we in an air-raid shelter? Did something happen?

Charlie slips his hand into mine, and his green eyes stare down at me, full of tender concern. Despite my confusion, I can't help smiling. Those eyes always make me smile.

"Charlie," I murmur.

Charlie frowns. "Jackson, it's me. *Riley*."

The name is a slap. It knocks the drowsiness from my brain. And everything comes into focus.

"Riley?" I hear myself say.

Right. Shit. Of course. He's Riley. And I'm Jackson. And we're in Orlando. Not London. London was... a dream? Right. Yeah. A dream. And now I'm awake.

Aren't I?

Shaking the uncertainty from my head, I force myself to concentrate.

I'm in Heartbeats. On the floor. I don't know how I got here, but there's a crowd gathered around me. Duy, Tala, Audrey, and several curious drag queens are staring down at me with bated breath like I'm some sort of sideshow attraction.

"What happened?" I ask.

"You fainted," Duy, Tala, and Audrey answer in unison.

"I what?"

"You passed out," Riley explains, still looking concerned. "In the middle of my song. You don't remember?"

I remember Riley singing. Something by Queen, I think. Then I remember getting lightheaded.

No. Wait. That's not right. Before the dizziness, there was something else. A feeling. Like déjà vu. Like I'd remembered something, something important. What was it?

"Okay, kiddies, am I calling an ambulance or what?" Miss Understood asks, waving her bedazzled phone in my direction. "Do we need to get this boy to a hospital?"

The entire room stares at me. I have no idea why I passed out or how long I've been unconscious, but I don't feel like I need to go to a hospital. If anything, I feel like an ass for causing a scene.

"Are you okay?" Riley asks, squeezing my hand. He still hasn't let go. It feels nice. Comforting. It feels—

Like we belong together.

"I'm good," I yelp, snatching my hand from his.

Riley looks taken aback. But I couldn't help myself. My cheeks are burning.

Despite the unsteadiness of my legs, I force myself to stand. I'm feeling claustrophobic—*trapped*. I need to get outside. Away from people. I need to—*think*.

"Sorry I ruined the show," I mumble to the crowd. Then, without waiting for a response, I push my way through the onlookers and hurry to the exit.

Riley calls my name, but I don't stop. I'm too ashamed. And confused. By my fainting. By my dream. But mostly by the things I felt for Riley in that dream. Things I'm pretty sure a guy doesn't feel for another guy unless . . .

The afternoon sun almost blinds me when I step outside. It's disorienting. I'm expecting to see a full moon in the night sky and to feel a brisk chill in the air, and I can't understand why I don't until I remember they were part of the dream. The dream where Riley and I—where we—*belonged* together?

"Jackson, wait up!" Riley shouts, exiting the bar with Duy, Audrey, and Tala close behind. "Where are you going?"

"Sorry," I mutter, unable to look him in the face. "I needed some air."

"Are you sure you're okay?"

"Yeah. I'm fine," I lie, forcing a smile. "You guys should go back inside. Enjoy the rest of the show. Don't worry about me. I'm gonna head home."

I scan the parking lot for my Jeep, then remember that it was Riley who drove Duy and me to Heartbeats.

"I'll take you home," Riley says, fishing the keys from his pocket.

"No!" I snap. Riley stares at me like I've lost my mind. And maybe I have. That would at least explain everything that's happened today.

"I mean thank you," I say, trying to cover. "But you don't have to do that. I'll get a Lyft."

"Jackson, you *fainted*. I'm not letting you take a Lyft."

I can't exactly argue with that. Not without making it seem like something really is wrong with me. Which there isn't. I just had a weird dream. That's all.

I don't even know why I'm reacting like this. So I had some dream where Riley—or someone who looked like Riley—said that he and

I belonged together. So what? That could mean anything. It doesn't have to mean—*you know*. And even if it did, it was a dream. *This* is reality.

"Jackson?" Riley says, his eyes full of concern.

"Okay, yeah, sure," I concede, too exhausted to argue anymore. "You should probably drive me home."

Riley nods, looking relieved. Then he turns to Duy and asks, "Are you ready to go?"

Duy hesitates and looks back toward Heartbeats. "Um, *actually*, if Jackson's good now—and he does look so much better, so *yay!*—I think I'm going to stay for a bit and hang with Caleb. We were kind of vibing earlier, so . . ."

Crap. I assumed Duy would be coming with us. If they stay, it'll be just Riley and me. In his car. Together. Alone.

"We'll give Duy a ride home," Audrey volunteers. "Tala and I are gonna stick around too. Maybe get another song in."

"Unless Jackson needs us?" Tala offers.

Not trusting myself to speak, I shake my head.

"Okay. Cool," Audrey says. "Well, feel better, dude."

"And text us if you need anything," Tala adds. "We can always bring soup."

There's a round of hugs. Then Duy, Tala, and Audrey head back inside.

"Right, let's get you home," Riley says, placing a supportive hand on my shoulder. It takes all my strength not to pull away. Still, something in my face must betray how uncomfortable I am. Riley looks confused, then slowly retracts his hand.

"Do you think there's something going around?" Riley asks as we drive down I-4. Even though it's almost ninety degrees outside, we've got the windows down because Riley thought the fresh air might help me feel better.

It doesn't.

If anything, my head is more of a mess now than it was when I came to. Because as hard as I try to block them out, the words from my dream keep playing on a loop in my head.

We belong together. We belong together. We belong together.

"What do you mean, going around?" I ask, keeping my voice even and my eyes fixed on the road ahead.

"I mean, maybe there's a fainting bug? I know that sounds crazy, but how else do you explain the fact that we both passed out in public for literally no reason. Unless it's the heat?"

"Yeah. Could be the heat," I answer without much conviction. I'm less interested in figuring out why I fainted than I am in forgetting that it ever happened.

Thankfully, Riley seems to get that I'm not in a mood to talk. He falls into a silence, and for one blessed minute, I'm convinced the conversation is over. But I'm wrong.

"You didn't happen to have any dreams when you passed out?"

I feel the color drain from my face.

"What?" I ask, unable to hide my surprise.

"Did you have any dreams?" he repeats. "I'm asking because when I fainted, that's when I had that bizarre nightmare about Pompeii."

"I thought you had that dream the night after we went skating?"

Out of the corner of my eye, I see Riley's cheeks redden. "It was actually a two-part dream. The first part happened when I fainted at the carnival. The second happened after we went to Rink-O-Rama."

"Oh." So Riley's had two dreams about me?

"Anyway, I was just wondering if you had any," he presses. "Dreams, I mean."

"No," I lie, shutting my eyes the way I'd like to shut out this entire day.

I don't know why I had the dream that I had, but I do know I'm not telling anyone about it, least of all Riley. It might give him... ideas. Not that I think he'd ever try anything. He knows I'm not... There's just no point in discussing it.

I mean, I like *girls*. I've always liked girls. It's never even occurred to me to look at another guy.

Clearly my subconscious got its wires crossed. I mean, I know people keep mistaking us for a couple. I know Riley and I have been spending a lot of time together, and we've grown really close really fast. It makes sense that some part of my brain might have gotten a little "confused." But the truth is, there's nothing to be confused about.

Riley is my *friend*. Period. Sure, I like spending time with him. But that doesn't mean I want to date him or—do anything else with him.

We're just friends.

"Are you okay?" Riley asks. The worry in his voice catches me off guard. I can feel his anxious eyes studying me. It's like he's trying to peer inside me. Like he knows there's something to see.

"I'm fine," I mutter, refusing to take my eyes off the traffic in front of us.

"You're just kind of quiet. And you're grinding your teeth. Are you sure you—"

"I'm *fine*," I bark. "I'm just tired, okay? So can we stop talking?"

"Okay." The word comes out in a whisper, but the hurt in his voice is deafening. It's like a sucker punch to my gut.

What is wrong with me? Why am I being such an ass? It's not Riley's fault I had that stupid dream. Why am I being such a baby about it? I mean, so what if I had a dream about us belonging together? I also dreamed I was some sort of cat burglar in London. The entire dream was nonsense. It's not fair to take out my frustration on Riley just because I have an overactive imagination. He hasn't done anything wrong. I'm the one being a dick.

"Sorry," I sigh, finally turning to look at him. "I didn't mean to bite your head off. Today's just been . . . a lot."

"It's okay," he answers, shooting me a tentative smile. It's a small thing, but it makes my heaviness feel a hundred pounds lighter. "I should've told you we were taking you to a gay bar. I know from experience your first time can be stressful. I didn't mean for you to get overwhelmed."

Despite the awkwardness of everything I'm feeling, Riley's comment makes me laugh out loud. "Dude, I know you think I'm some caveman jock, but I didn't pass out because you took me to a gay bar. I'm not that fragile."

At least I hope I'm not. Then again, considering the way I've been acting, maybe I'm not as secure in my masculinity as I thought.

"I was actually having a good time before I fainted," I add, hoping to make up for my piss-poor attitude. "And I'm sorry I ruined your song. For what it's worth, the part I heard was great."

Riley shoots me a smirk. "Yeah, sure. You liked it *so much*, you decided you'd rather be unconscious."

"Hey, now," I retort, "if that's the way you want to play it, then I'm the one who should be insulted."

"Why?"

"Because I might've fainted when I heard you sing, but you fainted when you saw my *face*."

Riley chuckles. And if his earlier smile put my entire body at ease, then his laughter makes me feel like everything is right with the world.

By the time we pull into my aunt's driveway, things are pretty much back to normal between Riley and me. Though I still want to kick myself for letting things get weird in the first place.

I can't believe I got so worked up over nothing. *Less* than nothing.

I mean, I played football for three years. I probably saw more dicks in the locker room than Riley's seen in his entire life. Did that freak me out or make me question my identity? No. Because I'm confident and comfortable in my sexuality, and one stupid dream doesn't change anything.

"Thanks for the ride home," I say as Riley walks me to my front door.

"No problem. What are you going to do for the rest of the day?"

"Probably just take it easy. Watch some TV."

"Cool. Well, if you need anything, let me know."

I start to unlock the front door, expecting Riley to head back to his car. Instead, he shuffles in place, staring down at his scuffed-up Chucks like he's working up the courage to speak.

"You okay?" I ask.

"Yeah, I'm fine. I just . . . I just wanted to say that I'm glad you're all right. When you passed out in the middle of my song, I got worried. Really worried." He shoots me a small, heartfelt smile. Then, as if embarrassed by his sincerity, he adds, "Purely for selfish reasons, of course."

"Of course," I say, playing along.

"Obviously, I've invested a lot of time and effort into this friendship despite your multiple shortcomings, and I've gotten used to having you around, so it would just suck if for any reason you—weren't."

This might be the most grudging compliment anyone has ever given me. But coming from Riley, it feels like scoring a touchdown.

"Don't worry," I assure him. "You're not getting rid of me anytime soon."

Without thinking, as if by instinct, I reach out and pull him into a hug. Maybe it's on account of the sheer weirdness of this day, but I'm almost overwhelmed by how much my body needs this.

I don't really understand it. But holding Riley in my arms feels right. More than right. It feels familiar. Like coming home. Like—

Like we belong together.

Without warning, Riley pulls away. "I'll see you later."

Before I can say anything, he darts into his Prius and drives away. And I'm left here, standing at my door, wishing he were still in my arms, and wondering what it would be like if I never had to let him go.

CHAPTER 21

RILEY

Jackson Haines gives incredible hugs, and they're fucking *killing* me.

I don't know what just happened on his doorstep, but it felt like I'd died and gone to gay heaven. I couldn't even look at him afterward. I was too afraid he'd see how much I liked it, and then things really would've gotten awkward between us.

Not that things haven't been awkward all day, I remind myself as I drive home, my skin still tingling from Jackson's touch. Awkward and insanely confusing.

I have no idea what's going on between Jackson and me. On the one hand, obviously *nothing* is going on because Jackson is straight. I *know* he's straight. He has an ex-girlfriend back in Tallahassee. He calls me dude. He likes zombie movies!

He's basically the straightest boy I've ever met.

And yet that hug . . .

That hug was *everything*. Everything I wanted to tell him about how much he meant to me but couldn't bring myself to say without making it into a dumb joke, he managed to put into that hug. Without him saying a word, that hug spoke volumes.

Maybe more than Jackson intended?

Is that possible? Could Jackson actually *like* me?

There have definitely been one or two moments over the past couple of weeks when our banter and horseplay felt more like flirting. Like the time he told me I'd make a great boyfriend. Or the time he ate whipped cream *off my face*. And then today, the way he encouraged me to get up onstage and sing—that was above and beyond the call of friendship. That was next-level boyfriend shit.

No wonder everyone thinks we're a couple.

Okay, not *everyone*. Three people. But three is actually *a lot* if you consider the fact that we started hanging out only a couple of weeks ago.

I wonder if my friends have noticed anything.

Part of me wants to ask them. But Audrey would just call me a toxic self-hating gay for crushing on a straight boy, and Tala has a really unfortunate habit of forgetting that something is a secret (she's ruined every surprise party we've tried to throw). If Jackson is straight, I don't want it getting back to him that I've been lusting over him. It could ruin our friendship, and that is absolutely the *last* thing I want.

Seriously, these past few weeks with Jackson have been some of the best weeks of my life. And I can keep having more amazing weeks if I don't fuck things up. The fact that he's a good friend who cares about my happiness and who makes me feel like the most special person on the planet should be enough. To ask for anything more would be selfish.

Jackson is my friend. My straight friend. And I need to respect that. It's not going to be easy pretending I don't want more, but for the sake of our friendship, it's what I need to do.

Even if it does mean taking nothing but cold showers for the rest of the summer.

When I get home, I ignore Dad's questions about my day and head up to my room, where I collapse onto my bed. All I want to do is take a nap and not think about Jackson, but I'm too restless to sleep. I need some sort of distraction, so I take out my phone.

I'm about to check my Instagram when I notice I have a new text. And when I see who it's from, I sit up in shock.

ALEX: Hey. I know it's been a while and you probably never want to hear from me again, but I've been thinking a lot about you and about how things went down between us. I know I was a jerk, and I don't expect you to forgive me, but I wanted to tell you how sorry I am for how I treated you. I know it's a big ask, but I'm in town for the next two weeks. I'd love the chance to apologize in person if you'd be up for that. If not, I totally understand. But it'd be great to see you.

I have to reread Alex's message five times before I can process what I'm seeing.

That asshole wants to apologize? In person?

I can't believe it. In a million years, I never thought I'd see the day where he'd own up to his shitty behavior. I should feel ecstatic. Or vindicated. Or, at the very least, smug. But I don't.

All I feel is anger—white-hot simmering anger.

I used to pray that I'd receive a text like this. In the weeks after Alex dumped me, I'd stay up every night fantasizing that he would come crawling back to me, begging me to take him back.

Of course, in my fantasy, I'd refuse at first. I had my pride, after all. Alex would need to suffer for what he'd done. But only for a day or two. Eventually, after his all-consuming love for me had finally inspired him to come out and accept himself, I'd magnanimously relent. I'd take him back. And we'd live happily ever after.

But that's not what happened.

Alex never apologized. I never got my happy ending. I never even got closure. All I got was an eating disorder and a raging distrust of men, two issues I'm very much still dealing with today.

So, *no*, I don't want to meet up with Alex or hear whatever lame-ass apology he's concocted. He's three years too late. The damage is done. If he's feeling guilty for how he treated me, *good*. He should feel guilty.

It might stop him from hurting someone else the way he hurt me.

I consider texting *that* to Alex. But honestly, I don't want to engage with him ever again. Instead, I content myself with deleting his text and hoping that my silence speaks volumes about just how unforgiven he is.

Maybe that makes me a jerk, but I don't care. Sometimes petty acts of revenge are the closest thing we get to closure.

CHAPTER 22

JACKSON

"What's your good side?" Duy asks, staring me down through the long black lens of their digital camera.

I have no idea how to answer them. It's never occurred to me that my face might have a good or bad side. But as it turns out, the question is moot.

"Ha! Kidding! As if people like you have a bad side," Duy says as they shove their camera in my face and snap a flurry of photos.

I swallow uncomfortably. "I thought you wanted to shoot the clothes."

"We will. I just want to get a feel for your best angles before we start. The better I make you look, the better my clothes will look."

Duy keeps snapping away, and I do my best to follow their instructions, tilting my head or adjusting my posture as I pose inside the gazebo that Duy's selected as the backdrop for our photo shoot. Thankfully, the gazebo (as well as Duy's entire backyard) is surrounded by a tall red fence, so I'm not on full display to the world. Aside from Ms. Nguyen, who occasionally peeks at us through the kitchen window, I don't have to worry about an audience making me any more self-conscious than I already am.

And right now, I'm pretty self-conscious.

When I agreed to model for Duy, I assumed I'd be wearing something, well, normal. Like a T-shirt and jeans or a suit. But when I arrived an hour ago, Duy explained that they haven't decided yet whether they want to pursue a degree in fashion design or costume design, which are apparently two different things. Duy's plan is to create two separate portfolios so that they can keep their options open when it's time to start applying to colleges. And today we're focusing on their costume designs.

That's why I'm dressed like some dude in one of Aunt Rachel's Jane Austen movies. I'm talking tailcoat, waistcoat, breeches, cravat—which are all words I'd never heard until an hour ago and which I hope I never hear again after today.

Not that the clothes aren't incredible. Duy's mad-talented. I'm sure my outfit would've been the height of fashion in "Regency England" (whenever that was). But this is June in Florida. It's already eighty-five degrees, and I'm in three layers of very heavy clothing. If it gets much hotter, I'm legitimately afraid I might pass out. Again. And I really don't want a repeat of yesterday.

Or that dream.

"Relax your shoulders," Duy orders. "You've gone stiff."

No shit. I can feel the tension running through my neck, across my back, and down my spine. It's been there for the past twenty-four hours, ever since I hugged Riley goodbye and found myself more confused than ever about my feelings for him.

I barely slept last night. I just lay in bed trying to figure out what the heck was going on with me. So far, the only thing I've come up with—the only thing that makes sense—is that somehow, for some reason, I've developed a *very tiny* but perfectly natural "man crush" on Riley.

That has to be it. After all, he's been a great friend to me since I moved to Orlando. It makes sense that we'd develop a strong brotherly connection. But that doesn't mean that there's something more going on between us.

It doesn't mean that I'm—that we—

It doesn't mean *anything*.

"Can you relax your face and stop grinding your teeth like an ax murderer?" Duy huffs, lowering their camera to shoot me an exasperated glare.

"Sorry," I mumble. "Foot cramp."

I jump up and down for a few seconds, hoping to shake off some of this nervous energy. I used to do this whenever I got anxious before a game, and it usually did the trick.

"Better," Duy says, studying me through the camera lens once I've settled back into my pose. "Much better."

I do actually feel better—for a second. Then I hear the screen of the back door screech open, and my shoulders stiffen even before I see Riley stepping out of the house.

"Good, you're finally dressed!" Duy exclaims, mercifully taking the camera out of my face and bounding over to Riley.

In his suit and topcoat, Riley could be my twin. Our costumes are almost identical—except for one crucial difference. Duy's put me in a navy-blue tailcoat with cream-colored pants, while Riley is decked out in head-to-foot pink.

"You look *amazing*!" Duy gushes.

"Thanks," Riley answers, breaking into a sheepish smile.

"I was talking to the clothes."

Riley shakes his head and lets out a snort of laughter. I can't resist joining in, and for a second, all the tension leaves my body. Then Riley notices me laughing. Our eyes lock; his green eyes stare into mine a fraction too long before he turns away.

Things have definitely gotten weird again between us. Aside from a brief hello when we arrived this morning, Riley and I haven't spoken since yesterday. To be honest, I'm not even sure *what* to say to him. I considered bailing on this photo shoot to avoid that particular problem, but I don't want to start avoiding him. For one, that'd be a shit thing to do. And for two, avoiding him would mean that my man crush is something more than a man crush. And since it's not, I need to stop freaking out and just *be cool*.

"Looking pretty swank there, Jackson," Riley calls out, flashing me a somewhat strained smile as he and Duy make their way over to the gazebo. "Loving the Mr. Darcy vibes."

"The what?" I ask.

"He means you look hot," Duy explains.

Riley's face burns as pink as his outfit, and for a second, I think he's gonna strangle Duy.

"Thanks." I force myself to laugh, pretending not to notice his embarrassment. "You look good too, dude."

And he does. In his usual outfit of distressed jeans, faded T-shirt, and scuffed Chucks, Riley has a tendency to look like "an emaciated street urchin," to quote something Duy said earlier. But under three layers of British formal wear, he looks solid. Dapper. Handsome.

"Did guys really used to wear all this pink?" Riley asks as Duy fluffs his cravat.

"No. Well, actually, *yes*," Duy answers. "In the 1600s, before colors got gendered, pink was incredibly common for men. Especially rich men who didn't have to worry about getting dirty. It was a status symbol. But by the time the Regency period rolled around, which was about two hundred years later, pink had become exclusively for women."

"So why do I look like Barbie picked out my wardrobe?"

"Great question! I was thinking about what I could do to set my portfolio apart from all the other aspiring costume designers, and I thought it would be savvy to show that, yes, I can create authentic

Regency menswear in my sleep—hence what Jackson is wearing—*but* I can also think outside the box and play with color and textiles to do a more fashion-forward, fantasy-inspired take on Regency wear, which is what you're wearing. Fantasy and reality. See?"

"Yeah," Riley says, looking suitably impressed. "That's smart."

"I know, right? If I were any more of a genius, I'd be *obsessed* with myself. Now, let's make some art!"

Riley sighs and shuffles obediently into the gazebo next to me. I try to shoot him a look of commiseration, but he avoids my gaze, so I turn to Duy and await my instructions.

"Okay, so, for these first couple shots, I want some classic Colin Firth broodiness."

"Uh . . . translation, please?"

"Just stand shoulder to shoulder, hands behind your back, and stare out at the camera like you're not sure if you want to kill it or make love to it."

I can't stop myself from guffawing at such insane directions. And neither can Riley. United in our awkwardness, we collapse into a fit of giggles.

"Hey, focus!" Duy barks, impatiently stomping a foot on the ground.

"Sorry," we both mumble, swallowing our silliness.

We then straighten up, stare out at the camera, and do our best to brood as Duy begins snapping away. Considering how much real brooding I've done over the year, I'm surprised at how difficult it is to brood on command. But I glower at the camera, trying to look sexy and bored at the same time, and it seems to work.

"That's it, Jackson. Keep smoldering. Just relax your shoulders. Riley, chin up a bit, but keep looking down your nose at me."

For the next hour, Duy issues an unending stream of instructions from behind their camera, pausing only to mop the sweat off our brows or adjust a strand of hair. It gets significantly warmer as the morning wears on, but Riley doesn't complain.

"I'm used to suffering for Duy's art," he quips on one of the rare boba breaks we're allowed.

By noon, Duy has taken almost a thousand shots of us in every conceivable pose at every conceivable angle. There are shots of Riley and me together, apart, standing back to back, sitting in the gazebo, leaning against the gazebo, staring into the camera, gazing off into the horizon, lying on the grass, sitting under a tree, holding a book, holding a rose, and a hundred other variations that I can't even remember at this point because I am so damn *tired*.

Duy, though, isn't satisfied.

"Some of these are okay," they concede with a sigh as they sit under the shade of a dogwood tree, scrolling through the morning's photos on the camera's viewscreen. "But I'm not sure I've gotten the shot."

"What shot?" I ask, fanning myself with a book.

"*The* shot," they answer, not making things any clearer.

"I'm sure you've got *something* you can use," Riley gripes, shooting me a sympathetic smile. If there's an upside to being this hot and tired, it's that we're both too worn out to be uncomfortable around each other. The easiness has returned between us. And as long as I don't think about that dream or hug, there's no reason things can't stay easy.

"No. This isn't good enough," Duy complains. "There's not enough fantasy. Not enough romance." Releasing a groan of frustration, they slump over their camera in defeat. Then almost as quickly, they bolt upright as a look of inspiration flashes across their face. "I know! Go back to the gazebo!"

Riley and I exchange a weary glance and shrug, partners in

exhaustion. But we do as we're told. We trudge back to our place under the ivy-twined arch.

"What do you want us to do now?" Riley asks.

"I want you guys to face each other, gaze into each other's eyes, and look like you're about to kiss."

Despite the hot afternoon sun blazing down on us, I feel the color drain from my cheeks.

"Sorry, what?"

"Face each other, gaze into each other's eyes, and look like you're madly in love," Duy repeats, completely oblivious to my distress.

I turn to Riley, who looks equally tense, but he doesn't say anything.

"Oh my gosh, *seriously?*" Duy groans when neither of us moves. "You guys don't have to *actually* kiss. Just get close to each other and look like you *want* to kiss."

Riley shoots me a questioning glance that says *Your call.*

I'm not sure what to do. Considering how confused I've been since yesterday, the last thing I want to do is put myself in a position that's even remotely romantic.

Then again, it's only romantic if I *let* it be romantic. If we can pose together like lovers or *whatever*, and it's *not* a big deal, isn't that proof that everything's actually fine between us and we really are *just friends?*

"What do you think?" Riley asks, his eyes unable to meet my own.

"I'm down if you're down," I answer.

"Great!" Duy chirps. "Now, put your arms around each other and stare into each other's eyes like you've just found the love of your life and you can't wait to rip each other's clothes off."

Riley curses under his breath but takes a tentative step closer. Cautiously and clumsily, I slide my arm around his waist and pull his body against mine.

"Is this okay?" I ask him.

He's stiff in my arms, unsure what to do with his hands or where to look, but he nods.

"Okay, Riley, you look like you're being molested," Duy calls out unhelpfully. "Can you, like, try to pretend that Jackson is hot?"

Riley reddens. I feel his chest expand against me as he forces himself to take a deep breath. Then he tilts his face upward, and his green eyes stare into mine with such a look of longing, they take my breath away.

"Good!" Duy shouts. "That's what I want. Keep looking at each other like *that*."

I hear the *click-click-click* of the camera shutter, but all my attention is on Riley. My eyes drink in his face: his long black lashes, the smattering of freckles across the bridge of his nose, his surprisingly full lips. How have I never noticed how handsome he is?

"Turn your face a bit to the left, Riley," Duy orders. "And, Jackson, can you lean your forehead closer to Riley's? That's it. Closer. Closer. *Closer.*"

My face is so near Riley's that there's scarcely an inch of space between our lips. I can feel the heat on his cheeks and the pounding of his heart. Or maybe it's my heat and my heart. With our bodies pressed together, it's hard to know where Riley stops and I begin. What I do know is that I don't want this moment to end. Because for the first time in my life, I feel like I'm exactly where I belong. And where I belong is with Riley.

Oh, fuck . . .

This isn't a man crush, is it?

I feel my body start to panic. My legs are shaking. They're itching to make a run for it. But at the same time, all I can think about is Riley and what it might be like to actually kiss him. His lips are so close. I'd only have to tilt my head . . .

"Yes, this is amazing, guys! Keep doing what you're doing!"

What would Riley do if I kissed him?

Would he kiss me back?

Do I want him to kiss me back?

There's only one way to find out.

I'm gonna do it. I'm gonna kiss Riley. I'm just gonna lean forward and—

"Okay, we got it!" Duy announces triumphantly. "We got the shot!"

Before I know what's happening, Riley slips out of my arms. He darts out of the gazebo, dashes over to the pitcher of boba, pours himself a glass, and chugs it down like a man dying of thirst. But even when he's done, he refuses to look in my direction.

"That was *so good!*" Duy gushes as they scroll through the images on the camera. "Look at these shots!"

I don't move. I can't move. All I can think is that I missed my chance. I missed my chance to kiss Riley, and I don't know if I'll ever have another.

"That's great. That's great. That one's *really* great," Duy comments as they shove the camera's viewscreen in Riley's face. "My clothes look amazing, *obviously*. But you guys? You guys look *so hot*. I was, like, totally convinced you were going to kiss!"

I can't see the photo, but I can see Riley's face.

"Yeah," he says, his expression not giving anything away. "We look good together."

Then slowly, deliberately, he looks at me. Our eyes lock and just for a moment, neither of us looks away.

CHAPTER 23

RILEY

I need two things right now: to get as far away from Jackson as humanly possible and a shower. My body is drenched in sweat from being baked under the sun all morning. God knows what I must smell like under all the suffocating layers of this costume. Actually, I don't need to guess. As I make my way to Duy's bedroom to change, I catch a whiff of myself and cringe.

I'm *ripe*.

How did I not notice the smell earlier? How did Jackson not notice? We were standing so close together in that gazebo, we were practically sharing the same skin.

Then again, Jackson was sweating just as much as I was, and I don't remember him smelling too bad. I don't actually remember much of anything, if I'm honest. Except how much I wanted him to kiss me.

Why did I agree to this stupid photo shoot?

Seriously, if I was trying to get my feelings for Jackson under control, I couldn't have picked a more self-sabotaging way to spend the day. I might as well have asked him to go skinny-dipping or mud wrestling. I was five seconds away from losing what's left of my self-control and sucking his goddamn face off. And if I didn't know better, I'd swear that Jackson felt the same.

Only I do know better. Which is why I need to change and get the hell out of this house before I do something I'll regret—like throw myself at Jackson and ruin our friendship *forever*.

I slip into Duy's bedroom and shut the door behind me, relieved to be alone at last. I then strip off the heavy layers of my pink prison and toss them to the floor. The air-conditioning feels so refreshing against my skin that for a full minute, I just stand in my underwear, letting my body breathe in freedom.

Then I hear the bedroom door open behind me, and my heart starts to race.

In my feverish state, I'm just delusional enough to think that I'm right about Jackson's attraction and that he's followed me here to Duy's bedroom to give me what we've both been craving.

But Jackson simply walks over to his pile of clothes and starts to change.

"Man, who knew modeling was such hard work?" he asks with a strained laugh as he peels off his topcoat.

"I'm pretty sure I warned you," I force myself to answer.

"Yeah," he concedes. "You did."

Jackson strips down to his underwear, and it takes all my strength not to stare at that stupid body of his that I want to cover in honey and then lick clean with my tongue. I consider grabbing my clothes and changing in Duy's bathroom. But that would practically be announcing to Jackson that I can't trust myself to be alone with him. Which, to be clear, *I can't*. But he doesn't need to know that.

"So, um . . . you got any plans this afternoon?" he asks, mercifully slipping on his cargo shorts so I'm no longer tempted to stare at the all too prominent bulge in his underwear.

"Nope," I squeak, zipping up my jeans.

"Do you maybe want to come over and . . . hang out?"

My heart stops. I don't know why this question feels so loaded, but it sucks the air out of the room. It's as if, instead of inviting me over to watch a movie or play video games, he's inviting me over for something else. Something . . . *more*.

But that's absurd, right?

The very fact that I think more is even an option is proof of how out of touch I am with reality and how out of control my feelings have gotten. I need to go home. I *am* going home. Right now.

But then I catch a glimpse of Jackson's abs before they disappear under his shirt, and all that comes out of my mouth is "Sure, I'd love to."

Jackson's aunt isn't home when we get there. Apparently she's hitting up the farmers' market over in Winter Park, which means we have the entire house to ourselves. This fact alone is enough to bring on a full-blown panic attack. But when it looks like Jackson is about to lead us to his bedroom, I swear I feel my heart stop.

Thankfully, he seems to reconsider, and instead he deposits me on the living-room sofa before heading to the kitchen to fetch us some water.

"Are you hungry?" he asks when he returns and hands me my glass. "Do you want to order something for lunch?"

"I'm good. Just dehydrated."

"For real," Jackson chuckles as he plops down beside me. "I think I sweated off twenty pounds today."

Then he polishes off his glass of water in one long, seamless chug that leaves me thirstier than ever. I can scarcely bear to look at him. I'm about ten seconds away from throwing myself into his arms.

But then . . . maybe that wouldn't be the worst thing in the world?

I know I've been trying (albeit very ineffectively) to put some emotional and physical distance between us, but that's because I've been operating under the assumption that Jackson likes me only as a friend. But if he likes me as something more—and based on some of the looks he was giving me during our photo shoot, I can't help thinking he does—then maybe it's okay if something more happens.

But what if more happens, and Jackson doesn't like it? What if I'm just an experiment to him? An itch that he only *thinks* he wants to scratch but that he'll actually regret if he does? He wouldn't be the first curious person to make that mistake.

What if he freaks out afterward? Or ends up hating me? What if I hate him?

"Are you okay?" Jackson asks, the concern in his voice pulling me back to the present. "You seem kind of distracted."

I sip my water so I have an excuse not to look at his face. "I'm fine. I was just wondering if we should invite the others over."

"Oh." Maybe it's my imagination, but does Jackson sound disappointed?

"I think Duy said they were going to a movie this afternoon," he adds. "With that Caleb guy."

"Oh, right." Duy did tell us that.

"But if you want to invite Audrey and Tala over, that's cool."

"I'll just see what they're up to," I say, quickly pulling my phone out of my pocket. I need a buffer. Or a chaperone. Someone to keep me from making a fool of myself.

I open my texts, but before I can start typing, I notice I have a message waiting for me.

> ALEX: Hey again. Guessing you didn't write back because you're still angry with me. I don't blame you. But I'd still like the chance to apologize. To be clear, you don't have to accept my apology. You can spit in my face and tell me to fuck off when I'm done. But I'd really appreciate the opportunity to give you the apology you deserve. Is there any chance we can meet up?

"Jesus Christ," I groan as I toss my phone aside in disgust.

"Is everything all right?" Jackson asks.

I shake my head and let out an exasperated snort. "This guy that I used to date keeps texting me. He's in town and wants to meet up so he can apologize for being such a shitty-ass boyfriend."

"Oh." Jackson blinks. "Are you gonna see him?"

Again, maybe it's my imagination, but does Jackson sound jealous?

"No, I am definitely *not* going to see him."

"Why not?"

"Because I don't believe in second chances."

Jackson flinches like I've hit him. I'm not sure why until I realize what I've said.

"I didn't mean that," I backtrack. "Of course I believe in second chances. But even if I didn't, my situation with Alex is completely different from your situation with Devon. Those are two totally different scenarios. Alex was a shitty person who did shitty things. You're a good person who made a mistake and owned it."

Jackson nods but doesn't look convinced.

I wish I could take back my words. I hate that I've let my bitterness toward Alex hurt Jackson. I guess this is why literally every therapist in the world says it's not healthy to hold on to resentment.

"I'm sorry," I say.

"Don't be," Jackson says, rallying slightly and forcing a smile. "You're allowed to be mad at this Alex guy. Especially if he hurt you."

"He did. But he hurt me because he was scared. He didn't want anyone to know he was gay and that fear really messed him up. I know I should forgive him, but dating Alex kind of kicked off the worst year of my life. And part of me wonders if a lot of the shit that I went through could've been avoided if I'd just never met him."

"What shit?" Jackson asks, his eyes narrowing in concern.

Crap. I was really hoping to avoid this conversation. It's never much fun introducing new people to your old trauma. But after my "I don't believe in second chances" comment, I feel like I owe Jackson the truth. Besides, if I'm worried about any lingering sexual tension between us, a trip down memory lane to the worst year of my life seems like a surefire way to kill the mood.

"This is going to sound way more dramatic than it was," I say, hoping to play down what I'm about to tell him. "But basically, after Alex dumped me, I kind of got depressed and stopped eating for a bit, and I wound up in the hospital."

As I expected, Jackson looks horrified by my announcement. "Shit, Riley. I'm so sorry."

"It's fine," I insist, hating the pity in his voice. "*I'm* fine. This was almost three years ago. I'm okay now. It's not a big deal. It's just something that happened."

Jackson nods. "You must have really liked this Alex guy."

"I guess I did," I concede with a shrug. "But if I'm being honest, the whole not-eating thing wasn't entirely his fault. There were other factors. I was being bullied at school. The teachers weren't really doing anything to stop it. And Florida had just passed yet another fucking awful anti-gay law that was bringing all the homophobes out of the woodwork. Basically, there were a lot of crappy things happening in my life at the exact same time, and Alex was just the final straw."

"So you stopped eating?"

"My therapist at the time told me that when people feel like they don't have a lot of control over their lives, they try to take back control by imposing a sense of order. And one of the ways that some people do that is by deciding not to eat. I know it doesn't seem like that makes sense, but by refusing to eat, you kind of feel like you're in charge of your body.

"You might not be able to control anything else in your life—like which of your classmates is going to call you a faggot on any given day or which of your rights the government is going to take away—but you can control what you eat. You can control your weight. You can control how much of you actually exists in the world. It's not healthy—obviously—and you absolutely shouldn't do it. But it does make you feel like you have a certain amount of control over your life. Like you're not just spiraling through chaos. And sometimes you need that."

Jackson doesn't say anything. Instead, he runs his eyes over my body, and I can tell he's asking himself the same question that my dad and my friends have asked themselves every day for the past two and a half years.

"I don't have a problem anymore," I tell him, answering his unspoken question. "I'm just thin."

"I know," he protests, attempting an unconvincing smile.

"Really, Jackson, you don't have to worry about me."

"Maybe I like worrying about you."

He says it with a slight laugh, but his eyes aren't joking. I'm about to ask what he means when his face clouds over. "What I mean is, if you were feeling stressed or like your life was out of control again because of something—or someone—you'd tell me, right?"

Something or *someone*?

"Alex isn't stressing me out," I assure him.

"I didn't mean Alex." He swallows. "I mean me."

For the second time today, it feels like all the air has been sucked out of the room.

"Why would you be stressing me out?" I ask.

Jackson opens his mouth to say something but stops himself. He stares down at his hands and shakes his head like he's debating whether to answer. Finally, after a deep breath, he looks at me and says, "You've been a really good friend to me since I moved here. Hell, you might be one of the best friends I've ever had. I know that's a weird thing to say. We only met, like, two weeks ago but—"

"I feel the same," I tell him, unable to stop myself.

Jackson looks surprised, then relieved. Like I've just lifted a huge weight off his shoulders. But his relief is fleeting. After a few seconds his eyes lose their confidence and his face darkens.

"That's... good to know. But what I'm trying to say is... if we're friends, the last thing I'd ever want to do is stress you out or make you feel bad about yourself, you know? I don't... I don't want to *hurt* you."

I'm not sure what's prompting Jackson's concern about his behavior toward me or why it's coming out now, but I hate seeing him so distraught.

"I know that," I assure him. "I know you wouldn't hurt me."

"Not intentionally, no. But Duy told me you have a hard time trusting people and letting them in, and I'm worried that I might... do something that would make you regret being my friend. And I don't want to screw you up or make you think that you can't trust people just because I don't have my shit together or know what I want."

What he wants? Does that mean me?

"Sorry," he says, shaking his head in frustration. "I know I'm not making any sense. I just—I don't want to be another Alex. I don't want to be another shitty thing that happens to you and causes you to have another worst year of your life. I want to be one of the good things— one of the best things. Because... because that's what you are to me. You're one of the best things in my life, Riley. And I don't want to lose that. I don't want to lose *you*."

Jackson looks at me, his face a roiling mixture of sincerity and confusion, and I have no idea what to say. What can you say to someone who tells you that you're one of the best things in their life? There aren't words.

But maybe the time for words is over.

I reach out and take Jackson's hand in mine. Much to my relief, he doesn't pull away. He just looks at me, his eyes full of tenderness and something else. Something that I feel welling up inside myself.

Something that I'm pretty sure is longing.

I bring my face closer to his until our lips are only a breath apart. With a tilt of my head, I start to close that distance when, without warning, the front door swings open.

"Oh, hello!" Jackson's aunt exclaims. She's standing at the front door, her arms straining under the weight of half a dozen canvas grocery bags. "I didn't know anyone was home."

"Hello," I squeak, my voice barely a whisper.

I wait for Jackson to say something. Anything. But the color's drained from his cheeks. He stares at the floor, unable to look at me, his face an unmistakable portrait of shame. And I know with every fiber of my being that I have truly and irrevocably fucked up.

"I have to go," I mumble, rushing toward the door.

Jackson doesn't stop me.

He doesn't say a word.

CHAPTER 24

JACKSON

"Was it something I said?" Aunt Rachel asks, setting her groceries on the floor.

I don't know what to do. My brain is shouting at me to go after Riley, but my body refuses to move. I don't think Rachel saw anything, but the thought that she could have has me frozen on the sofa in a cold sweat. I don't understand what just happened. One minute Riley and I were talking and the next we were about to kiss. At least, I'm 99 percent sure Riley was about to kiss me. Was I about to kiss him?

"Riley had to go," I hear myself answer, my mouth on autopilot.

"Is he okay?"

"Yeah. He was just . . . late for something."

Aunt Rachel looks dubious. Thankfully, one of her overstuffed bags tips over, spilling several bright red tomatoes across the floor. I jump off the sofa and start gathering them up.

"Here. Let me help you."

"Thanks," she says, hoisting up her bags again with a laugh. "I kind of went overboard on kale."

We take the groceries into the kitchen, where my aunt launches into a story about some drama that went down at the farmers' market. Something about a fistfight that broke out between two farmers because one of them accused the other of passing off Smucker's as his own homemade organic jelly. I don't know. I'm only half listening.

All I can think about is Riley.

Less than an hour ago, in that gazebo, I was so certain I wanted to kiss him. Just once. Just to see how it felt and find out if there really was *something* between us.

But now? I don't know what I want. The fact that I'm on the verge of a heart attack because my aunt almost caught me making out with a boy isn't a great sign. It's pretty much proof that I am not ready for anything more complicated than friendship with Riley. Not if this is how I'm reacting.

Then again, who knows how I'd be reacting if I'd actually gotten to kiss him? Maybe if Aunt Rachel hadn't come home, I'd still be doing it. Maybe a kiss would've changed everything.

Is that what I want, though? For everything to change?

If so, why does the thought of that terrify me?

"*Jackson*," my aunt barks, snapping me out of my head. "Did you hear me?"

Blinking in confusion, I turn to see her staring at me with an expression of amused exasperation. I think she's been trying to get my attention for a while.

"Sorry, what did you say?"

"I said, 'Don't go into the light, Carol Anne.'"

I'm so lost. "Carol Anne?"

"The little girl in *Poltergeist*? She falls into a trance and gets sucked into the light of her TV?"

"*What?*"

"Oh, for goodness' sake, Jackson, *shut the fridge*."

I have no idea what my aunt is talking about until I feel the chill on my skin and realize that I'm standing in front of the open refrigerator. I must have spaced out in the middle of putting away the kale.

"Sorry," I mumble, shutting the door.

"You okay, kiddo?"

"Yeah. I'm fine. Duy just had me standing in the sun all morning. I'm a little wiped out. If it's okay with you, I'm gonna go lie down."

Without giving my aunt a chance to respond, I hurry to my room.

I need to talk to Riley. Regardless of how freaked out I am, I need to make sure he's okay. He looked really upset when he left. And I don't blame him. He must think I hate him.

I pull out my phone. But just as I'm about to call, it occurs to me that I have no idea what I'm gonna say.

Am I calling to tell him that everything's cool between us and we can just pretend nothing happened? Or am I calling to tell him that I'd like to try again?

Would he even want to try again after the way I acted? And what happens if we do try again and I decide I don't like him in that way? That's not fair to Riley. He's already had one guy in his life who played with his head and fucked with his heart. I can't put him through that again.

Unsure what to do, I lie back on my bed and stare up at the ceiling as a nauseous feeling opens up in the pit of my stomach.

I can't call Riley until I figure out what I want. But I can't figure out what I want without talking to Riley. I'm stuck. And I don't know how to get unstuck without potentially hurting the one person in the world I'd do anything to protect.

So what do I do?

I shut my eyes and try to think, but it's no good. Maybe it's the stress of this impossible decision or maybe I'm just drained from this impossible day, but I'm suddenly *so tired*. I can feel my body sinking into the bed as my mind surrenders to the sweet oblivion of sleep. I don't fight it. I welcome it.

At least if I'm asleep, I don't have to think about today. Or the fact that I might just have lost Riley forever.

LONDON, ENGLAND

(MAY 10, 1941)

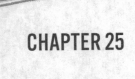

CHAPTER 25

JACK HARTNELL

"Jack, are you sure about this?" Charlie asks when he notices where we're headed.

The moon's so full and bright in the sky that I can see the worry in his eyes plain as day. It's no wonder the Germans decided to have a go at us tonight. It's the best flying weather they've had in months. And they're certainly making the most of it. Even here in Mayfair, where we've come for our latest bit of adventure, I can still hear the low buzz of their planes as they drop bomb after bomb on the other side of the river.

"Don't worry," I laugh, giving Charlie a reassuring pat on the back. Though he's not wrong to be nervous.

Strolling through a posh neighborhood like this, with our dirty faces and ratty jackets, the two of us must stick out like a pair of tarts at a christening. Or we would if anyone was here to see us. But that's the thing about people with money, innit? They don't have to see us. They don't have to see anything that's inconvenient. And war is pretty bloody inconvenient.

That's why when the bombs started falling back in September, anyone who could scrape two shillings together got themselves out of London. Not that I blame 'em. I'd pop off to my house in the country too if I could. But since I can't, I reckon I ought to make the best of a bad situation.

I lead Charlie past a row of tall white-brick homes with big windows and fancy columns. It's funny, but just walking down a street like this makes me feel kind of grand. Important-like. Charlie's still a bit anxious, but I can tell from the twinkle in his eyes that he's excited. He's always liked fancy things. And since it's his birthday, I figured I'd treat the lad to a night out.

"Wait here," I tell him, jumping the waist-high iron gate of the house we've stopped at. I scamper down the stone steps of the servants' entrance, which, like most servants' entrances, is conveniently out of sight of the rest of the street.

"All right, it's clear," I call back to Charlie, picking up the bottle of lager I left outside the door a few nights earlier.

It's an old trick one of the Bermondsey boys taught me: If you're casing a joint, and you want to know if anyone's about, you leave a bottle of beer outside the servants' entrance. If the bottle's gone when you come back a few days later, you know someone's been about the place. But if the bottle's still there, untouched, then odds are no one's home.

I pocket the lager as Charlie pads down the stairs, then I get to work trying to budge the door. I'd like to boast that I have a sophisticated approach to dealing with locks, but the truth is, all I've got is my hammer and chisel. Not very subtle, I know. But between the bombs in the distance and the sirens wailing at the end of the street, I ain't too worried about making a ruckus. Four good strikes, and Charlie and I are in.

The air in the kitchen is stale and musty-like. Another sign no one's been home for a while. Hopefully it's not been *too* long a while. I'd like to find something to eat that ain't spoiled over and covered in mold.

"You check the icebox, I'll see what's in the cupboards," I instruct Charlie as I pull open the pantry doors.

I know it's not exactly patriotic to be stealing food in the middle of a war. But the way I see it, if you can afford to toddle off to the country while the rest of us get pounded by the Germans every night, you can afford to make a contribution to the Jack and Charlie Emergency Food Fund. Consider it doing your bit.

"Icebox is empty," Charlie says, shutting the door.

"Thought it might be." I slide some tins of veg and a couple of packets of biscuits into my sack. It ain't much, but we've only just started. "Why don't you take a look around upstairs, see if there's anything valuable lying about?"

Most of the time, people fleeing the city have the sense to take anything that's worth anything. Especially when they don't have any idea if their house will be standing when they get back. But every once in a while, you get lucky, and someone leaves behind a piece of jewelry or a fancy bauble.

Charlie heads up to the first floor while I keep rummaging through the cabinets. It's pretty slim pickings. Whoever lived here must've cleared out a while ago. In fact, I'm starting to reckon this house is a proper bust when I notice an alcove under the stairs. I almost missed it in the darkness, but as I light a match I'm pleasantly surprised to spot six bottles of wine.

That's more like it. Personally, I'm a Guinness man myself. But these bottles will fetch a pretty price down at the black market tomorrow. They look old. Expensive-like. We won't have no trouble finding someone to take 'em off our hands.

I shove the bottles in my sack, then hurry upstairs to show Charlie my score. I can hear him humming (Charlie's always humming something), so I follow the tune to the library, where I find him squinting in the moonlight as he tries to read the titles on the spines of books.

"Look what I found," I announce, pulling one of the bottles out of my bag.

"Oh, good," Charlie says, barely glancing my way before turning back to the shelves.

I have to laugh. Here I am, showing him a fortune, or what *will* be a fortune, and he's more interested in a bunch of bloody books. But that's my Charlie. Never met a book he wouldn't stick his nose in.

Me, I never really saw the point of books. I mean, they just sort of clutter up a place. But then, I'm not much of a reader, am I? Not like Charlie. He'd read a new book every week if he could. And he knows all sorts of big words that I've never heard before.

I don't know if he learned all those words before we met or if he picked them up along the way, but he's got a pretty impressive vocabulary when he chooses to use it. Sometimes at night, if we're staying in a place where there's a lamp (which ain't always the case), he reads to me before bed. I can't say I always understand what he reads, but I don't mind listening.

I could listen to Charlie for hours.

"Anything good?" I ask.

"Mm-hmm."

"Well, don't take more than you can carry. I'm not lugging a bunch of books across the river. My bag's heavy enough and we haven't even searched the bedrooms. Speaking of which, we should get cracking."

"I'm looking for Shakespeare," he says, standing on his tiptoes to reach the topmost shelf. "There was a play my mum used to read me. It was a comedy about fairies putting spells on people. It was my favorite. I think it's called *Summer Dreams* or something like that. It had *Dream* in the title."

"Right, well, I'm going to scrounge around upstairs."

"I'll be there in a minute."

He won't. He'll still be looking over these books when I've turned this entire house over. But it's his birthday. He might as well enjoy himself.

Before heading upstairs, I do a quick pass through the dining room and parlor. I grab a pair of candlesticks that look like they might be silver and a decorative jade elephant that's the size of my hand. There are some posh-looking paintings on the wall, sunsets over green pastures and the like, but it's always a bit of a gamble with art. I mean, you never know if a picture's going to be worth something or if it's just pretty, so best not to bother.

Charlie's still in the library when I head up to the top floor. There are three bedrooms, which I make quick work of. There's no money or jewelry lying about, but I do find an ivory comb, a small box of cigars, and one very special item that'll make for a nice surprise for Charlie when we get back to our digs.

As I'm making my way back to the stairs, I decide to pop my head in the loo just to see if it's as grand as the rest of this house. It's not. It's bloody grander. Or at least grander than anyplace I've ever had a piss in before: white gleaming tiles, gold faucets, an enormous porcelain tub resting on four gold lion paws. I can't believe the nonsense rich folks'll spend their money on. I could feed the whole of East Ham for a week with what it must've cost to fix up this hoity pleasure palace.

That being said, it does seem a shame not to take advantage of it.

I try the hot-water tap, and after a minute of ice-cold water pouring out, the temperature starts to warm, bit by bit, until there's a lovely layer of steam rising out of the tub.

"Charlie!" I lean my head out the door and shout.

"Yeah?" he calls from downstairs.

"Get on up here!"

"Why?"

"We're having a bath!"

He doesn't have to be told twice. If there's anything Charlie likes more than books, it's baths. I hear him padding up the stairs, and seconds later he's standing beside me, hopping excitedly from one foot to the other.

"Gosh!" he gasps, taking in the boat-size tub full of steaming water.

"Come on, then. Strip off."

I toss my jacket to the floor and start to undo the buttons on my shirt while Charlie kicks off his shoes. Once I'm down to my birthday suit, I slip into the bath and dunk my head in the near-scalding water that would hurt if it didn't feel so good. It's been months since I've had a proper scrub, and as I lean back into the water, I can feel every one of those dirty, grimy days peel away from my body.

Charlie hops into the other end of the tub, covering himself with his hands as he does. I have to laugh. All these years, and he's still the timid sort.

"Here now, how's this for a birthday?" I ask, giving him a splash.

Charlie lets out a purr of pleasure and sinks himself up to his ears. "It's amazing, Jack."

I can hear the air-raid sirens wailing outside like wolves. In the distance, another bomb rocks the city. But here, soaking in this tub with Charlie, I ain't never been so relaxed in all my life.

"Jack?" Charlie asks, sitting up in the tub and only half looking at me, the way he does when he's shy.

"What is it?"

"I was wondering . . . since it's my birthday and all . . ."

"Yeah?"

"Can we?"

I don't have to ask what he means.

"All right," I say, shooting him a grin. "Since it's your birthday."

Charlie blushes in the moonlight. Then he slides down to my end of the tub and gently climbs on top of me. His legs straddle my hips as his arms wind 'round my neck. I run a hand through his damp hair and trace my fingers over his ears and down his throat.

Charlie closes his eyes and rests his forehead against mine. I can tell he's nervous. He's always nervous, even after all these years. I take his left hand and kiss it, then the right, and then I place both his hands over my heart.

"Happy birthday, Charlie Dawes," I whisper.

Charlie lowers his lips to mine and fills my mouth with kisses.

I guess you could say this is something else I've gotten used to.

Not that you'll catch me broadcasting that fact to the world. I mean, it's nice, innit? But it's not exactly the sort of thing you want getting out. I've enough to deal with trying to make it from one day to the next without people giving me dirty looks or whispering rotten names behind my back.

But that's the thing about Charlie. With him, it don't feel dirty. Mad as it sounds, it feels clean. Pure. Sometimes I think it's the purest thing in my life.

Even so, Charlie still asks my permission every time. He knows this don't come natural to me the way it does to him. Though if I'm being honest—like, proper honest—there's nothing he could ask of me that I'd ever refuse him. Refusing him would be like refusing happiness. And who'd be daft enough to do that?

"Am I your boy?" Charlie asks, panting, between kisses.

His hunger for me fills me with my own hunger. A hunger to always be with him. Like this. With him in my arms. A hunger to keep him safe and never let him go.

"You're my boy," I whisper, almost breathless.

"For always?" he presses.

"For always," I promise.

I mean it too. Charlie might've chosen me first that day he followed me home from the market. But I've chosen him every day since. And I'll never stop choosing him. Because there is no choice. We're Jack and Charlie. We're forever.

"Why haven't they sounded the all-clear?" Charlie asks, cocking his head to the wind as we haul our loot over Waterloo Bridge. We've been making our way to our digs for a while now, and aside from the wail of the air-raid sirens, the night is quiet, and the sky is empty. There's not a plane in sight.

"What time is it?" I ask.

"Almost midnight."

"They'll be sounding the all-clear soon enough, then," I say, shifting the weight of the sack on my back from one shoulder to the other.

Between the wine, the books, and the trinkets, Charlie and I made quite the haul tonight. All we've got to do is find someone to take this loot off our hands at the market tomorrow, and we'll be sitting pretty for weeks. We can ditch the dump we've been dossing in and find ourselves a proper room to rent. Maybe somewhere with our own private bath so we can have ourselves a repeat of tonight whenever we fancy.

"Look at those colors," Charlie says, leaning against the railing to peer down the river where Southwark and Tower Bridges are still burning. Fire crews are trying to put out the blazes as ribbons of flames paint the purple sky with slashes of orange and gold.

"It's sort of beautiful, isn't it?" Charlie asks, the distant fires flickering in his eyes.

I can't help smiling. I know the world's gone mad. I know people are dying, and not just here in London. I should be angry or frightened. But standing here, watching the colors dance across the sky, I feel nothing but peace. Because I have what the rest of the world doesn't. I have Charlie.

"Oi, before I forget, I nabbed you something," I tell him as I dig his present out of my pocket. "Happy birthday."

Charlie's eyes go wide as he stares down at the book I nicked off a bedside table.

"*A Midsummer Night's Dream*! You found it! Thank you, Jack!"

Charlie throws his arms around me and crushes me in one of his wiry hugs. I don't normally go in for such public displays of affection, but as there ain't much public about, I don't see the harm.

I hug him back, breathing in the fresh scent of soap on his skin. I swear I'd stay like this forever if I could: The air crisp. The sky a painting. And Charlie in my arms.

Then his shoulders stiffen, and he pulls away with a start. "What's that noise?"

It takes my ears a second to clock what he hears, and when they do, my blood runs cold.

Charlie gasps in horror, and I follow his eyes to the sky. A sky full of planes. German planes. Not one or two stragglers, not the dozen or so raiders we've come to expect, but forty—no, fifty planes. The night sky is thick with them, so thick they almost block out the moon.

I don't understand. The Germans *never* attack twice in the same evening. And they *never* send this many planes. There's no need. Not for a few strategic strikes. I mean, you wouldn't send all these planes unless . . .

Unless you were planning to wipe London off the map.

"Jack," Charlie gasps.

I grab his hand. But it's too late. The bombs are already falling.

ORLANDO, FLORIDA

(THE PRESENT)

CHAPTER 26

RILEY

"No plans tonight?"

I glance up from my bed and see my dad leaning in the doorway. He's nonchalantly cleaning his glasses with a handkerchief, a move I've seen him use in court whenever he wants to appear casual or disarming to the witness he's about to question.

"Nope," I answer, turning back to my phone on which I've been half-heartedly scrolling through TikTok since dinner. "No plans."

"You're not seeing your friends?"

I shake my head. Audrey and Tala are on a double date with Duy and Caleb tonight. They invited me to tag along, but I figured the only thing more pathetic than staying home on a Friday night was going out and being someone's fifth wheel.

"You want to watch some *Doctor Who?*" Dad offers. "It's been a while since we've cracked open the Blu-rays. I was thinking either Jon Pertwee's fourth season or Sylvester McCoy's third?"

It's not lost on me that the seasons he's suggesting are two of my favorites. Just like it's not lost on me that Dad has been going out of his way to cheer me up for the last week. Not that he has any idea why I need cheering up. I've been too mortified to tell him (or anyone else) what happened between Jackson and me, so I've just been letting him think I'm in one of my teenage funks. Given my history, it's not a hard sell.

"Maybe some other time," I tell him.

"Oh." Dad's brows furrow in disappointment. "You sure? We can watch the extended cut of *The Curse of Fenric* with the updated CGI."

"I'm actually really tired," I answer, forcing a yawn. "I'm just going to go to bed early. Can you close the door on your way out?"

Dad bites his lip. I can tell he wants to say something. But whatever it is, he decides it's not worth pressing the issue. At least not right now.

"Sure, I'll let you get some rest," he says. "Maybe we can watch some *Who* together later this weekend."

"Yeah. Maybe."

Dad shoots me a weak smile. Then, with some reluctance, he leaves and shuts the door behind him.

I let out a tired sigh and collapse back against my pillow. It's exhausting having to pretend that nothing's wrong—that I haven't been sick to my stomach thinking about Jackson.

Not that my brooding has been particularly subtle. Aside from going into the ACLU office every morning (where I do the bare minimum to avoid getting fired), I haven't left my room all week. I've been sullen and uncommunicative at dinner. And I've barely responded to any of my friends' texts.

I know I need to pull myself together and stop acting like the goddamn world is ending, but I can't.

It's been five days since I tried to kiss Jackson. *Five days*, and I haven't heard a word.

He must really hate me. Not that I blame him. He had literally just finished telling me in no uncertain terms that I was his *friend* and that he never wanted anything to jeopardize that—and what did I do? Nuked our entire relationship by attempting to shove my tongue down his throat.

How could I think that was okay? Or that Jackson would want that?

When I close my eyes, I can still see the horror on his face when his aunt walked in on us. He couldn't even look at me. That's how disgusted he was.

Is it any wonder I haven't heard from him?

I betrayed his friendship. I betrayed his trust. I betrayed him.

Of course he's never going to speak to me again.

I've ruined *everything*.

CHAPTER 27

JACKSON

"Okay, *enough*," Aunt Rachel announces, yanking back the curtains and flooding my room with blinding light. I pull my sheets over my head to block out the morning sun, but my aunt stomps over to my bed and whips them back.

"Get up. We're having breakfast."

"I'm not hungry," I grumble.

"Too bad. You've been moping in this room for almost a week, and I'm sick of it. Get your butt out of bed *now*."

"I'm in my underwear."

Aunt Rachel folds her arms across her chest. "Jackson, either you get up and join me in the kitchen where we can talk about whatever's turned you into this reclusive, lethargic *slug* while we enjoy some delicious Belgian waffles and fresh-squeezed orange juice that I've spent all morning preparing *or* I can call your parents and you can tell *them* what's going on. Your choice, kiddo."

Aunt Rachel pulls out her phone and waits for my decision.

"Fine," I groan. "I'll get up."

"Good. Get dressed and I'll see you in the kitchen in five minutes. Or else."

Aunt Rachel leaves, and I grudgingly pull on a pair of rumpled cargo shorts and an old T-shirt. After days of barely leaving my bed, I feel like a zombie. But I force myself to trudge to the kitchen, where I find my aunt sitting at the table next to a pot of steaming coffee.

She slides two waffles covered in sliced strawberries off a decorative serving platter and onto a plate that she sets in front of me, then pours some coffee into my mug.

"Sit. Eat."

The aroma of fresh coffee and waffles makes my stomach growl, and for the first time in days, I realize I'm famished. I sit down across from my aunt and tuck into my breakfast. Before I know it, I've cleaned my plate.

"Nice to know my cooking is appreciated," Aunt Rachel says as she dishes out seconds. "Now, let's talk."

I set down my fork and stare at my plate as my appetite vanishes.

"You've been sullen, moody, and, frankly, a real buzzkill for the past week. So talk to me, kiddo. What's going on?"

I shake my head, unsure where to begin. Do I start with the fact that I almost kissed Riley? Or do I start with that batshit-crazy dream I had immediately after, the one that left me so freaked out, I haven't wanted to leave my room all week? The one I can't stop thinking about no matter how hard I try?

And not because of the sex. If it had been only a sex dream, I think I could've handled that. It would've been weird, for sure, but at least it would have been a pretty clear message from my subconscious about what I want. But it wasn't only a sex dream. It was a sex dream that ended with Riley and me being blown up.

By *Nazis*.

What the fuck am I supposed to do with that? Is my brain trying to tell me that if I have a relationship with Riley, I'll blow up both our lives? Is it a warning?

But if that's the case, why did my brain dream about us having sex in the first place? Because honestly, I can't get that image out of my head.

For the past week, I've been thinking nonstop about what it might be like to kiss Riley—to hold him in my arms and do exactly what we did in that dream.

At the same time, I also can't stop thinking about us dying on that bridge.

I know it was only a dream, but it was fucking *terrifying*. And I think that fear was a message. A message that I'm not ready to deal with these feelings and that I need to stay away from Riley.

Even though right now, staying away from him is fucking killing me.

"Okay, let me rephrase the question," Aunt Rachel says when I continue to stare at my coffee in silence. "Does this recent bout of brooding have something to do with what happened back in December?"

I shake my head.

"Okay. I didn't think so, but good to rule it out." She takes a sip of her coffee, and I can feel her eyes studying me. "So, if this sudden funk isn't football related, would I be right in assuming it has something to do with your friend Riley?"

Despite my intention not to tell my aunt anything, I find myself nodding.

"Did you guys have a fight?"

"No, nothing like that."

"Okay. So . . ."

I consider lying or telling her it's none of her business. But if there's one person who might actually be able to help me make sense of everything, it's Aunt Rachel. She knows me better than anyone.

"So . . . Riley's gay," I begin, starting with the simplest part of the story.

"Yeah, I got that from the skinny jeans."

When I don't laugh, she stops smiling and sets down her coffee. "You don't have a problem with that, do you?"

"No, of course not," I say.

"Okay. Just checking. I love my big brother, but I know better than anyone that Wyatt doesn't have the most progressive views on certain subjects. I'm allowed to make sure that he's not passing on his toxic, macho bullshit to my favorite nephew."

"I'm your only nephew."

"Take the win, kiddo."

I smile, and Aunt Rachel plucks a strawberry off her waffle, pops it into her mouth, and considers what I've told her. "So if you don't have a problem with Riley's sexuality, what *is* the problem?"

I take a deep breath. It's now or never, I suppose.

"Riley likes me," I explain. "He *likes me* likes me."

Aunt Rachel starts to reach for another strawberry but stops. Her expression doesn't change but there's a definite shift in her energy as she turns her full attention to me.

"I see. And how do we feel about that?"

The way she poses the question, I know exactly what she's asking. It's the same question I've been asking myself for the past six days.

"I don't know," I tell her.

Aunt Rachel nods, and I can see her picking her next words carefully.

"Well, one of the great things about being young, maybe the only great thing—aside from being able to drink like a fish and roll out of bed the next morning without a hangover—is that you don't have to have all the answers. Contrary to what my brother believes, you don't need to have your whole life figured out by the time you're eighteen. That goes for your professional life *and* your personal life. You're allowed to take as much time as you want to decide who you are, how you want to spend your life, and *who* you want to spend that life with. The only thing you need to know right now is that, whatever you decide, I am always, always, *always* going to be here for you."

Aunt Rachel reaches across the table and squeezes my hand. My relief is overwhelming. After days of suffocating under the weight of my fear, I feel like I can breathe again.

"What do I do about Riley?" I ask once I trust myself to speak. "What do I tell him?"

"Tell him what you told me. That you don't know how you feel, and you need time to figure things out. If he cares about you the way he should care about you, he'll understand."

Despite how reassuring her words are and how much I want to believe them, I can't shake the memory of my dream. Or what it might mean.

"I'm afraid I'll hurt him," I confess. "Not intentionally but . . ."

Aunt Rachel nods sympathetically.

"When you care about someone, there's always a chance you might end up hurting them. Or getting hurt yourself. But that's no reason to stop caring about them. Pain is an inevitable part of life, Jackson. There's no way to avoid it. But love? Love isn't inevitable. Love is a choice. We have to choose love. And when we do, it doesn't erase the hurt or shield us from pain, but it does make it bearable. More than bearable. Love is one of the few things that make life worth living."

I nod. Everything she's saying makes sense. And yet . . . "I'm afraid."

"Oh, Jackson." My aunt laughs, giving my hand another squeeze. "There are so many things in this world to be afraid of. But love? Love isn't one of them. *Never* be afraid of love."

CHAPTER 28

RILEY

Someone keeps ringing the doorbell. I want to break their fingers. Instead, I bury my head under my pillow and try to block out the noise. I don't understand why Dad doesn't answer the door. It's almost ten o'clock. He must be awake.

"Are you going to get that?" I shout.

Dad doesn't respond, at which point I vaguely remember him saying that he was going to some work event or charity breakfast this morning. I'm not sure of the exact details. I wasn't listening.

The doorbell grows more insistent. Whoever's outside clearly isn't going to stop ringing until they get an answer, so with a groan, I kick off the bedcovers. Despite being dressed in only a T-shirt and boxers, I march downstairs, fling open the front door, and bark, *"What?"*

Jackson jumps back. He guiltily yanks his finger away from the doorbell as his face turns red with embarrassment. But he's not the only one momentarily at a loss for words.

"What . . . what are you doing here?" I stammer when I finally find my voice.

But I know what he's doing here, don't I? He's come to tell me off. To tell me our friendship is over and that he never wants to see me again.

"Sorry," he says, looking surprisingly contrite for someone who's here to eviscerate me. "I was gonna call before I came over, but I wasn't sure if you'd . . ." He blushes again. "What I mean is . . . it's been a while. Since we hung out. And I thought I might as well come over. You know? So we could talk."

"Oh." I swallow.

"Can I come in?"

Jackson's energy is definitely more "polite nervousness" than "angry retribution." Which means this is going to be the nicest telling-off in the history of tellings-off or I'm wrong about why he's here.

"Sure," I answer cautiously. "Come in."

Jackson steps inside, but instead of moving farther into the house, we linger in the entranceway, neither of us quite able to look at the other.

"How are you?" he asks after an awkward silence.

"Good," I lie, because what the hell else can I say? "How are you?"

"Good."

We both nod stupidly at each other, and I can feel another awkward silence looming on the horizon.

"What did you want to talk about?" I force myself to ask. If this friendship is over, I might as well rip the Band-Aid off and put us both out of our misery.

My question, though, seems to throw Jackson. He clears his throat, stares at his Nikes, then clears his throat again.

"I just wanted . . ." he begins, then abandons the thought. He opens his mouth to try again but, at the last second, seems to think better of it and settles for shaking his head.

His nervousness is making me nervous. In fact, it's safe to say that I'm on the verge of a full-blown freak-out when, without any warning, he looks at me with his clear blue eyes and asks, "Have you had breakfast?"

"Breakfast?" I'm not sure I heard him right. "Um . . . no. I just woke up."

Jackson nods eagerly, like that was the answer he was hoping for. "My aunt just cooked up this huge breakfast. For real, we've probably got enough waffles to feed the Miami Dolphins. Do you want to come over and have some? Then afterward, if you're not doing anything, maybe we could hang out?"

I am so confused. This is why he dragged me out of bed and nearly broke my doorbell? For waffles?

But maybe this is a good thing. After all, if he was going to end our friendship, I doubt he'd insist on feeding me first. But are we really not going to discuss what happened?

"Are you . . . are you sure?" I ask.

Jackson nods so vigorously, I'm afraid his head might snap off. "Absolutely," he says, flashing me a smile so bright, it's like the sun burning through the early-morning haze. And all at once I understand. He didn't come over this morning to offer me breakfast. He came over to offer me a second chance.

The relief that I feel is so immediate and so intense, it almost knocks me off my feet. I thought I had ruined any possibility of having Jackson in my life. But here he is, grinning down at me and asking for my friendship. And this time I won't screw it up.

If he needs to discuss what happened last Sunday, I'll have that conversation and own my mistake. If he wants to pretend the whole thing never happened, I can do that too. Because whatever my feelings are for Jackson, the most important thing is our friendship. And I won't do anything to jeopardize that again.

"Okay," I say as my heart fills with hope for the first time in days. "Waffles sound great."

I shower and dress in record time, then Jackson drives us back to his aunt's house in his Jeep. Along the way, I decide to text Duy, Audrey, and Tala to see if they want to meet up with us later this afternoon.

I've barely responded to any of their texts this week, and I want to make it up to them for being such a moody, melodramatic dick. Also, it probably wouldn't hurt to have other people around—just in case there's any lingering awkwardness between Jackson and me, and we need a buffer.

Sorry I've been MIA, I text my friends. Anyone got any plans this afternoon?

To my surprise, Audrey texts back almost immediately. What do you mean, "got any plans"? We're seeing the Glorious Peccadilloes. REMEMBER?

I have no idea what Audrey is talking about, though her angry capitalization seems to suggest I should. Sure enough, scrolling back through our group text, I see that a few days ago she sent out a reminder that one of her favorite bands is playing a free concert at the Lake Eola amphitheater.

I don't have any memory of agreeing to go, but I keep scrolling and see a later text from Audrey in which she laid out the exact details of when and where we'd be meeting up this afternoon and to which I apparently responded with the thumbs-up emoji.

"Everything okay?" Jackson asks when he notices me engrossed in my phone.

"Yeah. Slight change of plans, though," I say as we turn onto his aunt's street. "After breakfast, how would you feel about going to a concert with my friends?"

"Oh. Uh, sure," he says. "Who's playing?"

"The Glorious Peccadilloes."

"Who are the—"

Without warning, Jackson brakes sharply and brings his Jeep to an abrupt stop in front of his aunt's house. I'm not sure why until I see that the driveway is occupied by a sporty silver BMW.

Beyond the BMW, two people are lounging in lawn chairs and

sipping iced tea in the shade of the garage. One is Jackson's aunt. The other is a very pretty Black girl with flawless skin and long box-braided hair. She looks about my age, and her outfit is like something out of the closet of Elle Woods in *Legally Blonde*: pink blouse, pink skirt, pink blazer. She's deep in conversation with Jackson's aunt, but when she spots Jackson's Jeep, her face breaks into the most radiant smile I've ever seen outside of a toothpaste commercial.

"Jackson!" she shouts, leaping out of her chair.

I turn to Jackson, who's staring like he can't believe his eyes.

"Micaela?"

CHAPTER 29

JACKSON

"Surprise!"

I've barely started walking up the driveway before Micaela bounces over to me and pulls me into a hug. Out of instinct I hug her back, but I'm so shocked I barely understand what's happening.

"What are you doing here?" I finally manage to ask her.

Micaela steps back and flashes a triumphant grin. "Well, you told me you didn't have any plans this weekend, so I thought I'd drive down and surprise you. And before you say anything, yes, I know the big day isn't until tomorrow. But who wants to celebrate their birthday on a Sunday?"

My birthday? I totally forgot. I've been so distracted with Riley and that dream that it completely slipped my mind.

"Oh. Um. Thanks," I answer. "You shouldn't have."

"Of course I should have. You can't celebrate the big one-eight all by yourself."

The door of my Jeep slams behind me, and Micaela and I turn to see Riley lingering at the end of the driveway. He stares awkwardly at his shoes, too nervous to approach or interrupt.

"Who's that?" Micaela asks.

That might be the most loaded question I've ever been asked. "That's Riley."

"Hi, Riley!" Micaela waves, and Riley slowly trudges up the driveway.

"Hi."

"I'm Micaela."

"Nice to meet you," he mumbles.

I try to catch Riley's eye to let him know that I'm as surprised as him, but he won't meet my gaze.

"So Jackson finally made a friend, huh?" Micaela teases. "I was getting worried. He made it seem like he was all alone down here."

Riley's face falls. I can tell he's hurt, and I don't blame him. He probably thinks I was deliberately keeping our friendship a secret. Which, in all honestly, yeah, I suppose I was. I did crop him out of that photo I sent Micaela. And in the few times that she and I have texted since then, I haven't bothered to correct her assumption about my lack of friends.

I thought I was doing it to spare her feelings. But looking back, I think I knew from the very beginning that there was something between Riley and me. Something I wasn't ready to admit to anyone. Not to Micaela. And definitely not to myself.

"Riley and I were just making plans to go to a concert this afternoon," I announce, putting my arm around his shoulder. He flinches at my touch, but that makes me more determined to show him that I'm not embarrassed by our friendship. Even if I still don't understand the exact nature of it.

"Oh. Fun!" Micaela exclaims. "What concert?"

"Um..."

"The Glorious Peccadilloes," Riley answers, pulling away from me. "But I can just go with my friends. You and Jackson should spend the day together."

I feel my heart stop. I don't want to spend the day with Micaela. I know that's fucking selfish, considering she drove all this way to make sure I wouldn't spend my birthday alone. But I'm not alone. I have

Riley. And we've only just started talking again. I don't want to lose any more time with him. Not when I'm finally starting to figure out my feelings for him.

"Oh my gosh, for real? I *love* the Glorious Peccadilloes!" Micaela gushes. "Are there still tickets available?"

"It's a free outdoor concert," Riley answers.

"Perfect! We can all go together! I'll drive."

I'm not sure what to say. I can't tell Micaela not to come, not without sounding like the world's biggest jerk. But inviting her along feels like a huge slap in the face to Riley. I turn to him to see what he thinks of Micaela's plan, but he refuses to look at anything other than the ground.

In a last-ditch effort, I look over at Aunt Rachel for help. She's been silently watching this entire exchange from the shade of the garage, but all she can do is shake her head and shrug helplessly.

"Great," I tell Micaela, the word catching in my throat like barbed wire. "That'll be fun."

CHAPTER 30

RILEY

The sudden appearance of Jackson's ex-girlfriend was admittedly a surprise. What isn't surprising is the speed with which Duy has become obsessed with her.

In the hour since the two of them met, Duy hasn't stop bombarding her with compliments on everything from her hair ("fabulous") to her skin ("radiant") to her nails ("fierce"). Micaela, in return, has declared Duy her new favorite person. Normally I'd find such a mutual lovefest nauseating, but at least it's helping to distract them from the fact that Jackson and I have barely said two words since leaving his aunt's house.

"So, Micaela, how long are you in Orlando?" Duy asks as the four of us stroll the path around Lake Eola that leads to the amphitheater. "And if you say anything less than a week, I will literally die."

"Alas, I'm only in town for the day," Micaela says with a sigh as she loops her arm through Jackson's and smiles. "I have to head back to Tally tonight."

"Ugh. *I'm dead*," Duy groans. "You would look stunning in the backless periwinkle gown I've been designing. Tell me you're planning to visit Orlando again soon. I would love to get some shots of you in the gown for my portfolio."

"Your portfolio?"

"Duy's a designer," Jackson explains, finally breaking his long and awkward silence. "They're putting together a portfolio of their work so that they can apply to fashion programs."

"Amazing!" Micaela's enthusiasm is undeniably genuine. As is her sweetness, vivacious spirit, and generous heart.

Even so, I wish she'd fall into the lake.

I know I said I was going to keep my romantic feelings for Jackson in check—*and I am*—but I can't help feeling jealous of Micaela. Not to mention betrayed by Jackson. In all our discussions, he never once mentioned that he was still in touch with his ex. Now it turns out that not only has he been texting her on the regular, he's also been keeping our friendship and my entire existence a secret.

I've tried to convince myself that he must have some perfectly reasonable excuse for not telling Micaela about me. But the only explanation that makes sense is the simplest one.

He's embarrassed.

Yes, he likes me. Yes, he wants to be my friend. But he's also Jackson Haines, star athlete and former dude-bro. He can't let his friends back home know that he's spending all his free time with some queer little gay boy.

Then again, Jackson was strangely insistent that we spend the day together even after I gave him multiple opportunities to bail on our plans. Would he do that if he was ashamed of me?

I don't know.

I don't know anything except for the supremely frustrating fact that every time our friendship takes two steps forward, we immediately take three steps back. It's like the universe is deliberately fucking with us.

"Speaking of my portfolio," Duy says as they pull out their phone. "I have to show you the shots I took of Riley and Jackson. They are *fire*."

Jackson stops in his tracks, and the color drains from his face. At the sight of his distress, my frustration with him instantly evaporates, and I'm left with an almost instinctive desire to protect him from any potential humiliation—like having to explain incredibly homoerotic photos to his ex.

"You got Jackson to model for you?" Micaela exclaims, her eyes going wide with excitement. "Oh my gosh, you have to show me!"

"We should actually get to the amphitheater," I say. "Audrey and Tala are waiting."

But Duy lets out a dismissive snort. "It'll just take two seconds. Besides, the concert doesn't start for, like, half an hour. Audrey needs to chill."

Jackson looks at me helplessly, but there's nothing I can do. Duy is already shoving their phone in Micaela's face, showing her the photo of me in Jackson's arms, our lips about to kiss.

"Is this the sexiest thing ever or what?" Duy boasts.

Micaela's smile falters. If Duy notices her reaction, they don't let on. Instead, they launch into an enthusiastic recap of the modeling session, pointing out specific details about the authenticity of the Regency design. Micaela nods and makes appreciative comments as the smile gradually returns to her face.

"So hot, right?" Duy asks, managing to be completely oblivious to the awkwardness they're inflicting.

"Yeah, so hot," Micaela echoes. She then turns to Jackson and adds, "I had no idea you had such an exciting life here in Orlando."

"We were just fooling around," Jackson mumbles, waving off the compliment that also sounds like an accusation. "It's not a big deal."

I know he's talking about the photos, but I can't help feeling like he's also talking about us. This morning when he came to my house, I thought I finally had confirmation that, if nothing else, our friendship was solid. That it was important to both of us. But maybe I was wrong. Maybe Jackson has just been fooling around with me until something or someone better comes along.

"We should find Audrey and Tala," I say, heading off to the amphitheater before anyone can see the hurt on my face.

I don't look back to see if anyone follows. In an effort to get control of my emotions, I keep my head down and my eyes glued to the sidewalk in front of me. Which is how I end up walking straight into someone's back.

"Ow! Watch it!"

"Sorry," I mumble without looking up. I try to go around the person, but a familiar voice stops me in my tracks.

"*Riley?*"

I glance up and can barely believe my eyes. Clearly, the universe isn't done messing with my life because standing right in front of me is Alex fucking Vargas.

"What are *you* doing here?" I ask, not even trying to hide the horror in my voice.

"I swear I'm not stalking you," Alex protests, throwing his hands up in a display of surrender.

Despite my shock, I can't help noticing how much taller he seems to have gotten. Do people keep growing after high school or did I just remember him as being short because his shitty behavior made me think of him as a small, insecure person? He's also let his black hair grow out into a thick, luxurious mane, which is actually quite flattering compared to the macho buzz cut he always insisted on having because he thought it made him look straight.

"I was just on my way to the amphitheater," Alex explains. "This band I like is giving a concert."

"*You* like the Glorious Peccadilloes?" Jesus Christ, is everyone in Florida obsessed with this band? I'd never even heard of them until this morning, and now they're *everywhere*.

"Yeah, they're not normally my thing," Alex confesses with a self-conscious chuckle. "But last year, my roommate got me into them. I'm at the University of Miami, which is where the band's originally from, so everyone down there is legally obligated to worship them."

"Cool," I reply. Because what else are you supposed to say to someone who once broke your heart and who now wants to swap music trivia?

The answer to that is nothing. But before I can think of a way to extricate myself from this clusterfuck of a conversation, Duy, Jackson, and Micaela are on top of us. Which means I now have the utter delight of introducing my friends to my least favorite person on the planet.

"Everyone, this is Alex," I tell the group, straining to keep my tone civil. "He used to go to my school."

I'm surprised by the warm greeting Duy gives Alex until I remember that Duy started at Olympus the year after the whole Alex debacle. Of course Duy's heard the story, but that was years ago. I don't think they're making the connection that the Alex standing in front of us is the same guy that Audrey vowed eternal vengeance against.

Jackson, though, knows exactly who Alex is. And from the way he clenches his jaw and greets him with a tight-lipped "Hey," it's clear that he's about as thrilled to be having this chance encounter as I am.

"You went to school with Riley?" Micaela asks, oblivious to both the death glare that Jackson is aiming in Alex's direction and how uncomfortable that glare is making Alex.

"Uh, yeah."

Micaela's face breaks into a mischievous smile. "Were you guys friends or were you . . ."

Alex turns bright red and stares at me like a deer in headlights.

"We were just friends," I lie. I might not be Alex's biggest fan, but I'm also not about to out him to a total stranger.

Micaela nods, but from the knowing smirk she throws my way, I can tell she doesn't believe me. In fact, it's pretty clear that Micaela is determined to play queer matchmaker because she turns back to Alex and asks, "Are you here for the concert? Because if you are, you should totally join us."

Now it's my turn to look at Jackson for help. I can just about survive spending the day with *his* ex, but the idea of also spending it with *mine* is enough to send me into a full-blown panic attack.

Thankfully, Alex appears equally uncomfortable with Micaela's invitation.

"Oh, thanks, that's really nice but . . . I think I'm just going to do my own thing. You guys have fun, though. Enjoy the concert."

Alex gives me a timid wave and starts to back away. For a second, I'm relieved. But before he turns to go, his eyes catch mine, and something about the way he looks at me—the pitiful mixture of longing and regret—fills me with something I never thought I'd feel for the boy who ruined my first year of high school: sympathy.

Part of me knows that I should let go of my anger and accept Alex's apology. Or at the very least, hear him out. But another part of me finds it hard to believe that people like him are really capable of change.

Then again, if I'm willing to accept that Jackson isn't the same person who allowed Devon Sanderson to be bullied so badly that he ended up in a hospital, don't I owe Alex the chance to prove that he's not the same person who broke my heart?

Besides, if my only options for today are hanging out with Alex or watching Jackson get cozy with his ex, there really isn't a choice, is there?

"Alex, wait up!" I shout.

He stops, and I see his shoulders tense as he turns back to me. He must think I'm about to tell him off or, worse, out him in public, so I force myself to smile. Then, ignoring the look of confusion on Jackson's face, I take a few quick steps toward Alex to close the distance between us.

"Do you want to go somewhere and talk?" I ask. "Just the two of us?"

The effect of my words is immediate. Alex's entire body relaxes, and a grateful smile spreads across his lips.

"Really?" he asks.

"Yeah," I say. "It's about time, don't you think?"

CHAPTER 31

JACKSON

A sinking feeling opens up in the pit of my stomach as I watch Riley disappear down the path with Alex. It's the same feeling I get when I watch a horror movie and some scantily clad cheerleader hears a strange noise in a basement and goes off to investigate.

Every instinct in my body is telling me to go after him—to stop him from wandering off with the asshole who messed up his life.

I know it's irrational. I know that he and Alex have unfinished business. But the possibility that Alex could do or say something—*anything*—that might hurt Riley is enough to make me want to chase him down and beat the shit out of him.

"I thought I noticed a spark," Micaela says, grinning proudly as she hooks her arm around mine.

"What do you mean?"

"Did you not pick up on the sexual tension?" She laughs. "Those two *clearly* have a history."

I'm aware of their history. I'm also aware that the "tension" is anything but sexual. Even so, Micaela's words knock the wind out of me. The idea of something happening between Riley and Alex, no matter how unlikely, fills me with *dread*. Not because Riley might get his heart broken but because I know that it would break mine.

Aunt Rachel said it could take time for me to figure out who I am and what I want, but if the panic I'm experiencing is any indication of the truth, then two things have become abundantly clear.

One, who I am is someone who can't bear the thought of Riley being with anyone else, because, two, what I want is him.

"Ugh, Audrey's getting impatient," Duy groans as their phone pings with a slew of incoming texts. "She's saving us seats in the front row, but some of the hard-core fans are giving her the stink-eye. We better hurry before she has a meltdown and decks someone."

"Why don't you go on ahead?" I suggest. "Micaela and I will follow in a minute."

My feelings for Riley might finally be clear, but the situation with Micaela is anything but. Maybe she really did drive all this way so I wouldn't have to spend my birthday weekend alone, but from the smiles and touches and private glances, I get the impression she's hoping something more will happen. If that's the case, if she still has feelings for me, then we need to talk. I need to be honest with her. About everything.

"Okay," Duy sighs. "But don't be *too* long. Audrey will give your seats away to more deserving fans if you're late."

"Copy that. We've been warned."

Duy winks at me, then heads off toward the amphitheater. When they're gone, I motion for Micaela to have a seat on one of the benches overlooking the water. It's another ridiculously sunny day, not a cloud in the sky, but for once there's no humidity, and the breeze coming off the lake is surprisingly refreshing.

"Your friends are hilarious," Micaela says approvingly. "And *very* interesting."

"Yeah." I blush. "They're pretty different from the guys back home."

"I'll say."

Micaela laughs, and her smile is brighter than the sun over our heads. A part of me wishes we could stay in this moment: the sun on our faces, the breeze in our hair, and not a single worry in our heads other than getting to a concert on time. But there are things I need to say to her. Things she deserves to hear.

"Thanks again for driving all this way to see me," I begin. "It was super-thoughtful."

"What are friends for?"

"Except I haven't been a good friend, have I? I definitely wasn't a good boyfriend."

Micaela shakes her head in protest. "You had a *really* tough year."

"I know, but that doesn't excuse how I treated you."

"We don't have to get into all that."

"Yes, we do. I want to apologize." Micaela looks about to protest again but stops herself. I suspect because she needs to hear this apology as much as I need to give it.

"You're one of the best people I know, Micaela. You're smart and funny and kind—so kind. And you are a beast of a cheerleader. I'm sorry I didn't appreciate that when we were together. After what happened with Devon, you stuck by me when so many people turned their backs on me, and all I did was push you away. I treated you like shit when all you wanted to do was help me, and I'm *so* sorry for that."

Micaela nods, unable to meet my eyes, and stares down at her lap. "Thank you for saying that."

I reach out and take her hand. "You're an incredible person. And I know someday you're gonna meet an amazing guy who appreciates just how fucking incredible you are, and you are gonna be ridiculously happy. Because that's what you deserve. You deserve all the happiness in the world. You really do."

"I know," she retorts with a laugh. "You don't need to tell me what a prize I am. I am well aware that I'm a catch."

"Of course you are," I chuckle. "And given what a catch you are, I want you to know that I'm *incredibly* flattered that you still care about me. I really hope that we can stay friends. That we'll *always* be friends."

"I hope so too."

"Right. But also . . ." I take a deep breath. Once again, it's bite-the-bullet time. "A lot has happened over the past year. We've both changed a lot, I think. I know I have. And as tempting as it might be for us to go back to the way things were, I don't think—"

"Whoa, whoa, whoa!" Micaela protests, snatching her hand away from mine. "I'm gonna stop you there. I am *not* looking to get back together."

I blink in confusion. "You . . . aren't?"

"Seriously?" She shakes her head, and her whole body rocks with laughter. "Jackson, you broke my heart! I do *not* get back together with boys who break my heart. I have a one-strike-you're-out policy. So, as much as I care about you and as much as I will always care about you, I'm sorry, babe, *you're out*."

"Oh," I say, feeling both completely embarrassed and oddly relieved by her rejection.

"I'm sorry if me driving all the way down here to surprise you gave you the wrong impression," she continues, wiping tears of laughter from her eyes. "But like I said, I was legitimately concerned you'd be spending your birthday alone. If you'd told me that you had all these new friends, I never would've come. In fact, why *didn't* you tell me?"

"I don't know," I confess. "I guess I thought maybe you wouldn't . . . approve?"

Micaela pulls a face. "Why? Because they're all gay or queer or whatever? You know that half my aunts are lesbians, right? And though she'd totally deny it if you ask her, my mom would definitely go bi under the right circumstances."

Now it's my turn to laugh.

"Well, I'm glad you like my friends," I tell her. "And I'm glad we're both on the same page about—"

"*Totally*," Micaela agrees. "Although, since you brought it up, can we maybe unpack that a little more? I mean, I know why I don't want to get back together with *you*. But just out of curiosity, why don't you want to get back together with me? Do you seriously think you can do better?"

"Never," I assure her.

"Well, don't tell me that you've met someone else."

I know she's only teasing, but that doesn't stop the heat from rising in my cheeks.

"Oh. My. Gosh." Micaela's jaw drops. "You *slut*! Tell me *everything*. Who is she? What's she like? More to the point, when can I meet her and warn her that she is making the biggest mistake of her life?"

Something in my panicked expression must alert Micaela to the earthquake of anxiety that's threatening to shake me apart from the inside out. Her eyes go wide with concern, and her tone instantly softens. "Whoa, relax! You know I'm joking, right? I would never talk shit about you to someone you're dating. For real, babe, I'm just excited to meet her."

"You've actually already met," I force myself to say.

If I want a relationship with Riley—a real relationship where we're more than friends and where he's more to me than just a secret—I have to get comfortable telling people about him. Because if I can't do that, if I can't be honest about who I am with the people I trust and love, then I don't deserve him.

"Met who?" Micaela asks.

I take a deep breath. "Riley."

"Riley?" Micaela stares at me in confusion. Then her eyes fill with understanding. "*Oh.*"

"Yeah."

"*Wow.*"

"Yeah."

"So you're . . ."

"I don't know," I tell her. "I'm still figuring that out. Although I kind of like 'bi under the right circumstances.'"

"And those circumstances are Riley?"

"Yeah," I answer honestly. "I think so."

"Well... congratulations!" Micaela exclaims with a baffled laugh. "I did not see this coming. But, hey, if Riley makes you happy—"

"He does."

"Then I'm happy for you," she concludes with a decisive nod. And despite the lingering look of surprise in her big brown eyes, I know she means it. After all, we were friends long before we started dating, and we'll be friends long after.

"So give me all the details," she says, practically bouncing in excitement. "How long have you guys been together?"

"Oh, we—we're not together," I stammer.

"You're not?"

"I haven't exactly told him how I feel."

Micaela throws her arms up in the air in exasperation. "Why the heck not?"

"I was gonna. Today. Over breakfast. But then—"

Micaela gasps and covers her mouth with her hands. "But then I showed up. *That's* why you looked so freaked out when you saw me in your driveway. I thought you were just surprised to see me, but no, you were bringing Riley over to tell him how you feel, and I totally cockblocked you!"

"It's okay."

Micaela shakes her head. "No, babe, it's not okay. Because now your boy is off with another man."

"Oh. No. That's just Alex. He's not—I'm not worried about him," I explain, even though only a few minutes ago I was panicking at the idea of the two of them together. "He's Riley's ex."

Micaela glares at me like I'm too dumb to come in out of a thunderstorm. With an exasperated sigh, she grabs her purse, hops off the bench, and starts to power-walk back toward her car.

"What are you doing?" I ask as I chase after her.

"I'm giving you your birthday present a day early. I'm leaving."

"What? No. You can't go. You just got here!"

Micaela stops and claps back at me. "Jackson, your boy is off with his *ex*."

"So? That doesn't mean anything. I'm here with you."

"Yeah, and if things had gone differently, I might totally have hooked up with you."

I blink in confusion. "But you said you didn't want to get back together."

"I *don't*. But that doesn't mean I don't miss your dick."

"Oh." The certainty I'd had about nothing happening between Riley and Alex evaporates, leaving behind a suffocating sense of dread.

Micaela shoots me a sympathetic smile, then stands on her tiptoes and kisses my cheek. "Sorry to be crass, babe. I'm just laying down facts. Now stop being an emotional fuckwit, and go get your man."

CHAPTER 32

RILEY

"How's college?" I ask Alex, wondering how much small talk two people can make before one of them goes insane.

The park overlooking the amphitheater is busier than usual. Some people are hurrying to score seats on the extremely limited benches while others are laying out picnic blankets on the surrounding lawn, but Alex and I have managed to find a somewhat secluded spot behind a cluster of palm trees where we can talk in private. Not that we've said much in the past ten minutes that's worth overhearing.

"College is good," he answers, still glancing at me sheepishly as if he half expects me to bolt at any second. "*Very* different from high school. Everyone's a lot more chill. You don't have to worry about people always being in your business."

Translation: It's easier for him to hook up with guys on the down-low.

Despite wanting to bury the hatchet with Alex, I'm finding it difficult to let go of my resentment. And my cynicism. Mainly because I'm still waiting for my apology.

Alex must pick up on my impatience. He blushes nervously and, in a timid whisper, adds, "I've come out to a few people."

"Oh."

Over the years, when I've wanted to indulge in a bout of self-pity, I've occasionally allowed myself to stalk Alex on social media. Nothing in his carefully curated profiles or in any of his posts has ever indicated that he is anything other than 100 percent straight (aside from the notable absence of a girlfriend). So the news that he's started to come out is a genuine surprise.

"I told my roommate last year," he continues. "And a couple of friends. I even told one of my professors."

"That's great," I say, somewhat taken aback to discover I mean it.

Alex nods, smiling bashfully. But a second later, his face clouds over. "I still haven't told my parents. Or my brothers. Nobody here in Orlando knows."

"That's okay," I assure him, my right hand instinctively reaching out to clasp his shoulder. Regardless of our complicated history, I can't help being proud of him. He's taken a huge first step. A step I've always hoped he'd take but never imagined he would. Which means whatever our beef in the past, in this moment, I want to support him.

"You'll tell your family when you're ready," I add. "You don't have to come out on anyone's schedule but your own."

Alex doesn't say anything. He just looks at my hand, then at me. When we were together, he had an absolute no-touching-in-public rule, so I half expect him to pull away in a panic. Instead, he smiles, his eyes filled with gratitude.

"Thanks. I appreciate you saying that. Especially after how I treated you."

"Yeah," I say, pulling back my hand. "Not exactly great memories."

Alex hangs his head. "I really am sorry. I was such an asshole in high school. And I want you to know that if I could go back in time, I would do everything differently. But I can't. All I can do is tell you how fucking sorry I am. For *everything*. I'm sorry I forced you to keep our relationship secret. I'm sorry I didn't stick up for you when the guys on the football team harassed you. I'm sorry I didn't visit you in the hospital after I made you anorexic."

"Okay, hang on there, you didn't *make* me anorexic," I correct him. "I did that to myself. And there were a lot of factors."

"Yeah, and one of those factors was *me*," he insists. "I was a horrible boyfriend. I used you and threw you away. And I hate that I did that, because I really liked you, Riley. I liked you *so much*. But I was so messed up and so scared that I honestly would've rather died than let anyone find out about me.

"That's not an excuse," he hastens to add. "I just need you to know that I'm really trying not to be that person anymore. I never want to hurt anyone the way I hurt you. Going forward, I want to be a better person. Even if you never forgive me. Even if I never forgive myself. I want to try."

In all the fantasies that I used to have about Alex and me getting back together, I always dreamed he'd make a speech like this. Now here he is, in the flesh, saying everything I've ever wanted him to say, and it's somehow better than the fantasy.

Maybe that's because in the fantasy, Alex's apology was almost irrelevant. It was just a task on a checklist, a penance I needed him to perform so that I could take him back without looking like a total doormat. It had nothing to do with his own personal growth and everything to do with me getting what I wanted—that is, an openly out boyfriend.

The Alex standing in front of me right now, though, isn't apologizing so I can finally claim the prize that I've decided I deserve. He's apologizing because he's trying to become a better person. Because he doesn't want to make the same mistakes or hurt anyone else, including himself.

"Wow," I say. "You really have changed."

"I'm trying to."

"Well, keep it up," I joke, hoping to lighten the tension after Alex's rather intense confession. "This new-and-improved version of you? He seems like a good guy."

"For real?" he asks.

"Yeah. And for the record, I do forgive you."

Alex's hazel eyes go wide. "You do?"

"Yeah," I say, a little surprised myself at how easily I'm able to say the words. "We're good."

The relief on Alex's face is so palpable, it brings a lump to my throat. Or maybe that's just my own relief as my body is finally able to let go of three years of anger, resentment, and recrimination.

"I want you to be happy," I tell him. "It's all I've ever wanted for you."

Overcome with emotion, Alex pulls me into a hug. It's jarring at first to feel his arms around me after all these years. At the same time, though, my body still recognizes and responds to his. The warmth of his skin, the tautness of his muscles, the musky scent of his cologne—it's all familiar. Like an old sweater you find in the back of your closet that still fits.

It's not like hugging Jackson. Nothing is like hugging Jackson. Even so, it feels good to be held. Alex was the first, last, and only boy I've ever hooked up with. Since then, it's been one long self-inflicted dry spell. If Jackson hadn't come along, I probably wouldn't have realized how starved I was for this kind of affection.

It's my own fault. After Alex, I didn't want to get hurt again. I've been telling myself that I can live without a boyfriend, without sex, without love. But I was wrong. I want all those things.

"Fuck, sorry!" Alex says, pulling away as his face turns bright red. At first, I think he's referring to the hug. Then I see him cover his groin, and I realize that the lump I'd felt pressing against my thigh a second ago wasn't his phone.

Guess I'm not the only one starved for affection.

"It's okay," I tell him, unable to stop myself from laughing at the absurdity of the situation. "I totally take it as a compliment."

Alex stares at the ground in mortification. But I can still see the slight hint of a smile when he says, "I guess it's true what they say. Old habits die hard."

"Really hard, apparently."

This time we both laugh. It feels surprisingly good to share a joke with Alex. It's a new experience for us. There wasn't much laughter when we were together.

"Since we're on the topic," he says, a coy glint twinkling in his eyes, "are you seeing anyone?"

I'm not about to delve into the whole Jackson situation with Alex. Mainly because I still don't understand what exactly our situation is. So I shake my head.

"No, I'm not seeing anyone."

"What about that guy you introduced me to? Jackson? I felt like I was getting definite angry-boyfriend vibes from him."

"Jackson's just protective," I explain, trying to convince Alex as much as myself. "There's nothing between us. We're just friends."

Alex looks skeptical. "Are you sure?"

"Yes, I'm sure. Trust me, I am totally and pitifully single."

Alex nods, then shoots me a meaningful look. "Me too."

In the pregnant silence that follows, I can tell where this conversation is headed even before Alex opens his mouth.

"I don't suppose you'd want to skip the concert and maybe go back to my place?" he asks, taking a step closer and lowering his voice. "My parents are out of town on a cruise. That's why I'm here. I'm house-sitting while they're in the Caribbean. We'd have the place to ourselves."

I know what he's asking. And I'd be lying if I said I wasn't tempted. After weeks of being emotionally jerked around by my feelings for Jackson, I can admit that the chance to hook up with a cute boy who is unambiguously into me is doing wonders for my self-esteem (and my libido). Also, the more I think about it, there is a certain poetic justice in having one last fling with the guy who broke my heart. In terms of closing this chapter of my life, it'd be incredibly satisfying to send Alex off into the sunset with one last romantic hurrah.

Only I don't want Alex. I want Jackson.

I know that's completely delusional and totally self-sabotaging. I know that right now, somewhere in this park, he's probably getting back together with his ex. I know I'm setting myself up for nothing but heartache and disappointment. But I don't care. Because regardless of how he feels about me, I know how I feel about him. And it's *absurd* to pretend otherwise.

Screw the vow I made this morning. I need to stop being a coward and tell Jackson how much he means to me. Yes, it might ruin our friendship. But maybe—just maybe—it'll lead to something more. Either way, it's time to find out.

"So . . . what do you think?" Alex asks, his grin faltering in my silence.

"I think, as much as it might be fun to hook up for old times' sake, it's probably not the healthiest idea."

"Oh," he says, unable to hide his disappointment.

"It might make things complicated. And given our history, you and I should probably avoid any more complications. Especially if we want to be friends."

Alex looks surprised. "Friends?"

"Yeah. I know you have your friends at U of M, but it never hurts to have more. Also, I know you're still coming to terms with your sexuality.

There are things you're figuring out, so if you ever need to talk—about anything—I'm here for you. Because I meant what I said earlier. I want you to be happy. I want us both to be happy. And right now, I think our best shot at making that happen is for us to be friends."

Alex considers for a second and then nods. "I'd like that."

This time, I'm the one to pull Alex into a hug. It's far less intense than our previous one, but still, I make sure to keep our pelvises apart to avoid any confusion.

Despite these precautions, though, when I hear a nearby voice aggressively and pointedly clearing its throat, I feel like I've been caught red-handed in an illicit tryst. I pull away from Alex and see that the voice belongs to Jackson. He's standing a few feet away, staring at me with an intense but inscrutable expression.

"Can we talk?" he asks somewhat abruptly.

He doesn't acknowledge Alex, who looks at Jackson, then me, then breaks into a sardonic smirk. "Just friends, huh?"

Before I can answer, Alex backs away and heads toward the amphitheater, making a tactical and tactful retreat.

Alone with Jackson, I feel my body start to panic. I'm not sure how much he saw or overheard before announcing his presence, but I'm low-key freaking out that he might've misconstrued my moment of reconciliation with Alex as something romantic.

"Sorry," Jackson says, his eyes and tone softening as soon as Alex is out of sight. "I didn't mean to interrupt."

"You didn't," I assure him. "Alex and I were just deciding that going forward, we would try to be friends. *Just* friends."

Jackson's face relaxes. "Really?"

"Yeah."

"Good." He nods excitedly, barely able to conceal his smile. "That's . . . good."

It is? I mean, it *is*. But why does Jackson look so relieved? Is it because he's happy that Alex and I are friends again? Or because he's happy that Alex and I aren't *more* than friends?

"Where's Micaela?" I ask as my heart begins to pound quicker.

For some reason, the question makes him blush. "Micaela went back to Tallahassee."

"What? Really?" I ask, a little too eagerly. My mind is racing as I consider what this might mean, but I don't want to get ahead of myself. "Did something happen?"

Chewing on his lip, Jackson lets out a nervous chuckle. "Sort of. We were talking about our relationship and about all the reasons why she and I could never get back together."

I'm not sure what a heart attack feels like, but I'm pretty certain I'm about to have one. But a good heart attack? Is that a thing?

"You were?" I ask.

Jackson nods. "She said she could never date a guy who'd broken her heart. And I told her . . ." He swallows nervously. "I told her that I liked someone else."

All the oxygen leaves my lungs. "You did?"

"Yeah," he whispers, timidly staring down at the grass.

"Who?" I'm almost too afraid to ask. If his answer isn't the answer I'm hoping for, I think it might honestly kill me.

"You."

With that little word, he looks up into my eyes and smiles. He looks incredibly proud but also slightly terrified. Like he's scaled Mount Everest and just now realized what a long drop it would be to the bottom.

"Me?" I can scarcely believe my ears. Or any of my other senses, for that matter. What's happening now is the kind of thing that only happens in movies or dreams. But if this is a dream, I don't ever want to wake up.

"Yeah. You." Jackson nods. "Is that . . . okay?"

I'm smiling so hard, I think my cheeks might crack. "Very okay. Very, *very* okay."

The anxiousness vanishes from Jackson's eyes as a triumphant grin spreads from one ear to the other. He takes a step forward and gently cups my face in his hands. "Can I kiss you?"

"Are you joking?" I almost shout. "Fuck, *yes*, kiss me!"

We laugh, both of us drunk with joy. Then without caring if anyone might be watching, Jackson leans forward and presses his lips to mine. And we kiss like it's what we were born to do.

CHAPTER 33

JACKSON

When I think of the time that I spent *not* kissing Riley, it feels like such a colossal waste. I don't mean the past few weeks. I mean my entire life. Because nothing in the past eighteen years can compare to this kiss.

It's like I've been sleepwalking, like I've only been half alive. But standing here in this park and holding Riley in my arms as our lips find each other over and over again, it's like I'm finally awake. More than awake. For the first time in my life, I feel alive.

"The concert's starting," Riley murmurs between kisses.

I cock my head and hear the riff of an electric guitar wail over the amphitheater's sound system. It's followed by a thunderous burst of applause.

"We should find the others," I say, still unable to pull my lips from his.

"Or," he teases, "we could go back to your place?"

"And what would we do back at my place?"

Riley grins and bites my lower lip. "Everything."

He doesn't have to ask twice. I grab his hand and lead him out of the park, both of us laughing like punch-drunk idiots. I order us a Lyft while Riley texts the others to tell them we're skipping the concert and to ask Audrey to give Duy a ride home. Then we're making out in the back of a silver Nissan while our blank-faced driver pretends not to notice.

Part of me is shocked at how comfortable I am kissing Riley. Given that until a few days ago, I was pretty certain I was straight, I thought I might have more apprehension about kissing another guy in public. But I don't.

Maybe I'm just intoxicated with infatuation, but right now I don't care what anyone thinks about me. Riley and I are together. That's all that matters. And I'm not gonna waste another minute feeling guilt or confusion about that.

By the time we get back to my house, our faces are practically glued together. We stumble through the front door, tripping over each other's limbs and giggling like schoolgirls. Aunt Rachel is vacuuming in the living room but stops long enough to raise an inquiring eyebrow at us.

"Someone's home early," she deadpans.

"We decided to skip the concert," I say, panting so hard I'm almost breathless.

"I can see that." Then, turning her knowing gaze to Riley, she adds, "It's nice to see you again, Riley."

"You too, Miss Haines."

"We're gonna hang out in my room," I announce, shutting down any additional conversation. I then pull Riley down the hall as my aunt breaks into a satisfied smirk.

"Have fun! Be safe!"

I'm not gonna lie, I don't love the idea of hooking up in a house with such thin walls and such a nosy aunt, but I'm too horny to care.

As soon as we're in my room and the door is locked, I pull up a playlist on my phone, connect it to my sound system, and hope the music is louder than whatever Riley and I are about to get up to.

"Good call," he laughs as he pulls me onto my bed.

Now that we're alone, my hands and lips are itching to explore his body—to touch him in all the places that I've been aching to know ever since that dream showed me what was possible.

I pull his T-shirt off over his head, and kiss his neck and chest before working my way down to his stomach. I unzip his jeans and yank them off in one quick tug. In response, Riley tears off my polo and unbuttons my shorts.

I start to reach for his boxers, at which point it occurs to me how quickly things are escalating.

"Are we moving too fast?" I ask, suddenly nervous that I'm rushing him.

Riley pauses and looks up at me, his green eyes full of longing. "Honestly, Jackson? I feel like I've been waiting for this my entire life."

Much to my surprise, I find I know exactly what he means. I might have met Riley only a few weeks ago, but in my heart, I feel like we've known each other for a lifetime. More than a lifetime. Gazing into Riley's eyes, I'd swear we've known each other *forever*.

"Me too," I say, placing my hand over his heart.

"Good." Riley grins. "Then shut up and kiss me."

I do as I'm told. I take him into my arms. And my body finds its purpose in his.

CHAPTER 34

RILEY

For one soul-crushing second, I think it's all been a dream. Then I hear Jackson's soft breathing against my ear. I feel his strong arms wrapped around my body, holding me while he sleeps, and I know it was no dream. This is real. The realest moment of my life.

I lift my head off his shoulder and glance up at Jackson's sleeping face. It's pale and luminous in the moonlight. I want to cover it in kisses. I want to taste his lips and feel the heat of his breath against my skin. He looks so peaceful, though, so *content*.

I wouldn't dream of waking him. Instead, I settle for admiring all the wonders of his handsome face: the curl of his lashes, the slope of his nose, the light dusting of freckles that cluster on his cheeks.

He's a work of art. My work of art. My beautiful, wonderful, impossible Jackson.

"Are you watching me sleep?" he murmurs.

Caught by surprise, I feel my cheeks redden in embarrassment. "No," I lie.

Jackson opens one drowsy eye and studies me with a mischievous grin. "You weren't?"

"If you're asking me a question, then clearly you're awake, which means *technically* I wasn't watching you sleep."

Jackson chuckles and wraps his body around mine even tighter so that there isn't an inch of space between us. "You're lucky you're cute, you weirdo."

We cuddle in the moonlight, Jackson gently stroking my hair as I breathe in the intoxicating musk of his skin. I'm surprised how comfortable it all feels. Comfortable and familiar. Like this isn't our first time together like this but the fiftieth or the seven hundred and fiftieth. Like we've being doing this all our lives.

The holding, the stroking, the breathing each other in, even Jackson chiding me for watching him sleep—it all feels like part of some age-old routine that we've spent our entire lives perfecting.

"You know," I tell him, nuzzling my chin against his chest, "I actually had a dream where we had almost this exact conversation."

Jackson raises an eyebrow. "You did?"

"Yeah. You remember that dream I had about Pompeii?"

"The volcano dream?"

"Right. Only before it became a volcano dream, it was kind of a... sex dream."

"I knew it!" Jackson crows triumphantly. "I knew when I asked about that dream and you got all cagey that there was something you weren't telling me."

"Okay. Yeah. Fine. I admit it. We did filthy, unspeakable things, and we loved every minute of it. Also, you'll be happy to know that Dream You *also* complained when Dream Me watched him sleep."

"That's wild."

"Isn't it?"

Jackson lets out a little chortle. "Well, since we're sharing R-rated dreams, I guess I should tell you that I also had a sex dream about us."

"You did?" I gasp. The idea of Jackson having naughty dreams about me is almost more exciting than all the naughty things we actually just did to each other. "Was it also set in Italy?"

"No." He laughs. "London."

"London?"

"Yeah. And for some reason, we were both pickpockets who lived on the streets."

"You mean like Dickensian orphans?" I ask.

"Like what?"

"You know, like in the movie *Oliver!* 'Please, sir, can I 'ave some more?'"

"*What?*"

"Never mind," I sigh. "Just tell me about your sex dream."

Jackson shrugs. "It was actually pretty weird. We were in the 1940s, you know, during World War Two. And the Germans were bombing London. That's how we died."

"We died?" I ask, pulling back in surprise.

"Yeah. In the dream. We were standing on this bridge and a bomb fell right on top of us."

"I thought you said this was a *sex* dream?"

Jackson laughs. "It was. We had sex right before the Germans blew us up."

"On a bridge?"

"In a bathtub."

My entire body tingles at the thought of Jackson and me in a tub together. That's definitely something we'll have to try in the near future. Though for the moment, I want to hear more about Jackson's dream. It's interesting that he's been dreaming about us in England at the same time that I've been having those nightmares about Italy.

"Why do you think you dreamed about London?" I ask. "Have you been there?"

"No. But my father and I used to watch a lot of war movies. You know, *Dunkirk, The Darkest Hour, Saving Private Ryan*. It was our thing."

"Have you watched any recently?"

"No. Why?"

"No reason." I shrug. "It's just odd that we both had these elaborate sex dreams set in foreign countries. And that we died in them."

"I guess," Jackson says, not sounding particularly concerned. "Maybe we were both just stressed out, you know? And that was our brains' way of dealing with it."

"Maybe," I concede. Though I'm not sure I believe that. Two sex dreams that turned into death dreams *and* they both took place in another time and country? That feels like way too much of a coincidence.

Before I can give the question any more thought, though, Jackson pulls me to him and chuckles mischievously into my ear. "So tell me about some of these filthy, unspeakable things that we did in your dream."

"You tell me about yours," I counter.

"I'd rather show you," he purrs, slowly sliding his hands down my stomach.

"Haven't you had enough?" I ask, pretending to be scandalized at his voracious appetite. "You really need to learn some self-control."

"But it's my birthday."

"*Tomorrow* is your birthday. Today is—wait. What time is it?"

I sit up and grab my phone off the nightstand. Jackson peeks over my shoulder.

"Well, well, well. Look at that," he gloats. "It's after midnight. I'm officially eighteen."

"In that case," I say as I lie back against my pillow, "I suppose the birthday boy is entitled to a small treat."

"Not so small." He smirks.

"Put on some music."

Jackson doesn't hesitate. He hops out of bed like an excited puppy and hurries over to the oak bureau on the other side of the room where his phone is docked in a very sophisticated-looking sound system.

Still not believing my luck, I let my thirsty eyes drink in his body. In the pure white glow of the moonlight, he looks like a Greek sculpture: smooth and hard and timeless. I don't think I've ever seen anything so beautiful or wanted something as much as I want him.

Even these few seconds apart are agony. I'm longing for his lips, his hands, his heat. I want every part of him, and I'm going to have every part of him.

Just as soon as he stops fiddling with those speakers.

"Everything all right over there?" I ask when Jackson continues to linger by the bureau. I can't see what he's doing because his back is to me, but he seems to be staring off into space.

"Jackson?" I ask when he doesn't answer.

His head turns slightly in my direction. He looks confused. And tired. More than tired; he looks exhausted.

"I'm so . . . *hot* . . ." He groans.

Then he collapses.

With a cry of panic, I leap out of bed and race to his side. When I lift his head onto my lap, I can see he's unconscious but breathing. Just like he was at Heartbeats. I pat his face and call his name, but it doesn't have any effect. I can't bring him around.

With a sinking fear, it occurs to me that Jackson might have some medical condition. Something he hasn't told me about. If so, I need to get his aunt.

I slip on my boxers so I won't completely freak out Miss Haines when I wake her in the middle of the night and dash to Jackson's bedroom door. But just as I'm unlocking it, my head grows dizzy, and my vision blurs.

Jackson's room tilts around me. It's like the whole house is turning upside down. I feel seasick. Disoriented. Just like I did at the carnival. Right before I—

My legs give out, and I collapse to the floor.

Beside me, Jackson lies helpless and unconscious. I don't understand what's happening, but with the last ounce of my strength, I reach for him—and the world goes dark.

BRATTAHLID, GREENLAND

(DECEMBER 999)

CHAPTER 35

RORIK

The witch is coming. Whether to bring good tidings or ill, none can say. But my heart fears the worst. A wolfish winter has fallen upon our land. The cold stalks our longhouses, devouring all that is warm. Does not this make my Ragnar the choicest prey? My Ragnar, who burns with fire in his blood.

"Water," he groans, tearing the sweat-stained blanket from his body as if it were some poison-fanged serpent that meant him ill.

Perched on the edge of his narrow cot, I dip a cup into the wooden bowl that rests in my lap. It's almost empty. I'll need to fetch more snow to melt, though had I all the waters of the fjords, I doubt I could quench the terrible flame consuming my beloved.

With great effort, Ragnar props his tired body up on his elbows, and I bring the cooling cup to his lips. He drinks greedily, desperately, then sinks down again in weariness. His face and body are drenched with sweat despite the meagerness of the hearth fire.

I soak a cloth in the remaining contents of my bowl, then press its damp relief to his hot forehead and wipe his tired face. Even in sickness, my Ragnar is beautiful. The fever that rages in his bones can do nothing to mar his noble profile or dull the luster of his hair, which even now catches the light of the fire like burnished bronze. He is and always has been my most precious treasure. My golden love.

I know not what I would do if I lost him.

"You're worse than a wife," Ragnar chides, pushing my hand away. "You fret like an old woman."

"I haven't said a word."

"You fret with your eyes. I can hear them. The whole settlement can hear them."

Unleashing another groan, Ragnar sits up in bed. His body, made taut and lean with years of fighting, is as pale as snow. Too pale for one who burns like the sun.

"Help me to dress," he says, gripping my shoulder for support as he forces himself to stand. "Everyone has already left for the Great Hall. Our absence will be noticed."

"You're not well."

"It's nothing. Bad fish. It will pass."

"You need rest."

"Erik wants all his men at his side when the witch arrives."

"Erik will understand. I will tell him—"

"You'll tell him nothing!" Ragnar barks, grabbing my wrist. Even in illness, his strength is ferocious. "Erik is our chieftain. We serve at his command. Those who cannot serve have no place in this settlement."

This rage of Ragnar is nothing new; I have seen his fury in battle. But never in all our years has he aimed it at me. This is how I know he is scared. Not of Erik. Not of losing face among our brother-warriors. But of the sickness that has fallen upon him over the past three days, stealing his strength and making him a prisoner of his bed.

"Even Erik rests when he is weary," I remind him.

"Great men can afford such comfort. We are but swords. And swords must always be at the ready to serve their masters."

Ragnar releases me. Whatever strength he mustered in his fit of anger flees his body, leaving him weak on his feet.

"I'll help you to dress," I say, clasping his shoulder to steady him. "The chieftain will have his swords. All of them."

I turn to fetch his clothes, but before I can take a step, I feel Ragnar against my back. He wraps his arms around my chest and buries his lips against the nape of my neck.

"You are half my heart," he whispers, the words tearing themselves from his lips as if he cannot help them. The new hairs of what will be his first beard scratch my cheek, and his breath on my shoulders is hot and moist. Both fill me with remembrances of our stolen nights together. Nights when, safe from the prying eyes of men, our bodies twisted around each other in an attempt to discover the shape of desire.

"And you are mine," I tell him, lifting his left hand to my lips, then the right. Then I press both hands over my heart and hold them there. Ragnar sighs into my shoulder, crushing me in the desperate embrace of his arms.

My beautiful warrior. I have seen him stained with the blood of Norsemen when the battle rage blazed in his bones, more wolf sometimes than man. But I have also seen him gentle as the dawn, covering my body with kisses so soft, his lips might have been the breeze.

That Fate can bestow such a blessing has often made my heart rejoice. But tonight, in Ragnar's sickness, I see the cruelty of such a blessing. For I see now that what Fate bestows to a man, it can also take away.

I know not if Ragnar's fever will consume itself or consume him. I know only that if it be the latter, I shall not survive the loss. For no man survives with half a heart.

The Great Hall is silent as the sun sets over Brattahlid. The long fire burns strong and bright in the center of the room, keeping the hungry night at bay. Outside, a wailing moves through the valley, though whether it be the wolves who live in the mountains beyond our settlement or the winter wind raging over the fjord, I cannot tell. Sometimes I think they are one and the same.

In the high seat, flanked by wood-carved dragons, Erik sits lost in thought. He scarcely attends to the hushed whispers of his kinsmen, who have gathered on the fur-draped benches nearest their chieftain. *Great men have great worries*, I think as I watch him run a nervous hand through his long beard, stroking the rough red hairs that have earned him his nickname and that have not, with age, lost their luster.

Never have I seen Erik so quiet. Nor have my brother-warriors, who have taken their cue from our chieftain and shuffle uneasily to their benches. Silence among Norsemen is an unnatural thing. I have, on many occasions, heard this hall filled with such carousing, I thought the roof would collapse. Tonight, though, our earls and warriors are as mute as stones. It is as if they fear that one wrong word or careless utterance might unleash disaster upon our heads.

"She is not to be called a witch," Erik announces, his voice like sudden thunder. "If she addresses you, you will call her Seeress or Wise One. She must be accorded every honor."

The men in the hall nod in solemn understanding, and Erik sinks back into his chair to resume the worried stroking of his beard. When he discovered this island and laid claim to its southern shores, he must have thought himself the most fortunate of men to possess such an unblemished paradise. But he did not reckon on the brutal winters taking so severe a toll on him and on those who followed him here. Every year there is talk of abandoning the settlement. That is why Erik sent to Iceland for the witch—to see what the future holds for Brattahlid. Whether greatness or doom.

Ragnar coughs beside me and struggles to loosen his cloak. I wrapped him in the warmest furs I could find to protect him from the elements. But now that we are seated in front of the raging fire, the air around us thick with smoke, he is once again drenched with sweat.

"Let me," I whisper when I see the leather knot of his cloak defeat him.

He glares at me but says nothing as I remove his furs.

On the bench beside us, Thorsten looks Ragnar up and down with his one good eye. "Where have you been all day?"

"Bad fish," Ragnar answers.

Thorsten laughs and turns away, and Ragnar smiles at me as if he has claimed some victory with his deceit. Then he coughs and clutches at his chest in such desperation, I am certain it will bring all eyes upon him. But I am wrong. We are spared discovery by the bitter frost-wind that tears through the Great Hall when its large oak door is thrust open.

Erik's brother Asvald enters. He removes his cap and shakes the snow from his bear-fur cloak. Behind him, lingering in the shadows, a hooded figure waits.

"My lord." Asvald kneels before his brother. "I bring you Ulfhild the seeress."

Erik rises from the high seat, and every man rises with him. The seeress steps out of the shadows and pulls back the cowl of her black lambskin mantle that is finer than anything our women have here in Brattahlid. Her pale face is sharp and lean, and her kohl-black eyes have something of the wolf's smile in them. Were I to guess, I would say it is a face that has seen no more than forty summers. In youth, she would have been a beauty, and some of that beauty lingers in the bloodred hair that coils atop her head like knotted snakes.

"Greetings, Erik, son of Thorvald," the seeress says, nodding in deferment to our chieftain, her voice sharp and cold as ice.

"Greetings, Seeress. You are most welcome in Brattahlid. It was brave of you to make the journey. I know men in this room who would be afeared to traverse the sea in such a winter as this."

"That does not surprise me," Ulfhild replies with a short, hard laugh. "Men are often brave only when it is convenient. Life does not afford such luxury to a woman."

My brother-warriors tense, our eyes turning to Erik to see how we are to take this strange rebuke. To our great relief, he laughs.

"You speak true, Seeress," he declares. "Come, sit, we shall feast and toast your good health!"

A chair almost as finely and elaborately carved as Erik's is set beside him and draped in pillows and furs. The seeress nods in approval. In slow, unhurried steps, she makes her way across the long, narrow hall, nodding to each of Erik's men, who pay homage with words of greeting.

"You are most welcome, Great Seeress," I say as she passes before me. She nods and is about to continue her slow procession when her wolf-sharp eyes catch sight of Ragnar. I see her take in his labored breathing and his pale face stained with sweat. She holds him in her hungry gaze, and I feel a chill in my bones colder than any winter.

Then she turns away and resumes her journey to the chair of honor.

Once his guest is seated, Erik motions for us to do the same. Ragnar almost collapses in exhaustion, his body going slack like a sail that has lost the wind. Thank Odin for the swift arrival of the servants. Their entrance draws the attention of everyone in the room as they set out huge plates of food overflowing with bread, cheese, pork, and herring. Sweet mead flows in our cups, though wine and wine alone is offered to the seeress.

"You must eat," I whisper to Ragnar. I grab a haunch of pork from a passing servant and push it into his hands. But after a few bites, he grows weary from the effort.

"Tomorrow," he sighs. "I'll eat tomorrow."

I nod, but his breath is so short, I have no certainty that we are guaranteed a tomorrow. Only the seeress has that knowledge, and she is not here for me. She is here for Erik. Erik who seeks to know all that the future holds.

I have no such ambitions. My one desire is to know if my fears for Ragnar are merited, and, if so, what can be done to avert his fate.

I must speak with the witch. Whatever the consequences, whatever Erik's punishment, I must try. All of Ragnar's tomorrows depend on me, and though it cost me my life, I owe him nothing less.

I was nine when he and I became bond-brothers. The woman I called Mother for the first years of my life was a healer. She lived among women who practiced the healing arts in the forests outside Húsavík in Iceland. I had no father I knew by name. Men were not permitted among the healers, so when it was that I reached my ninth winter, I was given to Ragnar's family. They farmed in Húsavík, and they owed my mother a life-debt, for she had breathed life back into Ragnar's sister when she'd drowned as a child.

My life in Húsavík was good. Most of the families were farmers, for the soil was rich and the harvests bountiful. This made us a constant target for sea-raiders, whose swift ships would appear on the horizon and strike without warning. In preparation against this evil, the young boys of my village were taught the ways of the shield and the sword from an early age, and Ragnar was accounted a skilled fighter by the time he reached his ninth summer.

Raised by women and healers, I could scarcely handle a knife. This should have earned me Ragnar's scorn. Instead, he took it upon himself to forge me into a warrior. Whatever time we had for our own after we finished our chores, he spent teaching me the art of combat. I repaid him the only way I knew how: with songs I had learned from my mother and the women of her forest. I had a pleasing voice, and many were the nights when my songs would lull Ragnar to sleep in the bed we shared. He said my songs gave him the sweetest visions while he slept.

In this manner, six summers passed. Him teaching me to fight. Me teaching him to dream.

Then the day came. The day we had long prepared for. The day that still caught us unprepared. Sea-raiders fell upon our village, swift and merciless like the wolves of winter. They burned the farms, stole the summer harvest, and left so many bodies in their wake that the ravens could have feasted upon them until Ragnarök.

Ragnar fought with the savagery of a bear. He split the head of a raider with the ax his father used for chopping wood and gutted another with his sword. I killed no one, but I kept myself alive and fought the best I could. Even so, our farm was burned with the others. My bond-parents were killed, and Ragnar's sister was taken by the raiders along with many of the young women.

That night, after the raiders had gone, leaving our village in ruins, I bathed Ragnar's wounds in the sea and sang him songs to soothe his soul. His grief was great but silent. He did not cry. He never cried. But in the remains of our charred farmhouse, for the first time since we were children, he climbed into my bed and wrapped his body around mine as if he were afraid I too would be snatched away from him.

"If I had lost you, I would have let the raiders kill me," he said, whispering his confession into the back of my neck. "You are half my heart."

Not long after, Erik came to Húsavík—or what was left of Húsavík—in his great ship with sails that blotted out the sun. His settlement in Greenland was expanding, he said. He was seeking warriors to serve him and protect his territory. In exchange, such men would be well provided for.

The stench of death still hung in the air of Húsavík, so Ragnar accepted the offer. His one condition was that Erik take me as well.

"Can he fight?" Erik asked, eyeing me as if I were a fish not worth the filleting. "He looks small."

"He can. Even if he could not, he is my bond-brother. Where I go, he goes."

So it was that Ragnar and I came to Brattahlid, he to fight for Erik, and me to fight for him. Such are my thoughts when the seeress's sharp voice, like the breaking of glass, echoes across the Great Hall and calls me back to the present.

"Where are your women?" Ulfhild demands.

Her question is aimed at no man in particular and yet it strikes fear in the heart of every man who hears it. The raucous laughter of my brother-warriors, which had hitherto flowed as freely as the mead, shrivels and vanishes. The room plunges into silence, and all eyes turn to Erik, who shifts uncomfortably in his chair.

"Our wives have dined already," he answers.

"You will summon them," the seeress commands as if asking for another bowl of hazelnuts.

"Unfortunately, that will not be possible," Erik replies. "My wife has of late adopted the Christian faith. As have many of the other women here. It is a great inconvenience, to be sure, but my wife says it is not permitted for her or any Christian woman to be in the presence of a—" Erik catches himself before he can say the forbidden word. "It is not permitted that they dine with us."

"I see." Ulfhild's thin lips curl into a dangerous smile. She rises from her chair, approaches the long fire burning in the center of the hall, and warms her hands in front of it. Circling the flame in slow, deliberate steps, she says, "Tell me, Chieftain, if you seek to know the secrets of what is to come, why do you not have your wife ask her new god?"

Erik has no answer.

"Could it be that her god has no words for Erik Thorvaldson? Or perhaps her god is too new to have acquired the great knowledge you seek."

"It is indeed a strange religion," Erik says carefully. "But I have always thought it best to let women worship as they will. It could be that there are things their new god will reveal to them that we men as yet cannot understand."

"Perhaps it is so," Ulfhild assents. "But if you wish me to tell you of your future, I will need your women. The spirits that I call upon are not my servants. I am theirs. And they must be appeased with song before they will deliver their secrets unto me. Surely your wife or some woman here still remembers the songs of the old way, even if they have found a new one?"

"They remember, but they will not sing them," Erik answers solemnly.

"Then my journey has been in vain."

The seeress turns to leave the hall, and Erik rises in dismay. I hear Ragnar's breathing grow strained, as if each breath is a battle, and I am stricken with fear. The witch is leaving, taking with her any hope I might have of saving my beloved. That cannot happen.

"I know the old songs!" I shout, leaping to my feet.

Ulfhild stops at the door. Without a word, she slowly retraces her steps back to the fire and stares at me across the flames.

"How do *you* know the songs?" she asks.

"The woman who bore me was a healer. I was raised among women. They taught me their songs."

"He has a fine voice," Erik adds eagerly, though such praise he has never once offered before. "My men have oft remarked that his voice is sweeter than any of our women's."

I catch Thorsten and Asvald exchanging a knowing smirk. What Erik has told the seeress is true. What he has omitted is that when my brother-warriors made such remarks, they were not intended as compliments.

"We shall see," Ulfhild says. "What is your name?"

"Rorik."

"And how old are you?"

"Today marks the first day of my eighteenth year."

Ulfhild's eyebrows rise in pleasant surprise. "An auspicious day. You may serve me well. You know the Green Warlock's song?"

"I do." I sang it to Ragnar many nights in our childhood. It was one of his favorites.

"Begin, then," the seeress commands. "Let us see what you have learned from your women."

I look to Ragnar, and despite his fever, his eyes are bright with pride. If I can please the seeress, I am certain she will grant me the favor I seek. Just as I am certain that without her powers, Ragnar will die.

Erik resumes his place on the high seat and nods for me to commence. I take a deep breath, look once more at Ragnar, and let the song slip forth from my soul. It has been years since last I sang this particular song, but I have no trouble remembering the words. My voice comes out clear and strong, filling the Great Hall.

Ulfhild circles the fire. Chanting strange words under her breath, she pulls unfamiliar plants from a small black pouch that hangs around her waist and tosses them into the flames. Despite the warmth of the fire, I feel a sharp chill seep into the room. Something in the air shifts. I wonder if the other men feel it too. I think they must. Perched on his chair, Erik looks rapt, and all his warriors have fallen into silence.

I finish the song and look to the seeress to see if she wishes me to begin again. Her eyes are closed, but she seems to sense my question.

"Your women taught you well," Ulfhild purrs with her sly wolf smile. "The spirits are pleased."

"Will they speak to you?" Erik asks, leaning forward, his eyes shining in hunger.

"Ask your questions, Chieftain, and I will give you their answers," Ulfhild replies, turning toward Erik but keeping her eyes closed.

"First, I wish to know of my son Leif. A year ago, he took a ship and set out across the great ocean in search of a new land on the other side of the world. I wish to know if he has found that land, how he fares, and if he shall return."

The seeress tilts her head as if listening to music that only she can hear.

"Your son is safe. He found the new land that he sought. And you will behold his face before the next winter."

Erik sighs in relief, and my brother-warriors raise their voices in a cheer.

"What of Brattahlid?" he asks. "What of our future?"

Again, the seeress tilts her head in silent communion.

"Brattahlid will be strong as long as Erik the Red sits on the great seat."

Another cheer rises up, and Erik nods approvingly. "The winter will not be too harsh, then?"

"No harsher than you are accustomed to."

"And our crops?"

"Will thrive in the spring. As they always have."

"And what of the sickness?" Erik asks. "I have heard rumors that it has returned all along the seacoast and that no village is safe. I lost fifty men to it when it first struck Brattahlid three years ago. It nearly destroyed this settlement. I must know if it will come again."

Ulfhild's silence sends a shiver through my body.

"Well?" Erik asks, his voice edged in fear. "Will the sickness come to Brattahlid?"

"No," Ulfhild answers, shaking her head. I breathe a sigh of relief, as does every man in the hall, until the seeress opens her eyes and points at Ragnar. "The sickness is already here."

Ragnar rises in protest, his eyes wild, his face drenched in sweat. He opens his mouth to speak, but before he can utter a word, his legs buckle beneath the weight of his weariness. He collapses into my arms, dragging us both to the floor.

"It is true," Erik says, rising from his chair in horror. "Ragnar has brought the sickness upon us!"

The men scatter like rats as they flee to the far side of the hall.

"Please!" I beg, turning my tear-filled eyes to Ulfhild as I cradle Ragnar in my arms. "Help him. You must help him!"

Ulfhild shakes her head. Her eyes are not without pity, but her words are without mercy. "There is no cure for the sickness but death."

"Take him from here!" Erik commands, turning to his brother. "Light a pyre. We will purge the sickness out of Brattahlid with fire."

"No!" I shout, jumping to my feet and unsheathing my sword.

"Rorik, put down your blade!" Erik shouts. "Ragnar must die!"

"You will not touch him!" I answer, spitting the words in defiance. "None of you will touch him!"

I cannot defeat one of my brother-warriors in battle, let alone all of them. But the wolf is in my blood. I will die before I let harm come to Ragnar.

The men look to Erik. At his fatal nod, they will have their order to kill. I am ready.

But the nod does not come.

The witch moves to Erik's side and whispers in his ear. The Great Hall goes silent. All I can hear is Ragnar's labored breathing and the howling of the wind moving through the valley.

"Let them go," Erik pronounces.

His words should bring relief, yet I cannot believe them. Nor can my brother-warriors, who stare at Erik in amazement.

"Take Ragnar and leave this settlement," he commands, turning his terrible gaze on me. "You may try your fortune in the wild, but if you are found in Brattahlid hereafter, you will die. Now go!"

I do not hesitate. I sheathe my blade and help Ragnar lift himself off the floor. He has not spoken a word, and I know not if he even understands what is happening, but it makes no difference. I will be his eyes and ears. I will be his strength and his legs. Just as he has always been my heart.

The fear-struck men part for us as we make our way out of the Great Hall. At the open door, the winter wind bites at my face, hungry for my warmth. I turn back to the hall and take one last look at my brother-warriors, at Erik, and at the seeress.

"*Witch*," I say, spitting the word at her with all my contempt. "I helped you. I *sang* for you."

"And you sang well. But now your song is at an end."

I open my mouth to leave her with one final curse, something to bring the stars crashing down upon her traitorous head, but a strange smile plays across her lips and silences me.

"Do not despair," she says, her eyes shining as if lit by a fire that burned within her soul. "When one song ends, another always begins."

With a slow, deliberate nod, she bids me farewell, and I carry my Ragnar into the endless winter.

Of all the nights to be banished, we could not have been cursed with one more terrible than this. The snow falls upon us, as relentless as the wrath of an angry god, and the bitter chill that cuts through our bones is enough to drive a man from his senses.

Even so, I push forward through the storm and out of the

settlement, supporting my weary Ragnar, who wheezes in my arms like a dying flame.

"Stop," he groans against my ear. But I pay him no heed.

We must keep going. We've just made it onto the slope of the shallow mountain that edges our settlement. If we stop here, our tracks in the snow will be easy enough to follow for any man wishing us harm. Though I cannot imagine anyone will trail us into this wilderness. The snow is falling hard and fast tonight, burying the land in a freezing white death. Only fools would brave a storm such as this.

"Stop!" Ragnar shouts. His legs give out and he collapses to the ground. I kneel beside him and try to lift him, but my arms are too weary, and my breath is short. The strain of carrying Ragnar even this far has stolen what little strength I have.

"We cannot rest," I tell him, laying my body next to his to warm it against the brutal chill. "We must get over the mountain."

When Ragnar and I first came to Brattahlid, we discovered a small cave on the western slope. It was to there that we would steal on warm summer nights when we could not bear to be without the other's touch. If we can but reach that cave, there is hope he may survive the night.

Already Ragnar's skin is ice to my touch despite his burning fever. He will not last until dawn. Neither, in truth, will I. But in the cave, we will have shelter. There Ragnar may rest. Then we shall steal a boat from Erik and leave this land. Perhaps we will return to Húsavík. Or if not to Iceland, then to any place where my Ragnar will be safe.

"Rorik, listen to me," he urges, his voice straining to form each word. "You must go back."

"We cannot. Erik has banished us."

"Erik has banished me. You can still return."

"I will not leave you."

"Rorik—"

"No!" I shout, taking his face in my hands. "You are my bond-brother. Where you go, I go. Now and forever. Even unto the Field of Death."

I press my lips to his, sealing my oath with a kiss, but his lips are cold as stone.

"You are half my heart," he whispers, his sea-blue eyes twinkling as they did the day we first met.

"And you are mine," I tell him.

Ragnar smiles and closes his eyes. Then he is gone.

I lay my head upon his silent chest and hold him in my arms. Around our bodies, snow falls, unrelenting as a wolf. I no longer mind. The wolf-snow is our friend. It covers us in its great white fur, hiding us from all the evils of the night.

It buries us in a grave with our one full heart.

ORLANDO, FLORIDA

(THE PRESENT)

CHAPTER 36
JACKSON

The morning sun, bright and relentless, streams through my window. I can already tell it's gonna be another sweltering day. Even so, Riley shivers in my arms and pulls the bedcovers around us tighter. Neither of us can shake the chill from our bones.

"What the hell is happening to us?" he asks, his teeth chattering.

"I don't know."

When I woke up this morning, cold and confused on my bedroom floor, I found Riley lying next to me, unconscious. His skin was like ice, so I carried him to my bed and wrapped myself around him until the color returned to his cheeks and he opened his eyes.

It took him a full minute to understand where he was. Once he did, he immediately started telling me about his dream. A dream where he and I were Vikings, where a man named Erik the Red summoned a witch to predict the future, and where the two of us froze to death in a blizzard.

The more Riley told me, the more I felt like I was losing my mind. Not because I didn't believe him but because I already knew everything he was going to say. Because I'd had the same dream. The *exact* same dream. Down to the smallest detail.

Two identical dreams.

"Maybe we both saw the same movie and it got stuck in our brains?" I suggest.

Riley scoffs. "I've never seen a movie about gay Vikings. Have you?"

I shake my head.

"You don't have some medical condition, do you?" I ask. "I mean, nothing like this has happened to you before, right?"

"I was literally about to ask you the same thing."

"So the fainting and the dreams? They're new?"

"Yeah," Riley says. "They didn't start until . . ."

"Until when?"

Riley won't meet my eyes. "Until I met you."

A shiver steals down my spine, but I force myself to ignore it.

"Maybe the dreams are—shit, what's the word? Coach used it all the time. When you're sick but it's all in your head?"

"Psychosomatic?" Riley suggests.

"Yeah, psychosomatic. We've both been under a lot of stress. Maybe the fainting and the nightmares are just our bodies' way of coping."

"That doesn't explain how we could have the same dream."

No, it doesn't. "So what do you think is happening?" I ask.

Riley opens his mouth, then seems to think better of it. I watch him wrestle with his thoughts before surrendering with a defeated sigh. "Maybe . . . maybe they're *not* dreams."

"What do you mean?"

"Okay, don't laugh. But what happened last night, it didn't feel like a dream. It felt more like—a memory. Like I was remembering something that happened."

"How could it be something that happened?"

Riley shakes his head. "I don't know. But that dream I had about us in Pompeii felt the same way. It was like I was remembering something. Or *reliving* something."

"Reliving?" I can't help laughing. "What? You mean like a past life?"

Riley lifts his head off my chest and looks into my eyes. "Yeah."

I want to laugh again, but something in Riley's expression stops me. "You're serious?"

"I know. It's crazy," he concedes. "But think about it. Ever since we met, we've had this connection, right? At the time, I thought it was just a really intense crush. But maybe it's something more. Maybe we feel like we've known each other forever because . . ."

"Because?"

"Because we have."

Riley holds my gaze, his piercing green eyes practically daring me to tell him he's wrong. But he has to be wrong. What he's suggesting is impossible.

"That's a really sweet idea," I begin, trying to select my words carefully so as not to hurt his feelings.

"But?"

"But past lives? That's kind of a stretch, isn't it? I mean, you said you wrote a paper on Pompeii for school, right? And I've watched literally every movie there is about World War Two. It makes sense that stuff would bleed over into our dreams."

"I've never heard of Brattahlid," Riley counters. "Or that other place, the one in Iceland."

"Húsavík."

"Húsavík! Exactly. I wouldn't even know how to spell that. But I *remember* it. I remember the farm we grew up on. I remember the taste of the porridge that your mother used to make. I remember the smell of burning houses when the village was destroyed. At least . . ." Riley sighs in frustration. "At least I *think* I do."

To my surprise, I find myself nodding in agreement. Because as much as I'd like to deny it, I remember those things too. All of them. And that shouldn't be possible.

"Okay, so what exactly are you suggesting?" I ask as my resistance to his theory begins to waver. "That we knew each other in a past life? *Multiple* past lives? And, what, we keep getting reincarnated?"

Riley falls into a thoughtful silence. "Do you remember what that witch said when we were being banished? She said, 'When one song ends, another always begins.'"

"And you think *we're* the song?"

"Maybe."

I shake my head. I can't believe I'm even considering this. "But why us? What makes us special?"

"I don't know. Maybe we're just—" Riley stops himself and blushes.

"Maybe we're just what?"

"Soulmates."

The word surprises me. I wasn't expecting it. And yet as soon as I hear it, something about it sounds undeniably *right*.

"I know that's a bit intense," Riley confesses with a shy smile. "But honestly, that's how I feel about you, Jackson. Before you moved to Orlando, my life was—I don't know how to describe it. It just felt . . . *wrong*."

"What do you mean, 'wrong'?"

"I don't know. Everything just felt *off*. Like something was missing. Or incomplete. It was like . . . like that video I sent you, the one about the kid who was color-blind. Do you remember? He could see fine, but everything was brown and gray."

I nod. "I remember."

"That's what my life was like. It was fine but colorless. Only I didn't know it was colorless until you came along. Then suddenly, everywhere I looked there were rainbows. Which is such a fucking gay thing to say. But it's true. You filled my world with color, Jackson. You made everything feel alive. You made *me* feel alive. It was like, being with you, I was finally living the life I was supposed to lead. If that's not a soulmate, I don't know what it is."

Riley's words leave me speechless. Everything he's saying about the way I make him feel, I understand. More than he knows.

"Sorry," he says, withdrawing into himself. "That was a lot. I shouldn't have—"

"I feel the same."

Riley looks at me in surprise. "You do?"

"I told you when we first met that I felt like I was living the wrong life. I never knew why until I met you. Then it was obvious." I slip my hand into his. "Any life I had would feel wrong if you weren't in it."

Riley breaks into a smile that I swear must come straight from his soul. The beauty of it—of him—takes my breath away. I wrap my arms around him and pull him into a long, aching kiss. Whatever questions we have about past lives and reincarnation will have to wait. We have more important things to attend to now.

Riley climbs on top of me and devours my mouth with kisses. The hunger of his lips against mine makes me desperate to taste every inch of him. I'm almost feverish with desire.

Thankfully, I'm not so far gone that I don't hear the very loud and very abrupt knocking on my bedroom door or my aunt's voice calling, "Jackson, are you up?"

"Shit!" Riley gasps, scrambling off me and diving under the covers.

I'm 90 percent certain I locked the door last night, but just in case I didn't, I bunch the bedspread over my groin in an effort to conceal my very obvious erection.

"I'm up!" I answer, the irony of that phrase not lost on me.

"I hope I didn't wake you," Aunt Rachel apologizes. Her tone is innocent and oblivious, but it isn't fooling anyone. I can practically hear the smirk on her face. "I just wanted to see what you'd like for your birthday breakfast. Since we had waffles yesterday, I was thinking omelets?"

"Sounds great," I reply. "I'll come to the kitchen in a few minutes, okay?"

"Okay." My aunt pauses. "Will anyone *else* be joining us?"

Riley turns so pink he looks sunburned and buries his face in my shoulder.

"Yes, Aunt Rachel, Riley will be joining us."

"Oh? Riley's still here? What a nice surprise!" she exclaims, not sounding at all surprised. "Well, breakfast should be on the table in about twenty minutes. I'm also planning to do a load of laundry if your sheets—"

"Oh my God, Aunt Rach, go away!" I shout. As lucky as I am to have a sex-positive aunt, this conversation is about to end me.

"Okay, kiddo, see you in a few minutes."

Aunt Rachel's footsteps fade down the hall, and I shake my head in exasperation. Then I turn to Riley, who's cringing so hard, he looks like he's about to curl up into a tight little ball of shame.

"That was *mortifying*!" He groans into my shoulder.

"It's fine," I assure him. "Don't worry about Aunt Rachel."

"I'm never going to be able to look her in the face again!"

With a laugh, I wrap Riley in my arms and try to soothe his embarrassment with a few chaste kisses. My aunt's unsubtle but totally effective bit of cockblocking has definitely killed the mood. But I don't mind. It feels good to just lie here with Riley in my arms.

Maybe it's on account of it being my birthday, or maybe it's on account of knowing I'll be spending that birthday with someone as incredible as Riley, but right now I feel like I don't have a care in the world. In fact, in this moment, I'm so ridiculously happy that I can almost forget about our crazy dreams.

Almost.

"Do you *really* think we had past lives?" I ask, my mind still wrestling to understand what happened last night. I can just about swallow the idea that Riley and I are soulmates. But reincarnation? That's magic. Fantasy. It's not real life.

"I don't know," Riley sighs. "Maybe not? But something weird is definitely going on."

"Oh, for sure," I agree. "But there has to be a logical explanation, right?"

Riley doesn't say anything, and we sink into silence.

It's wild to think that an hour ago, I woke up shivering on the bedroom floor, dazed and disoriented and half out of my mind with panic. Now I can hear Aunt Rachel banging pans around in the kitchen. I can smell bacon sizzling. Nothing about this moment feels strange or supernatural. If anything, it feels normal. Blissfully and boringly normal.

Then Riley shudders in my arms.

"What's the matter?" I ask.

"Sorry. I was thinking about our dreams."

"What about them?"

Riley hesitates. "Well, if we do have past lives, and if the dreams we've been having aren't dreams but actual memories of those lives, then . . ."

"Then what?"

Riley lifts his face off my chest and studies me carefully. "What do you think it means that we always die at the end?"

CHAPTER 37

RILEY

There's a queasy feeling in the pit of my stomach. I keep telling myself it's because of the criminal amount of bacon that I scarfed down at breakfast. But I don't think that's true. Mainly because, no matter how hard I try, I can't stop thinking about my dreams.

I wish I shared Jackson's certainty that they're nothing more than the by-product of our overstressed imaginations. But I can't shake the feeling that they're something more. A glimpse of the past, maybe. Or a warning about the future.

"Maybe it's an unfinished-business thing," I announce more to myself than Jackson as we cuddle on his living-room sofa.

"Unfinished business?"

Jackson pulls his gaze away from the morning cartoons we've been "ironically" watching since breakfast and stares up at me with his clear blue eyes. He looks so comfortable with his head resting in my lap, I hate disturbing him with my paranoid speculations. Especially when I'm aware of how insane they sound. But I can't help myself. I need to make sense of what happened last night.

"Yeah. You know how in movies, ghosts are always haunting a place because they can't move on? Because they have unfinished business? Maybe it's the same with reincarnation," I theorize. "Maybe in our first lives, we had something important that we needed to accomplish, but we didn't get to do it before we died, so the universe gave us a second chance."

"And then a third chance and a fourth chance?" Jackson teases, not bothering to hide the skepticism in his voice.

"Maybe."

"So life is like a video game? And we both get multiple do-overs until we, what, win?"

"I don't know," I sigh. When he puts it like that, it doesn't sound particularly plausible. But then, what explanation would?

Jackson must sense my frustration. He sits up on the sofa, clicks off the TV, and turns his full attention to me.

"I take it we're not done talking about this?" he asks, flashing me a patient if somewhat condescending smile.

I shrug and look away. I held my tongue all through breakfast this morning. Mostly because I didn't want Jackson's aunt to think her nephew was hooking up with a complete nutjob. But now that Miss Haines is sculpting in the garage and we have the house to ourselves, I feel like the possibility of us having had *multiple* past lives deserves some additional discussion. And frankly, I'm surprised Jackson doesn't.

"You aren't the least bit curious about what's happening to us?" I ask.

"Dude, of course I'm curious. But like I said, there's got to be a rational explanation."

"Does there?"

Jackson shakes his head and laughs. "Look, I know you want to believe that something supernatural is going on—"

"I never said supernatural." Although I guess I didn't *not* say supernatural.

"Okay, just for the sake of argument, let's say you're right, and reincarnation is real, and Fate or Destiny or *whatever* is throwing us a bone by giving us extra lives so we can finish our unresolved business, whatever that is. Why didn't Fate reincarnate us somewhere safe? Why put us in a plague or the middle of a world war?"

That's a good question. And I don't have a good answer. "Maybe it's just bad luck?" I suggest rather lamely.

"Bad luck?"

"Or maybe that's the trade-off? We get extra lives, but we have to deal with crazy shit like Vikings and Nazis."

"Okay," Jackson concedes with an amused snort. "But what's our unfinished business?"

Fuck, that's another good question.

As far as I can recall, the only thing I really wanted in my dreams was to be with Jackson. That's it. But Jackson and I are together. We got our happy ending. Does that mean we've finished our unfinished business?

Personally, I'd love nothing more than to believe that Fate is some big queer matchmaker. That it's so invested in Jackson and me as a couple that it's willing to suspend all the rules of science to bring us together over multiple lifetimes. But the logical part of my brain knows that's absurd. Not to mention completely narcissistic.

I mean, what could possibly be so special about Jackson and me? Out of all the people in the history of the world, why would the two of us be given the opportunity to find each other over and over and over again?

Assuming that's even what's happening.

For all I know, Jackson could be right. There could be a perfectly rational explanation for the fainting and the dreams. Something scientific or medical, like brain tumors. That would be just our luck. Though in a way, brain damage would be a relief. It'd make a hell of a lot more sense than *reincarnation*.

"Hey, where'd you go?" Jackson asks. He slips his hand into

mine and gives it a comforting squeeze. I must have spaced out for a bit.

"Sorry," I tell him. "I'm just trying to figure out if we're dying, insane, or cursed."

Jackson erupts in laughter. "Why are those our only options?"

"What other option is there?"

"We're sleep-deprived? Stressed out? So in sync that we have the same dreams?"

"You really don't think it's anything more than that?"

Jackson shakes his head. "Look—do I know why we keep fainting and having these weird-ass dreams? No. But I do know reincarnation isn't real. And even if it were—even if we've somehow lived multiple lives together—would that necessarily be a bad thing? Why can't it be something good?"

"How could it be something good? It would mean we've died at least three times."

Jackson smiles. "True. But it would also mean that we got to live three extra bonus lives. And I kind of like the idea of spending more than one lifetime with you."

Oh. Wow.

That might be the most romantic thing that anyone has ever said to me. In fact, I'm pretty sure my insides just melted into a sappy gay soup that's about to spill out of me and ruin this sofa.

"I guess when you put it like that," I say, lacing my fingers through his, "reincarnation doesn't sound too terrible."

Jackson leans forward, and when he kisses me, I no longer care how many past lives we might have had. Because *this* life, the one I get to share with Jackson here and now, is more than enough.

It's everything.

I climb onto Jackson's lap, straddle his hips, and feel his strong hands slide up under my shirt. It occurs to me that we never got around to "celebrating" Jackson's birthday, and I am more than ready to correct that omission.

In fact, I'm just about to suggest that we head back to his room before we get too carried away when our make-out session is once again interrupted. Not by Jackson's aunt but by his phone. With a groan of frustration, he pries his lips away from mine and pulls the buzzing culprit from his pocket.

"Huh," he says, staring at the screen in surprise. "It's my mom."

"She must be calling to wish you a happy birthday," I say as I slide off his lap.

"Guess I'd better answer."

"Don't worry." I wink. "We can finish what we started when you're done."

"We'd better."

Jackson kisses me again, playfully biting my bottom lip. Then he hops off the sofa and heads to his room to answer the call.

I take out my own phone and decide it's time to answer some of the five hundred texts that I have. One is from Dad asking what time he should expect me home today and if I had fun at Duy's, which is where I sort of implied that I'd be spending the night yesterday when I texted him to say I wouldn't be coming home after the Glorious Peccadilloes concert.

The other four hundred and ninety-nine texts are from Duy, Tala, and Audrey, who for the past umpteen hours have been demanding to know why Jackson and I bailed on the concert and if we're okay.

I definitely owe them an explanation, but as I start to reply, it occurs to me that Jackson and I haven't really had the chance to discuss what he feels comfortable telling people about our relationship and his sexuality. Obviously, he doesn't have a problem with his aunt knowing about us. And he certainly didn't mind making out with me in a park full of strangers. Still, I don't feel right outing him to my friends without discussing it with him first.

It takes me a surprisingly long time to craft a response that's both honest and vague but not so vague that my friends will get suspicious and think I'm hiding something. Basically, I tell them that after my encounter with Alex and Jackson's reunion with Micaela, neither of us felt up for a concert, so we decided to crash at his place.

I wish I could tell them the full story. But that's something I'll have to do with Jackson. When he's ready.

"Sorry that took so long," Jackson mumbles when he wanders back into the room.

"That's okay," I say as I finish up my text. "I'm just letting the gang know we're still alive. How was your call?"

"Not great."

The tightness in Jackson's voice causes me to look up from my phone, and I see that his eyes are red. Has he been crying?

"What happened?" I ask, reaching for his hand as he slumps down beside me on the sofa. It's like someone's thrown a switch. All the light has gone out of his face.

"My parents asked me how I'd be celebrating my birthday. I didn't want to lie so I told them I'd be hanging out with you. They asked if you were a new friend, and I told them . . ." Jackson shakes his head and sighs. "I told them you were my boyfriend."

My jaw drops.

I'm not sure which of those two bombshells to process first, that Jackson used the B-word to describe me or that he just came out to his parents. Both should be cause for celebration. Instead, he looks devastated.

"You told your parents about us?" I ask, not quite believing my ears.

"Yeah. That's the part of the conversation that didn't go so well."

"What did they say?"

"Short version?" Jackson snorts. "My mother said I was being selfish, ridiculous, and immature. And my father asked why I was so hell-bent on ruining my life."

"Fuck. *I'm sorry*," I say, pulling him into a hug.

Jackson shrugs in my arms but I can tell how upset he is. "It's my own fault. I shouldn't have sprung it on them like that. I thought if I slipped it into the conversation like it wasn't a big deal, they wouldn't freak out, you know? But I should've known better. They're not like Aunt Rachel or Micaela. I should've known they'd react like this. I just..."

"Just what?"

"I just thought after six months of seeing me be utterly miserable, they might want to know that I'm finally in a good place. I thought they'd be happy for me. But no. They couldn't even give me that. Not even on my fucking birthday."

Jackson buries his face in my shoulder, and my heart breaks for him. I wish I could take his hurt away, but I can't. All I can do is be here for him and give him all the love and acceptance that his parents are incapable of.

"Maybe they just need time," I say, trying to reassure him. "When Tala first started dating Audrey, it took the Youssefs months to accept that she was queer. But they did."

Jackson doesn't say anything. He doesn't have to. I know all too well what he's feeling.

My mother didn't cut me out of her life because I was gay, but she did cut me out. And that hurt. It hurt for a really long time. If I'm honest, some days it still hurts. But I got through it. And so will Jackson.

And who knows? Maybe once they've had a chance to cool down, his parents will get their shit together and apologize. But even if they don't, Jackson won't be alone. He'll have me. He'll always have me.

And whether or not we've had past lives, I'm just thankful that I can be here for him in this life.

CHAPTER 38

JACKSON

After I told my father I wanted to quit football, change schools, and move in with Aunt Rachel, he didn't talk to me for a month. I wonder how long the silent treatment will last this time now that I've told him about Riley.

So far, it's been three days. No calls. No texts. Nothing.

Aunt Rachel got an earful, though. A few hours after he chewed me out on my birthday, Dad called her. She wouldn't tell me what he said, but I'm guessing it wasn't good. All she said afterward was "Your parents are going to need some time" and "You'll always have a home here."

So, yeah, not a great sign.

Thing is, I should've known my father would react this way. That one time I wore a dress for Halloween, he nearly lost his mind. And that was a joke.

But my mother? My mother has never had a problem with gay people. Her hairdresser is gay. So is her florist and her cardio instructor. And, yeah, I know that's fucking cliché, but it proves she's not homophobic. At least I *thought* it did.

But I guess it's one thing to have a gay hairstylist and another to have a gay son.

If that's even what I am.

I should probably figure that out at some point since it's costing me my relationship with my parents. But honestly? I don't care what I am. I care about Riley. So whatever that makes me, that's what I am.

If my parents can't get on board with that, that's their problem. I'm not gonna give up the one thing—the one person—that makes me happy just because they don't approve. They can give me the silent treatment all they want. I don't need their noise. I don't need anything. Except Riley.

"Wow, someone's in serious study mode," a voice calls from behind me, jolting me out of my thoughts.

I look up from the pile of books strewn across my table in the Winter Park library and turn to see Tala hovering over my shoulder.

"Oh. Uh. Hi," I say, surprised to see her. "What are you doing here?"

"Getting a head start on my senior thesis. What are you doing here?"

I'm not sure how to answer that. The truth is I'm here because I need the distraction. Sitting home all day waiting for Riley to get off work, I was starting to go a little stir-crazy. I kept replaying that conversation with my parents on a loop in my head, and I knew it was gonna drive me nuts if I didn't do something to take my mind off it.

That's when I thought about Riley and his whole theory about past lives and reincarnation. He hasn't mentioned it since my birthday, but I can tell he's still freaked out about the dreams. Some nights when we're hanging out or watching a movie, he'll just go *quiet* and get this intense, faraway look in his eyes like he's trying to solve some impossible puzzle.

I know he's gonna keep obsessing about these dreams until he gets answers, so I figured I might as well try to get them for him. It's the least I can do. Riley's been so incredible these past couple of days, calling me every morning before he goes to work and coming straight over when he's done. He's really been there for me. And I want to do something to show him how much I appreciate his support.

That's why I texted him this morning and asked him to recommend a library with a good history section. The way I see it, Riley's freaking out because he thinks our dreams might be memories, so if I can prove that the crazy shit in our dreams didn't actually go down the way we dreamed it—like if we got some major historical detail wrong—that'll be proof that our dreams aren't memories but random nonsense. Then Riley can stop worrying.

That's the plan, at least. Only I can't say all that to Tala.

"I have to write a report," I tell her after way too long a pause. "It's kind of embarrassing, but I got an incomplete in my history class last semester."

"Oh no!"

"Yeah. I never turned in my final assignment," I lie. "But my teacher said that if I wrote something over the summer, he'd consider changing my grade."

"That was really nice of him."

"Yeah. He's a cool teacher."

Tala grabs one of the books off my table and reads the title on the spine. "'The Life and Times of Erik the Red.' You're writing a paper about Vikings?"

"Yeah." I roll my eyes like it's the lamest subject in the world. "My teacher assigned the topic."

"Learn anything interesting?"

"Not yet. I only just started reading," I answer truthfully. "I keep getting distracted."

"Oh, sorry!" Tala says, quickly setting the book down. "I'll let you get back to your research."

"No, I didn't mean you," I assure her. "I'm just having trouble focusing this afternoon. It's kind of been a rough week."

Tala tilts her head in concern. "Is everything all right?"

I start to say no. I don't want to burden her with my drama. But then I remember what Riley said about her family and how they reacted when she told them she liked girls.

"Actually, do you have a minute to talk?" I ask.

"Sure," she chirps, sliding into the chair across from me. "What's up?"

"So, this might come a little out of left field," I begin, trying to sound as casual as I can, "but I wanted to ask you about your parents."

Her brow furrows. "My parents?"

"Yeah. Riley told me that when you first started dating Audrey, your parents weren't exactly on board. And I was wondering, you know, how you dealt with that?"

"Oh." My question seems to take her aback.

"Sorry. Is that too personal? I shouldn't have asked."

"No, it's okay," she says, recovering with a smile. "And Riley's right. It was a definite adjustment for my parents. It still is sometimes."

"What do you mean?"

"*Queer, Muslim,* and *Egyptian* aren't words that are typically used in the same sentence. At least, not in my family. I mean, the mosque we go to is somewhat progressive. But there's still a lot of shame and confusion in the Muslim community when it comes to queerness and homosexuality. And sometimes it's difficult for my parents to navigate that."

"Yeah. I bet."

"Don't get me wrong, my parents love me," Tala clarifies. "And they really like Audrey. In fact, on some level, I think my dad is actually relieved I'm dating a girl. He doesn't have to worry about becoming a grandfather before I graduate."

We both laugh, but a second later Tala's smile falters.

"Of course, my parents still refer to Audrey as my 'friend' no matter how many times I correct them. And sometimes my mom says things that make me think she's okay with me dating a girl so long as when I finally decide to settle down and marry, I end up with a guy."

"Oh. I'm sorry."

"It's a process. Some days my parents are totally fine with having a queer daughter, and we'll watch *Heartstopper* together, and everything seems great."

"And other days?"

"Other days not so much." She shrugs. "But the important thing to me is that they're trying. I see them putting in the effort to educate themselves. I know they want to understand me. Even if they still have certain hang-ups or they occasionally say things that make me want to pull my hair out, I know their hearts are in the right place. I know they love me. And that makes all the difference."

Tala smiles. It's a smile filled with hope. I want to return it, but all I can do is stare at my hands and wonder if my parents will ever make half the effort that the Youssefs are making. Given how they spoke to me on my birthday and how they haven't spoken to me since, it's hard to imagine they will.

"Did that answer your question?" Tala asks.

"Yeah. It did. Thanks."

"Great." She pauses. "Do you mind if I ask *you* a question?"

"Uh . . . sure."

"Does your question about what it's like to be in a same-sex relationship when you have conservative parents have anything to do with all the time you've been spending with my best pal Riley?"

I feel the heat rise in my cheeks. Even if I tried to deny the implication—which I don't want to do—Tala wouldn't believe me. My face is a dead giveaway. As is the oddly proud smile that I'm unable to hold back.

"Yeah," I hear myself confess. "We're sort of . . . dating."

Tala gasps and covers her mouth with her hands. "I *knew* it!"

I can't help laughing out loud, and Tala instantly blushes.

"Oh, sorry! I mean, congratulations!"

"I guess it's sort of obvious that we're into each other, huh?"

"*So* obvious. Duy wanted to say something, but I said no, let them figure it out themselves. And you did! I'm so excited!"

An old man at a nearby table shushes Tala, at which point we both remember we're in a library.

"This is such great news. We need to celebrate!" Tala whispers.

"Celebrate?" I shake my head. "*Wow.*"

"Wow what?"

"Nothing. I just wish my parents had had that reaction."

Tala's face falls. "Did they not take the news well when you told them? Is that why Riley asked me to come check on you?"

"He did what?"

"Oops." Tala once again covers her mouth with her hands. "I wasn't supposed to say anything. But Riley texted me an hour ago and said you were a bit down. He asked me to swing by here and check on you."

I shake my head. "That sneaky little . . ." But I can't even pretend to be angry. I'm too touched by Riley's thoughtfulness.

"As for your parents," Tala continues, "I'm sorry they didn't react the way you'd hoped. That *sucks*. But it just gives us more of a reason to celebrate, don't you think?"

The idea of celebrating the fact that Riley and I are a couple, while incredibly sweet, is something that Old Jackson would find totally embarrassing. But Jackson 2.0 is very much aware that having Riley in his life might be the most momentous thing that's ever happened to him. And if that's the case, why not celebrate?

Even if I don't believe in reincarnation or past lives, we still found each other in this life. And right now, despite what my parents think, that honestly feels like a miracle.

CHAPTER 39

RILEY

"Do you mind if I take off a little early today?" I ask my dad as I power down my laptop. It's only three o'clock, but it's Friday, and I'm eager to get a head start on the weekend.

Dad looks up from his desk, where he's reading over some depositions. "Got some exciting plans?"

"Duy, Tala, Audrey, and I are throwing Jackson a coming-out/belated-birthday party, since we weren't able to celebrate it properly last weekend."

"That's nice of you." Then, with a sly smile, he adds, "Should I expect to see you at home at all this weekend? Or will you be otherwise engaged?"

"I plead the Fifth."

I've gone over to Jackson's house every day after work and stayed until it was time for bed. Dad has a strict no-sleepovers policy during the workweek, but with the weekend coming, there's nothing to prevent me from spending the next forty-eight hours in uninterrupted bliss with Jackson.

Also, it's been a full five days with no nightmares or fainting spells, so I'm feeling cautiously optimistic that all that weirdness, whatever it was, is a thing of the past. Of course, I'll feel even better if we manage to get through the weekend without any incidents. Saturdays and Sundays, I've noticed, tend to be when things go sideways for Jackson and me. But if the next forty-eight hours are nightmare-and-fainting-free, I might finally be able to put all this past-life paranoia behind me.

"Well, have fun with your friends," Dad says with a chuckle as I get up to leave. "And tell Jackson hello for me. Maybe someday you'll bring him by the house so I can actually meet the boy my son is dating. Assuming, of course, it wouldn't be too mortifying for you to introduce your boyfriend to your tragically uncool and very put-upon father?"

In the doorway, I turn back to my dad, preparing a clever parting shot. But when I see the genuine smile on his face, my sarcastic comeback dies in my throat. As smothering as my father's love can be, I know I'm incredibly lucky to have it.

Not only do I have a parent who loves and accepts me as I am, but that same parent actively wants to meet my boyfriend. On top of that, Dad spends sixty-plus hours a week fighting for queer rights. If there was ever a son who won the parental lottery, it's me. And standing here in his office, I can't help feeling overcome with gratitude.

"What's this for?" Dad asks with a surprised laugh after I march over to his desk and throw my arms around him. "I already said you could leave early."

"You're a good dad," I tell him.

My sudden and very out-of-character display of affection must throw him because he doesn't say anything back. He just returns the hug in silence.

"Sorry," I say, wiping a tear from my cheek as I pull away.

"You never have to apologize for being nice to me," Dad jokes. "And for the record, Ri, you're a good son."

I shake my head. We both know that's not true.

"I'm sorry I've been such a shitty intern. I know you were really excited for me to come work with you, and I've been totally half-assing it. But I'm going to do better. From now on, I'm going to buckle down and work twice as hard. I promise."

Dad takes off his glasses and massages the bridge of his nose.

"I've actually been meaning to talk to you about that," he says. "I've noticed that you've been a bit low-energy around the office. A bit distracted. In fact, most days I've been getting the distinct impression that you'd rather be anywhere but here. So I wanted to check in and see how you were feeling about, well, everything."

With a pang of guilt, I feel my entire body deflate in my cobalt-blue suit. I should've known this conversation was coming. You can't show up for work every day acting like a depressed narcoleptic without people noticing. It's honestly a testament to Dad's patience that he didn't say anything sooner.

"I'm sorry," I mutter, too ashamed to look him in the eye. "I'll do better. I didn't mean to disappoint you."

"It's not about disappointing me," Dad says, putting a hand on my shoulder. "It's about making sure that you're somewhere you want to be doing something that you want to do. Now, me, I love being a lawyer. I love the work I do, and I love sharing that work with you. But if that's not what you want to do with your life, if there's something else you'd rather pursue, I hope you know you can tell me. I'm not trying to turn you into a mini version of me. I want you to be your own person. You know that, right?"

I literally don't know what to say. Dad always seemed so eager for me to follow in his footsteps. It never occurred to me that he'd be okay with me veering off on my own path. Especially when I don't even know where that path would lead.

Maybe that's why, even now when I'm being presented with this chance for freedom, it feels selfish to take it.

"The work you do is so important," I say as shame washes over me.

"It is," Dad agrees. "But it's work I choose to do."

"It feels wrong for me not to choose it too."

Dad's brow furrows in confusion. "Why?"

"Seriously? What kind of person would I be if I was like, 'Yeah, I know the world is full of suffering and injustice, but I'm going to let my dad fight all those battles for me. Later!'"

Dad puts on his glasses and shakes his head. "Ri, I knew the world was a mess when your mother and I chose to bring you into it. If anything, I'm the one with the responsibility to fight those battles and fix this country precisely so that you don't have to grow up in the same mess that my generation did. That's my job as a parent—to make the world a better and safer place *for you*. Your only job is to live your life however you want and with whomever you want. That's what I'm fighting for. For you to be the man you want to be. For you to be *happy*."

I don't have words to express everything in my heart right now. I pull Dad into another hug as a fresh round of tears stream down my face.

"Thank you," I manage to whisper between sniffles.

"You don't have to thank me," Dad says. "You just have to live your life. I'll be proud of you whatever you do."

CHAPTER 40

JACKSON

"This is the most horrifying thing I've ever seen!" Riley whimpers, turning away from the TV, where a horde of zombies are gleefully disemboweling the president of the United States in the Oval Office. I wrap my arms around him and let out a laugh as he buries his face in my chest for protection.

When Riley and his friends asked how I wanted to spend my birthday do-over/coming-out party, I told them I wanted a simple, quiet, low-key evening at home, no roller-skating, no karaoke, no carnivals. I just wanted to order pizza and watch one of my favorite horror movies, *Capitol Riot: Zombie Insurrection*. Which, it turns out, is a lot bloodier than I remembered.

"Do you want me to turn it off?" I ask.

Riley shakes his head but nestles closer. "No, it's okay, we can keep watching. But I think you might need to kiss some more courage into me?"

"Again?"

"Is that a problem?"

"Not for me." I tilt Riley's face up to mine and press my lips against his—which earns us a collective groan from the room. Then Duy, Tala, and Audrey pelt us with popcorn.

"Boo!"

"Gross!"

"Take it outside!"

I laugh and pick a salty kernel out of Riley's hair.

"You guys seriously need to cool it," Audrey chides us from the floor, where she and Tala are spread out on my aunt's homemade afghan and some cushions. "All the PDA was cute when we were having cake and opening presents, but this inability to keep your hands off each other is almost as nauseating as that scene where the First Lady got pecked to death by that zombie bald eagle."

"Are we being a lot?" I ask.

Duy raises an eyebrow. "You're being *the most*."

"Don't listen to them," Riley scoffs, wrapping his arms around me and kissing my cheek. "They're just jealous. They've never seen true happiness before."

This earns us another round of boos and an even more violent pelting of popcorn.

"Okay, okay, stop!" I laugh. "We'll cool it."

Duy and Audrey glare at us, but Tala lowers her fistful of popcorn and smiles. "Just for the record, we are genuinely happy for you guys."

"Obviously, we're *happy* for you," Duy grumbles as they lounge back in my aunt's recliner and resume texting Caleb, who's vacationing in Maine this week. "We just don't want you to be *more* happy than us."

This earns Duy an eye-roll and a popcorn-pelting from Tala.

"Well, if it evens things out," I tell them, "my parents still aren't talking to me."

The room goes silent (aside from the screams on the TV, where the zombies are now treating Congress like an all-you-can-eat buffet). My self-deprecating joke, which I thought was funny, has instantly killed the party vibe.

"You still haven't heard from them?" Tala asks, sitting up in concern.

"Oh. Uh, no," I mumble. "Not yet. But it's fine."

"It's not fine," Audrey huffs indignantly. "Your parents are assholes."

"Babe, let's maybe not call other people's parents assholes," Tala suggests.

"But they are! They're assholes!" Audrey doubles down. "Seriously, if you're a parent, you have one job—to love your child unconditionally. That's it. And if you can't do that, if your love comes with conditions about who your kid can be or who they can love, then you shouldn't have kids in the first place."

"I think what Audrey's trying to say," Tala adds diplomatically, "is that we're sorry your parents are still struggling to come to terms with the person you're becoming. But like I said before, sometimes it takes time."

Riley slides his hand into mine and squeezes. "And in the meantime, you've got me."

"And me!" Tala adds, hopping up onto the sofa and pulling me into a hug.

"Me too!" Duy shouts, vaulting onto the sofa and into my lap.

"Come on, Audrey," Riley calls as he wraps his arms around me. "Group hug!"

Audrey snorts. "You're all ridiculous." But a second later, she climbs onto the sofa and joins our popcorn-scented dogpile.

Someone's knee is in my groin. Someone else's elbow jabs my ribs. I don't think I've ever been this physically uncomfortable in my life. Or this happy.

"I am legitimately obsessed with your friends," I tell Riley a few hours later when we're cleaning up after the party. "You're really lucky to have them."

"I think it's safe to call them your friends too," he says with a chuckle as he sweeps some stray popcorn into a dustpan.

"I didn't want to assume."

"You're joking, right? At this point, I'm pretty sure my friends prefer you to me."

"That makes sense."

"Hey!" Riley barks as he swats me with his broom.

"What?" I laugh. "I'm being a supportive boyfriend. I'm agreeing with you!"

Riley scowls like an angry little hedgehog, so I set down the empty pizza boxes that I was about to carry out to the recycle bin and pull him into a bear hug. "All jokes aside," I say as he melts into my embrace, "tonight was just what I needed. So thank you. And you're right, I *am* lucky to have such incredible friends. Not to mention an even more incredible boyfriend who's smart and funny and very, *very* kissable."

"Good save." Riley gives me a quick peck on the lips, then rests his head against my shoulder.

I love seeing him so relaxed. I wish I could claim some of the credit for that, but so far, my attempt to put his fears about our past lives to rest hasn't yielded much success. I was hoping by now to have poked enough holes in the historical accuracy of our Viking dream to make him realize we'd made it all up. But from what I read about Erik the Red and Greenland, our dreams were surprisingly accurate. Even the witch's predictions about the future turned out to be spot-on. Erik's son did come home safely from America. And the settlement at Brattahlid did collapse after Erik's death.

Not that that *proves* anything. It just means I need to do more research.

Next week I'll start looking into London during the Blitz. If that doesn't turn up anything I can use to debunk Riley's theory, I'll move on to Pompeii. I know there's got to be something I'm missing, some obvious anachronism or detail that's just plain wrong and that'll prove without a shadow of a doubt that our dreams really are just that: dreams.

Then again, if Riley stays as happy and relaxed as he is right now in my arms, maybe I won't need to convince him of anything. Maybe he'll forget his crazy theory on his own. And we can just enjoy being together without anything hanging over our heads to spoil it.

Well, anything other than my parents.

"I'm sorry your mom and dad still aren't talking to you," Riley says as if reading my mind.

"Don't be," I tell him, gently pulling back so he can look into my eyes and see just how okay I am. "At this point, I'm with Audrey. They're assholes. And until they get their shit together and stop being assholes, I'm not gonna waste my time on them."

"Still, they're your parents. I feel like if they could just see how happy you are, they might change their minds."

"Maybe I should text them some photos," I joke.

But a second later, the idea of sending my parents proof of my happiness—of the amazing life that I've built for myself—doesn't seem so laughable. I plop down on the sofa and pull out my phone.

"You're not seriously going to do it?" Riley asks, sitting beside me.

"Why not? The whole reason my parents aren't talking to me is because they want to punish me, right? They want me to feel bad so that I'll come crawling back to them and apologize for daring to defy them. But if I show them that I'm doing just fine without them, maybe they'll realize that I'm not the one who needs to change."

"Or it might piss them off even more."

I shrug. "So it's win-win."

I start scrolling through my photos, trying to find the perfect pic to send them. There's a group shot of Duy, Tala, Audrey, Riley, and me eating pizza that Aunt Rachel took before she cleared out for the night so we could have the house to ourselves. Then there's a photo of Duy presenting me with the rainbow cake they baked. There are also a bunch of selfies of Riley and me kissing and snuggling on the sofa. In almost every photo, I'm smiling harder than I've ever smiled in my entire life, and I want my parents to see that happiness. I want them to see me.

"Fuck it," I say with a laugh. I select every photo from tonight as well as the unedited photo of Riley and me from Rink-O-Rama and send the entire batch to my parents.

Riley gasps in disbelief. "I can't believe you just did that."

"Believe it. Your boyfriend has zero fucks to give."

Riley leans forward and nuzzles his face against mine. "Have I ever told you how hot it is when you refer to yourself as my boyfriend?"

"No. Tell me."

"How about I show you instead?"

Riley takes my face in his hands and pulls me into a kiss. Not to be outdone, I bury my face in his neck and kiss his throat, which I've recently discovered is his favorite place to be kissed.

Sure enough, he lets out a little moan, and his breath comes out in hot, quick gasps against my ear. I feel the heat rising off his skin as he wraps his arms around me and runs his fingers through my hair.

I'm about to suggest we continue things in my bedroom when Riley goes stiff in my arms. I feel a shiver run down his spine and his shoulders tense, and I pull back to see what's wrong.

Riley is staring at the TV. We left it on while we were cleaning up but neither of us were paying much attention to it. Now, though, Riley can't take his eyes off it.

"What's the matter?" I ask.

Riley grabs the remote and turns up the volume. A commercial is playing, some low-rent ad for a cheesy psychic named Jocasta

Devereaux. Apparently, she's gonna be in town tomorrow at the Hilton offering some sort of seminar on "how to unlock the power of your past lives."

That gets my attention, but I'm still not sure why Riley is so mesmerized. Not until I take a closer look at the psychic. With her bright red hair, pale skin, and high cheekbones, Jocasta Devereaux looks oddly familiar. Then it hits me.

"It's her." I gasp, the blood running cold in my veins. "It's Ulfhild."

CHAPTER 41

RILEY

"What are we gonna do if we can't get in to see her?" Jackson asks as we storm into the gleaming, sun-dappled lobby of the Hilton.

"Don't worry. We're going to see her."

Jackson looks unconvinced, and I don't blame him. At this very moment, Ulfhild or Jocasta Devereaux or whatever she's calling herself these days is giving a demonstration of her "psychic abilities" on the stage of the hotel's largest auditorium. Unfortunately, when Jackson and I went online to buy tickets last night, we found the show was completely sold out. All five hundred seats.

Thankfully, I have a plan to get us in. Or, rather, I have Farouk.

"Hey, Farouk," I call out, marching over to the concierge desk where Tala's brother is working. Farouk is five years older than Tala, and if I'm honest, I used to have a slight crush on him despite the overwhelming evidence that he is 100 percent straight. With his clear olive skin, sharp jawline, and head of luscious black hair styled in a very sexy pompadour, he looks like someone you'd see playing the romantic lead in a movie, not someone who spends his days helping the hotel's incredibly entitled guests book tickets to Orlando's various theme parks.

"Hello there, Riley," Farouk says, cocking his head to the side the same way that Tala does when she's surprised. "What are you doing here?"

"We need your help," I answer, getting straight to the point: "We need to see Jocasta Devereaux."

Farouk raises an eyebrow, looking very sexy and faintly amused. "Jocasta Devereaux? Really? You never struck me as someone who went in for all that astrology nonsense."

"I'm not. We're not. This is Jackson, by the way. But we really need to see her. It's kind of an emergency."

Farouk shakes his head and chuckles. "I'm sorry. I'd love to help you, but the event is completely sold out. Besides, it started forty-five minutes ago, so you've already missed half of it."

I know we've missed half of it. That's because we sat in traffic for ninety minutes due to an overturned truck that shut down I-4. But I don't really care about whatever show Jocasta is putting on for her fans. I've had a front-row seat to her magic act before, and I'm not exactly eager to repeat that experience.

That being said, Jackson and I want answers. And right now, the only person who might have those answers is the witch who stabbed us in the back a thousand years ago. Assuming, of course, that Jocasta *is* Ulfhild. Which we won't know for sure unless we talk to her.

"We just need to see her. Just for a few minutes," I explain to Farouk. "If you could get us backstage so we could meet her—"

"Sorry, Riley. I can tell that you and your friend are big fans, but I can't get you backstage. It's against hotel policy. If anyone found out, I could get in big trouble. You understand."

"We understand," Jackson says, putting a hand on my shoulder, a signal for me to let the matter go. But I'm not ready to give up. Not yet.

I let out a deep sigh in an attempt to do my best impression of a defeated but gracious loser. "Yeah. Of course. Sorry for bothering you." Farouk nods, and I start to turn away. Then, as if the thought only just occurred to me, I say, "Oh, by the way, how's Becky?"

Farouk's smile falters slightly. "Uh... Becky's good. Thanks for asking."

"Cool. That's really cool. Tala says you guys are ridiculously cute together. She's really rooting for the two of you."

"I'm rooting for us too."

"You must be," I continue. "I mean, you got her name tattooed on your chest, right?"

Farouk nervously clears his throat. "What?"

"That's what Tala told me. She said that's how she knew you must be really serious about Becky. Because tattoos are haram, right? And if your parents ever found out that you had one, they would totally lose their shit. At least that's what Tala told me."

I can see Farouk working out the implications of what I'm saying, and though I feel bad for blackmailing my friend's brother, I don't have a choice. I'm not leaving this hotel without speaking to Jocasta. Of course I would *never* in a million years actually tell the Youssefs about Farouk's tattoo. I'm not the world's biggest asshole. But I'm counting on him not knowing me well enough to call my bluff.

"Riley, what exactly are you saying?" Farouk asks, narrowing his eyes.

"I'm not saying anything. I'm just complimenting you on being a really good person. Like, you know how important it is to follow the rules, right? But you're also not afraid to bend the rules. You know, when something's *important*."

Using his electronic key card, Farouk unlocks the backstage door of the auditorium so Jackson and I can slip inside. "If anyone asks," he whispers sharply, "I've never met you, I have no idea who you are, and you snuck in here on your own. Got it?"

Without waiting for a response, Farouk closes the door. I feel incredibly guilty about blackmailing my way backstage. Hopefully when this is all over, I can find a way to make it up to him (and to Tala, who's going to be pissed when she finds out that I used something she told me in confidence to extort her brother).

Right now, though, my priority is Jocasta.

There aren't very many people milling around backstage, which is convenient. It's also dark, which further decreases the chances of someone spotting Jackson and me and kicking us out. Not that anyone would notice us even if all the lights were on. The few people who are standing in the wings seem too engrossed by what's happening onstage.

There, seated in a large wooden chair decorated with ornately carved wolf heads, is Jocasta. Her eyes are closed, and her palms are turned upward in that rather stereotypical pose of spiritual communion. She's wearing a pink Chanel power suit and her red hair has been styled into an angled bob, but there's no denying that the woman onstage has the same sharp cheekbones and the same gaunt figure as the woman from our dreams.

"It's definitely her," Jackson whispers.

I nod, and a familiar chill creeps down my spine. A part of me was hoping that we'd made a mistake about Jocasta. If we'd been wrong, if our eyes had been playing tricks on us and she *wasn't* the woman from our dreams, there would have been a good chance that I was also wrong about everything else—the past lives, the reincarnation.

But I wasn't wrong. About any of it. A woman from our nightmares who should've died a thousand years ago is standing in front of us. Which means either she really is a witch or she's been reincarnated like Jackson and me.

I'm not sure which option scares me more.

Trying to stay calm, I peek out into the packed auditorium and scan the audience. There's a pretty even mix of men and women, of old and young, that spans almost every race and ethnicity. The only common denominator is that every audience member is riveted to their seat, waiting breathlessly for Jocasta to speak.

"There's someone here today who's name begins with a *D*," she announces suddenly, her voice breaking the silence of the auditorium and surprising me with its unexpected Southern drawl. It has nothing of Ulfhild's cold, austere tone. In fact, she sounds less like a mystical seeress and more like a posh socialite from Atlanta.

"It's a woman, I believe," Jocasta continues, eyes still closed. "A woman facing a difficult decision about not one man but two?"

In the audience, a woman gasps and cautiously rises from her seat. She looks about thirty and has long stylish locs cascading over one side of her head; the other side is buzzed almost bare. Duy would describe her look as "effortlessly and intimidatingly cool," though right now, she's completely in awe of Jocasta.

"I think that's me," the woman says. "I'm Dionne."

Jocasta opens her eyes. She nods and beckons the woman to the stage. It's only then that I notice the second, smaller chair next to hers. Dionne sits in the chair, and Jocasta tilts her head as if listening to something that only she can hear.

"You find yourself at a crossroads," Jocasta announces. It's not a question but the woman nods in agreement. "Two men are vying for your heart, each with an equal claim to your affection."

Dionne blinks in amazement. "Yes."

"These men—you feel a strong connection with them both. Both support your dreams and inspire you to be your best self. You believe that with either of these men at your side, you could accomplish great things. Especially in your career. Both of these men work in the same artistic world as you, I believe, which means that a union with either would be both a romantic partnership and a professional one. This, of course, is something you have always craved."

Again, it's not a question, and Dionne's mouth falls open. "How did you..."

Jocasta waves dismissively as if to say how she knows what she knows is as obvious as it is irrelevant. "The only difference between these men is that one is someone you have known all your life and the other is a more recent acquaintance. With the former there is a sense of stability, security, and comfort stemming from a life of shared experiences. With the other, there is a passion and an intensity that comes from the newness of the relationship. But there is also a fear and distrust of that passion."

Dionna looks like a bobblehead. She hasn't stopped nodding since Jocasta started speaking. "Exactly."

Jocasta chuckles to herself as if she's impressed with her own abilities. "This is not the first time that you have found yourself in such a dilemma. Throughout the many lives that you have lived, you have often been pursued by men who recognize your greatness. Your strength, your intelligence, your beauty—men are drawn to it like moths to a flame. They want to possess you. But a queen can never be possessed."

Dionne blinks in confusion. "A queen?"

Jocasta nods solemnly. "You have the blood of the Ptolemys in your veins. You have stood on the shores of the Nile and breathed its perfumed air. You have been hailed as a god and you have held the asp to your breast in death."

Dionne's eyes go wide with amazement. "Are you... are you saying I was Cleopatra?"

Jocasta nods, and a wave of excitement ripples through the audience. "Cleopatra was the name you first called yourself. Since then, you have had many. Many names and many lives. But in all those lives, you have faced the same question: What man is worthy of a queen? Cleopatra loved the great Julius Caesar and Mark Antony. But did she force herself to choose? *No.* She took them both. And with both of those loves, she and her kingdom flourished."

"Yes, but—"

"But what?"

Dionne laughs nervously. "Well, I can't ask these men to share me."

"Why not?"

Dionne is speechless.

"All your life, you've known that you are destined for greatness. But greatness isn't given. It's taken. If these two men have what you need—stability from one, passion from the other—don't be afraid to take it. If they find the arrangement unorthodox, get rid of them. They are unworthy of your greatness. But if they can stand by your side and give you what you need so that you can achieve all that you are capable of, you will have found men worthy of your love as well as partners worthy of a queen."

To my surprise, Dionne nods in agreement, and the entire audience bursts into applause. The two women stand, and Jocasta embraces an overcome Dionne before sending her back to her seat.

"What the hell was that?" Jackson whispers.

"I think Jocasta just told that woman it was okay for her to be in a throuple because she used to be Cleopatra."

Jackson shakes his head in disbelief, and I find myself more confused than ever.

I know a lot of weird stuff has happened in the past couple of weeks—enough to make me question the very nature of reality and my own sanity. I've conceded that past lives and reincarnation might be real and that Jackson and I might have known each other in Pompeii, Brattahlid, and London. But asking me to believe that Cleopatra—*the* Cleopatra—is here in Orlando getting a psychic reading because she's having trouble with her love life? That's too much to swallow. Not least because Jocasta's got her history wrong.

Cleopatra never had to choose between Julius Caesar and Mark Antony. Cleopatra was with Caesar first and got with Mark Antony only after Caesar died. She was never part of some ancient Roman power throuple. Anyone who's seen the Elizabeth Taylor movie or read Cleopatra's Wikipedia page would know that.

So why doesn't Jocasta?

Despite my misgivings, Jackson and I watch for the next hour as Jocasta continues to summon audience members up to the stage. One by one, she explores their past lives before offering them advice about their current dilemmas. She tells a short, balding man that he used to be Napoleon and that he should demand a promotion at work. She tells a silver-haired older gentleman wearing a rainbow Pride pin that he used to be Oscar Wilde and that he shouldn't give up on the play he's been writing for the past ten years.

Even the people who don't discover that they were once big names like Frederick Douglass or Joan of Arc still seem to have led extraordinary past lives. Each and every one was a brave soldier or a gifted artist or a brilliant scholar. No one leaves the stage without being told that they were exceptional in a former life and (more important) that they can become exceptional in this life *if* they follow Jocasta's advice—advice that is in her new book, which is conveniently on sale in the hotel lobby.

"She's a fraud," Jackson scoffs, shaking his head in disgust.

I nod. Though, annoyingly, no one else in the auditorium seems to share our outrage or our disillusionment. When Jocasta brings her show to a close, the entire audience leaps to its feet, showering her with deafening applause.

Part of me wants to run out on the stage and yell at the crowd for being so gullible. It doesn't seem possible that so many people could be this delusional.

Then again, who am I to judge? I just blackmailed my best friend's brother because I was as desperate as everyone in this room to meet the woman who I thought could magically solve all my problems.

"What do we do now?" Jackson asks.

"I don't know."

Jocasta's definitely a liar, a fraud, and an opportunist. She's also undeniably the same woman from our dreams. That can't be a coincidence.

I suppose it's possible that she's both a fraud *and* a reincarnated witch. That would explain why she hasn't aged in a thousand years and why she's still doing the same hocus-pocus shtick that she did when she was calling herself Ulfhild. Who knows. If Jackson and I keep reincarnating because we're soulmates who are meant to find each other, maybe Jocasta keeps reincarnating so she can scam people out of their money. It seems like an insane waste of such an amazing opportunity, but maybe that's how it works. Maybe whatever happens in your first life you're forced to repeat over and over in all your future lives.

"We should talk to her," I say as Jocasta starts to make her way backstage. "She might be a con artist, but right now she's our only lead."

Jackson nods. "So how do you want to do this? Do I just go up to her and say, 'Hey, remember us? We used to be Vikings and you told everyone I had the plague.'"

Before I can answer, I see Jocasta marching in our direction. She's deep in conversation with a young woman holding an iPad who I assume is her assistant. Instinctively, I pull Jackson farther into the shadows and out of Jocasta's line of sight.

"What time's my flight?" Jocasta asks the young woman.

"Not until seven thirty."

"Good. I'm going to head up to my room and take a nap. Make sure I'm not disturbed."

"Of course, Miss Devereaux. I'll wake you up when it's time to leave for the airport."

Jocasta strides toward the exit but then stops and turns back to her assistant. "What room am I in again?"

"Room ten thirteen."

Jocasta nods and slips out the door, and the assistant hurries off to harangue some stagehands who are clumsily attempting to carry Jocasta's ornate chair offstage.

"So," Jackson says, putting a hand on my shoulder. "Room ten thirteen?"

Five minutes later, Jackson and I are standing outside Jocasta's door. And for the first time, I wonder if we're about to make a huge mistake.

We could be completely wrong about her being Ulfhild, in which case, she'll probably call hotel security when she finds two teenagers outside her room insisting that she's a witch. But if we're *not* wrong, then we're about to confront the woman who once got Jackson and me killed.

"You don't think she's dangerous?" I ask, surprised that this thought is only now occurring to me.

Jackson snorts. "I think we'll be okay." A second later, though, he swallows uncertainly. "Just to be safe, though, we should watch our backs."

I nod. Then, before I can chicken out, I take a deep breath and knock.

"Yes?" Jocasta calls from inside.

"Room service," Jackson improvises when I'm too tongue-tied to speak.

"I didn't order any."

"It's champagne. Compliments of the hotel."

The door swings open and reveals Jocasta's eager, excited face—an expression that instantly collapses into a scowl when she sees Jackson, me, and no champagne.

"No autographs," she barks, starting to close the door.

Jackson thrusts out his hand to stop her from shutting it in our faces. "Wait!"

Jocasta's nostrils flare, and her eyebrows rise in indignation. "Young man, I suggest you remove your hand from my door or I will call the police and have you escorted from the premises *in handcuffs*."

"Sorry," Jackson says, dropping his hand. "We don't mean to scare you. We just need to talk to you."

"If you'd like to book a private spiritual consultation, you can do so through my website."

"We don't want a consultation," I reply. "We want to know if you recognize us."

Jocasta looks from me to Jackson and back to me, then shakes her head in confusion. "Why on earth would I recognize you?"

"You've never seen us before?"

"Never."

"Are you sure?" I press. "Look at us. Really look at us."

Jocasta snorts. "I *am* looking at you. And all I see are two hooligans who are wasting my time and ruining my nap."

My heart sinks in disappointment while at the same time a strange relief passes over me. We're wrong—Jocasta isn't Ulfhild. Which means all the crazy things that have been happening to Jackson and me aren't supernatural occurrences, just bizarre coincidences.

"You really have no idea who we are?" I ask one last time to be certain.

"No. Should I?"

"We met in Greenland," Jackson jumps in. "In a place called Brattahlid."

Jocasta scoffs. "I've never been to—"

She doesn't finish her thought. Instead, a flicker of recognition flashes across her eyes. It's faint, almost imperceptible, and a second later she pushes it away with a shake of her head as if trying to dismiss an unpleasant memory.

"I'm sorry. You have the wrong person. Now, if you'll excuse me."

She tries to shut the door again, but this time I'm the one who stops her. "You *do* know who we are," I exclaim in amazement.

"I do *not*," she insists, taking a quick step back like a cornered animal. "I have never laid eyes on you—either of you—in my life."

"Well, we've met you," I say, growing more certain with every second. "And we know your real name: *Ulfhild*."

Jocasta freezes, her cheeks turning paler than the snows of Brattahlid. She stares at Jackson and me in disbelief, and the flicker of recognition in her eyes explodes into a brilliant, burning flame.

"You," she snarls. "It's *you*."

CHAPTER 42

JACKSON

I'm no expert on witches, but based on every Disney movie I've ever seen, I'm pretty sure that if one invites you in for a snack, you're supposed to run for the hills. Not Riley and me, though. We're seated at a table with a platter of multicolored macarons in front of us waiting for our witch to finish making a pot of tea in her suite's kitchenette.

"So, what did you think of my little show?" Jocasta asks as the kettle whistles shrilly. She lifts it off the stovetop and brings it over to our table, where she proceeds to fill our cups with a murky brown liquid.

Riley and I exchange a nervous glance. In the span of two minutes, our hostess has gone from belligerent to welcoming, which is frankly more disturbing. Neither of us touches our tea.

"It was *interesting*," Riley replies diplomatically.

Jocasta or Ulfhild—I'm not sure what to call her—laughs.

"It's embarrassing, I know." She shakes her head and takes a seat across from us. "But what I can do? We've all got to make a living."

"So it *is* a scam?" I ask.

"Of course it's a scam. You think Oscar Wilde, Cleopatra, and Napoleon are all hanging out in *Florida*?" She sips her tea. "Years ago, when I was first starting out, I tried to use my gifts to help people without all the hocus-pocus nonsense. I'd see someone with a problem and give them incredibly profound—not to mention *practical*—advice, and nine times out of ten, do you know what they'd do? Ignore me! Or, worse, they'd go off and do the exact opposite."

Jocasta lets out a rueful chuckle. "It didn't take me long to realize that if I wanted to be taken seriously, I'd have to embellish my routine. Now I still give customers sound advice, only first I put on a little show for them. I weave stories about their past lives, about the great, important people they used to be. That's *crucial*.

"You've got to flatter their egos if you want them to listen to you. It's like hiding your dog's medicine in peanut butter. You give the customer a treat, you make them feel special, like you and only you can see their true potential, and *voilà*. Suddenly they're willing to listen to what you have to tell them. And pay handsomely too."

Grinning in triumph, Jocasta takes another sip of her tea. At which point she notices the untouched cups sitting in front of Riley and me.

"It's not poisoned," she says. "It's oolong."

I don't want her to think I'm frightened, so I take a sip. The liquid is strong and bitter, but I think that's how tea is supposed to taste. I wouldn't know. I'm a coffee guy. "Doesn't anyone ever call you out?" I ask as I grab a red macaron off the platter. I take a bite of its sugary shell hoping to get the tea's bitter aftertaste out of my mouth.

"Call me out?"

"For being a phony."

Jocasta shakes her head. "There's nothing phony about the advice I give. Everything I tell a client is something I truly believe they need to hear."

"Really?" Riley scoffs, dunking a blue macaron in his tea. "That woman, Dionne, she *needed* to hear that she should have a threesome?"

Jocasta smirks. "You'd be surprised how many of life's problems can be solved with a threesome."

"But you're telling people they used to be Cleopatra and Napoleon," Riley continues. "And you're getting basic historical facts wrong. Doesn't anyone get suspicious?"

"Sometimes. But the human capacity for self-delusion is excelled only by its narcissism. Once I told three different men in the same night that they had each been George Washington just to see if I could get away with it. Not a single one batted an eyelash."

Riley bites his macaron in half and snorts scornfully. "That's insane."

Jocasta shrugs. "Human beings need to believe they're special. And I suppose, in their own ways, they are. Life, after all, is always a miracle. Nonetheless, the simple truth is that most people walking this planet are just average individuals living very average lives."

"But not you," I say.

"No." Jocasta grins—the same wolfish grin from my dream. "Nor you."

Riley shakes his head. "Look, Ulfhild, we don't care what sort of scam you're running. Jackson and I are only here because—"

"I'm not Ulfhild," she says, cutting him off. "Ulfhild was my great-great-great-great-great-great-great-great-great-grandmother. I've probably left out fifty or so *great*s, but you get the point."

I look at Riley in confusion, then back at Jocasta. "But you look exactly like her."

"The women in my family have always borne a striking resemblance to each other."

"But you recognized us," Riley insists.

"I did. But only from the stories passed on from generation to generation by the women in my family. A story of two boys, always together, one with eyes bluer than the sea and hair like polished bronze and the other with hair like midnight and eyes as sharp and green as glass."

Riley stares at her in awe. "Who are you?"

"I come from a long line of seeresses," Jocasta explains. "My lineage stretches all the way back to the Oracle of Delphi. No one knows how or why the women in my family acquired our particular gifts, but we've always had a special relationship with the universe. We can see the direction in which it wants to move. And we help steer it from time to time when things go off course. Though what its ultimate goal is, if indeed there is a goal, I couldn't begin to speculate. Nor could the women who came before me. But we serve the universe when we're called upon. And when we're not, we're free to do as we like."

Jocasta smiles like that's the end of her story. But I have more questions than ever.

"You said your ancestors—the women in your family—they've met Riley and me before?"

She grins. "Quite a few times. You're rather infamous in certain circles. Of course, it's been a while since any of my lineage have run into you. Almost a century, in fact. To tell you the truth, I was starting to think you two were just an old wives' tale. But here you are."

"Wait—how many times have your ancestors met us?" Riley asks. "Jackson and I only remember meeting Ulfhild in Greenland. Are you saying we've met your ancestors in other past lives? That we've had other encounters with your family?"

"Oh, yes. Ulfhild was just one of many. The two of you have crossed paths with the women of my lineage on several occasions. At least a dozen, if our family records are to be believed. Though there may have been more encounters that we don't know about."

This conversation is making me dizzy. It's hard enough wrapping my brain around the idea that I might've had three past lives. The fact that I might've had a dozen or more makes my head swim.

"So past lives *are* real, then?" Riley asks. "Reincarnation is real?"

"Yes. Very rare and very unusual, but real."

"What do you mean, 'unusual'?"

Jocasta sighs, and for a second, I'd swear she looks disappointed. "I mean it's not supposed to happen. And if it does happen, you're certainly not supposed to remember it. None of the versions of you boys that my ancestors encountered ever recalled their previous lives. As far as I know, you two are the first."

Something about the way she says that last part sends a shiver down my spine.

"If reincarnation isn't supposed to happen, why is it happening to Jackson and me?"

Jocasta considers. "Do you recall any of your past lives other than your time in Greenland with Ulfhild?"

"Jackson remembers us living in London during World War Two. And I remember living in Pompeii right before Mount Vesuvius erupted."

"But nothing earlier than Pompeii?"

"No."

"Interesting." Jocasta sips her tea. "I had an ancestor in Pompeii. A high priestess of the Sibylline Oracle. She died in the destruction of the city, and her death has always been one of the great mysteries of my family."

"You mean because she didn't see the volcano coming?" I ask.

Jocasta shakes her head. "Because she *did*. She sent her daughter and all her handmaidens out of Pompeii a day before the eruption. Yet for some reason, she stayed behind. I've always wondered why."

Out of the corner of my eye, I see Riley color and stare down at his lap.

"I think . . ." He hesitates. "I think . . . we met her."

I look at Riley in surprise. In our discussions about our dreams, he never mentioned any high priestess. But then, I haven't really pumped him for information about Pompeii. I've been more focused on Greenland since that's the only past life we both remember.

"Tell me," Jocasta says eagerly, leaning forward in her chair. "Tell me what happened in Pompeii."

"There's not much to tell," Riley answers defensively. "Jackson and I were—a couple. When the volcano erupted, we ran from our families to find each other. We couldn't make it out of the city, so we took shelter in a temple. That's where we found the high priestess. She was trapped under a column and dying. But right before she passed away, she told Jackson and me that we had to die. She was pretty insistent about it. Then the temple collapsed, and that was it. We died."

Jocasta nods and leans back in her chair. "Except you didn't, did you? You clever boys found a way back."

"But how?" I ask, my tired brain still struggling to understand what I'm hearing.

Jocasta sets down her tea and considers. "How old were you when you died in Pompeii?"

"We were young," Riley answers. "Teenagers. I think I'd just turned eighteen."

"And you were in love?"

The question makes Riley blush. "Yeah. We were in love."

Jocasta sighs. "That could do it. Two souls in love cut off in their prime, wanting more time. It's been known to happen."

A shudder passes through my body, causing my skin to break out in goose bumps. "We died young in our other lives too," I add. "In London. And in Greenland."

"Did you?" Jocasta sips her tea and stares at us in unnerving silence.

I turn to Riley, whose eyes reflect my own apprehension. "If your family has run into us a dozen times," he says, "do you know if we died in those lives as well?"

Jocasta shrugs. "Everyone dies."

"But did we die young?" Riley insists.

Jocasta studies him, and something in her dark piercing eyes makes me wish he'd never asked. "You were eighteen when you died in Pompeii?"

"Yes."

"How do you know you were eighteen?"

"Because it was my birthday."

An icy chill roots me to my chair and fills my chest with dread. "The day that we died in London, it was also your birthday," I remind Riley. "And in Greenland."

"His eighteenth birthday?" Jocasta asks.

I nod.

"Interesting."

"Why is that interesting?" Riley asks.

"It seems as though each time the two of you are reincarnated, you're given the exact same lifespan that you had in your first life."

Riley's face goes white. We're both thinking the same thing.

"How old are you now?" Jocasta asks.

"Seventeen," Riley answers.

"And when do you turn eighteen?"

"In two weeks. July thirteenth."

"Ah." Jocasta doesn't say anything more. She doesn't need to.

"Hang on," I say, shaking my head in disbelief. "Are you saying that in two weeks, Riley and I are gonna—what—*die?*"

Jocasta sighs. "I told you. Reincarnation is highly unusual. Human beings are meant to live one life and one life only. Each time the two of you come back, you're breaking the rules."

"What rules?" I demand.

"The universe's."

"It's not like we're doing it on purpose!" I shout.

"But you are," Jocasta says simply. "At some point in that first life of yours, you bound your souls together. And in every life since, you've continued to join your souls in a bond so powerful that it has overcome death itself."

"That's insane," Riley scoffs. "You're saying that every time Jackson and I are reincarnated, the universe starts actively plotting to kill us?"

"You're an aberration to the natural order. You're chaos. It can't permit you to exist."

"So what are we supposed to do?" I ask. I'm trying to stay calm even though my head is swimming in confusion. "If what you're saying is true, how do we make sure we don't end up like we did in our past lives? Aside from avoiding volcanoes and Nazis?"

Jocasta reaches for a macaron, then reconsiders.

"I'm not sure there's anything you can do. On July thirteenth, there's a very good chance that you both will die. I'm sorry, but that's the truth. Furthermore, after you die, the cycle will begin anew. You'll be reincarnated, you'll find each other in some future time and place, and you'll die. Over and over. On and on. Until the end of time. Unless . . ."

"Unless what?" Riley asks.

"You break the cycle."

Riley shoots me a nervous glance. "And how do we do that?"

"You break the very thing keeping you trapped in the cycle. You break your bond."

"Our bond?" I repeat.

"Your love is a bond that has kept you coming back in search of each other time and time again across the millennia. Break that bond, and the cycle breaks with it."

Riley shakes his head and stares at Jocasta incredulously. "You're telling us we need to *break up?*"

Jocasta nods. "If you renounce each other—truly renounce each other—and stay away from each other for the rest of your lives, then the bond you made in Pompeii and have reaffirmed in each of your subsequent lives will fail to renew itself. It'll be broken, in which case the universe will no longer have a reason to cut your lives short. You'll both go on to have very long, very full lives, after which your souls will be free to move on from this world and never return."

"Bullshit." Riley snorts. "Do you actually expect Jackson and me to believe that if we don't break up, the universe is going to kill us on my birthday?"

"I think it would be more accurate to say that if you don't break up, the universe will find a way to maneuver you both toward a pre-determined historical tragedy that has already been set in motion."

Riley scoffs. But I can't shake the feeling that every word Jocasta is saying is true. It's too impossible not to be.

"More to the point," she continues, "I think that—for whatever reason—the universe is giving you a very rare opportunity to learn from your mistakes and choose a different path for yourselves."

"Says you," Riley sneers.

"Do you think it's a coincidence that you two are the first ones in all your many lives to have access to your past memories? The universe has been swatting you like flies for two thousand years and you still haven't gotten the hint that it's time to let go of each other. So now, if I'm right—and I usually am—the universe has changed its strategy. It's given you a glimpse of your past so that you learn from your mistakes and put an end to this cycle of death once and for all."

"And I say, where's your *proof?*"

Jocasta's thin lips curl into a patronizing smirk. "You mean aside from the fact that *you* tracked *me* down because you thought I was a witch that you'd encountered over a thousand years ago when you were Vikings?"

Riley shakes his head. "I'm not saying weird shit isn't happening. Weird shit is *definitely* happening. But that doesn't mean Jackson and I need to break up. And it certainly does not mean we're going to *die*."

Jocasta arches an eyebrow. "Enlighten me, then. What does it mean?"

"I don't know. But I do know that you're a self-admitted fraud, even if you do claim to be helping people. I also know that your great-great-grand-whatever got Jackson and me killed, so your family's track record when it comes to helping us is pretty much shit."

"It's not my job or my family's job to help you. Our job is to carry out the will of the universe. And the will of the universe is and always has been quite clear. You must die."

"Jesus Christ, you sound like that crazy high priestess," Riley growls.

Jocasta bristles, and her pale cheeks color in anger. "That crazy high priestess sacrificed her life for you. Don't you understand? She foresaw what you were about to do, and instead of fleeing Pompeii when she had the chance, she stayed behind and gave her life trying to stop you from making a terrible mistake. A mistake that you will spend eternity repeating unless you choose a different path!"

Fuming with animosity, Riley stares across the table, his eyes shooting daggers at Jocasta. He's so angry, he looks like he might erupt. But instead, he goes dangerously still.

"I. Don't. Believe. You." He enunciates each word so clearly that there's no mistaking the contempt in his voice. "Come on, Jackson. We're leaving. She's wasted enough of our time."

Riley pushes himself up from his chair and stands defiantly. Almost immediately, though, he stumbles and has to lean against the table for support.

"Are you okay?" I ask, watching him shake his head like he's fighting off a dizzy spell.

"I'm fine," he answers. "I just . . . stood up too fast."

He sits back down and massages his temples as if he's trying to ward off a migraine. Maybe it's the stress stemming from everything we've just been told, but I can feel a headache of my own building behind my eyes.

"I understand that what I'm saying is difficult to believe," Jocasta says with a sigh. Her voice has taken on an air of good-natured patience, but something behind the forced pleasantness makes my skin crawl. "However, if you won't listen to me, perhaps you'll listen to yourselves. Consider it a parting gift."

I have no idea what she means by that, but I've no intention of sticking around to find out. Every nerve in my body is telling me that we're in danger and we need to get out of here. But when I try to stand, my body feels as though it's fighting to move through wet concrete. Before I know what's happening, I collapse back into my chair.

Beside me, Riley groans and slumps over. He rests his head against the table as his eyes flutter shut. I know I need to wake him, but my own head feels impossibly heavy. It's a struggle just to keep my eyes open.

I reach for Riley, but my hand is an anvil. It falls to the table like a dead weight, knocking over my tea.

Of course.

"The tea..." I gasp. "You put something... in the tea..."

Jocasta blinks innocently and sips from her cup.

"Don't be absurd," she scoffs. "I put something in the macarons."

PARIS, FRANCE

(AUGUST 24, 1572)

CHAPTER 43

GASPARD

There are two ways to be drunk—with wine and with love. For the first, God created grapes. For the second, He created Thierry. Tonight, I've had my fill of both and can attest that such a heady mixture is the closest any man can come to tasting heaven here on earth.

Blasphemous? Certainly. A mortal sin? To be sure. Still, how sweet damnation will be with Thierry by my side. And hell can't possibly be hotter than Paris in August.

"Can we open a window?" Thierry sighs beside me, his pale, lithe body made almost golden in the candlelight. "It's stifling in here."

I pull myself out of bed, sticky with perspiration, and open the window of the cramped, airless room we've been renting. I suppose we should count ourselves lucky we were able to find even a hovel like this. Half of France has poured into the city to witness the princess's wedding. Though I suspect, like me, most of them are placing bets on how long the marriage will last.

A Catholic princess and a Huguenot rebel? I'd not have believed it if I hadn't seen it with my own eyes. For how many years have our two faiths been at each other's throats? How much blood has been spilled? Frenchman against Frenchman.

Now, though, with one seemingly impossible wedding, all that strife is at an end. Now we are expected to set aside our swords and clasp hands in friendship with those who only last week were our sworn enemies.

It's a bold strategy for peace, I'll give King Charles that. If indeed it was his idea and not his cunning mother's. But it cannot end well. Such things never do. I may have only eighteen years on my back, but I've lived in this world long enough to know that man's ability to hate his fellow man is an unquenchable hunger. In the end, it will devour everything.

But why dwell on such unpleasantness? I've been drinking all night—all week, in fact—to forget such painful realities. And yet Paris is too quiet tonight.

This stultifying heat that has fallen upon the city is nothing compared to the tension in the streets. I can feel it emanating from the thatched houses and cobblestones, choking the air with resentment and animosity.

This city is a powder keg. And one match will set Paris ablaze.

Thank God we're leaving.

"Is that the matins bell?" Thierry yawns as I slip back into bed beside him. If I cock my head, I can just make out the tolling coming from the Cathedral of Saint-Germain.

"Yes, I'm afraid we've been quite wanton. It's almost dawn."

"What day is it?"

I laugh. "How much did you have to drink last night?"

"Too much."

"It's Sunday."

"Sunday," he repeats, breaking into a coy smile. "And do you have anything in particular that you'd like to say to me on this day?"

"Such as?"

Thierry fixes me with his languid eyes, the green of his irises now glowing with a mischievous glint. "Felicitations are the traditional custom on the day of one's birth."

"Felicitations," I say, sliding my hand through his luxurious black hair as I lower my lips to his. Despite the two of us having spent the entire evening in ecstasy together, I find myself wanting nothing more than to forget all the troubles of the world by once again losing myself in the sweet oblivion of his embrace.

"I suppose it's too much to hope you got me a present?" Thierry teases between kisses.

"I believe I already gave you your present," I inform him as I climb on top of him. "In fact, I believe I've been giving you your present all night."

"I was hoping for something more original." He smirks. "You've been giving me that gift for years."

"I've never heard any complaints."

Thierry's mouth devours mine, but before I can drink my full pleasure, he pulls away.

"How about a song, then?"

"A song?"

"For my birthday."

"You want me to sing? Now?" I ask, glancing down at our bodies' rather rigorous declarations of desire.

Thierry shrugs. "Don't I deserve something exceptional on my special day?"

I sigh and shake my head. "Did you have a particular ballad in mind?"

"Singer's choice. Surprise me."

I rack my brains for something suitable and (more to the point) short.

"My lover's lips are as soft as his kisses," I sing painfully off-key. Unlike Thierry, I'm incapable of carrying a tune—a fact he perversely enjoys reminding me of whenever the opportunity presents itself.

Still, I have a plan to use this humiliation to my advantage. I slowly trace a trail of kisses down to his neck, and his laughter melts into quick gasps of pleasure. Silly boy. I learned long ago that there is no part of his body that elicits such passion from him as his sweet and tender neck.

> *My lover's skin is as soft as my breast,*
> *My lover is soft in all the right places,*
> *But it's where he is hard that I like him best.*

My right hand slides down his stomach, and Thierry breaks into laughter.

"And where, may I ask, did a well-respected mayor's son learn a filthy song like that?"

"From a very witty tart," I answer.

"Oh, dear, I hope you haven't been consorting with riffraff. Your father will be so disappointed."

"What can I say? I'm a man who craves a certain variety in his life. It's hard to keep me satisfied."

"Is it?" Thierry asks, taking hold of me. "I've never found it so."

I pull his face to mine and bite his lips, and the familiar hunger awakens in me: To taste every inch of him. To consume him with kisses. To devour him body and soul until we are one body, one soul.

Sometimes my craving frightens me. It's like a fever that ravages my body, stripping me of reason. Yet I've long stopped looking for a cure.

It was three years ago that Thierry first came into my life, and to this day I do not know if it was a gift from heaven or a temptation from hell. My father had recently broken with the Church of Rome and converted our family to the teachings of Calvin and his Reformed Church. Our new minister, a man of great influence, encouraged my father to dismiss all the Catholics from our household lest they spy on us or plot against us. So it was that Thierry's father, Old Broussard, a lifelong and committed Huguenot, became my father's steward at Thouron, bringing with him his son to live on our estate and provide me with constant companionship.

I still remember the first time I laid eyes on Thierry. When he stepped out of the carriage that delivered him to the doorstep of our estate, I felt like I was seeing the sun for the first time after a life of living under the earth. His beauty blinded me. And his green eyes, sharp as glass, unnerved me. Even his touch when we shook hands seemed to burn my skin. I could scarcely stand to be in the same room with him for fear of what would happen if ever I forgot myself.

I was by no means a pious or moral young man. Quite the contrary, in fact. My father frequently fretted for my immortal soul. But up until that time, my sins had been of the standard variety that boys in the country enjoyed. That is to say, nothing I couldn't boast about to my friends late at night in some tavern where we traded tales of our debaucheries.

But the sin I wanted from Thierry was different. I knew it would damn me. Not because it would send me to hell but because I was there already from the sheer want of it.

Thus began the longest year of my life.

By day, Thierry was the perfect companion. We would ride or hunt, taking endless delight in each other's company and conversation. Then by night, alone in my room, I would burn for him until I was exhausted with desire.

I thought I would go mad. I slept with every girl in the village who would raise her skirt for me in the hopes of purging this fever from my blood. I tried to forget him with drink and dice and (worst of all) prayer. Nothing worked.

Then on his sixteenth birthday, after everyone had gone to bed following a modest celebration befitting the steward's son, I found myself bold with too much wine and too much longing. I stole from my room and crept through the humid night until I arrived outside his bedroom door.

Without knocking, I slipped inside. The candles were out, but in the light of the full moon, I saw him sit up in bed. He did it quite calmly, quite naturally, as if he'd been expecting me. As if he'd always been expecting me.

He asked what I wanted, and when I was unable to speak, he rose from the bed, beautiful and perfect as Apollo, and came to me. Without saying a word, he took my left hand and brought it to his lips, then my right. Then he placed both hands over his heart and said, "Don't you know there's nothing you could ask of me that I would not give?"

His lips tasted of honey. His hair smelled of lavender. My nightshirt fell to the floor, and a second later we joined it there, discovering new and exquisite ways to astound each other.

Thus began the happiest two years of my life.

Two years in which I've never stopped asking for him, and he's never stopped giving himself. Two years in which the fever between us has burned so true and strong that, were I not at heart a cynical beast raised in a cynical age, I could almost dare to call it holy.

"Do you hear shouting?" Thierry asks, pulling his lips from mine.

Intoxicated as I am by my craving for him, it takes me a moment to return to my senses. I cock my head toward the window and at first hear only the tolling of more bells. There's nothing unusual in that. Except the louder they clang, the less it sounds like tolling and the more it sounds like a warning. Or an alarm.

A scream pierces the night, baleful and desperate. It's followed by another. Then a third.

"Something's wrong," Thierry whispers, sliding out from under me and moving to the window.

I'm about to join him when our chamber door is rocked by the insistent pounding of an impatient fist. It swings open, and the inn's proprietress, Madame Montague, enters frantically. She's dressed in her nightgown, her white hair wild and erratic, her wrinkled face twisted in fear. Every muscle in my body tenses in apprehension.

"What is the meaning of this?" I demand.

Madame Montague glances nervously out the door and wrings her hands. "Oh, messieurs, you have to go! You're in danger!"

Her panic is palpable. Without hesitation, I leap out of bed and start to dress. "What's the matter?" I ask, pulling on my breeches.

"You must leave the city. Now! There's no time to delay."

"But why? What's happened?" Thierry asks, rummaging on the floor for his own clothes.

"The king—God forgive him—the king has declared war on the Huguenots. His soldiers are searching the city. They have orders to kill any they find!"

My blood runs cold. I look to Thierry, who stands in stunned silence, the color draining from his face.

"There must be some mistake," he protests. "The king—he wouldn't do that. He wants peace. That's why he married his sister to a Huguenot!"

"The princess and her husband have been arrested."

"No. No, that doesn't make any sense," Thierry exclaims, shaking his head in disbelief. "The king's the one who arranged the marriage. He's the one who invited all the Huguenots to come to Paris and celebrate the wedding!"

"It was a trap," I say, the cruel truth dawning on me with terrible certainty.

Thierry turns to me, horror-stricken. "What?"

"It was a trap," I repeat, spitting the words in disgust. "To lure us to the city. To trap us within the walls like rats so they can pick us off one by one."

Thierry's knees go weak. He grips the bed to steady himself as Madame Montague crosses herself. "I must warn my other guests."

Before she can take a step, though, a loud and violent pounding erupts from downstairs. Someone is beating against the door of the inn.

"Open up!" a voice shouts.

"It's the king's soldiers," Madame Montague hisses. "You must hide!"

I want to laugh at the absurdity of her suggestion. There's nothing in our room to give us shelter except a spindly table and a wooden bed. But I grab Thierry and pull him and our rapiers under the bed with me. Madame Montague hurries downstairs, and for a moment there is no sound but Thierry's panicked breathing beside me. I put my hand over his mouth to muffle the noise, and when I do, I feel his entire body trembling.

Why did we come to Paris? Why didn't I listen to my father? He tried to talk us out of it. He said there would be danger. But I laughed and called him a paranoid old fool. I wasn't about to miss the wedding of the century. I wasn't going to be the one Huguenot who sat at home while the rest of his countrymen celebrated such a momentous event.

And poor Thierry followed me. Because how could he not? He'd follow me to hell if I asked him to. And that's where I've led him.

"There are no Huguenots here," Madame Montague shouts in the stairwell. I wonder if she's lying to save our necks or her own. More to the point, I wonder what she'll do if she's forced to choose between the two.

"I don't rent rooms to Huguenots. I never rent rooms to Huguenots. I'm a good Catholic."

I hear her approaching footsteps followed by the heavy clomp of several pairs of boots.

The door to our room swings open, and Thierry goes stiff in my arms.

"Whose room is this?" I hear a soldier bark. I can't see his face, only his feet, but his voice alone is sinister enough to conjure the specter of death.

"No one's," Madame Montague answers, stepping between the soldier and the bed to obscure his view. "There were some country boys staying here for the wedding, but they left last night."

The soldier scoffs. Whether it's because he doesn't believe her story or because he's disappointed at not finding two Huguenots to slaughter, I can't say. But he storms out of the room. Madame Montague hesitates, then follows, shutting the door behind her.

I hear the soldiers moving through the inn, banging on doors, demanding papers. Someone pleads. Someone screams.

Thierry covers his ears and buries his face in my shoulder. I want to comfort him, but I don't dare move. One creak of the floorboard might bring an army of soldiers crashing through our door. And as romantic as it might be to die in Thierry's arms, I want to live.

I want to live.

The scream continues—then ends in an abrupt and fatal silence. Minutes pass. Or perhaps hours. Who can tell? When you're waiting to die, every second is an eternity.

Finally, the door of our room scrapes open again. I hold my breath until I hear the soft tread of Madame Montague shuffling across the floorboards. She stops and stands without speaking for a long, terrible moment. Then quietly, simply, she says, "The soldiers are gone."

A sob of relief escapes my throat, and Thierry heaves a sigh beside me.

"You must go," Madame Montague says sharply, turning on her heel.

Her words renew my dread. Up until ten seconds ago, my only thought was to survive the soldiers' search. But now that we've done that, I realize our dangers are far from over.

"What are we supposed to do?" I ask, scurrying out from under the bed.

"Get out of Paris," she answers, refusing to look at me.

"How?" I demand. "Surely they'll have locked the gates to the city. We're *trapped*."

"Even so."

"But, Madame—"

"I said *go*!" She spits the words, and for the first time I notice how exhausted she looks, as if a great weight were pressing down upon not just her body but also her soul.

Is it possible for a person to be so transformed in so short a time? I think it must be. This tired, broken woman is a far cry from the laughing, irreverent hostess who rented us her very last room because, as she put it, "Huguenot or Catholic, the money's all the same." Madame Montague has seen things tonight. Things that have changed her. Things, I suspect, that will change everyone in Paris.

Or at least those of us with the good fortune to survive.

"Thank you," I say, taking her hand in gratitude.

She pulls it away as if my touch were fire. "Go," she whispers. Then, looking up at me with tears in her eyes, she says it again. "Go."

The sun has just started to paint the dawn red when we slip into the alley behind Madame Montague's inn. Thierry hasn't said a word since

I pried him out from under the bed. His eyes are wide and wild with panic, but his body is like a marionette whose strings have been cut. I have to keep my arm around his waist to stop him from collapsing with every step.

The alley we're in is dark and cramped and reeks of a hundred emptied chamber pots, but it's safer than the open streets. Alarm bells still clamor in the distance, calling the city to battle, and the morning air is thick with screams.

If Thierry and I can but get across the Seine and then out of Paris, we'll have a fighting chance. The Catholics may outnumber us here in the city, but in the countryside, we'll find safety. We just need to get back to our families in Thouron.

It's a desperate hope, but right now hope is all I have.

"What's that?" Thierry gasps, stopping abruptly and staring at a large mass lying on the ground a few paces in front of us.

It's a body. A man's body. His eyes are open but lifeless, as if surprised by his own death. His gray beard and nightshirt are covered in blood, a fresh pool of which congeals around his body. I look up at the neighboring building, at the window ajar on the third floor, and I can't help but wonder if he died before or after he was thrown from it.

Thierry buries his face in my shoulder and weeps, his body trembling as if it contained a great earthquake that longed to shatter his entire being.

"We're going to die," he says through his sobs. "We're going to *die*!"

I'm no less horrified by the slaughter in front of us, but panic and sorrow are not luxuries we can afford. We have to keep moving.

"Listen to me," I tell him, taking his face in my hands and forcing him to meet my eyes. "We're not going to die. We're going to get out of Paris and get back to our fathers, and we're going to live. Do you understand? We're *not* going to die.

"Besides, even if we did," I add with a miserable laugh, "do you think death could keep us apart? I would tear down the gates of heaven and wade through the fires of hell to find you."

I don't know where I find the confidence to believe these words, let alone speak them to Thierry, but my certainty calms his terror.

"Do you swear it?" he asks.

I put my lips to his and, in the kiss that follows, he has his answer.

Our courage revived, we set off into the city, winding our way through its haphazard streets like Theseus in the labyrinth.

We turn down an excrement-stained alley, then another, only to find ourselves at a dead end. We backtrack and try a different alley and a different direction, but a minute later another dead end blocks our path. Despite my earlier words of assurance to Thierry, I can feel my panic quicken. I don't know Paris well enough to navigate it by these furtive little backstreets. We need a main thoroughfare. It may expose us to danger, but it's the only way we'll be able to find our way out of this infernal maze.

I pull Thierry in the direction of what I believe is the nearest boulevard in order to get my bearings. He doesn't resist, but when we finally turn onto a wide, open street and see what awaits us, I almost wish he had.

Corpses litter the cobblestones like a graveyard vomiting up its dead. Men, women, children: No one has been spared. Their bodies lie mutilated, as if savaged by marauding beasts, their gaping wounds staining the ground in a thick river of blood.

Hell has truly come to Paris.

"No, please, let me go!" a terrified voice cries.

I turn and see a group of men dragging a young woman in her nightgown from an inn. The men aren't soldiers. Their clothes are simple and plain, like that of ordinary citizens, but each is wearing a white cloth tied in a makeshift band around his right arm and a white cross pinned to his hat. A few carry knives, but the rest have fashioned weapons out of rakes and shovels.

"Huguenot whore!" the thick-bearded ringleader shouts, throwing the woman to the ground.

"Please!" she pleads, her face smeared with blood, her eyes searching wildly for pity in a pitiless crowd. "Spare me! I'm with child!"

Thierry grips my hand, but there's nothing we can do. The men snigger in disgust as the ringleader grabs the woman by the back of her head and pulls her up to her knees.

"With child, are you? Then we'll be doing the world a favor by ridding it of another heathen bastard!" Before the woman can respond or I can look away, the ringleader unsheathes a dagger from his hip and plunges it into the woman's belly. She collapses to the street with a wail, and the men howl with laughter, circling her body like wolves moving in for the kill.

"Let's go," I whisper, pulling Thierry in the opposite direction and breaking into a run. Stealth is no longer an option. Speed is the only thing that will deliver us from this nightmare.

We turn east and follow the sun, passing more corpses. Then we turn south onto an avenue that should take us across the Seine and out of the city. The streets are surprisingly deserted, and I'm about to offer a quick prayer of thanks for this unexpected mercy when up ahead I spot half a dozen men pouring into the intersection. They're wearing white armbands and crosses, and one of the men, a giddy youth with orange hair, is dragging the mutilated corpse of a naked man behind him like it's a speared boar he's carting home for dinner.

I grab Thierry, stopping us in our tracks, but it's too late. The men see us, and it takes only one look at our frightened faces for them to realize what we are.

I start to pull Thierry back in the direction from which we've come, but another group of men marches onto the avenue from a side street and blocks our retreat.

Thierry gasps. "We're trapped!"

Both groups begin to advance, their bloodstained faces breaking into eager smiles at the sight of fresh prey. I draw my rapier, but Thierry clings to my side, too terrified to reach for his blade.

"Stay behind me," I say, backing us up against a wall.

The two mobs close in around us and become one. I count twelve men, some old enough to be my father, others too young to grow beards. I wonder who taught them to hate at such an early age.

"Heathen devils," one of the men spits at us. He grabs a large stone off the street and hurls it at my head. It misses, but the next one doesn't. It slices open my cheek, and in blinding pain, I drop my rapier. It's only a second of weakness, but it's all the men need to press their advantage. In an instant, they're upon us, pulling Thierry from my arms.

"Gaspard!" he shouts, but a rain of fists and sticks falls hard and fast upon my body, pummeling me to the ground. A knife pierces my back. The blade is like ice, but the pain is fire. I taste blood in my mouth. And in an instant, the raging animal instinct to fight for my life is replaced with the cold, grim certainty that I am going to die.

I raise my battered and bloody face off the cobblestones to look for Thierry. A group of men have him on his knees, just like the pregnant woman whom I was equally helpless to rescue. The orange-haired boy twists Thierry's arms behind his back with one hand, and with the other he forces his head up, exposing his neck. That neck that I have covered in kisses. That neck that I will never kiss again.

My Thierry. My other half. My world.

Unable to move, unable to speak, unable to do anything as my life drains out of me, I watch in horror as the bearded ringleader stands before my love and unsheathes his dagger. He holds it over Thierry's head as he offers up a short prayer to his bloody, merciless god. The blade glistens in his hand under the cruel August sun.

Then he brings it down and ends my world.

ORLANDO, FLORIDA

(THE PRESENT)

CHAPTER 44

JACKSON

Riley is shaking in my arms. He's gasping and fighting back tears, clinging to me like his life depends on it. I hold him tight, fighting back my own tears, as we huddle on the floor of Jocasta's kitchenette.

I don't know what time it is or how long we've been out. The sun is setting, casting its dying orange light and long purple shadows across the empty hotel room. There's no sign of Jocasta or her things. Not even an overturned teacup.

"They were killing us," Riley whimpers, his voice choked with fear. He clutches me even tighter. Like he's afraid that if he lets me go, even for a second, I'll slip away forever. Or he will.

"It's okay," I tell him, my own voice little more than a whisper. I'm still in too much shock to say or do anything more, so I find myself repeating that phrase as much for Riley's sake as my own. "We're okay. It was just a dream. We're okay."

My words are hollow, though. I don't believe them.

Riley and I both know we are far from okay. Just like we know that that excruciating dream wasn't a dream. It was our past.

And unless we listen to Jocasta, it's our future.

CHAPTER 45

RILEY

It's surreal and not a little disorienting to be sitting under the harsh fluorescent lights of the Mall at Millenia food court when less than an hour ago, Jackson and I were being murdered in the streets of Paris. Neither of us, though, could bear the thought of going home. His aunt and my dad would only have to take one look at our red eyes and haggard faces to know something was wrong. And what could we possibly tell them?

I don't even know what to tell myself.

"Do you think it was a coincidence?" Jackson asks, looking up from the cold plate of chicken teriyaki that we ordered from Wok N Roll to share but that neither of us has touched. The mall is almost empty at this hour. Jackson and I are the only people in the food court, but he speaks in a whisper as if he's afraid of being overheard.

"Was what a coincidence?"

"Everything that happened last weekend with our exes."

"With our exes?" I repeat, unable to follow his train of thought.

Jackson nods solemnly. "You and I were starting to get close, then out of the blue both of our exes suddenly appeared and almost derailed us from getting together. Do you think that's a coincidence or do you think it was . . . the universe? Jocasta said it wanted to keep us apart. Do you think—I don't know—do you think it was using our exes to steer us away from each other so it wouldn't have to . . ."

Jackson trails off, but I know what he's saying.

So it wouldn't have to kill us.

"I think if the universe wanted to keep us apart," I say as my frustration rises, "it wouldn't have let you move to Orlando in the first place. And it certainly wouldn't have let you move next door to one of my best friends."

Jackson blinks in surprise. "You don't believe Jocasta, then?"

"I don't know what I believe," I sigh as I throw my plastic fork down in disgust.

Ever since waking up on the floor of Jocasta's hotel room, I've been ricocheting between dread and denial. I know it was only this morning that I was the one insisting that our past lives were real. But that was when my theory was just that—a theory. Now that I know I'm right, all I want is to be wrong. And for Jocasta to be wrong. She has to be. Otherwise...

My hands start to shake. Jackson reaches across the table and takes them in his. His touch is warm and comforting. But when I try to smile, my mouth can't hold the shape.

"Riley, we need to face facts," Jackson says, looking at me with a mixture of pity and defeat. "We've seen ourselves die *four* times. And Jocasta said we've died at least a dozen other times. We need to consider—"

"We don't know it'll happen again," I cut him off. Because I know where this conversation is going. Maybe I'm being stubborn and unreasonable, but I've spent my whole life waiting for someone like Jackson. I'm not about to give him up because of a few bad nightmares or because some scheming witch thinks the universe is out to get us.

"You aren't worried about what's gonna happen when you turn eighteen?" Jackson asks, his voice almost pleading.

"*Nothing* is going to happen," I insist, snatching my hands away in annoyance. "We don't live next to a volcano. The Germans aren't going to bomb us. Nobody's getting the plague. We're going to be *fine*."

I'm not sure who I'm trying to convince, Jackson or myself. I don't think it matters. Neither of us believes it.

"I'm going to the bathroom," I announce, pushing my chair back from the table. I need to clear my head. To think. And I can't do that with Jackson staring at me like we're doomed passengers aboard the *Titanic*. "I'll be right back."

Forcing myself to stay calm, I walk briskly across the deserted food court, then down the long corridor that leads to the men's room. There's a sharp antiseptic smell of bleach that burns my nostrils when I step inside, but at least the bathroom is clean. It's quiet and empty and gleams with a polished whiteness. Like the snow-covered fields of Brattahlid.

Where I died.

Pushing the thought out of my head, I lean over one of the motion-operated sinks and splash cold water on my face. I'm hoping the jolt will snap me out of the nightmare that I've found myself in. Only I'm not in a nightmare.

Jocasta, Ulfhild, my past lives—they're all real. It's impossible, but apparently impossible things have been happening to Jackson and me for the past two thousand years.

But even so, we don't know for sure that we're going to die on my birthday. Jocasta said that none of our previous selves were able to remember their past lives, that Jackson and I are the first. That has to *mean* something.

Maybe Jackson and I have been shown our past so that this time around we can learn from our mistakes. Not the way Jocasta thinks, not so we can break up and escape whatever awful death the universe has planned for us, but so we can find some way to escape death *and* stay together.

That has to be a possibility, doesn't it?

I hear the universe's answer before I see it—a raucous, wild laughter that echoes down the hall and makes my stomach turn.

I look up from the sink, and the bathroom door flies open as the guys from the Olympus High Thunderbolts bound inside like a pack of hysterical hyenas.

"Barbie Boy!" one of them shouts in surprise. It's Rex Miller. He was one of the jerks who Audrey had to rescue me from freshman year. Only Audrey isn't here now. No one is.

My hands start to stake again, and my body breaks into a cold sweat. Every instinct is telling me that I'm in danger, that I should *run*. But the seven varsity-jacket-clad footballers are a wall of meat and testosterone between me and the door.

"What are you doing here?" Rex asks. "Trolling for some weekend mall dick?"

Keeping my head down, I try to push past him, but Rex blocks my way.

"Um, rude." He snorts. "You can't say hello?"

I look up from the floor so I can tell him to his face to fuck off. But when I do, my breath catches in my throat.

It's Rex's hair. It's the exact same shade of orange as the boy's hair in Paris. The one who was dragging the naked corpse through the streets. The one who pinned my arms behind my back and . . .

My blood runs cold.

Are Rex and his friends going to be the ones who kill me? Are they going to jump Jackson and me on my birthday? Is that how we're going to die? The victims of some fucked-up hate crime?

"Hey, Earth to Iverson." Rex takes a step toward me. "I said—"

"Don't touch me!"

I scramble backward, and my foot slips on the polished bathroom floor. My legs slide out from under me, and I crash against the tiled wall, banging my head against the metal casing of the paper towel dispenser.

"Holy fuck!" Rex gasps, stifling a laugh.

There's a sharp pain on the side of my head. I touch it, and when I pull my hand away, my fingers are red with blood.

"Yo, are you okay?" one of the other boys asks.

Run, my mind is screaming. *Run!*

Clutching my head, I stumble toward the bathroom door. This time Rex lets me pass.

Blind with panic, I race down the corridor and into the food court, stopping only when someone steps in my path.

"Riley? What's the matter? What happened? Are you all right?"

I throw my arms around Jackson.

"I don't want to die," I cry as every part of my body trembles with terror. "I don't want to die!"

CHAPTER 46

JACKSON

I drive Riley back to his house in silence. Both of us know what has to happen next but neither of us wants to say it. Even after we've pulled into his driveway and I've killed the engine, we continue to sit in silence, neither of us daring to look at the other.

Finally, after what feels like an eternity, I say the words that one of us has to.

"We need to break up."

Riley doesn't answer. He doesn't even look at me. He stares straight ahead at his house. Through the large bay window, I can see a man who must be his father sitting at the dining-room table in front of a laptop.

"If there was some way that we could be together and I knew you'd be safe, I'd do it in a heartbeat," I continue, pulling each word out of my throat like a fishhook. "But we can't take the risk. If something happened to you because of *me*, I would never forgive myself. *Never*."

My body is shaking almost as much as my voice. I have to look away from Riley to stop myself from completely losing it. I know ending things with him is the only way to keep him safe. To keep us both safe. But that doesn't make it any easier.

I feel like I'm ripping out my own heart.

"Maybe . . . maybe we could just break up for a month," Riley suggests, his voice smaller than I've ever heard it. "Until I'm eighteen. Or maybe—"

He stops himself. There's no point in pretending we have any option but the one Jocasta laid out for us. Not if we want to live to see nineteen.

Besides, even if we were able to trick the universe by breaking up and then getting back together after Riley's birthday, we'd still spend the rest of our lives looking over our shoulders, wondering who or what might be coming for us. Riley already had a full-blown panic attack when he thought those guys at the mall were after him. I can't put him through something like that again.

"We probably shouldn't have any communication with each other for a while," I force myself to say. "And we should avoid each other as much as possible at school in the fall."

Riley nods, but I can see him struggling to hold back tears.

"We'll have to tell the others that we had a fight. Maybe you could tell them about Devon. You could say that once you found out, you decided to break up with me. Tell them you confronted me, and I was a jerk about it, and you realized I wasn't a good person."

Riley shakes his head. "I could *never* say that."

"We'll have to tell them something."

Riley looks back at his house. He's silent for a long time. Then his face crumples and his voice cracks. "I can't believe this is happening. You're literally my fucking soulmate. How am I supposed to spend the rest of my life without you?"

I've been wondering the exact same thing. But I hold my tongue. One of us has to be strong. "You'll find someone else."

Riley looks at me like I've punched him in the face. It's all I can do not to take him into my arms and kiss away his pain. But before I can let myself break, Riley slides out of my Jeep and hurries to his house. I watch him disappear inside, and as I do, a strange relief washes over me.

He's safe now. That's all that matters.

Even so, I rest my head against the steering wheel and let the tears pour out of me until I'm as empty and lonely as the night.

CHAPTER 47

JACKSON

My phone buzzes. Again. Then again. Every few seconds, I hear it vibrating on my nightstand. With a groan, I pull my bedspread over my head to block out the noise. Whoever's messaging me, I know it can't be Riley. And if it's not Riley, I don't care who it is.

Even though it's only a little after seven and the setting sun is still streaming through my window, I try to will myself to sleep. But it's no use. The constant buzzing assaults my ears like a persistent mosquito.

With a sigh, I drag my head out from under the covers and grab my phone. I'm debating whether to silence it or hurl it across the room when I see I have a string of missed texts from Duy, Tala, and Audrey.

After three days of stalling, Riley must have finally told them we've broken up. They're all asking what happened, if I'm okay, and if I need anything. Whatever reason Riley gave them for our split, I must not have come off as too much of an asshole. They're being incredibly kind, insisting that they'll be here for me whenever I want to talk.

Who knows, Tala writes optimistically, maybe this is just a bump in the road and you guys will get back together.

Even if it isn't, Audrey follows up, you're still our friend.

We LOVE you!!! Duy adds.

Messages of support continue to roll in faster than I can read them. In any other scenario, my heart would be swelling with gratitude. But my heart's too broken to swell.

Besides, I need to be realistic. Cutting Riley out of my life means cutting Duy, Tala, and Audrey out too. Trying to hold on to them while avoiding Riley would be impossible. I have to let them go.

They may be three of the best, funniest, weirdest friends that I've ever had, but what can I do? I have to make a clean break. Riley's life depends on it. Not to mention my own.

Although right now, that life feels pretty fucking meaningless.

"Jackson?" My aunt's voice, followed by a gentle knock on my door, startles me. "Are you sure you don't want any dinner? I made sausage and peppers."

I turn off my phone, pull the covers over my head, and pretend to be asleep.

I hear the door open and then my aunt sigh at the foot of my bed.

"Kiddo, I don't know if you're really asleep or if you're just sick of me trying to cheer you up, but if it's the latter, you should know that I am never *ever* going to stop trying to cheer you up," she says, patting my foot through the bedspread. "How about you get up, and we'll watch one of your terrible zombie movies? We don't have to talk. We can just make popcorn and watch people get their brains eaten by the undead. How does that sound?"

I don't bother to answer.

"I was also thinking that maybe this weekend, we could drive over to Daytona and hit the beach. It's been a while since I've dipped my toe in the ocean, and I've been meaning to try out my new two-piece. Although when I bought it, the fetus who rang me up at the register had the nerve to suggest I might be more 'comfortable' in a one-piece. Can you believe it?"

When I don't respond, my aunt lowers her voice in what I can only assume is an attempt to mimic mine. "'Oh, but Aunt Rachel, you're so young and beautiful. I'm sure you'd kill it in a two-piece.'"

"Aww, thank you, Jackson," she answers herself. "That is so sweet of you to say. You really are a kind and considerate young man. Whatever would I do without you?"

I don't know if Aunt Rachel is trying to get a rise out of me or make me laugh. Either way it doesn't work. I hear her sigh in defeat, and the next time she speaks, her forced breeziness is gone.

"Look, kiddo, I don't know what happened between you and Riley. You don't want to tell me, and I don't want to pry, but please know that whenever you're ready to talk, I'll be here. Okay?"

When I don't say anything, she pats my foot again, shuffles out of the room, and shuts the door behind her.

I know I'm gonna have to get out of this bed and face the world at some point. But the thought of living in that world without Riley feels like an impossible task.

Imagining the rest of my summer, the rest of my senior year, the rest of my life without the one person who's finally made that life worth living is impossible. I feel hollowed out. Empty. Like a husk. Like a thing that used to be Jackson Haines but now is nothing.

That's what I see when I close my eyes and try to picture a future without Riley.

Nothing.

CHAPTER 48

RILEY

"I wish you'd tell me what happened," Dad says as he studies me across the dinner table. It's Friday night, and he's made this complaint or some version of it at least fifty times over the past week.

This time, like every time before, I ignore him. Avoiding his reproachful gaze, I push the lukewarm chicken and potatoes around on my plate in an attempt to make it look like I'm eating. I haven't had an appetite since Jackson and I ended things, and mealtime with the Food Police has become the bane of my already baneful existence.

"Riley?" Dad persists when I continue to stare at my plate in the silence that has become my default since last week.

"Nothing happened," I grumble. "Jackson and I just decided we shouldn't be together."

Dad shakes his head and sets down his fork. "But something had to have happened to make you come to that conclusion."

I shrug and continue to devote my full attention to pushing around my potatoes.

There have been a couple of times over the past week when I've almost broken down and told my dad everything. About Jocasta. About our past lives. About the death sentence hanging over our heads if Jackson and I stayed together. Thankfully, I had enough sense to realize that the quickest way to get myself institutionalized (or at the very least sent to a shrink again) would be to start ranting about witches and reincarnation.

So I kept my mouth shut. I forced myself to get out of bed and go to work every day even though Dad insisted I take some time off. I figured if I pretended everything was okay, he might get off my back and stop checking on me every five minutes. But I was wrong. If anything, he's been keeping a closer eye on me than ever.

I know that his constant attempts to get me to open up about what happened are because he wants to help. But his questions and concern are suffocating. They're too much to deal with. *Everything* is too much. My friends, my job, my life.

All I want to do is lie in bed and disappear from the world until I stop missing Jackson. Until the pain in my heart stops reminding me every second of every day of what I've lost.

But that's never going to happen. I'm never going to stop missing Jackson. That pain is never going to go away. It's going to be a part of me. Forever.

"Son, I have to ask . . ." Dad says, his voice taking on a strange, strained inflection that I've rarely heard before, "Did Jackson . . . *hurt* you?"

A burning furnace of rage erupts inside me and my hands begin to shake. "Jackson would *never* hurt me."

Dad blinks in surprise, visibly taken aback by the vehemence in my voice.

"How could you even *ask* that?"

"I'm asking because it's clear something happened," he pushes back. "A week ago, you were the happiest that I've seen you in months. You were walking around the office with a smile on your face and a bounce in your step. Then you came home Saturday night, and it was like someone had flipped a switch. Now you're hiding in your room, avoiding your friends, and walking around like a robot."

I shrug. "I'm a teenager."

"You're also not eating," Dad adds, pointedly holding my gaze.

"Oh my God," I scoff. "Is that what this is about? You think I'm developing an eating disorder again?" I spear the chicken breast with my fork, bring it to my mouth, and tear off a huge chunk with my teeth. As with everything else I've tried to eat over the past few days, the meat tastes bland and flavorless. It's like chewing plastic. But I force myself to swallow.

"There? Happy?" I ask. I know I'm lashing out at the person who least deserves it, but I can't help myself. I'm hurting. And right now, all I want to do is pass that hurt onto someone else.

Dad removes his glasses and massages the bridge of his nose like he's fighting off a migraine. "Riley, you're clearly in pain. I'm trying to help. I'm your father. I'm allowed to be concerned about your eating habits. The last time something like this happened, you wound up in the hospital."

The fact that my father is comparing Jackson to Alex makes me even more furious. Alex was a closeted jerk who used and discarded me. Jackson is—was—the best thing in my life. And every other life. Those two names don't belong anywhere near each other.

"I'm tired," I say, pushing away from the table and starting to rise. "I'm going to bed."

"Sit *down*." Dad's voice is hard and sharp. Out of instinct, I obey, even though I'm certain he's about to lay into me like he's never laid into me before.

Instead, Dad just stares down at his half-eaten dinner and sighs. In his exhaustion, I can see the toll that the past few days have taken on him. With his pinched expression and tired eyes, he looks almost as shattered as me.

"I know you're upset about Jackson," he says, struggling to keep his voice under control. "I know you're hurting. But, Riley, you need to take care of yourself."

His request is so urgent, so full of concern, that it breaks what's left of my already broken heart. I feel my ice-cold anger melt away, leaving behind only a rising tide of remorse.

"I will," I hear myself say, much to my own surprise. "I'll start eating more. I promise."

"It's not just the eating. When something's wrong, you need to tell me about it so that I can help you. I know you're an independent person and you think you need to face all your problems on your own, but it's okay to ask for help. I want to help you. Your friends want to help you. But you have to let us in."

"I know," I whisper. "I'll try."

Dad nods. I'm not sure if he believes me. I'm not sure *I* believe me. But after a week of worrying about me and my diminishing diet, he's eager to accept any win he can get.

"It'll get easier, Ri, I promise," he says, reaching across the table and squeezing my hand. "I know you don't want to hear this, but there will be other boys. Right now, you're hurting, and you probably feel like you'll never find someone as amazing as Jackson, but you will. Trust me. You're a thoughtful, considerate, incredible young man, and you're going to have so much love in your life from so many wonderful people. But in the meantime, son, you need to remember to love yourself."

I nod and force myself to smile.

I know Dad is only trying to help me. I know everything he's saying is something I need to hear. And if Jackson really were just another Alex, Dad's words would make me feel a thousand times better.

But Jackson isn't another Alex.

He's my soulmate. He's the one and only person on the planet that I'm meant to spend the rest of my life with. And I don't know how I'm supposed to live without him.

How does a person live with only half a soul?

CHAPTER 49

JACKSON

"Jackson? Can you wake up?"

My ears must be playing tricks on me. If I didn't know better, I'd swear that if I opened my eyes, I'd see my mother standing at the foot of my bed. But that's about as likely as the Jacksonville Jaguars making it to the Super Bowl.

A second later, though, my mattress sags under the weight of someone sitting beside me, and I feel a hand squeeze my shoulder. "Jackson? Baby?"

The word *baby* sends a jolt through my body. Nobody calls me baby. No one except—

I open my eyes and, sure enough, my mother is leaning over me, her blond power bob framing a face pinched tight with worry. At least I assume it's worry. Years of Botox and cosmetic surgery have gradually stripped my mother's face of its ability to express the most basic human emotions. Staring into it can be a lot like looking at one of those Rorschach tests. You see what you want to see.

"Hello, Jackson."

My mother runs an immaculately manicured hand through my bedhead, pushing my hair out of my eyes. It's meant to be affectionate, but her touch makes me flinch. I don't know what she's doing here, but after the way she and my father treated me, she's the last person I want to see.

Across the room, I notice Aunt Rachel lingering in the doorway in her blue dungarees. She avoids my eyes with a guilty sideways glance, and suddenly my mother's appearance makes a lot more sense.

"You called my parents?" I growl.

"Of course she called us," my mother answers, still attempting to fix my unruly hair as if that's her greatest concern. "She told us that you haven't gotten out of bed in ten days."

"It hasn't been ten days," I scoff.

I catch the pitying look on my aunt's face, and it occurs to me that I have no fucking clue what day it is or how long it's been since I left my room to do anything other than take a piss.

"Has it?" I ask.

Before Aunt Rachel can answer, my mother is tossing back my sheets. "Baby, why don't you get up, take a shower, and get dressed? Hmm? Then we'll have a nice lunch and talk. Just you and me. How does that sound?"

Maybe it's because I'm too exhausted and confused to argue; maybe it's because I know there's no point in refusing my mother when she sets her mind on something. But against my better judgment, I hear myself mumble a short, defeated "Okay."

"Great." My mother beams, smoothing down her fuchsia blazer as she stands. She looks like she's just closed the sale of the century and is already spending the commission in her head. "We'll see you in the kitchen."

Once she and Aunt Rachel are gone, I pull myself out of bed and drag my body down the hall to the bathroom. My first shower in over a week is a revelation. I let the hot water blast down on me until it scalds my skin, but the pain feels good. It's a relief to feel something other than constant numbness.

When I get back to my room, I dry off and put on a clean pair of shorts and a T-shirt. Then I make my way to the kitchen, where my aunt and mother are talking in hushed tones over a platter of fresh fruit and finger sandwiches. Actually, Aunt Rachel is talking. My mother is smiling and pretending to listen, but I can tell that she's mentally redecorating. It's a habit she's picked up from years of staging open houses to entice potential buyers. She's constantly revising the world in her head, making everything and everyone over in her own image.

"Oh, Jackson," Aunt Rachel exclaims, rising from the table with a start when she notices me hovering in the hall. "Come on in. Have a seat. I was just on my way to the store."

"You're leaving?"

"We're out of milk," she says, giving me a lame shrug to go with her even lamer excuse. "But you should enjoy lunch with your mom. You two have a lot to discuss."

When my aunt passes me in the archway, she squeezes my shoulder and musters an unconvincing smile. Then she's gone, and I'm left to face my mother on my own.

"Your aunt has made us a nice little spread," Mom observes cheerfully as she fixes me a plate. "I always forget how handy she is in the kitchen. It's criminal she hasn't been able to land a husband."

Digs disguised as compliments are nothing new from my mother. Over the years I've learned not to engage with them. I slump down into Aunt Rachel's empty chair and take the plate she's prepared for me without a word.

Faced with my silence, Mom smiles uncertainly and plays with her sliced kiwi. Now that we're alone together, she seems less confident than she was when she had an audience to watch her perform the role of doting mother.

I wonder how long it will take her to ask me what's wrong. Then again, it wouldn't surprise me if she didn't ask at all. Mom's never met a problem she couldn't sweep under the rug. It's why she let me move in with Aunt Rachel in the first place.

"Your father and I got the pictures you sent," she announces as she sips at her iced tea. "You've certainly made some interesting friends."

I'd almost forgotten the photos I'd texted her. That night and my birthday seem like a lifetime ago.

"I'm assuming the rather emaciated-looking boy who seems to always have his arm around you is the one who ... the one that you've been ..." She trails off, unable to bring herself to finish her thought. For a second, a part of me enjoys seeing her squirm as she tries and fails to acknowledge my relationship with Riley.

Then I remember that I have no relationship with Riley.

"That's all over," I tell her.

"Oh." My mother blinks in surprise. Whatever Aunt Rachel told her to get her to come to Orlando must not have included the breakup. "Do you mind if I ask what happened?"

"We realized it was a mistake," I say with a shrug, and leave it at that.

My mother nods, and I can practically see the gears turning in her head. She's trying to work out what this piece of news means for her. And for me. A gleam of excitement flashes in her eyes.

"Well, that's okay!" she gushes, unable or unwilling to disguise her relief. "Baby, we *all* make mistakes. Especially at your age. High school and hormones? It can be *very* confusing. But there's no shame in trying something new and realizing it's not for you."

I want to laugh. What my mother has chosen to hear (*I'm straight again*) and what I actually meant (*I broke up with my boyfriend*) are two very different things. Before I can correct her, though, she pushes forward.

"You have had such a trying year, Jackson. And I know you feel like your father and I haven't supported you in the way you'd have liked. But I hope you know that we have only ever wanted what's best for you. We know the kind of man you are and the kind of man you're capable of becoming. And it just kills us, baby, when we see you doubting yourself and making certain life choices that, frankly, don't make any sense."

I shake my head in exasperation, and Mom throws up her hands defensively.

"I know, I know. I'm the one who supported your decision to come here and live with your aunt. But, baby, I have been regretting that decision *all* summer long. I mean, let's be realistic. Your aunt is a very kind, very generous woman, but she isn't capable of taking care of you or giving you a stable home. Look at the people she's letting you consort with!"

I open my mouth to defend Aunt Rachel and my friends, but my mother stops me.

"Not that they aren't pleasant enough kids in their own way, I'm sure," she backtracks. "But, Jackson, look how confused they've made you. And look how unhappy you are. Even at the height of that whole Devon Sanderson fiasco, you never refused to get out of bed for days on end. You never stopped showering and eating and taking care of yourself. You never had your whole family worried you might do something—*drastic.*"

The word *drastic* catches in her throat. For the first time, I see the fear in my mother's eyes. And despite all the awful, ignorant things she's said about Aunt Rachel and Riley and my friends, I can't help feeling *grateful.*

All I've wanted since the day that I told her about Riley was to know she still loved me. And even though she hasn't said the words, I can tell from the way she's looking at me with desperate panic that she's terrified of losing me.

"That's why," she continues, "your father and I think you should come home."

It takes a second for my brain to catch up with my ears, but when it does, my jaw drops. "You *what?*"

"We discussed it last night, and we really feel like it's the only solution. I know you wanted to move here so you could escape everything that happened last year. But don't you see? You're only making things worse for yourself. You're not thriving here. You're flailing. Even your aunt can see—"

"Wait," I interrupt. "Does Aunt Rachel know you want me to move back home?"

"Of course she does."

"And what does she think?"

My mother tilts her head in confusion as if Aunt Rachel's opinion is about as relevant as a stack of expired coupons. "Your aunt wants you to be happy, Jackson. We *all* want you to be happy."

"You think I'll be *happy* in Tallahassee?"

"I think you'll be a lot better off at home surrounded by a family who loves you and *real* friends who want the best for you, instead of wasting away in a strange city with well-meaning but dubious people who have confused you and made you miserable."

"They didn't confuse me," I protest. "And they didn't make me miserable."

"Then why am I here, Jackson? Why am I getting frantic phone calls from your aunt telling me she's at her wit's end because she's worried sick about you? Why do you look like a walking corpse?"

I don't know what to say. I want to tell her about Jocasta, tell her the only reason I'm miserable is because I had to break up with Riley to save our lives. But I can't. That would only convince her that I'm even more screwed up than she thinks I am.

"Baby, just *think* about it," she says, her voice gentle but insistent. "If you came home, you could finish your senior year with all your friends, you could rejoin the football team—maybe you could even get back together with Micaela. Everything could go back to the way it was, and we could forget all about this confusing summer and just move on with our lives."

My mother stares at me with wide, pleading eyes. They're the same shade of blue as my own, a reminder of the bond we share. As mother and son. As family. But I have zero desire to return with her to Tallahassee.

That old life, the one she looks back on so fondly, the one that made me utterly miserable, is something I will never return to. Not as long as I have any say in the matter.

I open my mouth to tell her that, but the words stick in my throat.

Returning to my old life might very well be hell, but it's not like there isn't another hell waiting for me here in Orlando.

Come the fall, every day will be its own special purgatory. Every day I'll have to see Riley at school and pretend that he means nothing to me. That my arms aren't aching to hold him. That my heart isn't empty without him.

How am I going to survive that? How am I going to survive seeing him over and over again and not die a little every day?

At least in Tallahassee, I'd be spared that torture. In Tallahassee there wouldn't be the constant daily reminder of what I've lost. Of what I can never have.

My mother senses my wavering. Quick as a flash, she leans across the table and takes my hand in hers, her eyes shining with hope.

"Jackson, baby, *come home.*"

CHAPTER 50

RILEY

"Consider yourself kidnapped," Audrey announces, eyeing me in her rearview mirror as I buckle myself into the uncomfortably tiny back seat of her Volkswagen Beetle.

"But fun-kidnapped," Tala adds, turning around in the front passenger seat to flash me a reassuring smile.

The two of them showed up at my house this morning just as I was finishing breakfast and informed me that I'd be spending my birthday with them. I'm pretty sure they arranged the whole ambush in advance with my dad. Normally he insists on us spending birthdays together as a family, especially when a birthday falls on a weekend and he's not consumed with work. This morning, though, he couldn't have been happier to see Audrey and Tala carry me out the door.

I should've seen this coming. I haven't spoken to my friends in almost two weeks, and I haven't left the house except to go to work. It makes sense then that Audrey and Tala's impromptu birthday kidnapping feels less like a celebration and more like an intervention.

"Where are we going?" I ask suspiciously as we merge onto I-4.

"It's a surprise," Audrey answers.

"Where's Duy?"

"Duy and Caleb are meeting us there."

I nod and stare out the window at the passing hotels and outlet malls. I should be excited to spend my eighteenth birthday with my friends on some mystery adventure. But as with everything else in my life right now, I can't muster much enthusiasm for it.

"Are you still missing Jackson?" Tala asks, studying me carefully in the rearview mirror.

I sink down into my seat to avoid her gaze. "I don't want to talk about Jackson."

"No problem," Audrey says. "We won't mention him for the rest of the day."

That's a very agreeable and thus very un-Audrey answer. I narrow my eyes in wariness. "You promise?"

"Hey, your birthday, your rules."

"Says my kidnapper."

Audrey rolls her eyes. "Please. It's not kidnapping if nobody wants you."

My mouth drops open.

"Audrey's kidding." Tala laughs. "We want you. And we love you."

"Eh." Audrey shrugs.

"We do. We love you, Riley. And we are going to have the best day at Dizzy World."

I sit up in my seat. "Dizzy World?"

"Oops!"

"Wow, babe, really?" Audrey groans, casting an exasperated glance at her girlfriend.

"Sorry! It just slipped out."

Audrey shakes her head and sighs. "Well, cat's out of the bag. Surprise, we're taking you to Dizzy World."

Despite my all-consuming sadness about Jackson, a small part of me can't help feeling a smidge of excitement. Dizzy World has the distinction of being Central Florida's "most affordable" theme park. It's also, as the name suggests, an unrepentant knockoff of Disney World. Instead of Space Mountain, they have Galaxy Peak. Instead of Thunder Mountain, they have Lightning Canyon. Instead of Splash Mountain, they have Waterfall Drop.

Even their mascot, Mackey the Mole, in his red overalls and white gloves, looks a lot like a certain cartoon mouse.

It's honestly shocking that Disney hasn't sued. And maybe they will. The park opened only a few months ago, but as soon as their sketchy commercials started airing on TV, my friends and I became obsessed with going. It just seemed like such a clusterfuck of bad taste and copyright infringement, we couldn't resist.

"Well, is it everything you were hoping for and more?" Audrey asks half an hour later once we're standing in Ye Old Town Square (which is definitely not a knockoff of Disney's Main Street, U.S.A.).

"It's fucking glorious," I answer as I take in the cheap and gaudy storefronts designed to look like shops in a colonial village despite the fact that they sell burgers, ice cream, and an endless supply of Dizzy merch. A man in a Daryl the Drake costume waves at some kids, but the lopsided wild eyes sewn into his headpiece make him look like he's either drunk or rabid, and the children scream.

"I can't believe this is an actual place," Tala whispers in awe.

"It's a trainwreck," I agree, basking in the bad taste. "I love it."

Audrey smiles and puts a hand on my shoulder. "Happy birthday."

I smile back, and to my surprise, it's a genuine smile, my first since Jackson and I broke up. Maybe it's because Dizzy World is a bigger shitshow than me, but for a moment, I don't feel the endless crushing sadness that's been pressing down on me since the breakup. Or maybe the emotional reprieve has more to do with Audrey and Tala, my two best friends, still caring enough about me to take me out on my birthday even though they've been on the receiving end of my shitty attitude for the past two weeks.

"I'm sorry I've been such a mess," I say, turning to them with a guilty sigh.

Audrey shrugs. "Breakups are hard. We get it. But you know you don't have to go through it alone, right?"

"You sound like my dad."

"Good. Your dad is smart as fuck. You should listen to him."

I nod. I don't know why it's always been so hard for me to ask for help—and even harder to accept it. I guess it's because I never feel like I deserve it. I never felt like I deserved anything—until Jackson came into my life. That was the first time I let myself want something.

"I'll try to be better about asking for help," I say. I know I made a similar promise to my dad only a week ago, but this time, I think I mean it.

Audrey and Tala pull me into a three-way hug, and once again, the numbing weight on my soul lifts for a moment. I know, of course, that it's only a matter of time before it returns. But I also know that the only way I'll have any chance of getting through the rest of this year, not to mention the rest of my life, is if I have my friends by my side.

"So, should we ride some rides?" I ask, pulling back from the embrace and wiping a tear from my eye.

"Actually, Duy and Caleb just texted," Tala says, looking at her phone. "They should be here any—ah! There they are."

Tala points to the entrance of the park, where I see Duy and Caleb strolling through the wide gates hand in hand. They spot us, and Duy waves excitedly. I'm just about to return the gesture when my eyes catch someone following in their wake, and my heart stops.

Duy and Caleb aren't alone. A third person is walking behind them. He's in such a daze, overwhelmed by all the absurdities of this insane amusement park, that he doesn't register my presence until he's right in front of me.

"Riley?" He gasps, stopping dead in his tracks.

"Jackson?"

CHAPTER 51

JACKSON

When Duy and Caleb showed up at my house this morning and insisted that I go ride some roller coasters with them, they didn't mention anything about Riley. In fact, the only reason I agreed to go was because I knew today was his birthday, and I was afraid that if I didn't do something to distract myself, I'd go crazy thinking about him.

Now here he is, standing in front of me and staring at me like a deer in headlights. I can tell from his panicked eyes that every instinct in his body is telling him to run, but he's too startled to move. And honestly, so am I.

"What the hell is he doing here?" Riley demands once he remembers how to speak. His voice is choked with fear, but Audrey simply smiles.

"Surprise!" she exclaims, beaming at us both. "Welcome to your intervention!"

"Our what?" I ask.

"A relationship intervention," Tala clarifies.

"That's right," Audrey agrees with a nod. "We have no idea why the two of you broke up, but we do know that you've both been miserable. So we decided it was time for you two to stop avoiding each other and figure out your shit because you both clearly regret splitting up. And you can be as mad as you want at us for tricking you when you get home tonight, but right now, you two need to talk. So *talk*."

Spending time with Riley—even only a few minutes—is all I've wanted for the past two weeks. Given what's at stake, I know it's the stupidest thing we could do—especially on his birthday—but there are things I have to tell him. And I don't know when I'll have another opportunity. So despite every fiber of my being warning me that this is a *terrible* idea, all I say is "Okay."

Riley's eyes go wide with surprise. For a second, he looks like he's about to protest. Then he shrugs in defeat, too tired to fight a battle against his own heart.

"Great! We're gonna get some ice cream at Ye Old Ice Creamery. You two sit down and talk," Audrey orders, pointing to a nearby picnic table shaded by a red-and-white-striped umbrella. "We'll be back to check on you in a bit."

Riley nods, but it's not until we both sit down across from each other that Audrey and the others look convinced that neither of us is gonna pull a runner. Slowly they drift across the street and into the ice cream parlor, leaving Riley and me to stare at each other in awkward silence.

"We shouldn't be doing this," he says, gazing down at his hands in an effort to collect himself. "It's not safe."

"We're only talking. We're not . . ." I can't bring myself to finish that sentence. Obviously, we're not getting back together. But if I have to say those words out loud, it will break my heart all over again. "How have you been?" I ask.

"Awful." Riley snorts. "You?"

"Awful."

Riley looks up at me, his eyes wet and wretched. "I've really fucking missed you."

"I've missed you too."

My body is aching to reach across the table and take his hand. It's killing me not to.

"What are we going to do about the others?" he asks, wiping away a tear. "They're going to keep pestering us to get back together."

"Don't worry," I tell him. "After today, that's . . . that's not gonna be an issue."

Riley's eyes narrow in suspicion. "Why not?"

"Because." I take a deep breath. "I'm moving back to Tallahassee."

Riley's face falls. "You're what?"

"My mother came to see me. She asked me to move back home. I told her I needed a few days to think about it. But I've . . . I've made my decision. I'm moving back to Tallahassee."

Riley shakes his head. "I don't understand. Your parents weren't even talking to you, and now they want you to come home?"

"Yeah."

"And, what, they're suddenly okay with you liking guys?"

Now it's my turn to avoid Riley's eyes.

"No, of course they're not," he scoffs. "Let me guess—they want you to come home so they can watch you and straighten you out?"

"It's okay," I insist. "I'll be fine."

"No, it's not okay, and you won't be fine!" Riley shouts. "I don't care if they're your parents. You can't live with people who don't accept you for who you are. They're going to spend all their time trying to change you, trying to make you into something you're not, and you're going to be miserable, Jackson. You're going to be *miserable*."

He's right. But what can I do? "I can't stay here."

"Yes, you can! You can stay with your aunt, and you can hang out with Duy and Audrey and Tala!"

"Riley—"

"Please stay. I know we can't be together, and I know it'll be hard seeing each other when school starts up, but you can't go back to Tallahassee. You'd be throwing your life away!"

The tears are streaming down his face faster than he can wipe them away. Unable to resist the urge any longer, I reach across the table and take his hand. He doesn't pull away.

"This is so stupid!" he exclaims, his words coming out in something that's half a laugh and half a sob. "How is this happening to us? How is *this* our life?"

"I don't know."

He squeezes my hand, and it's like a jolt of electricity. It fills me with recklessness and something like hope. We're getting strange looks from all the sunburned tourists, but I don't care. Being with Riley, even if we're both fucking devastated, is still a million times better than the past two weeks of unrelenting emptiness without him.

"Promise me you won't move back to Tallahassee," he insists. *"Promise me."*

"Okay," I hear myself agree.

"Okay?"

"I won't move back to Tallahassee."

Riley smiles up at me, and I swear it's like staring into the sun. His happiness is blinding. It doesn't seem possible that I'll have to spend the rest of the year—the rest of my *life*—without that smile. Without that happiness. Without him.

"All I think about is us getting back together," I tell him, the words spilling out of me.

Riley nods and wipes away more tears. "I know. Me too."

His sharp green eyes peer into mine, and before I know what I'm doing, I say the impossible. "So why don't we?"

Riley snatches his hand away like he's been stung, and his whole face clouds over in shadows. "We can't, Jackson. You know we can't."

But seeing Riley in front of me after two weeks of agony, I don't know anything anymore. Except how much I need him in my life.

"Jocasta said if anything was gonna happen, it would happen on your birthday. Maybe if we can just get through today—"

"We can't trick the universe!" Riley snaps. "We can't break up just for my birthday, then get together tomorrow and expect the universe to be like, 'Oh, well, guess you guys got me on a technicality. Guess I'll have to let you live.'"

"We don't know what the rules are. Maybe if we get past today, we're in the clear."

"Jackson—"

"These past couple of weeks without you have been the worst fucking weeks of my life," I confess. "I thought I could let you go if it meant we'd both be safe, but I can't."

"You think I don't feel the same?" Riley shakes his head. "Not seeing you is *hell*. But we know what's going to happen if we stay together."

"No, we know what Jocasta *thinks* will happen if we stay together."

"And I believe her!"

"I know you do."

"And you don't?" Riley throws up his hands in exasperation. "Because you were pretty fucking certain two weeks ago when you dumped me."

"I know," I answer, feeling a fresh stab of pain at the memory of that night. "And all I can say is, at the time, I thought we were doing the right thing."

"And now?"

Truth be told, I don't know what I believe anymore. Maybe Riley and I are doomed if we stay together. But it feels like we're also doomed if we stay apart.

"Look," I say, "Jocasta said if we stayed together, something bad would happen on your birthday, right? Well, it's your birthday. We're together. Nothing's happened."

"There are still twelve hours left in the day."

"Right. And what I'm saying is, if nothing happens in those twelve hours, then maybe we consider getting back together."

"Something could still happen after I turn eighteen."

"Yeah," I concede. "Maybe. Or nothing could happen."

Riley doesn't say anything to this, so I keep going.

"I know what I'm asking is a lot. Especially considering how fucked we are if I'm wrong. But I don't care. Living to a hundred—living a long, full life—that's gonna mean nothing to me if I don't have you."

Riley looks at me helplessly, his eyes swimming with confusion. I can tell he's wavering.

"You don't have to answer right now," I tell him. "You can take as much time as you need. As much time until you feel safe and certain that nothing bad is gonna happen. If that's a day or a week or a month or a year, that's okay. I can wait. I can wait forever as long as I know that at the end of that waiting, you and I will be together."

Riley is silent, so I reach out and take his hand again. "Please, Riley. Just tell me you'll think about it."

He hesitates. Then, looking deep into my eyes, he nods. "Okay."

CHAPTER 52

RILEY

I can't believe I just agreed to consider getting back together with Jackson. I must be out of my mind. At the same time, I can't deny how incredible it feels to hold his hand again. It doesn't just feel good, it feels right. Not that I'm surprised. Being with him has always felt right. And I'm finding it harder and harder to believe that we're going to be punished for that feeling.

Even if we are, part of me thinks it might be worth it.

"Aww!" Tala coos as she bounces over to our table. She's holding an enormous waffle cone loaded with ice cream, pistachios, and whipped cream. "Did it work? Did we *Parent Trap* you into getting back together?"

I snatch my hand away from Jackson's and wipe my eyes as the rest of our friends make their way over to us.

"No, we're *not* getting back together," I announce, jumping up from the bench. Out of the corner of my eye, I see Jackson flinch, so I add, "At least, not right now."

"Right," Jackson says, also rising from the table. "We still ... uh ... we still have some stuff we need to figure out."

Audrey rolls her eyes. "Ugh, seriously?"

"Look, we really appreciate what you guys are trying to do," Jackson says. "Riley and I just need more time."

"How much time?" Duy huffs.

Jackson casts an uncertain glance my way, then puts on a brave smile. "Like Riley said, we're still figuring that out. In the meantime, though, I should give Riley his space, so I'm gonna go. I'll order a Lyft to take me home."

As I'd expected, Jackson's decision to leave is greeted with cries of protest.

"You can't go. You just got here," Tala insists. "You haven't even ridden any rides."

"That's okay," Jackson answers, already edging toward the exit. "I'll come back another time."

"Oh my gosh, don't be ridiculous," Duy exclaims. "You already paid fifty bucks to get in. And you were so excited to go on Galaxy Peak! Right, Caleb?"

Caleb looks taken aback. The poor guy clearly has no idea what he's gotten himself into. I suspect that all he wanted out of this day was to ride some roller coasters. Now here he is, caught up in the messy relationship drama of two guys he barely knows. To his credit, though, he gamely plays his part. "Uh...yeah. You've gotta ride at least one ride, man."

"I don't want to crash Riley's special day," Jackson counters. But Duy is already wrapping a hand around one of his arms and halting his retreat.

"Riley won't care if you ride *one* roller coaster," they insist. "He doesn't even have to come with us! It'll just be you and me. And Caleb, of course! The three of us can go for a spin on Galaxy Peak and then afterward, if you still want, you can go back to your boring life of not hanging out with us and being sad all the time."

"I can't—"

"It'll be super-quick. Come on, Caleb. We're taking Jackson to the stars!"

Caleb dutifully grabs Jackson's other arm, then he and Duy proceed to drag Jackson into the bowels of the park.

Releasing a sigh of exasperation, I turn back to Audrey and see a satisfied smirk spread across her face.

"You have to stop," I tell her.

Audrey arches an eyebrow and licks a dribble of strawberry ice cream from her fingers. Under the hot July sun, her and Tala's cones are already melting into a sticky mess.

"And you need to get back together with Jackson," she responds flatly. "You obviously miss each other."

"It's not that simple."

"It fucking is."

"Riley, maybe if you explained to us what the actual problem is, we could help," Tala suggests diplomatically. She sits at the picnic table and then gestures for me to do the same.

"You wouldn't understand," I sigh as I flop down beside her.

"Why wouldn't we understand?"

"Because you'll both think I'm crazy."

"We're not going to think you're crazy," Tala assures me.

"Yes, you are."

"Riley, we love you. You can tell us anything."

Tala and Audrey stare at me with pleading eyes. They both want to help me so much. And right now, I do need help.

I take a deep breath. "Okay. I'll tell you everything. But for real, you're going to think I'm crazy."

"Riley, look at me," Tala says. "I promise: This is a safe space. No one is going to think you're crazy."

"You're fucking *crazy*," Audrey exclaims.

I just finished telling her and Tala about everything that's happened to Jackson and me over the past month, and (unsurprisingly) Audrey is now staring at me like I've either lost my goddamn mind or never had one to begin with.

"Witches? Reincarnation? *Past lives?*" Audrey throws her arms up in the air like she's asking the universe if it also sees how ridiculous I am.

"I know," I sigh. "It's a lot."

"It's bananas!"

"Babe," Tala gently chides her, "remember what we discussed about respecting other people's beliefs even if they differ from our own?"

"T., he's talking about being a *Viking*. That's not a belief. That's brain damage."

"I knew I shouldn't have told you," I grumble.

"No, you shouldn't have let some con artist convince you to break up with your boyfriend because you guys had a couple of bad dreams!"

"They weren't dreams. They were—never mind. It doesn't matter. You're never going to believe me."

"Riley, wait!" Tala says as I start to rise. "We believe you."

"We do?" Audrey asks.

Tala kicks her under the table, then flashes me a reassuring if somewhat artificial smile. "We believe that you believe that your life will be in danger if you date Jackson. That's not crazy."

"It's not?"

"No," Tala insists. "I feel the same way about dating Audrey."

I sit back down. "You do?"

"Sometimes," she clarifies. "I see the looks we get when we're together in public. I hear the comments. It can be scary. And even though I try to stay positive and not let that fear affect me, a part of me is always a little afraid—afraid someone won't like seeing two girls kissing and decide that they need to do something about it."

Despite the noon heat, Tala shivers. Audrey reaches out and takes her hand.

"What I'm saying is, it's not crazy to be afraid," Tala continues. "When you're queer and in a relationship, you're always going to be a target. Especially in Florida. But that doesn't mean you should be afraid of love. Love is how we get through the fear to something better. Love is how we get to hope."

"Exactly," Audrey agrees. "That's all I was trying to say."

"Sure, babe." With a chuckle, Tala leans over the table and kisses Audrey's cheek.

Seeing their love for each other and how happy it makes them, I want to believe Tala's words more than I've ever wanted to believe anything. Because if she's right, if on the other side of fear there's hope, then despite Jocasta's warning and all our visions of death and doom, there's still hope for Jackson and me.

Maybe I just need to stop being afraid. Because regardless of all the things that I don't understand about my life right now, there is one thing that I know is true.

I love Jackson Haines.

"I think . . . I think I'm going to go find Jackson," I say, once again rising from the bench.

Audrey nods approvingly. "And I think *that's* a great idea."

"Do you know which way I go to get to Galaxy Peak?"

"Yeah, I think you just—"

Audrey doesn't finish her sentence. She's cut off when a large, deafening crash shakes the air like thunder, almost knocking me off my feet.

"What the fuck was that?" Audrey shouts, leaping up from the table.

Over the tops of the faux-colonial storefronts, a dark plume of smoke rises from somewhere deep in the park.

"Is that a fire?" Tala asks, nervously reaching for Audrey's hand. "Did something explode?"

A chill runs down my spine.

Before I know what I'm doing, I'm tearing down the street, winding through groups of confused tourists as I race past whirling rides and blinking lights. Somewhere behind me, Audrey calls my name, but I keep running.

I have to find Jackson.

My heart is racing. A cold sweat clings to my skin. But those things are nothing compared to the bottomless pit of dread that opens in my stomach.

I know what's happening. And why it's happening. Despite this, I still hope against hope that I'm wrong.

But I'm not wrong.

When I turn onto one of the wider thoroughfares, I see the cause of the commotion and it stops me in my tracks. It's Galaxy Peak. From the corny commercials, I instantly recognize the enormous, futuristic-looking silver pyramid that houses the massive indoor roller coaster. Only the pyramid in front of me is very different from the one on TV. It's lost its gleaming tip. That's collapsed, leaving a massive hole at the top of the structure through which a raging column of black smoke is being belched into the air by the fire below.

"Holy fuck," Audrey exclaims as she and Tala appear beside me, both of them panting for breath. "What happened?"

The three of us stare at the nightmare in front of us. People and families are scrambling out of the exit at the pyramid's base, screaming in terror as more of the silver structure collapses in on itself.

Tala covers her mouth as her face goes pale. "Duy, Jackson, and Caleb are in there . . ."

"We don't know that," Audrey says, trying to reassure her.

But of course they're in there. I know that with an absolute and crushing certainty.

Jocasta warned us that something would happen on my birthday if we didn't stay away from each other. We didn't listen. Now it's too late.

Jackson and I are out of time.

CHAPTER 53

JACKSON

The first thing I notice is the smell. Sharp and metallic, like burning wires. Then I hear a moaning followed by a soft whimpering. I can't tell which direction it's coming from. There aren't any lights in this part of the ride. It's like being lost in a black hole. I can't get my bearings.

Though that might have more to do with the fact that my head feels like it's about to split open. I must have hit it against something when our rocket coaster jumped the track and crashed. There's a throbbing on the right side of my skull. And the ringing in my ears is making it difficult to concentrate.

"Duy?" I call out. "Caleb?"

In the darkness, I hear someone groan, but no one answers.

What the hell happened? One second, we were zooming through black starlit tunnels. The next, we're screaming and crashing.

Did we hit something? Or did something hit us? I remember our rocket-shaped carriage shaking uncontrollably right before things went sideways, but I thought that was part of the ride.

Something wet and sticky trickles down my face. I don't need to see it to know it's blood. I wonder if I have a concussion. The searing pain in my head is growing worse.

"Hello?" I shout. "Is anyone there?"

Again, there's no answer, only more groaning.

I have no idea if anyone's coming to help, and I don't want to wait around to find out. Despite my entire body aching like it's been tackled by ten linebackers, I try to stand. But when I go to draw up my legs, I find I can't move. My legs won't budge. A tight, viselike grip is holding them down.

Trying not to panic, I fish my phone out of my pocket. The screen is cracked, and I can't get a signal, but the flashlight still works. I aim the beam at my legs, and suddenly it makes sense why I'm having so much trouble moving.

It's our crashed rocket coaster. Its heavy overturned frame is lying across my legs, pinning me to the floor with its crushing bulk. I don't know how I didn't feel it before. I must have been in shock.

I try to pull my legs out from under the coaster, but it hurts too much to move them. I then try to lift the rocket. All I need is an inch to free myself. But I can't budge the massive weight. It's too heavy. And my arms are too weak.

I'm trapped.

CHAPTER 54

RILEY

"They're not picking up," Audrey growls as she stares at her phone in frustration. She's tried calling Duy, Jackson, and Caleb more times than I can count, but no one's answered. Not that I thought they would. That would mean that they're safe. And today no one is safe.

Even so, my heart surges with hope every time a bruised and bloody park guest staggers out of the base of the crumbling pyramid. Some of the traumatized stragglers are limping. Others are crying and clinging to loved ones for support. All their faces are twisted in disbelief and terror, but none of those faces belong to my friends.

"Keep back! Everyone, please keep back!" a park employee barks at the large crowd gathering to watch the grisly spectacle. More of the pyramid collapses in on itself with a horrifying crunch, and another entire floor disappears. At this rate, it's only a matter of minutes before the entire building implodes.

"What happened?" a woman asks in a stunned voice behind me.

"I don't know," another woman answers. "I heard someone say something about a total structural collapse."

"What does that mean?"

I know what it means. It means Jackson and Duy and Caleb and anyone else who doesn't make it out in the next few minutes will be buried alive. Assuming there's anyone inside who's still alive.

Why didn't we listen to Jocasta?

She told us something like this would happen. She fucking *warned* us.

As soon as I saw Jackson walk through the park gates, I should've run in the opposite direction. I should never have let him convince me to get back together. We knew what would happen. We knew the universe would try to kill us.

Except...

Except the universe isn't trying to kill *us*, is it?

Jackson's the one in danger. He's the one about to be crushed under twelve stories of roller-coaster rubble. Not me. I'm safe.

How is that possible?

In all our past lives, whenever we died, Jackson and I always died *together*. I thought that was the rule. I thought that was the whole point. We die together and then we come back together. But if Jackson dies and I don't, what happens then?

A chill creeps down my spine, turning my blood to ice.

Jocasta said that the reason Jackson and I were allowed to remember our past lives this time around was because the universe wanted us to understand what would happen if we didn't break the cycle. She thought it was giving us a choice: We could stay together and die or break up and live. But maybe she was wrong.

Maybe this is the choice.

Jackson is going to die. I know that with every molecule of my being. And I can watch it happen and break the cycle and never see him again in this life or any other life, *or* . . .

"Where are you going?" Audrey barks, grabbing my arm as I start to slip through the crowd toward the burning pyramid.

"It's okay," I say, flashing her and Tala as brave a smile as I can muster. I want them to remember me smiling. "Everything's going to be okay."

Before she can say anything, I pull free and race toward Galaxy Peak.

"Hey, what are you doing?" a park employee shouts as I barrel past him. "Come back here!"

Above me I hear the tearing of metal and the shattering of glass as more of the silver structure collapses. I force myself to block it out, just like I block out the sight of the wounded park guests trickling out of the pyramid and the sound of Audrey's and Tala's cries begging me to come back.

I race to the entrance of the roller coaster and dart inside. There I find myself in a large, cavernous room cheaply decorated to look like a cross between NASA's Mission Control and the Death Star. It's an odd, disjointed mash-up of two worlds made all the more ominous by the fact that the room is deserted and almost completely dark. Only a few red emergency lights flicker overhead.

With the fire alarm blaring over the speakers and the pungent smell of smoke wafting through the air, I feel like I've stepped into some crazy sci-fi disaster movie. I should be terrified. But as I make my way down the long winding corridor that leads to the roller-coaster tracks, I'm too full of purpose to be frightened.

All that matters is finding Jackson and my friends.

I reach the boarding zone of the ride, where several empty roller-coaster carts shaped like rocket ships sit on a track that leads into a pitch-black tunnel. I take out my phone, turn on the flashlight, and aim the beam into the winding darkness. Then I carefully step onto the tracks and set off into the heart of the pyramid.

The air grows staler and smokier the deeper I move into the tunnels. Every twenty feet or so, I pass overturned rocket ships that have been abandoned in the chaos. I assume everyone who was in them got out safely because I don't see any bodies. That's a good sign.

Then again, I'm still on the lowest level of the ride. There are probably eight floors of track between where I am and what's now the top of the pyramid. Jackson, Duy, and Caleb could be on any of those floors. And if they were on one of the levels that's already collapsed...

No.

I push the thought out of my head. I have to believe they're alive.

I climb up a steep incline of track, passing cheap papier-mâché models of Jupiter and Saturn. The passage levels off as I reach the next floor, where I have to climb over two rocket ships that must have collided because they're both overturned and blocking the track. There's just enough room for me to squeeze over their bulky frames, and when I do, I spy a flicker of light coming from around the curve of the tunnel up ahead.

"Hello?" I call out.

"Hello!" a familiar voice shouts back.

"Duy!"

"Riley?"

Hope courses through my veins. I scramble down the tracks and around the curve, and the sight that greets me almost makes me weep for joy.

In the light of their smartphones, a very-much-not-dead Duy is leaning over a very-much-not-dead Jackson attempting to lift an overturned rocket ship off his legs.

"You're alive!" I shout as a sob of relief bursts from my throat. I'm so overcome, I can hardly believe my eyes. Neither can Jackson. He looks at me like I'm a ghost.

"What are you doing here?" he asks.

"I came to find you."

"Are you out of your mind?"

"Clearly. Are you all right?"

"Of course he's not all right," Duy snaps. "This stupid spaceship weighs a ton. So maybe save the conversation for later and help me get this off him."

They don't have to tell me twice. I drop to my knees, and together we put our backs into trying to shift the overturned rocket. But after a few minutes of grunting, straining, and pushing with every ounce of our strength, Duy and I have nothing to show for our efforts except cramped muscles and a heavy coat of sweat.

"It's no use," Jackson says, letting out a defeated sigh. "I told you, it's too heavy. You're not gonna be able to lift it."

"We just need more help. Where's Caleb?" I suddenly remember to ask.

"Over here," a feeble voice answers. I cast my phone's light farther down the tracks and see Caleb huddled against a wall. Blood trickles down his face from a nasty gash across his forehead. And his right arm, clutched against his chest, is bent at such an unnatural angle, it must be broken.

"Where the hell is the park staff?" Duy asks. "Aren't they coming to help?"

I shake my head.

"Why not?"

As if in response, a violent crash shakes the entire pyramid down to its foundation.

Jackson looks at me nervously. "What was that?"

"Galaxy Peak is collapsing," I answer. "The whole roller coaster is imploding floor by floor."

"What? Why didn't you tell us?" Duy demands. "We have to get out of here!" But as soon as the words are out of their mouth, Duy remembers Jackson, and their face falls.

"It's okay," I assure them. "I'll stay and help Jackson. You get Caleb out of here. There are a couple of overturned rockets blocking the tracks, so you're going to have to help him climb over them. But other than that, the path is clear."

Duy shakes their head. "We can't leave you."

"It's okay. We'll be okay. Right, Jackson?"

I catch Jackson's eye, hoping he understands my meaning.

"Right." He nods. "You should get Caleb out of here."

Duy opens their mouth to protest, but Caleb lets out a low moan and clutches his broken arm.

"Okay," Duy concedes with a reluctant nod. "We'll send someone to help you guys as soon as we're out."

I force myself to smile as if Jackson and I have all the time in the world. "Don't worry about us. We'll be okay." A second later, though, my confidence falters. "But just in case, if for some reason you see my dad before I do, would you tell him . . . tell him I love him. And tell him I finally figured out what I want to do with my life."

In the light of my phone, I can see Duy working out the implications of what I said. I'm afraid they're going to insist on staying with me or try to convince me to leave with them. Instead, Duy pulls me into a hug and holds me tighter than their tiny frame should allow.

Nearby, something heavy and metal collapses with a deafening *bang*, and we jump apart.

"You need to go," I tell them.

Wiping their eyes, Duy nods. Without wasting another second, they hurry over to Caleb and help him stand. Then the two of them carefully make their way down the track toward the exit.

"You should go too," Jackson says, his voice gentle but firm.

In the dim light of the tunnel, I can see his blue eyes are filled with a placid resignation. It's impossible for me to look away from them as

I listen to the metal bones of the roller coaster snap and sag under the weight of its collapsing body.

"I'm not going anywhere," I answer as I sit on the floor beside him.

"Don't be stupid," Jackson protests. "You know what's gonna happen. There's no point in both of us dying. I'm the one who screwed up and pushed us to get back together. This is my fault. I'm the one who deserves to die. Not you. You need to go, okay? Before it's too late. *Please.* Just go."

"And what am I supposed to do after I go?" I ask.

"You live."

"Without you?" I shake my head.

Given the circumstances, I'm surprised at how calm I feel. Maybe because, despite how inevitable this ending is for Jackson and me, I know it's not an ending. Jackson and I have no ending.

When one song ends, another always begins.

"Riley, listen to me," Jackson pleads. "If we die together, we're just gonna end up reincarnated again. And then we're gonna *die* again. And again. And again."

"I know," I answer. "But we'll also get to live again. And again. And again."

"Even so, I can't ask you to do this."

"You're not asking, I'm offering. Besides, you would do the same."

Jackson sighs and shakes his head, but he doesn't contradict me. He knows he could never leave me if our roles were reversed. Despite this, I can tell he's still conflicted about my decision, so I take his hand in mine and smile.

"You are half my soul, Jackson. You are the person that I am meant to spend my life with. Not just this life. *Every* life. And I don't care if that pisses off the universe or if we're breaking its precious rules. I don't care if it keeps swatting us like flies. I can take the swatting.

I can die a million times if it means I get the chance to live a million more lives with you. Because I'm not afraid of dying. The only thing I'm afraid of is having to live one minute of my life without you."

Jackson is silent as he struggles to find his words. When he does, he looks at me with so much tenderness, my heart can hardly bear it.

"Are you sure?" he asks.

"I'm sure."

Jackson takes both my hands in his and squeezes them. "We only got to be together for a few weeks this time around. What if in the next life it's even less? What if we only get a few days? Or a few hours?"

"What if we get the full eighteen years?"

The thought of us sharing almost two full decades coaxes a grin from Jackson. "You know there's a good chance we probably won't remember any of this. We're gonna be starting from scratch again. We might not even recognize each other."

I bring his left hand to my lips and kiss it, then the right, and then I press both his hands against my heart. My heart that will always be his.

"I'll find you," I promise. "Whatever happens, wherever we end up, no matter how many times we die or how many times we come back, I'll find you."

"Not if I find you first."

The tunnel around us shakes as more of the roller coaster implodes overhead. Under the weight of who knows how many collapsed floors, the roof buckles and groans above us. A sound like a low, desperate moan echoes in our ears, then slowly and steadily builds into an angry scream. Like a wild beast dying. Like the universe howling.

With an earsplitting screech, the tunnel finally collapses. Jackson throws his arms around me, pulls me to his chest, and holds me so tightly that it becomes impossible to know where he ends and I begin.

"I love you," he says, pressing his forehead to mine. "In this life and every life."

"I love you too," I answer. "In this life and every life."

Shutting my eyes, I listen as the universe roars. It sounds like crashing metal, shattering glass, and an eternity of outrage. Over all of that, though, I hear Jackson. His voice is strong and clear and full of the future.

"Don't let me go."

HISTORICAL NOTE

When it comes to the historical events depicted in this book, I've tried whenever possible to report history, not revise it. Occasionally the demands of the plot required me to take a few creative liberties (for example, there was no Temple of the Sibylline Oracle in Pompeii). But on the whole, I've attempted to be accurate in my portrayals of the past despite the sometimes scanty or contradictory accounts in the historical records. Even the encounter between Ulfhild and Erik the Red, while fictional, is based on an old Icelandic legend.

For the reader wishing to learn more about the cities, cultures, and events recounted in Riley's and Jackson's past lives, I strongly recommend the following books, which provided the backbone of my research: *The Fires of Vesuvius* by Mary Beard; *The Saga of the Greenlanders* and *Erik the Red's Saga* (authors unknown); *The Age of the Vikings* by Anders Winroth; *Catherine de Medici* by Leonie Frieda; *The Saint Bartholomew's Day Massacre* by Barbara B. Diefendorf; and *The Longest Night: The Bombing of London on May 10, 1941* by Gavin Mortimer.

ACKNOWLEDGMENTS

Thank you to my agent, Tanusri Prasanna, and my editor, Carolina Mancheno Ortiz. Without you both this book would not exist.

Thank you to Noah Dao for the beautiful cover. If I wasn't already gay, your artwork would make me gay.

Thank you to the copyeditors and proofreaders who had to wrangle my creative spelling and my even more creative grammar into something resembling coherent English.

Thank you to my first readers, Mashuq Deen, Kirby Fields, Don Nguyen, Vickie Ramirez, and Pia Wilson, who gave me incisive but encouraging feedback. Thank you for also explaining how football works.

Thank you to Dr. Darcy Krasne for fact-checking my details about Roman life in Pompeii.

Thank you to Stella Fawn Ragsdale for feeding me a continuous supply of chicken pot pies and for providing me with anecdotes about the drama that goes down at a farmers' market.

Finally, thank you to the television series *Doctor Who* for instilling a love of history in me at an early age. If reincarnation exists, I look forward to watching the special edition of "The Curse of Fenric" in all of my future lives.